SOLAR SENSATIONS

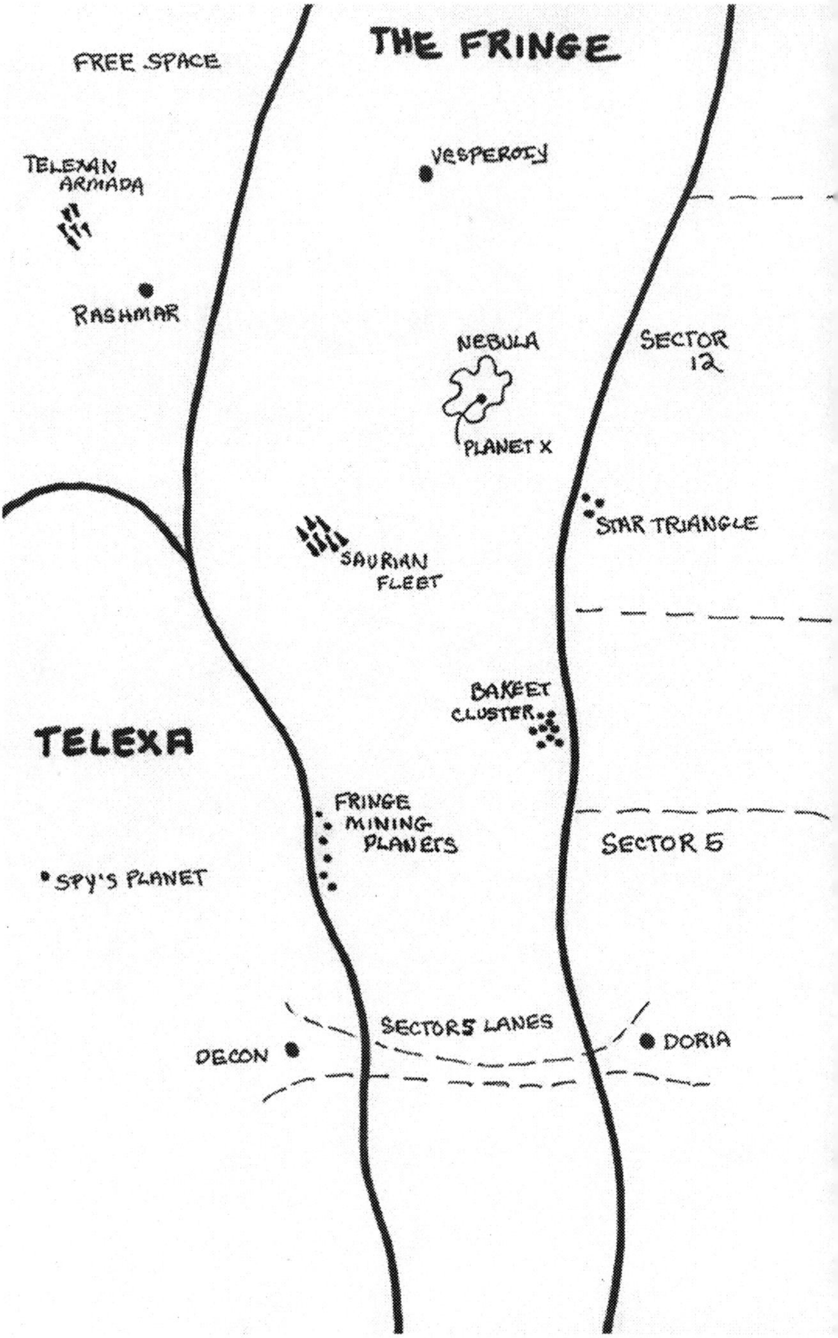
THE FRINGE
FREE SPACE
VESPEROFY
TELEXAN
ARMADA
RASHMAR
NEBULA
SECTOR
12
PLANET X
STAR TRIANGLE
SAURIAN
FLEET
BAKEET
CLUSTER
TELEXA
FRINGE
MINING
PLANETS
SECTOR 5
SPY'S PLANET
SECTOR 5 LANES
DECON
DORIA

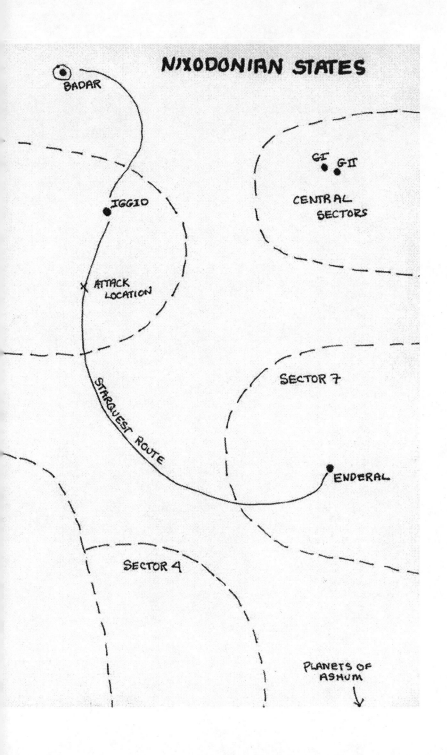

NIXODONIAN STATES

BADAR

IGGIO

G·I G·II

CENTRAL
SECTORS

✗ ATTACK
LOCATION

SECTOR 7

STARQUEST ROUTE

ENDERAL

SECTOR 4

PLANETS OF
ASHUM

SOLAR SENSATIONS

L.A. Taylor

iUniverse, Inc.
New York Lincoln Shanghai

Solar Sensations

iUniverse books may be ordered through booksellers or by contacting:

iUniverse
2021 Pine Lake Road, Suite 100
Lincoln, NE 68512
www.iuniverse.com
1-800-Authors (1-800-288-4677)

ISBN-13: 978-0-595-36162-5 (pbk)
ISBN-13: 978-0-595-80606-5 (ebk)
ISBN-10: 0-595-36162-5 (pbk)
ISBN-10: 0-595-80606-6 (ebk)

Printed in the United States of America

PROLOGUE

The steel sterility of the detention corridor echoed the General's crisp click of the booted heels. He stopped in front of the death chamber where his aide, Lieutenant Page, greeted him. The aide's thin frame was withered with age but his mind was still sharp and his loyalty to General Angel Keem, unwavering. The General peered through the portal of the solid door and smiled. The woman spy they'd captured pounded hard against the thick glass, screaming obscenities at them.

"Page," the General said, "Let's hear what our prisoner has to say."

When Page thumbed the intercom switch, the woman's voice exploded through the speaker. "You bastards! You won't get away with this!"

The General's smile widened. "Oh, I'm afraid I will, Captain Moasin."

"You're destroying Telexa! I know it was you who murdered those government officials. And you who annihilated an entire planet. How dare you!"

"Dare? It's quite simple. The democracy you uphold is weak and inefficient. It will soon see its end. And, the planet you speak of? It would not yield to my demands. Others shall see the same fate if they choose to defy my power."

The spy gasped. "Power? Being Telexa's self-appointed dictator will not bring you power! If you haven't noticed, sir, half the nation is already in revolt. Your TRA can't annihilate half its systems!"

The General brought his pug nose closer to the glass. "You overestimate the ability of your alliance. The nation is quickly learning that my Telexan Revolutionary Army cannot, and will not, be stopped."

Her voice trembled with doubt. "Oh, yes it will." She stood in the small chamber, fists clutched at her side. "I know your secrets. You won't get away with it." She lunged at the chamber door, fists slamming against the glass. Instinctively, the General pulled away. He glanced at Page who smiled and muted the intercom. Page said, "She thinks she's in an interrogation chamber and that her people are negotiating her release."

General Keem chuckled. "Well then, let's find out what she thinks she knows."

He turned to the woman. The intercom reactivated. "And what secrets are these, Captain?"

Her bleeding fingers splayed against the glass. "You plan to take over Telexa then move into Nixodonian States. The idea is so ridiculous, it's laughable, but we've learned how you think you're going to achieve this."

The General played with her. "My dear, Nixodonia is ten times the size of Telexa. It has enjoyed an elected government for nearly five hundred years." He shrugged. "Surely a freedom fighter like yourself recognizes the weakness of Nixodonian States' democracy."

"General," she scoffed, "anyone who isn't Nixodonian understands what's happening there. The Nixodonians are too arrogant, too blind, to realize that the Knabon administration is hardly democratic. Pao Knabon is a fourth generation president. That makes Nixodonian States empirical at best."

"True. And as weak as Telexa is now."

Moasin shoved her chin toward the glass. "Not for long! I know your secrets. And I've passed them on." She sneered at the two men in the corridor. "You've found yourself a traitor over there—that stupid woman who thinks her fashion statements will enlighten the galaxy."

"Ah, yes, Marie Flechette. And what have you learned of her?"

The woman was so loud that Page thumbed down the volume. "She's that supermodel who somehow got so popular that most of Telexa has heard of her. I used to admire her, until I learned of her association with you! It seems that a lust for power has spoiled even Nixodonia's appointed *princess*. To think!" Captain Moasin tossed her head. "It's a title her fans gave her, and that stupid president of theirs goes along with it!"

The General glanced at Lieutenant Page who smirked with understanding. Page had been there in the early days of the TRA when the council had tried to disagree with Angel Keem's idea concerning the heiress. After all, Marie Flechette was merely the young child of a wealthy family. However, as time went on, the council began to concur with Keem's sense of foresight. With less influence than was originally expected, the beautiful Marie Flechette managed to spread her influence right to the level of the Presidential House. Her philanthropic ways expanded from there as she promoted herself until she was better known than the First Lady.

Keem taunted the prisoner. "She's about to become a movie star. Did you know?"

Captain Moasin was visibly taken aback.

"Ah. You've heard?"

The spy's shifting eyes betrayed panic. That cheered the General a great deal. So, Captain Moasin hadn't learned all the TRA secrets. It was obvious, watching the spy's raw fingers trail down the window that her flushed features were beginning to pale. She was realizing that she'd missed something.

Captain Moasin's voice warbled. "What's that got to do with anything? The movie isn't even released yet."

"Oh, but when it is—in just a few weeks time—everyone will know what Nixodonia's princess is really all about."

"It's a stupid romance!" the spy spat out, then hesitated. "Isn't it?"

"Unfortunately, you won't be around to find out."

"You can't hurt me! I'm a ranking officer of the Telexan Navy and you're holding me illegally. You will release me."

The General laughed. "Release you? From this ship?" He raised his arms. "This is the *Reliant*, the largest and most awesome destroyer in the entire galaxy."

"And it belongs to the Nixodonian Space Navy."

"You're very observant, Captain," he said, rolling his eyes. "I suppose we'll find the time to change its marking after the war. This ship—and the others."

"How many ships have you pilfered from Nixodonia?" she asked, horrified.

"Oh, dozens. It's quite easy with my men virtually controlling the Nixodonian Space Navy."

"You traitor!"

"Ah." His lips pulled into a sardonic curl. "Being a traitor all depends on whose side you're on. If you'll look around, you'll see that I have no intention of releasing you. The TRA never releases traitors."

Captain Moasin glanced about the chamber, her gaze darting to the ceiling. Her eyes widened as she noticed the gas-releasing nozzles. Although trembling, she stood tall. "You won't win. Before you caught me, I dispatched a transmission about Miss Flechette and the mission of this destroyer to a secret location. Your war will soon be over."

The General grunted. "Our war has just begun. Your war is over. We intercepted your transmission. We therefore learned the location of your secret base. In fact, we've just arrived in that planet's system. You can be sure that your secret base will pay the price for your recklessness."

The woman lunged at the glass, clawing at it with fury. "Noooo!"

The General's eyes shifted to the detention officer at the chamber's controls. "Terminate her."

The screams quickly waned as the chamber exploded in a swirl of white smoke. Keem waited. As the chalky powder cleared, he smiled, seeing for himself the spy's body crumpled on the death chamber's floor. "Page," he said casually, "shall we watch the battle from the bridge?"

"A splendid idea, sir."

As the men walked toward the bridge, General Keem muttered to Page. "Are you sure no original copies of the movie have been distributed?"

Page glanced at the General. A beaked cap shadowed the aide's determined features. "None sir. All of the original copies are secure with the director."

"Good. And the Flechette Benefit Concert festivities are underway?"

"Yes, General."

"With all of our primary members present?"

Page smiled. "As you have orchestrated."

The two men stopped on the command deck of the Reliant. Through the massive view port, a crystalline blue-green planet hung against the velvet black of space. General Keem shifted his gaze to admire the portion of his fleet that could be seen within the range of the curved window. The muscular warships completely dominated the scrawny flotilla rising from the planet's surface in a useless attempt at self-defense. The planetary shield was ancient, showing several weak points on the holo display that floated above the strategics console. One carefully directed turbolaser would take the shield down, completely exposing all those pitiful little ships and the planet behind them to his armada's firepower.

"How sure are we that Moasin's transmission was fully intercepted?" Keem asked.

"We're ninety percent certain that no one received the message, sir."

"That isn't good enough," the General growled. "No one must know of our plans. Another few weeks and the entire galaxy will learn of our intentions. Until then, secrecy is of the utmost importance."

"I agree, sir," Page said. "We mustn't take a single risk."

General Keem turned and walked curtly to where the ship's admiral stood. The admiral gave a sharp salute.

Without hesitation, Keem gave the order. "Destroy the planet."

CHAPTER 1

"You look wonderful, Marie," Anne Amaaka said approvingly. Marie glanced at her prime coordinator, noticing that the accolade was delivered with a look of impatience. Anne glanced at the beautician." Javid, that's good enough. Get that headpiece on or we'll get behind schedule!"

"Yes, yes, Miss Amaaka," the beautician muttered absently. "He's almost finished," Marie defended, sweeping her hands down her perfectly tailored sheath gown. She let her fingers trace the swirls of pearl and diamond beads so well placed that one barely noticed the sheerness of the creamy satin beneath.

Marie shifted her famous aqua-blue eyes to watch her beautician work. Javid was the only humanoid-alien on staff, still an enigma to the public after his twenty years with Flechette Cosmetics. His short, thin frame was agile, his long fingers deft as he tucked the last of Marie's copper locks into the mass of curls on her head. Oddly, Marie felt nervous. She'd been a public figure her entire life, with the annual Post-Benefit Concert Gala held every year here at the family estate, but this year was different. Waiting for her outside her private marquee was half of Nixodonia's High Court members, and shortly they'd be joined by the President himself. This would intensify the itinerary of the day, already packed with a series of important events. Not the least was her debut as a movie star. Marie flushed with tension through her expertly applied make-up. "Where is my father?" she asked Anne.

"He's coming."

"How is he?"

"Moving slowly, but the ground car is taking him and your mother right to their booth. He won't have to stress himself at all."

"He's been out of bed only a day. He'll be stressed no matter what," Marie grumbled. Her father had been struggling with a horrible disease that no one could diagnose. They said it was always changing, the mutations in his blood altering with every attempted treatment. It had kept her father confined to his bed for nearly two years, causing Marie and her mother endless worry.

At least Paul was supportive, other than his ill-timed recklessness these past few months. "Where's Paul? Are you done yet, Javid?"

"In one second," Javid said, working in a bejeweled headband until it was perfect by his standards.

"He'll be here soon," Anne said.

"He was supposed to be here an hour ago!" Marie complained.

"I'm not your fiancé's babysitter," Anne ground out.

Marie glanced sideways to catch Javid's eye as he gave her another of his I-told-you-so looks. His long face and tufts of unruly hair were apparently signs of beauty on his far-away home planet of Rashmar, but in these parts no one found him especially attractive except Marie, and maybe Anne. Those warped eyebrows and equally twisted mouth were sending yet another sign of disapproval of her choice of life mates. Javid had been her secret spiritual advisor over the years and he had yet to misguide her. This time though…

"I know, I know!" Marie lamented. "You think those rumors about Paul are true, don't you?"

"I've said nothing of the sort," the Rashmarian chirped, his palms flying up in a gesture of innocence.

Marie glared at him. "Not in so many words."

"All right you two," Anne scolded. "We've got exactly one minute."

"Well," Marie huffed, "I agree that Paul could be a little more responsible in some areas, but it's just nerves. If things weren't so busy with his new project, he'd be out there greeting the guests like he's supposed to."

Javid opened his mouth but Marie interrupted. "A case of nerves is far from cheating, Javid. Please! There're only two weeks before the wedding and you're dishing out doom."

"Only what's been entrusted to me by my gods," Javid mumbled.

"Enough, you two," Anne said with more resolve. "We're stepping out. Now."

Marie's entourage, a collection of the nation's fashion and entertainment elite, met in the anteroom before the group stepped from the pavilion into a wedge of Enderal's sunshine.

"Your mother is doing Paul's job by the looks of it," Anne muttered.

Although the planet of Enderal was edging on its mild winter season, the guest pavilions of the Flechette estate had the air beneath the marquees warmed to summer-like conditions. A wide vista spread before the two women, dominated by the four acres of covered gardens. The ceiling of carapace-like layers of brilliant white triangular shapes allowed airflow yet complete protection from the elements.

On such a glorious day as this, parts of the roof had been rolled back to allow wedges of sunshine to penetrate to the grounds beneath. The sunlight sparkled against pools, fountains and statues. Around those were paths and small bridges, dining sections, meeting areas and entertainment corners. For the many guests staying at the adjoining villas, the likes of casinos, spas and shops provided for every need while the guests enjoyed the lavish Post-Benefit Concert Gala. The most prominent feature of the gardens was Theater Square with its plush booths and large screen showing a continuous rerun of the recent Flechette Cosmetics Benefit Concert. This year it had been held on the prestigious planet affectionately called G2; Nixodonia's Second Governing planet.

The immensity of the area seemed smaller now as it milled with nearly a thousand of the galaxy's most prominent and powerful. Marie lifted her chin, hoping to spot her mother's lush golden hair. The elegant Genevieve Flechette was meandering through the crowd, greeting the guests. Paul was supposed to be there doing the same! What on earth had gotten into him lately, Marie wondered? Surely he wasn't getting jumpy just days before their wedding!

Nerves, that was all. Marie would need something to calm her own if he didn't show up! Someone touched her arm. She glanced sideways to see her personal bodyguard, Bill Tripp. Bill forewent all pretense of the fashion world and sported his balding head with pride. His wide shoulders and strong body were somehow incongruous with his ever-beneficent smile. He'd been her primary agent since she was six years old.

"Bill," she breathed with relief.

Paul has arrived," he said. "He's changing in his quarters at the house."

She smiled and touched his arm. "Thank you. Will you get him here the minute you can?"

"Sure. I'll get the boys to keep an eye on you."

It was always the same two "boys" whom Bill had within his physical radius. They took a step closer as Bill spoke to them. Marie thought quickly. "No, Bill. Send your boys for Paul. President Knabon is due to arrive at the pier and I need you there with me."

"Done," Bill said, turning to organize his men on yet another mission to fetch Paul. Anne immediately organized Marie's entourage for the slow, welcoming walk through the concourse towards the river's docking bay.

One of the events tonight would be the handing over of the Solar Sensations Cup to Marie a fifth and unprecedented time. Marie knew that it was no more than a popularity contest run by the most prestigious of the fashion magazines but she didn't belittle its significance. Ken Lass, owner and editor of *Celebrity Quest*, ran the annual contest. He'd followed her career since her birth, along with the stupendous growth of her father's company, Flechette Cosmetics. The FC logo was now a universal symbol, known in nearly all fourteen sectors of the great nation of Nixodonian States.

Paul was supposed to be taking care of making FC a household name in Nixodonia's god-forsaken Fifth Sector, but *that* little pet project had taken him away far too many times lately.

Concerns over the project niggled at her mind. A new research lab to produce new products with a multitude of yet undiscovered plant life on a nearly unknown planet called Doria seemed far too ambitious at a time like this.

But Paul would not wait until after the wedding. He needed to prove himself seeing as he'd come from the beggar planets of Ashum to rise to the top of the FC executive ladder. He was desperate to eradicate the apparent condescension of FC's aristocratic executive.

Two weeks, she thought, taking in a breath. Then the wedding, then the much-needed month-long honeymoon, a surprise holiday planned by Paul. Then she and Paul would travel to Doria to attend the grand opening of Paul's precious new FC plant, the only thing he seemed to talk about these days anyway. While on their honeymoon, she and Paul would quietly enjoy the release of her first movie *Angel's Test*. She'd sung its theme song, and its success would be honored tonight as well.

Her heart suddenly shuddered painfully. In less than a second, Javid appeared at her side. Despite the entourage of twenty around her, she felt the need to grasp her beautician's hand, not caring what they might think. "Javid," she whispered down to him, a head shorter than she, "I'm so overwhelmed!"

He closed his eyes and squeezed her hand. A little steady moan, a sound Marie recognized as a calming technique he'd learned years ago on his home world, sent a ray of peace straight into her aching heart.

"Just tonight," he whispered. "Think of only tonight, and all these wonderful people here to celebrate so many events with you. You have only to take one step in front of the other."

She nodded, taking in a deep breath as he'd taught her.

He gave her a teasing grin, flipping to his mischievous side with an ease that always surprised her. "Go ahead," he said. "Have a ball!"

With a liberating smile on her face, she nodded to Anne, who started the procession deeper into the arms of the cheering crowd. With Javid's little portent invigorating her, it didn't matter that Paul wasn't at her side. It was an exhilarating time. Marie had the pleasure of seeing some good friends, many of whom she'd been too busy to contact in recent months.

Mareeee!" squealed an excited friend. Marie accepted the hug from President Knabon's granddaughter, Keeta Abby. Keeta's auburn hair flounced in large natural curls at her back as she hugged Marie exuberantly.

"My turn to congratulate the Princess of Nixodonia!" Keeta said beaming.

"Stop that," Marie scolded. "You know how I loathe that pet name, especially seeing as I'm a High Court member of a *democratic* nation."

Keeta waved a hand. "Oh, don't give me that administrative talk. I hear enough of it at home. We need a little charm in this country and you, my princess, are the chosen one."

Marie's heart warmed. "From you, Keeta, I'll take it as a compliment."

Keeta's features unexpectedly sobered. She bent to Marie's ear. "I was sorry to hear those dreadful rumors about Paul."

Marie flushed despite herself. "They're not true. You know that!"

"Of course, but it's nasty business anyway. Even *Celebrity Quest* has an article about it in this morning's issue."

"They do!"

It was Keeta's turn to flush. "You...haven't seen it?"

"No!" Marie lowered her eyes, hiding her embarrassment. Abruptly, she took Keeta by the hand and led her into the fold of her entourage. "What did the article say?" Marie asked.

Keeta swallowed. "Ah...that Paul was seen in Sector 5 fondling a...another woman."

The muscles in Marie's neck were visibly taut. "Did it say *where* he was seen?"

Keeta blinked, obviously surprised at the question. "Well, no—"

"Good," Marie cut in stridently, "at least that's still a secret!"

Keeta let out a long breath. "Was he at his new lab?"

"Yes, and we wanted its location kept secret until the grand opening."

"I'm so sorry. Especially because of me and Joe."

Marie sighed. "You're sorry because you're happily married and I'm engaged to an apparent philanderer?"

"Well, yes, I suppose that's it," Keeta agreed sadly.

"Don't worry, Keeta, "Marie assured. "Paul was just playing with the press as a way to release his tension. It makes me angry, but there's no philandering going on. Be assured of that." Suddenly Marie wasn't so sure anymore. Had she been throwing herself into a sea of denial as the wedding approached? Was she drowning with her prince charming? This was the third time after all.

Anne broke her train of thought. "We must move along, Marie." Then she added, "Did I hear that right about Paul?"

"You should have known about it, Anne!"

"I didn't have time to read this morning's issue," Anne defended. "But, I can't believe their audacity! If you want to ask Ken Lass about it, I've been told he's arrived."

Marie had given *Celebrity Quest* sole rights to the day's events seeing as they were presenting her with their coveted Solar Sensations award. "Yes, I'll speak with Ken, alone! As soon as you can arrange it."

"I'll get on it immediately," Anne replied.

Congressmen and senators milled in the lounge areas, sampling exotic drinks and chatting politics, a hot topic these days with an impending crisis in one of their neighboring countries—an issue Marie hadn't had a minute to consider. In another area, Marie noticed Enderal's governor talking with Keeta's husband, Joe Abby. Joe was Nixodonia's secretary of defense, a position that kept him close to President Knabon. Keeta had chosen well among her many admirers, Marie thought warmly.

Arriving at Theater Square, Marie was thunderously applauded as she took her seat to watch a small portion of the benefit concert. Her mind reflected back to the concert on G2. Moments after it was over, Marie had received an intergalactic hyperlink that sent her rushing home to her father's bedside. Again, he brushed with death. Again, he miraculously recovered. The entire ordeal was still a mystery to Doctor Hurd and his extensive staff who'd set up a ward at the estate. They were the galaxy's best, and yet...

Marie had accepted the acting role just prior to her father's illness. As she shook hands with dozens of dignitaries, she wondered what could have possibly convinced her to take on an acting career! But family, most notably Paul, had urged her to accept the coveted role offered by Henrie Marchand, Nixodonia's most successful director. In the end, *Angel's Test* had been fun, but a challenge to say the least.

Marie's attention was taken up by the sudden live appearance of the entire cast of *Angel's Test*, including her leading man, Ekeem Danderwood. Despite herself, she squealed with delight.

"Oh I'm so glad you could all come!" she cried, leaning over the golden railing of the booth to grasp Ekeem in a hug. He'd been her lover and defender in the action drama, deemed by critics to be the best movie of the year.

"Angel, Angel," he wooed. "You should adopt your character's name in earnest," he said for the hundredth time.

"Sorry, Ekeem," she grinned. "That isn't going to happen."

He sighed. "Well, then, my Princess, you'll be happy to know that I have a surprise for you."

"Really?"

"Yes, and you'll love it." He kissed her on the cheek and moved on. Marie wasn't as popular with all of the cast. Her FC duties had often caused delays and rescheduling. The director, Henrie Marchand, had always supported her, and for that she hadn't loathed him completely by the end of the shoot. Even to Marie, his methods of transforming her from a completely green actress into a supposed superstar had seemed rather strange. She'd found herself in private lessons with him trying all kinds of speech therapy, intonations, especially for her theme song, "Follow Me."

The strangest exercise had been learning to handle a weapon. Target practice was not something Marie had ever dreamed she'd pick up as a skill. She'd hassled Bill endlessly for help, to get it just right, and all for naught. The segment was eventually cut. Suddenly she spotted the director's tall frame in the crowd. He nodded, Henrie's indication that he'd send an envoy to schedule a proper greeting later.

Paul Lambert.

Henrie Marchand.

The two names had sparked something deep within her soul. She was of ancient French descent, something that didn't exist anymore except in family names, the odd expression, or bits of trivia found only in rare historical manuscripts stored in the government archives. Hervos Nixodonia had quelled the endless wars among a vast number of star systems by amalgamating the whole lot into Nixodonian States. The hundreds of state colonies eventually restructured into the present fourteen sectors but the old name of Nixodonian States remained along with an elite board of statesmen. These law-making members still acceded to their positions from a group of original ruling families, the only governing remnants of the ancient empires to which both her parents had family ties. Perhaps Hervos had done the galaxy justice, but the price was egalitarianism—death of cultures as they were once known. Egalitarianism had been law and had taken hold until the millions of planets were somehow all the same. It saddened Marie, making Paul's equal interest in their ancestral roots a strong bond between them. Even though Henrie claimed to be nothing more than Nixodonian, she could see physical features in him that matched with profiles she'd dug up in the musty books of the government archives. Even her parents were unable to trace their cultural roots back more than a few generations before they, too, were lost to Hervos Nixodonia's social equality. And so, Marie and Paul were determined to find something to tie themselves to history itself, to help them cherish more than just national idolism.

Finally Marie met with her parents. Her eyes misted as she saw her father, standing, but with the help of a body brace beneath his elegant black attire. Raymond Flechette was stunning even as the ravages of the disease creased his face and contorted his previously proud and erect frame. Genevieve surpassed mere natural beauty. She was his pillar, her pillar! Marie grasped both of their hands.

"A wonderful party!" Raymond's hoarse voice crooned.

"Maman, thank you—"

Genevieve smiled forlornly. "We'll have to remind Paul of his manners," she said simply.

"How are you feeling, Papa?"

"Grand! Genevieve and I are busy making up for not being at the concert with you."

The redeeming factor for Marie was the concert's success. The Foundation could now pour money into this year's proposal; a series of four hospitals for children on less fortunate planets, including one in Paul's birth system of Ashum.

Marie was suddenly faced with a group of the nation's leading men. She knew them all, some on a more personal level, like Joe Abby, who'd reunited with Keeta. With them walked Senator Ormo Black of Sector 4. She knew Senator Black mostly by reputation. He owned the exclusive rights to build spacecraft for the Nixodonian Space Navy. The rich planetoids of Sector 4 had favored the senator, who was now, in his own right, one of the richest men in the galaxy. Despite an air of sociability, his piercing gaze looked straight through her with a hard edgy intelligence. "You look ravishing, Miss Flechette," he breathed against the back of her hand as he kissed it.

"Your factories must be very busy these days, Senator, with the crisis in Telexa." Marie found herself sifting through bits of information she'd picked up mostly through social gossip.

"My dear, the brutal spats of such uncivilized nations don't concern us much."

"Oh?" Marie said, a little surprised. "But, Telexa is our largest neighbor, is it not?"

"True," Ormo Black returned, "and still no threat to Nixodonia. Be assured that your national security advisor is keeping a watch on the situation, as courtesy to those interested, of course."

"Our security advisor?" Marie questioned. "Is he here?" She'd met Ray Lapp years ago during her political studies at the prestigious universities of G2.

"Yes," Black said, turning. "Ray, the lady would like to say hello."

Ray Lapp stepped forward. "Marie! So good to see you. Gosh it's been, what—since Joe's wedding, I think?"

"I'm afraid so. How have you been?"

Ray's hallmark blond hair and blue eyes caused all too many women to swoon. "Not as lucky as you, it seems." He grinned lopsidedly. "I hear the Princess of the Galaxy has finally captured Prince Charming."

"Oh, Ray," she groaned. "The only reason you're not captured yourself is because you love your playboy life."

He laughed heartily. "You know me too well, Marie. But, we'll miss you."

Her eyes widened. "You're not getting rid of me! You just might not see me as often." She lowered her voice. "Paul and I are going to raise a family."

"Really? What about FC?"

"Oh, I won't give that up! Just the parties." Marie glanced longingly at her father. "I think Papa will retire soon, but Maman and I will carry on. I'll be taking on the presidency soon—" The words caught in Marie's throat.

"Ah, Marie, we're all praying for Raymond. But, you wait! He'll recover and head FC for another fifty years."

Marie nodded solemnly. "I hope so, Ray."

Bill Tripp kept one eye on Marie while listening to his earpiece. He turned to Anne. "The President's ship will be landing in exactly ten minutes." Anne nodded and moved the group along. The afternoon sun glittered across the rippling river as the luxury Presidential craft hissed in its descent to a soft landing inside the walls of a secluded riverside landing site. Hovering above were dozens of other vessels, all in the same striking black and gold presidential colors. Marie knew that those ships might look handsome, but they housed enough firepower to secure the entire planet of Enderal if the need arose. Cheers exploded as President Knabon and his wife, Leea, were lowered smoothly by a ramp to the tarmac. Marie forced her stiff smile to soften. She'd never grown to like Pao Knabon much, found him a bit spineless, a bit of a "yes man," whereas his father, Ismal, had been powerful and disciplined. Ismal had been the man to grant her an honorary membership to the High Court, one of Marie's most valued achievements. Ismal was gone now. Marie would always mourn him.

Marie greeted Pao, then the First Lady. Leea Knabon was a beautiful, but misguided woman in Marie's eyes. Surely Leea could have married better than the likes of Pao! She leaned toward Leea. "I have a tiara to return to you," she said.

The comment caught the President's attention. "You mean the tiara you wore for the concert belongs to my wife?" His smile surrendered to laughter.

"I honestly didn't mean to toss it off like that when I started my dance. I assure you that it survived intact."

Leea laughed. "Forget about acting, Marie. Live theater is for you."

"Oh, I don't think so," Marie guaranteed. "I'm following in your footsteps, Leea. At least four children."

"I'll hold you to that. By the way, Johnas came with us."

Marie groaned inwardly. Johnas? How unfortunate. At that moment, he stepped towards her, his eyes seeking hers. Just like his father, his frame was tall and thin, his features aquiline. Marie found him completely unattractive, certainly not someone she would court, let alone marry, but this had been Johnas' quest since they were children. He approached her, slipping a hand around her waist and inappropriately pulling her close. "You haven't, by any chance, changed your mind about that commoner you're marrying?" It was obvious he wasn't joking.

Marie smiled brightly. "Quite the contrary. I can't wait."

"That's too bad. Paul Lambert is a nobody who'll remain a nobody! Trust me, Marie, I could offer you so much more, but you wouldn't even agree to court me." He gave her a stupid pout.

"That's the disadvantage of being so far away, Johnas. I know Enderal isn't on the other side of the galaxy, but it isn't next door, either. You've just made the trip, so surely you understand?"

"Who was talking about a lengthy courtship? All I needed was to hear yes. And presto! No more grueling space flights."

She refrained from gasping. "Johnas, there are millions of women just hoping to catch your eye."

"I don't want those millions of women."

She rolled her eyes. "Please. You're like a brother to me." She could only return his pout.

Johnas frowned. "He's a lucky man, but beware, my love. I've been hearing rumors."

"You're not the one spreading them, are you?"

He gasped. "Now come, Marie. I'd do anything to win your heart, but I'm an honorable man." The beguiling grin that followed was a feeble attempt to inveigle her. "However, if my rival is about to fall from your graces, do remember my proposal."

She looked at his homely features and tried to smile genuinely. "I will, I promise."

Following Johnas was Senator Yousef Phoebe and his wife, Lola. Yousef Phoebe was the only man who could truly intimidate her. He was tall and large, with the physique of a wrestler. His gentle smile and pale gray eyes should have softened his appearance but his carriage had the means to make her cower. Nevertheless, he and Lola were still the largest private donors to the Benefit Foundation.

She'd never understood Senator Phoebe's choice of wives, other than the theory that opposites attract. Lola Phoebe was short and squat with a shrill voice that could be heard clear down the tarmac. "Marie, so good to see you," she squealed, her lavish gown rivaling Marie's own. "Your performance of 'Follow Me' was such a surprise to everyone. It was an absolute treat."

"And, as I predicted," Yousef's baritone voice added, "the final total was a record."

"Yes," Marie confirmed. Her performance of *Angel's Test's* hit song for the closing act had been Yousef Phoebe's idea. He apparently loved the tune and swore that a personal performance by the singer herself would increase donations. Why, she couldn't imagine. It was Marie's first attempt at being a pop singer. Yet, despite what she felt were mediocre talents, the song was presently a top hit in twelve of Nixodonia's fourteen sectors.

Within minutes, the entire assembly was escorted back under the protection of the canopies. "Have you talked to Ken yet?" Marie asked Anne as they proceeded.

"Yes. But," Anne glanced at Marie, "Paul has arrived. I thought you might like to see him first. I've arranged ten minutes for you at his pavilion."

"Good." Marie lifted her chin. "Take me there now."

CHAPTER 2

Marie dreaded her encounter with Paul. She entered his pavilion and froze. Her fiancé's disheveled look sent her anger sizzling. Considering he was one of the most handsome men she knew, he somehow looked like he'd just gotten out of bed and forgotten to wash his bleary eyes.

"Where have you *been*?" she hissed.

"Wow, what's with you? Such a loving hello. I was at the office trying to straighten out the last computer foul-ups from Doria."

"Doria? Will I ever hear the end of it!" She closed her eyes to hold back her temper.

"Not yet, sweetheart, but soon." His voice settled. "I mean that."

He did it to her again, and she nearly succumbed. His whole countenance softened as he sidled up to her, taking her in his arms and kissing her ever so gently, massaging her lips until she yielded. "Babe, I've missed you," he murmured. "But this was terribly important. The whole thing could fall apart just because we can't get the hyperlink working, and you know what that would mean."

"No. What?"

He sighed. "That FC wouldn't have contact with its soon-to-be biggest manufacturing plant, that's what. Still—" His lips were against hers again.

She pushed him away. "Paul! Not now."

"But, I've barely seen you since I got home."

"That's not my fault," she shot back. "You've been back for two days and yet Doria, which is about a trillion light years from here, keeps you away—mind, body and soul."

His shoulders slumped beneath the lapels of his tailored Duval suit. "You're right. I'm so sorry, Love. I promise I'll make it up to you."

"Too late. You missed the presidential greeting. Everyone noticed you weren't there."

"So I'll stick to you like glue for the rest of the evening."

Marie huffed. "That would be a good idea."

"In two weeks, we'll get a break. And just you wait and see what I have planned for us."

"I don't want a honeymoon with too much travel—"

"My love, you'll be so relaxed, you'll be like a wet noodle in my arms."

She smiled stiffly.

"So, let's get out there and meet our guests."

"Fine. Then afterwards, you can tell me what the tabloids caught you doing on your precious journey." She turned and marched toward the door of the pavilion where Bill stood guard.

"Just one minute!"

She turned to see Paul's face stricken with fear. His voice lowered. "What are you talking about?"

"You know what I'm talking about. And, if you don't, you can read about it in this morning's *Celebrity Quest* issue."

Paul's nostrils flared. "Those lousy bastards!" He pointed a defiant finger at her. "The tabloids have no right following me—Ken Lass and his hoodlums included!"

"Paul! You're engaged to me! They're going to follow you to the bathroom if they get a chance. So what did they catch you doing?"

"It's a lie, Marie."

"Don't insult me, Paul. I agree that the tabloids sometimes twist the truth a little, but to formulate an entire story with no factual basis?…No!"

Paul huffed. "I'm really sorry it happened this way, Honey."

"So am I."

From across the expanse of the pavilion their gazes held, hers stormy and determined, his timid and begging forgiveness. He threw up his hands. "Yes, I admit it. There were reporters, and pictures were taken, but it was for diversion. Nothing more!"

Marie said nothing.

"Okay," he said, nodding his head in resignation. "I gave a woman a ride home—and I got defensive and gave them something to write about, seeing as they had come all that way!"

"You *what*?"

Paul's voice rose to match hers. "Well pardon me, but I don't deal well knowing the entire universe scrutinizes every little move I make simply because of my association with you."

"Really?" She grinned stiffly. "Well then, if it's all too much for you, perhaps you should consider severing your *association* with me, as you call it."

Paul suddenly gave in, letting out his breath while running fingers through his jet-black hair. "Oh Creator, what have I done. I'm so sorry." He walked over to Marie and pulled her into his arms. "God forgive me, Honey. I didn't mean any harm. Mostly, I was angry that it wasn't *you* getting into that vehicle. Ah, Sweetheart, I'll do everything I can to turn this around. I'll talk to the press and think of something brilliant to mollify them with."

Marie nearly snorted. "No. No more brilliance from you tonight."

Paul pulled her back, seeking her gaze. "Does that mean you'll forgive me?"

A frown touched her lips. "I'll think about it. Meanwhile, please be a gentleman."

He straightened. "Of course! Come on. Let's go show the guests who we really are, hmm?" He took her by the hand and led her to the door. Outside the crowds greeted them with loud cheers. The couple smiled. Paul raised her hand in such a way that it displayed his fiancée's immense diamond ring.

Inside her pavilion office, Anne Amaaka read the *Celebrity Quest* article with eyes wide open.

"…She's a sensation! She's a Solar Sensation!

Marie Flechette's performance of "Follow Me" at the Benefit Foundation concert was, to say the least, a huge success. Such professionalism does not come as a surprise to those of us continually astounded by Marie's abilities. It's unfortunate that we cannot expect the same from the man she is about to marry. An outpost reporter witnessed Paul Lambert indulging in behavior not becoming of one about to wed into the distinguished Flechette family. A man in his position should have his eyes riveted on his more than solid future. It seems, rather, that his eyes riveted to the buttocks of a Sector 5 working girl…"

Huffing, she threw the magazine down. "Outpost reporter?"

Ken Lass sat on the edge of Anne's desk, an ankle pulled over his knee, his demeanor unperturbed. His flaming red hair and boyish energy had hung on with rare tenacity. He wasn't old, Anne thought. It just seemed that he'd been in the business since the beginning of time.

"I'm telling you the truth." Ken said. "I didn't authorize that article—"

"You're the chief editor of this tabloid."

"*Tabloid?* We're talking *Celebrity Quest* here, Anne."

"Still a tabloid."

"Fine, whatever you want to call it. I'm telling you the truth."

"Well, you can tell Marie that yourself. She wants to see you."

"Good, when?"

"Five minutes."

"Even better."

"Bill Tripp will escort you."

"That's bad," Ken grumbled. "That man makes my life miserable."

"He's a bodyguard, Ken."

"Oh, he's much more than that, Anne, but like the rest of them, he's blind as a bat to what's ahead."

Anne's expression flattened. "What's that supposed to mean?"

Ken moaned. "Ah, not you, too?"

"Me, too?"

"Don't you see? Marie's popularity has grown to proportions never before achieved in our history. There's never been a nation as big as Nixodonia for a single person to conquer, but she's done it! What's ahead for FC is more than anyone is prepared for."

"Aren't you going a bit too far?"

"No, and now that she's performed the likes of 'Follow Me,' there'll be a whole nation ready to do just that. Where is she going to lead them?" His eyes shifted from Anne's to Bill Tripp's who now glared at him from the doorway. "You'd better figure it out soon, because keeping the frenzy down is going to be FC's primary concern in the very near future."

Anne gave a short laugh. "You're crazy!"

Ken looked dead serious. "That attitude will be your undoing, Anne." He glanced at Bill. "And your biggest security risk, Mr. Tripp."

Ken was no less than tossed into a meeting room with Marie. She spun to face him, her arms crossed defiantly across her chest. "I can't believe you had the guts to show up here tonight, Ken. I want you off the estate. Now."

"Sure. What do I do with the hundred staff here to cover the event?"

"Put someone else in charge."

"I know what you must be thinking—"

"Good. Then you can leave. Now."

"Wait, wait!" Ken's fingers splayed in a pleading gesture. "Just give me one minute to explain. I have a couple of guys on staff who are hard-core fans of yours—but not especially of Paul."

"So you're blaming them?"

"No. But at least they honored their bargain with Paul not to disclose Doria as the place where they found him. Sector 5 is the only location disclosed."

Marie's stomach churned. Paul had bargained with the reporters?

"I'll take full responsibility," Ken assured. "In fact, I'll make an apology here tonight."

"You really are a class act, Ken."

"Marie. That apology will be heard galaxy-wide. But please, tell Paul not to be so obvious!"

"He's explained it to me. That's all I need. So, you speak with your staff or this will be the last time you ever cover an event of mine. Understood?"

"Understood. But I was right when I encouraged you to perform 'Follow Me.'" Ken's tone rose. "You were sensational. When did you learn to dance like that?"

"Out, Ken!" her voice snapped. "I'm warning you. Tread lightly."

Bill appeared. He clamped steely fingers over Ken's shoulder and shoved the editor out of the tent and into the custody of his boys. Bill turned back to a distraught Marie. "Are you all right?" he asked, his eyes studying her.

Her shoulders shuddered. "Bill, could I be all wrong about Paul?"

Bill frowned. "This is a stressful time, Marie."

She knew he was biting his tongue. Paul wasn't one of Bill's favorite people, either. In fact, it seemed that her parents were the only ones who approved of him. A company man, one who'd started from the bottom and was now making upper management's heads spin. No matter how much potential Doria's botanical assets proved, Paul could have chosen a smaller project closer to home and still proven himself to the company executives. Marie drew in a breath. "Could you call Javid for me. I think he'd better freshen me up."

A minute later, the beautician was touching up Marie's lips, but Javid knew it was consoling she needed most. She murmured pleadingly. "Javid, do you think we could do one of your prayers now? The kind that sees the future?"

Thin eyebrows rose up his long forehead. "Now?" His voice was full of surprise. "But, this isn't a very good place, my lady."

She sighed. "You're right. How about at my office in the morning?"

"Of course, my lady!"

She squeezed his hand, knowing the gods of his faraway home world would support her until then, even if it was just in her imagination.

At Paul's request, they sat in Theater Square to watch her performance of "Follow Me." On the large screen she watched herself urge the audience on. For months before the concert, *Celebrity Quest* had suggested that the ticket holders ask for a special performance by thumping out the rhythm of the Marie's pop song against the stadium floor. There'd been no hesitation from the crowd. She'd barely made her closing remarks when the thumping rhythm began. Paul squeezed her hand. "Now there's a sexy dame," he said as they watched Marie on-screen undo the skirt portion of the gown and toss it aside. The crowd went wild as she revealed skintight leggings beneath. It was then that a national treasure, the First Lady's tiara, was tossed aside giving freedom to Marie's glowing curls.

Marie cringed as the sound-system picked up the clatter of the priceless diamond piece hitting the stage floor. She peeked over and shared a wincing grin with Leea Knabon. On screen, Marie spread her arms and bellowed, "*Follow Me!*" All those around her, Paul included, clapped and cheered as they watched Marie strut to mid-stage to begin her song:

> *"You asked me tonight, when the moons were up,*
> *Will we ever change, might we ever unite?*
> *I'll tell ya baby, listen…listen*

> *Life is a paradox,*
> *Untangle the mystery, untie the knot."*

Marie flushed as she watched herself thrust a hip to catch the glint of dancing laser light. As the song went on, the audience could be heard singing the words along with their hostess.

> *"I see the cries of my people,*
> *I see your empty hearts, I see the wreckage of your past,*
> *Listen, listen to the distance in your hearts,*
> *Listen to the sadness and your heart sinks so fast."*

She sang with passion, Fists to her bosom. Stepping to the edge of the stage, the hostess reached out to the hundreds of hands that begged for a touch. Marie found her eyes riveted to the screen, remembering the exhilaration of connecting with her fans, of letting them see her as someone real, not a fashion icon, not a concert hostess, or even a High Court member.

As her own words spilled out, the stage filled with a chorus of two hundred strong dressed in white flowing robes. They emerged from a thick backdrop of white smoke to form a semicircle behind her, all the while chanting the punctuating baritone chorus, "follow me, follow me…"

Marie's voice rose above theirs:

> *"Untangle the mystery, untie the knot.*
> *Come on, follow me—cause you know not the way,*
> *Don't fear for your life, I know the answers, can't you see.*
> *Follow me…follow me…follow me!"*

"Ekeem!" she gasped, suddenly remembering her leading man's promise for a surprise. Didn't he somehow get all two hundred of her back-up singers, dressed in their white robes, to converge in front of the screen and sing their parts? The effect was powerful, the base notes vibrating the ground around them. On the screen, Marie's body was raised in an electromagnetic tractor beam, her arms out wide, enveloped by a hologram of white wings that made her look like an angel, congruent with her character's name in the movie. Angel.

Paul laughed with delight and shouted above the noise. "What a performance!"

Moments later, the screening was over and Ken Lass stood at the podium. His promised apology was muted by the cheering of a well-relaxed crowd. Just moments later Marie walked up to receive the huge silver Solar Sensations Cup. Even President Knabon came on stage to be photographed alongside the Cup winner.

Soon after, Marie and Paul moved among the guests. Paul stayed within inches of his fiancée. "Hello Harin," he said, shaking hands with one of his business associates.

"Congratulations to both of you," Harin said. "Paul, we hear your new research facility is coming along well."

"Like a master plan."

"Rumor has it, that project is on a planet called Doria. I've never heard of the place."

Marie stiffened. So much for his bargaining skills, she thought.

Paul smirked. "Forget the rumors, Harin. The project's actual location is a secret."

Harin laughed. "Well, at least we know it's in Sector 5. Are you worried about the Telexan war?"

Marie's spine stiffened. "War? What war?" she demanded.

Paul threw her a glance. "It's all right, Honey, it doesn't—"

"I thought Telexa was in a state of civil unrest. That's a far cry from war!"

"Well, that civil unrest was declared war just a few days ago," Harin informed her. "It happened after those thugs who call themselves the TRA annihilated a planet said to harbor spies against its regime. Pretty radical, wouldn't you agree?"

Marie was aghast. "Paul, could the plant be in danger?"

Harin piped in. "Ah, yes, the Sector 5 lanes are pretty much the only way through to Telexa."

"We're not in danger."

She pulled back on Paul's hand. "I don't think it's a good idea to—"

"Don't *worry*. There's no danger. I've checked into it."

The conversation continued but Marie didn't hear it. Only minutes later the subject resurfaced with another group of guests. An alarming number of people seemed to think it was funny. "Can you believe it?" the Enderal attorney, Mr. Duva, spouted. "Once they topple the Telexan government, the TRA plan to trap some of Nix State's peripheral planets rather than start from scratch with exploration teams."

Marie cut in. "This sounds like a serious matter."

"Don't worry, Miss Flechette," Duva placated. "Joe Abby is monitoring the situation carefully. Besides, the TRA know better than to come anywhere near our borders."

"Yeah. That would be like putting a hand-blaster up the nose of a turbo-laser cannon."

Marie didn't join in the laughter. She could only hope to dig up something positive to relieve her sudden anxiety. "Isn't there a place called the Fringe between ourselves and Telexa anyway?" she asked. "Doesn't that offer us some protection?"

"Well, not that we need protecting, but yes, the Fringe is quite a wide band of space, and quite tough to navigate. It's rumored that some pretty good freighter pilots come from there."

"True," Paul added. "You see them in Sector 5 all the time."

"I thought no one lived in the Fringe," Marie said.

"Oh, not folks like you and me are familiar with," he answered. "I took to hanging out at the local establishments just to hear the stories. Now that's entertainment!"

"Really?" Marie huffed.

"I even heard stories about pirates that would make your skin crawl," Paul laughed, enjoying the surprised expressions of his peers.

Marie began to pull him away. He looked at her then gasped. "Aw, Sweetheart! I didn't mean to scare you. They're just stories, of ancient times. There hasn't been trouble with pirates for years."

She could stand no more. She had Bill escort them to her private pavilion. There, she faced Paul again. "What is japanning to you?"

"What?" He shrugged as if bewildered.

"The local *establishments*?"

"There's not exactly a lot to do after hours on Doria, Marie," he said in a huff. "Look, Babe, I'm really tired tonight and it seems that I just keep messing up! I'm space-lagged, and I'm being a lousy host, plain and simple."

Paul's shoulders suddenly slumped. "Look, this is your party. Why don't I fake an emergency at the office and go to the villa and rest a while. Maybe you can join me later."

Although Paul had his own quarters here at the estate, he'd kept his private villa in the city for times of refuge. Marie sighed. "You know I can't go there. Bill thinks the villa is a security risk at the best of times."

"Bill should stay out of our affairs."

Marie's teeth clenched. "Don't start with that, Paul. Just go to the villa and I'll see you in the morning, okay?

"Okay" He sighed then shook his head as if in reverence. "Thanks, Babe."

CHAPTER 3

Late the next morning, Marie paced the plush carpet of her penthouse office located on the top floor of the tallest building of the FC complex. She stared out of her floor-to-ceiling windows at the other dozen matching ebony black towers that made up the FC headquarters. She wasn't really focusing on them, but at the river beyond, and Enderal Lake Park with its swimming beach that she'd never used—again, security risks. Her gaze moved farther, to the towers and spirals reaching above the envirobubbles of Enderal City. Somewhere in there, Paul was *still* at his villa. He called to tell her he'd be tied up for most of the day, but promised he'd be at the estate long before the guests began arriving for their engagement party tonight.

Marie propped a hip against her desk, her worried mind recalling yet another of the morning's events. Her day had begun with Javid and his prayer drum. The entire affair had frightened her, although she knew she shouldn't take it seriously. It seemed the gods of Rashmar thought the rumors about Paul were true, that she should protect both herself and FC vigilantly. "Be sure of Paul's motives," Javid had conveyed. "Be sure of your own."

The recollection had Marie trembling. Was she kidding herself? Was Paul just someone competent enough to manage FC with her after her father was dead? Did they really have mutual interests or did she merely crave to repeat her parent's husband-and-wife team success? Was it just the need for security, with children of her own to carry on the Flechette dynasty?

She lowered her forehead into her hands, easing the ruminations that drummed at her brain. At least Javid had said positive things—of sorts. He'd said, "More powerful than your troubles, I see brightness and joy in your future. Be courageous. There are never wrong choices, just choices."

"Right," she drawled beneath her breath. That *future* could be light years away and she might lose her mind before then.

CHAPTER 4

Henrie Marchand gave a deep pull on the fat Dorian cigar Paul had offered him. The director raised an eyebrow in satisfaction but the gift was obviously not enough to console the old man. Paul fidgeted restlessly in the chair facing the director's desk, angry that a little flirting had so riled Henrie, not to mention Marie. Henrie had obviously not appreciated the job of passing on a warning to Paul from Yousef Phoebe, but Paul couldn't understand how such a small incident could cause such an uproar.

He thought of Yousef Phoebe and supposed that carrying a dual leadership such as he did presented some logistical problems mastered only by the truly professional. Covertness, discretion, never attracting unnecessary attention—he could still hear Phoebe drill the surreptitious etiquette of an infiltrator into his head. Phoebe used his own success as an example, over twenty years holding a seat in the Nixodonian senate while maintaining his alliance to the TRA without suspicion. Sure, Paul could be a bit more careful, but they needed to remember how important he was and show a little leniency if not respect. Just the same, Paul wrung his hands, disturbed at how they'd become so uncomfortably clammy.

"Look," he said to Henrie. "The Dorian plant is running smoothly. The shipments are moving through without any trouble. Phoebe will have a copy of all the transactions in his file by tonight."

Marchand's gaze followed a bluish swirl towards the ceiling. "That's good. But things are going to move quickly now. Our timing needs to be precise. My job is to release *Angel's Test* on schedule. Your job is to get Marie on that honeymoon. To accomplish that, you have to keep your family jewels zipped up where they belong. Honest, Paul. You have two weeks left. Surely you can manage that!" Marchand huffed out the smoke and butted the cigar in the ashtray.

"Save your speeches, pal," Paul growled. "I said I've already fixed it."

"Neither of us is indispensable, Paul"

Paul drained the strong drink. Wiping a sleeve across his mouth, he pretended not to be afraid. "Wrong. I am."

"So I'm told. But you'll dispense with yourself if you don't get off those Dorian drugs. Sure, you developed some nice potions for us. That doesn't make you immune, my friend."

Paul smashed the empty glass against the polished top of the massive desk. "Drugs?"

Henrie watched his partner succumb to the exorbitant pressures they all felt these days. In earnest, Henrie hoped he could get the man some help before he destroyed himself, but it didn't look promising. Henrie leaned towards the flustered executive. "You think *Celebrity Quest* is on your ass? Be assured, Phoebe's men are watching you even more closely." Marchand held Paul's gaze a few interminable seconds before sinking back into the contour of his leather chair. Methodically, he lighted another of the exquisite cigars and pulled it to a bright glow. "Get home to your woman," he said in a tired voice. "Don't you have an engagement party to attend tonight?"

"Oh, yeah," Paul blinked. "That's tonight, isn't it?"

"Paul," Henrie sighed, "do yourself a favor. Be clean when you get there."

CHAPTER 5

The sun set behind the forests of Enderal Lake Park in a spectacular show of color. Some of the hues filtered through the tall narrow windows of the ballroom of the Flechette estate. The last of the golden light set aglow exquisite gowns and embroidered lapels of the three hundred guests milling about the floor. The presidential ship had left in the early afternoon, but many important people, including Senator Phoebe and his wife Lola had stayed to attend the much anticipated engagement party. The guests now waited patiently for the bridal party to appear at the top of the flaring staircase. Guests whispered concerns that the large ornate doors at the top of the stairs remained closed. The Flechettes were always punctual.

Marie stood in the anteroom above the ballroom, her face ashen, her hands trembling as she clutched the puffed layers of the silken dress. An hour! He was one bloody hour late! "I'm going to kill him, Papa!" she said to her father, who looked elegant again this evening.

Raymond frowned. "Perhaps he doesn't realize that such an event requires the presence of the groom."

Marie laughed bitterly. "Yes, in mind and body!"

Raymond strode toward her, revealing only a hint of the pain that had wreaked havoc on one of his hips earlier that day. He gathered her in his arms. "Oh, Sweetheart. I don't know what to say."

Marie pulled away from her father's embrace. "There are two possibilities," she said. "One, that there's been an accident. And two, that he's been...shall I say, distracted. I have Bill checking on both possibilities and it seems that the latter is most probable."

Raymond grimaced as Marie continued. "He's at the villa, and he's not alone. One of his friends was seen entering earlier. I still remember the security codes to the back gate so I'm going to go fetch the weasel. Then I'll mutilate him."

"You're a crazy woman, you know that?" Bill remarked as he squeezed his boys on either side of Marie in the back compartment of a small security vehicle.

"You were the first to agree that no one will suspect me in here," Marie said, embarrassed right along with the two agents who flushed as Bill piled the billowing gown inside the small craft.

"It looks like a meringue bomb exploded in here," she jested. The "boys" grinned sheepishly. Marie thought they looked like overgrown teddy bears with their huge muscles filling the security uniforms to capacity. She was suddenly troubled that these men, whose faces had become so familiar, were total strangers. Impetuously, she reached out a hand. Caught by surprise, the first agent reached over the folds of the gown to return the handshake, bobbing his head like a sewing machine in delighted response. She shared the greeting with the second agent, ignoring Bill's quick backward glance from the pilot's seat.

"I'm pleased to make your acquaintance," she said in a foolishly formal manner. "I'd like to personally thank you both for the excellent service you've provided to myself and my family over the years." Marie cleared her throat to break the subsequent silence. "What's your name, sir?" she asked the brute to her right.

"Spencer, my lady."

"And yours?"

"Rossgar." The man said. "We're pleased to be in your service this evening, my lady."

Marie smiled crookedly. "I'm not sure you'll say that later."

The craft gained security clearance into the city and wormed its way along the designated radar tracks that guided traffic in and out of the atmospherically controlled bubbles. They exited the busier thoroughfares and entered a quieter residential area. The craft came to a stop in the shadows of a narrow back alleyway formed by the high walls of adjoining villas. The craft bobbed almost imperceptibly as it hung a few feet off the ground at the back entrance to Paul's residence.

Marie accepted the assistance of the agents to disembark from the craft. The brutes gently tugged at the layers of material until they could pull her from the tiny craft. While patting to adjust the ruined form of the gown, Marie asked Bill to accompany her into the villa.

"This is out of my regular line of duty, Marie," Bill warned as he punched in the entry codes she'd recited to him "Are you sure you want to approach the matter this way?"

"It's the only way," she grumbled. "Personal confrontation...although I'll probably have to wake him up for the chat."

With a hollow thud, the large steel door opened and the two stepped into a spacious courtyard. Marie immediately realized they were not exactly alone. Lights blazed out of every window. Music pulsed through the thick walls. Marie spoke urgently. "Take off your jacket, Bill."

He hesitated a moment, then understood her plan to diminish his occupation. "That gown may throw them a bit, though," he warned.

She drew in a shaky breath. "We'll see."

Before they had taken two steps towards the back door, it crashed open. An entangled couple fell out onto the marble steps, squealing and groping and tearing off each other's clothing. The couple looked up with a start, but their attention was short lived. Beyond the couple, Marie was able to get a glimpse of the party going on inside. She smiled weakly at Bill. "The dress will do nicely."

Ignoring the couple, Marie and Bill stepped inside. Her wide eyes took in the horror before her. There wasn't a piece of furniture or stretch of wall that hadn't been sullied to some degree. The damage appeared cumulative. Over what? Months? The entire year she'd been away from this place?

A hundred people crowded the villa, most of them off in some drug induced world, or indulging in expensive, hundred year old Dorian champagne readily available from numerous crates scattered about the floor. Marie's gall rose when she remembered that Paul had promised to bring this rare champagne to the engagement party. Instead, it flowed freely into the glasses of these hideous guests. Marie could hear the whispered gossip over the rims of the stemware as eyes followed their walk through the kitchen and into the entertainment quarter. Marie stopped, her hard gaze surveying the hellacious playground.

Bill grasped her arm. "Let me get you out of here." he shouted over the blaring music.

"Don't stop me now, Bill."

"You're in danger here, Marie. I need to get you out."

"Danger of what? Finally accepting the truth?"

He wasn't sure if he should drag her out, or protect her on the quest she proposed next. "I need to see the bedroom," she told him. "Please, come with me." Her hands grasped the front of his shirt. "Promise not to be more than a step away."

Bill's shoulders dropped. Reluctantly, he nodded.

Tearing away from his supporting gaze, Marie turned towards the staircase and clawed her way through the inebriated mob to the second floor. She stopped before the large doors of the master bedroom, the room in which she'd first made love to Paul. She put up a palm, asking Bill to wait. Facing the door, she slammed her hand against the access plate, trusting that he wouldn't have bothered to delete her biological data. The panels parted, fully exposing the occupants on the bed.

"What the hell?"

Distorted as the voice was, Marie recognized it.

"That door is supposed to be sealed, so whoever is in here can get out!" Paul sat bolt upright in bed, as if to convey his request more forcefully. The look of shock that crossed his features was no match for the stone cold glare of his fiancée standing in the doorway. The trance was broken by an annoying whine from the naked woman who sat up beside Paul.

The woman pushed her unkempt hair from her eyes and squinted. "Who's this?"

Paul was frantic. He scrambled to cover his naked partner in a vain attempt to lessen the charge. "What are you doing here, Marie?" Paul demanded.

Marie wasn't even sure the words came from her lips. "You're supposed to be at our engagement party…but I see you're busy."

"What?" He slapped a palm to his forehead. "Blast! You're right, that's tonight, isn't it!"

Marie's voice blared, "I don't care what night it is. What are you doing with *her*?"

Paul scrambled out of bed, grabbing one of the sheets to wrap around his torso. Tripping and stumbling, he rushed towards her. "Ah, damned. This is *not* good. Listen, the guys wanted to throw a party for me. And…well." His voice fell to a whisper as he tossed his head in the direction of the bed. "The guys put me up to this. I guess I wasn't thinking."

They both jumped when the woman shrieked, "Put you up to it? Don't you dare, Paul. Get her out of here."

"Susie, shut up," Paul barked over his shoulder. "Oh, what rotten luck! Your poor father. He'll be devastated if you tell him about this, and with his illness, who knows what it could do to him."

Marie felt like she might choke. How could she have been so blind!

"Sweetheart, please. Don't tell Raymond. He's entrusting the company to me, and if he finds out about this—"

"Entrusting the company to *you*? You deranged maniac. The company is mine and always will be, so take your pitiful illusions and get out of my life!" She wrenched off the engagement ring and threw it across the room. It landed in Susie's lap.

CHAPTER 6

Marie hadn't slept by the time the prismed windows threw tiny shards of morning light against the library walls. She sat lifelessly on the couch, staring into the flames of the raging hearth. She and her parents celebrated all their victories in this room with its lined bookshelves full of ancient bound volumes, its glowing wooden floors inviting tranquility. They also came here in times of sorrow.

Genevieve entered the room and sat beside Marie. "Hi, Sweetheart. I hope you don't mind, but I contacted Cecilia."

"You did? But...that must have taken you hours," Marie gasped, knowing that intergalactic connections to the Fourteenth Sector were long indeed.

"I couldn't sleep, and I didn't think it would be right to have her come half way across the galaxy for a wedding that isn't going to happen."

Marie didn't want to express her disappointment. Cecilia was Marie's only aunt, her father's sister, a woman Marie adored.

"The two of us came up with an idea," Genevieve said with a mischievous smile.

"An idea?"

"Yes. She's wondering if you'd like to go visit her instead—get off Enderal, away from Paul, away from the press."

Marie blinked, thinking through the sudden change of plans. It had been a long time since she'd traveled to Cecilia's seaside home. Years before, Cecilia had taken up the near-lost art of oil painting. While traveling Nix States doing research, she fell in love with the water planet of Kutar 2. It was a long journey, but the thought of visiting the beautiful estate lifted Marie's dreary spirits.

Genevieve sighed. "Paul's been trying to reach you since early morning."

"That's probably how long it took him to clear his head and send his whore home."

Genevieve glowered. "At least he's agreed to stick to the story I made up for the press. I don't think you need to face him, or anyone. The galaxy may think this is their affair, but I think it is yours."

"Thank you, Maman," Marie whispered wearily.

"I hope you don't mind, but I checked on the next passenger liner to Kutar 2. Our own shuttle will be in service for another week and I couldn't get anything private on such short notice, so I reserved eight seats in the first class section of the *Starquest*. If you're interested, it leaves late this evening."

Marie sucked in a breath, struggling to assimilate all the new plans.

Genevieve took Marie's hand. "It will make only one stop, on Iggid in Sector 12. That should make for a fairly undisturbed voyage." Genevieve paused. "If you want to go that is."

Suddenly, Marie could barely contain her excitement. She thought fondly of the *Starquest*, an elegant, century-old cruise ship designed for luxury travel. Her head fell back against the couch and she laughed. "I'd love to go. I don't want to see Paul, I couldn't stand another social engagement, so yes! Absolutely." Marie threw her hands into the air. "I'll personally cancel my meeting with Henrie Marchand. I officially divorce him, too."

Genevieve laughed. "That's my daughter."

CHAPTER 7

Paul sat in the living room of his villa, not feeling any better about the fact that the maid with the heart-shaped ass left his needs temporarily satisfied and the villa half-ways respectable. The sun had long since risen since Marie had tossed the ring at him. He snorted and took another swig from the bottle of Dorian champagne resting on his middle. A shrill beep jolted him from his self-pitying thoughts. Damned! He didn't want to talk to anyone right now. He was about to ignore it when he realized it was his security line blinking. Paul reached over to the side table and punched in his password, swearing as he did so.

A voice exploded in his ear. "Paul! What the hell are you doing in the villa?" It was Marchand. Paul grimaced. "I can hear you, damn it. What do you think I'm doing here? I'm trying to reach Marie. It's suddenly like trying to talk to the president on election day."

"Have you talked to her at all?"

"Nope. Been trying since midnight."

"She's going to leave the planet, you ass. Did you know that?"

Paul sat bolt upright, slamming the wine bottle on the table. "What are you talking about?"

"If you were down here at control, you could be monitoring her yourself."

"Stop screwing with me. I don't need a lecture. She might call, and I'm sick."

"You're dead, Lambert."

He ignored that. "How do you know she's going anywhere?"

"She's booked eight seats on the *Starquest*."

"What!" Paul's attention was suddenly complete. This, he hadn't anticipated. "Where. Where is she going?" The *Starquest* was an intersystem ship. Now he did feel sick.

"Two stops: Iggid and the Kutar system."

Paul pushed rigid fingers through his unwashed hair. "Shit. She's going to her aunt's place on Kutar 2," he growled. "When is she going? I mean, how long before departure?"

"Late this evening," Marchand drawled.

"What?" He slid to the edge of the chair. "Wait...this evening? Like today?"

"That's what I said. So what are you going to do about it?"

"What's the matter with those fools down there? Why didn't we know this sooner?

"The tickets were just booked hours ago—under eight different names. To keep the press away, I presume."

Paul slapped his forehead. "Aw, shit! Tripp already has the estate barricaded like Hervos Nixodonia's High Palace, so I can imagine he's already done his thing at the Spaceport. God, I hate that man!" Paul's eyes darted about the villa, his mind formulating a plan. "We've got to stop her somehow. Right away. Wait there Henrie. Don't go anywhere. I'll think of something." He began to replace the receiver but slapped it back to his ear. "Stay right there. I'm coming down."

"I'm right below you," Marchand muttered in tired disgust.

"I've got a plan. It's already in my head so don't worry. I'll stop her. Problem is," he smacked his lips, "we probably can't actually stop her from leaving now, so we'll let her go, then I'll get her back later." Paul started to laugh and slapped his knee. "Wow! I've got a plan that'll blow your mind, Henrie. Wait right there. I'm coming down."

CHAPTER 8

She had no idea how the secret of her departure had leaked, but Marie was shocked to find a thousand crushing fans at the Enderal Spaceport. Bill reminded her of all those who'd attended the doomed engagement party. "There'll be a lot of waggling tongues in this town," he said as they moved through into the quiet of the Super Elite lounge. Within minutes, Marie and her escorts stepped into the transport tube that would take them towards the enormous bulk of the *Star-quest*. She relished the vague feeling of excitement that brewed within her as they approached the boarding hold. Suddenly, the sight of the liner represented an escape route, a lifeline, and they could *not* board her fast enough.

Through the transparent tube, Marie gazed at the *Starquest*'s bulk, which loomed ominously, like a gray mountain on the tarmac. It stretched over half a mile down the docking bay although it was classified a mid-sized luxury ship. As they approached, it suddenly occurred to her that this would actually be a holiday, one long overdue. Once beyond the stratosphere she would relax, knowing the ship wouldn't backtrack even if she changed her mind and gave in to the leniency she too often imparted to Paul.

No! No more Paul!

Her attention was diverted to the boarding procedures, made fluid for the four hundred passengers of the first class section. She stepped inside the space liner within the protective escort of Bill and his boys, Spencer and Rossgar. Following was her personal attendant, Reebe and her two assistants. Even though the three women could have handled Marie's cosmetic needs, she wouldn't think of being without Javid. She caught his eye. He returned with a furtive wink, bringing a mournful smile to her lips. His gods had been right again.

As they boarded, Marie was instantly surrounded by a dozen admirers. Her group was able to cocoon her until the bubble was burst by the voice of Lola Phoebe. The woman squealed with glee and waved frantically when she saw Marie. There was no avoiding the senator's wife. She must be on her way home to Iggid, in Sector 12. With an inner groan, she politely acknowledged Lady Phoebe with a smile and a nod, then sent Reebe to arrange a meeting with the lady for a later time. Marie noted that the senator wasn't at her side. Perhaps he'd stayed behind for business he often conducted on Enderal. Whatever the case, Lola's presence on this ship warranted a personal thank you and an apology.

A short time later, Marie chose to strap in for liftoff on the observation deck. Her three guards and Javid joined her. The women had stayed in the stateroom to prepare her cabin. The attendant secured the restraints as snugly as they would go around Javid's thin frame. He grinned endlessly through the procedure, loving the fuss, unable to hide his excitement at star-stepping once again. The journey would bring him closer to his home planet of Rashmar.

Marie was sorry that she couldn't send him there for a well-deserved vacation of his own, but Javid was in exile—twenty-one years already. He'd never expounded on the story more than to tell her that some very bad men had chased him and his people off their ranch lands. Eventually, he'd had to escape the planet or face death. Marie hadn't pried further. She was sorry he couldn't at least see his family but it seemed that the situation there still made it impossible. Javid had assured her that it didn't matter. Just being closer to Rashmar would give him a strong sense of communion with his gods.

A deep rumble vibrated in the heart of the craft as it sprang off the tarmac. Moments later, the ship broke through a thick cloud layer before silently stealing into space. They were blinded with a shard of raw sunshine blasting over the curvature of the planet as the ship executed a gentle roll. A breathtaking crescent view of Enderal enthralled the onlookers. The edge of the planet displayed swirls of emerald seas and ocher land formations, delighting the senses and stretching the imagination. Enderal City lay somewhere in the somber night of the dark side. The globe momentarily filled the view of the observation bubble before the next shudder marked their acceleration. The orb regressed, eventually to disappear from their field of view altogether.

Marie sat quietly, staring out the thick, clear walls of the observation deck. Just like that. They were all gone. She took in a ragged breath that joined the emotions of fear, loneliness, and excitement all churning in the stew pot of her heart.

To Marie's surprise, her vacation began with two days of near solid sleep. It took a third day before Marie regained some sense of self. Feeling refreshed, she craved to venture from her cabin. Another meal in her stateroom didn't sound appealing so Marie asked Bill to join her for dinner that evening seeing as he'd be right by her side anyway.

They entered the dining room together and were escorted to a table by the maître d'. Bill stepped ahead to pull back the chair for Marie. She gave him a radiant smile as they settled to order their meal. "Thanks for accepting my dinner invitation, Bill," she said as the champagne was poured. "You're at least someone who won't need a discourse on my entire, sordid affair."

"Oh? I thought you'd asked me so that I could ward off all the eligible men lurking about."

"Ha! *Lurk* better be as close as they get! I've been thinking carefully about some of the things my parents have said. Did you know Papa was near middle age when he met my mother?"

"Near middle age? Nice of you to put it that way," Bill muttered, aware that he was *near* middle age himself.

"You're welcome." She gave him a quick smirk while helping herself to the elegantly prepared meal. It tasted divine, making her realize how famished she was after eating so lightly over the past few days. Savoring another bite, Marie continued, "I've come to a realization that rushing is not only unnecessary, but dangerous. Much as it's hard to see this little dream die, I'm sure there are better things in store for me." She laid down her fork and looked at Bill. "You know, I'm just repeating every one of my mother's words and I don't believe a bit of it!"

Bill grinned widely.

"However," she raised a finger, "if I repeat it often enough, I'll believe it—eventually. Maman said that too." Wagging her head like a metronome, she recited more of her parent's counsel. "Time heals all wounds, so time is what I'll give this wound. Right?"

"Sounds to me like you've got it all figured out," Bill said. "I have nothing but faith that you'll bring the best upon yourself, and a good start is this holiday. I think it's long overdue."

"Well, thanks for your great faith in my ability to make wise decisions, but the holiday was Cecilia's idea." Marie dabbed at her lip with the silken napkin then let her wrist fall to the table. "Look at me Bill. Old enough to have two careers, yet I can't make decisions about my own personal affairs!"

"Don't be too hard on yourself. Not many of us can."

"I'm not sure I believe that." She paused. "But it makes me feel better to think that might be true. So...," Marie raised her glass, "I now solemnly acknowledge that this holiday will be one of self-discovery with Cecilia as my prudent teacher and guide. I know the minute I step into Cecilia's home the story will have to be told in detail, but that will be a way of putting closure on this whole ordeal. Besides, Cecilia has a way of injecting humor into everything, so by the end I shall be happy and completely self-assured."

"You're not saying that with a lot of conviction," Bill pointed out.

"Absolutely none," she said flatly.

He laughed. "Well then, just keep your focus on the present and enjoy a little freedom for a while. No more meetings or functions. No Henrie Marchand breathing down your neck, or mine!"

Marie frowned. "You were at odds with him from the beginning, weren't you?"

"Believe me, the feelings were mutual," Bill grumbled. "How many times did he literally kick me out of his little inner sanctum while he taught you his brand of acting lessons? Anything could have happened to you. I admit that I strongly disagreed with your father on this one, but Marchand had convinced him that his security was adequate and that *my* staff would be a distraction."

"And look, nothing happened," Marie soothed. "Let's just be thankful that neither of us will have to deal with Marchand for a while," Marie sighed. "Believe me, his archives have more holograms of me than were taken during my entire modeling career so I'm sure they'll manage their marketing campaign just fine. I wasn't looking forward to that part of it, anyway"

"I won't miss it either," Bill agreed. They gave each other a knowing look.

Marie gave a perky smile. "Enough of that! When I arrive on Kutar 2, I'm going to wear some old tattered clothing and take walks along the beach. Maybe I'll learn to paint. But mostly, I'm going to lounge about the estate and do nothing—be free of everything and everybody for a while."

He leaned forward. "Do I understand, then, that you're not disillusioned with the prospect of a little solitude?"

"No. I'm not disillusioned. I'm down right frightened. In fact I feel as void as the space outside this craft. I don't know if I'm happy or sad but I'm definitely frightened. I'm afraid I'll go from being Princess of the Galaxy to Spinster of Flechette Cosmetics because I can't find a man capable of handling the pressures of my lifestyle. So, you're right. Doing nothing is a pretty foreign concept to me. I'm not sure what to do with myself right now, let alone later."

Bill raised an eyebrow. "We could do a little sight seeing."

She looked at him quizzically. "Pardon me?"

"First, there's this ship and the space around it. It isn't just empty space out there, you know. There are hundreds of attractions to see along the way, if you know what to look for."

"I don't know what to look for," she admitted flatly.

"I'll show you. The observation deck is excellent on this craft and space geography is a small hobby of mine."

"Really?"

"Cross my heart."

Marie laughed. "Well then, you can start my education by sharing your secret knowledge of the stars with me."

"It's a date," he confirmed. As the meal was cleared away, Bill noticed that fatigue had begun to draw on Marie's shoulders. "Is there anything you'd like to do after dinner? The games room, theater?"

"No thanks, Bill. I have to get back to my stateroom."

He tapped the table. "You see? You do know what's good for you." He cocked his head. "If you're ready, the boys and I will escort you back."

Her smile waned. "Sorry, neither of us gets to rest just yet. Javid's going to get me ready for my meeting with you-know-who."

"Oh, dear. Is it time to visit Lola?"

"Yes. And, there's no avoiding it."

Javid cleverly tossed Marie's hair, creating a casual yet stylish look for Marie's meeting with Lola Phoebe. Their get-together was to take place in the opulent Stargaze lounge but Marie didn't plan on usurping Lola's garish styles. Nor would she condone them. Marie would dress in a semiformal fashion.

"I wish you didn't have to meet with that woman," Javid muttered. "She gives me the proper creeps."

"Thanks for you're concern, Javid," Marie said softly. "And one of these fine days I'm going to learn to take you seriously. You were right about Paul, you know. How do you do that?"

"It's not a matter of being right or wrong, my lady. I was simply giving you an omen. An omen is just a message. How you interpret that message is up to you. The omen itself is inert. However, now that the relationship is over, I want you to know that I share your pain."

Marie stopped the hand that worked feverishly at her hair. Grasping his long bony fingers, she squeezed them tightly. "Would you take a minute to call on your gods for me again? Tell me what's ahead? I'm frightened Javid. It would help to know that everything will be all right."

"Well," he drawled. "it's awfully soon since the last one, but for you, I'll certainly appeal again."

"Yes, please do," Marie begged.

Javid dropped the comb and excitedly dug through his bag of belongings and pulled out his small drum. The two settled on the plush sofa of the dressing chamber and Javid began a rhythmic beat. With eyes closed, his voice produced small mewing noises that Marie recognized as a chant that called upon his gods. All the years of treating this as a fortune game melted in the aftermath of the past few days. With renewed sincerity, Marie closed her eyes and imitated the odd sounding noises. Javid soon grew feverish. Marie caught herself up in the excitement more honestly than ever before.

The drumming stopped abruptly. Javid's eyes flew open. The two stared at each other, breathless. "It is confusing, my lady," he panted. "Yet the message is very clear. I see more devastation, yet in the midst of it there is a ball of light that radiates a presence. It is a source of—well, I'm not sure exactly, but it is not harmful. I would think it represents protection. Yes, I see that most clearly now, but you will not recognize this protection at first."

"Devastation?" Marie's voice quavered, ignoring the promise of protection. She wanted no part of further harm. "Oh, Javid I don't think I can take any more devastation." She looked at him in anguish. "Will I be harmed?"

"Possibly. But..." He blinked. His eyes stared somewhere into the back of his own head. "I do not foresee any lasting personal harm. That is clear."

CHAPTER 9

A sharp blow to the gut doubled Paul Lambert with as much surprise as pain. He gasped to regain his breath, but Yousef Phoebe slugged him again before graciously ordering a chair slid up behind him as he staggered backward.

"Congratulations, Paul," Phoebe snarled in his heavy central Nixodonian accent. "You've done a marvelous job of destroying your ties with Flechette Cosmetics and now your lady is off on some unscheduled holiday! That leaves our plan somewhat unbalanced, doesn't it." The rhetorical statement was delivered with another blow that sent Paul off the chair and sprawling onto the floor. A streak of blood followed him, then pooled beneath his head where his body stopped. Paul panted as he watched a scarlet circle expand on the mirror polished floor, slowly blotting out his reflection.

Paul caught his breath and wiped the blood from his mouth as he pulled himself to a kneeling position, a shaky hand grasping the lip of a console for support. "You can't take me down, Phoebe," Paul reminded through a swelling lip. "I know that, and you know that. So do me a favor and save your punches."

Yousef Phoebe walked purposefully across the floor, stopping inches in front of Paul who found himself staring directly at the man's crotch. "I may not be able to take you down," Phoebe agreed smoothly, "but I can make you regret you even remotely considered what you did."

Paul gripped harder to the console's edge and hauled himself to a standing position. He wasn't sure if his shaking was as much from pain, or fear of that threat. "You can't run Doria without me," he spat. "I've gained their trust, and they won't transport for anyone but me. One more threat like that and you'll find yourself having a talk with General Keem."

Phoebe countered the threat. "The General's favoritism won't last long if you don't get control of the heiress. In just a few weeks, you are supposed to be on your honeymoon helping the lovely lady memorize Act II. We *need* her to start the fundamental movement."

Phoebe had backed Paul against the computer console. The Alpha's angry breath cooled the blood tricking from Paul's nose. "And, I told you. I'll do it!" Paul retorted, pushing hard against the Alpha's chest. His blood stained hands left ruddy prints on the lapels of Phoebe's suit. The Alpha let out a howl and delivered a swing that would have knocked Paul over had he not noticed his blunder and immediately executed an evasive maneuver. The two stood at odds for a moment. Phoebe slowly removed the suit jacket. He handed it to one of his men. "Burn it."

Paul blinked, hardly believing that his death sentence hadn't been ordered on the spot. The knowledge that he was indispensable was momentarily shaken. Nevertheless, his heart pounded fiercely. "I have it all under control. My plan is already in effect." Paul's eyes shifted nervously from Phoebe to Henrie March-and, who stood in the shadows and refused to catch his eye. "I'll have her on Doria on schedule," he assured them, but his voice warbled maddeningly. "I talked to your wife, and—"

"You talked to my wife?" Phoebe roared.

"—I know! Lola is aboard the *Starquest,* but she won't be harmed. I promise you that."

Phoebe breathed heavily. "You had better not fail me this time," Phoebe warned. "And just to be doubly sure, I'll join you on Doria to personally coach the young lady in her expected duties."

Paul growled. "Fine. Whatever you want."

"Good. Then, carry on. I presume the teams you've put together are capable of executing your plan?"

"They're your men."

Yousef Phoebe's jaw remained taut while he donned a fresh suit jacket brought in by an aide. Abruptly, he turned to leave the room, first stopping to give Marchand a short, piercing glare.

Marchand stalked over to Paul who was wiping his bleeding face with a handkerchief. The director grabbed Paul's shoulder and shook it roughly. "You imbecile. Get a hold of yourself!"

A ridiculous look of glee lit beneath Paul's blood stained features. "The rat can't hurt me and he knows it," he chirped, roughly shrugging off Marchand's grip. "And you can bet he'll regret this little incident." Paul turned and marched out of the room.

Marchand caught up with him in the hallway and jerked him to a halt. "Listen my friend. I told you to get off those drugs. You found suitable ones for the job, now leave them alone! Look at you!"

Paul smiled happily. "Don't forget that my willingness to experiment gave us the solution to a very perplexing problem. You should be grateful."

Marchand reddened. "Lambert, if you go down, don't think for a minute that I'm going to go down with you." Marchand turned sharply and strode away.

Disconcerted, Paul shoved his hands into his pockets and fidgeted nervously as he watched Marchand disappear down the hall. "Don't worry, it's all under control," he shouted after Henrie, but his life-long partner was already out of ear shot.

Paul shook himself, both to regain his composure and to straighten his ruffled clothing. He slapped a hand to his jaw as pain shot through it unmercifully. Digging through his pockets, he found a small yellow pill and he held it tightly for a moment, convincing himself that this was the last one. He threw it to the back of his throat. If nothing else, the pill would get rid of this god-awful pain. Marchand was right about one thing. The stuff was killing him; but he didn't care. His entire life had been under the rule of these tyrants. Do this—do that. If the pills didn't kill him, these assholes would. At least the little yellow darlings gave him personal freedom.

Once begun, not even the Alpha could take away the euphoria. Paul's nostrils flared as he breathed in the placidity that the pill offered. Next came the exhilarating effects of illusionary speed and heightened clarity. In short order, any doubt he may have had about the habit vanished. With spurious self-control, he shot down the hallway and raced down a metal grated stairway that led to the massive central control room of the secret underground complex. His boisterous arrival was muted by the steady drone of machine and operator that marked the feverish activity of the military bunker.

A woman yelped when Paul pulled her from her chair. She quickly slapped a hand over her mouth when she realized her assailant was Agent Lambert. The sight of fresh blood on his face horrified her. She cowered, then meekly offered assistance but Paul vehemently informed her that he knew what he was doing.

With drug-induced speed, he flipped switches, cranked dials and punched in commands until one of the towering screens at the front of the control room came to life. He continued to massage the data until he was tapped into the flight plan of the *Starquest*.

"I couldn't stop you from getting on that thing," he grumbled, eyes darting back and forth between screen and console, "but I'm sure as hell going to get you off."

Finally, a smile lit his face and he blew a kiss towards the screen. "And voilá. There you are. Right on schedule in Sector 12, Iggid bound. The team's ready to roll; master plan in effect. Whoopee!" He jumped up from the chair, his sharp clap of exaltation startling the technicians next to him. Ignoring their annoyed glances, he quickly sat down again, a sinister smirk crossing his broken features.

"Nice try, dear, but you aren't finished with me yet!"

CHAPTER 10

Javid's concerns regarding Lola Phoebe were clear to Marie the moment she sat down across from her in the lounge. Marie couldn't quite get through the layers. There was something not quite real beneath the facade of her outlandish gown and painted face. All the wrong colors, Marie thought as a diversion to the woman's irritating voice. Lola alternated between low and devious tones when she spoke about interesting guests at the gala, to falsetto when she needed service from either her own staff or that of the liners.

Marie sipped on a fruit punch and listened with interest. It seemed Lola knew more about Marie's life than she did herself. Marie could only gaze wide-eyed as Lola forged on with gossip about every celebrity in the galaxy. She tried to hide her amusement, but Lola was simply too absurd.

Lady Phoebe ordered herself another champagne while reluctantly obliging Marie's request for a second glass of punch. "And where are you off to in such a hurry, my dear?"

"Oh, nowhere important," Marie offered quickly, catching the glint of Bill's eye from the shadows behind Lady Phoebe. "I'm taking a quiet holiday. I'd like to keep my destination hush-hush, you understand."

"Oh, I wouldn't tell a soul!" Lola huffed, waving a bejeweled hand. "But, I understand your silence. You need quiet at a time like this, you poor dear. How nasty that boy was to you."

"It was a mutual decision, Lola."

"Sleeping around doesn't sound mutual to me!" Lola scoffed.

"Our break-up had nothing to do with that *Celebrity Quest* article, Lola."

"*Celebrity Quest*? I'm talking about that party he had, and that woman! Oh, you poor dear! Perhaps I'm misinformed, but I heard there were a lot of people at his villa the night of your engagement party."

The smile on Marie's face froze with the force of sheer amazement. "I'm sorry. I'm not sure what you're talking about."

"Well, I'd heard he was at his villa. You didn't hear?" Lola's voice dropped off.

"No. And neither did Paul. He was with me the entire evening."

The conversation became awkward. After more uncomfortable gossip, Marie made her official apology and thanked Lola and her husband for making the long journey to Enderal for the occasion, doomed as it was. Lola insisted that she not worry. Her husband had to be there for extended business anyway.

Marie excused herself and left the lounge. Later, in the comfort of her large bed, with the humidity setting pushed to its limit, Marie lay awake in thought. How had Lola found out about the party? Remembering the quality of Paul's company at the villa, Marie guessed that some of them would be loudmouths, but why would someone in Lola's position hear of it? It was an uncomfortable mystery, but who knew what sources the likes of Lola had.

Marie dimmed the berth lights and put the whole embarrassing affair out of her mind. On her schedule, it was very late in the night, and she meant to be alert for her first astronomy lesson with Bill in the morning.

Other than referring to local time, one wouldn't know if it were day or night on the observation deck of the *Starquest*. The deck lighting was kept the same round the clock, only bright enough to locate a seat while not interfering with the view. An attendant with a torch was always present to assure passenger safety. It seemed strange to have just finished breakfast then sit attentively in the dark of night.

Bill had honored his date with Marie and they sat together gazing out the view plate which bubbled over them in a full semicircle. Sharing awe at the grandeur of the universe, they witnessed the jump from hyperspace back to normal space as they entered the core of Sector 12. Marie marveled at the feeling of internal rippling that accompanied deceleration. Simultaneously, they witnessed a brilliant, explosive burst of light as they entered normal space.

Bill told Marie that he'd begun his career in this sector, a satellite jurisdiction for a few of Nixodonia's highbrow institutions over which Senator Phoebe now presided. Both Marie and Bill were glad that the senator's obnoxious wife would part from their company at this port.

Bill explained to Marie that there were still almost two days of travel before arriving at the Iggid spaceport. It was necessary that ships come out of hyperspace early due to some strong gravitational pulls that marked one of the borders to the Fringe.

"The Fringe?" Marie raised an eyebrow. "You mean I've traveled all these times through here without ever knowing we came close to the Fringe?" She studied the long wisps of bluish haze emitting from the young star clusters that Bill pointed out to her. "In fact, until Doria was chosen as the location for the new laboratory, I never really thought of the place."

"Well, there you are. See those stars in a triangle formation to your left?" Bill pointed to three stars that poked their icy whites through the blue haze. "They mark the entrance to one of the trading lanes through the Fringe."

"I thought there was only one set of lanes through the Fringe, from Sector 5, near Doria."

Bill smiled. "The Fringe is a huge band of space marking a sort of intergalactic border between one star cluster that makes up Nixodonia and another cluster that's occupied by the Telexans. There are dozens of established lanes, but very few of them are widely known. It takes some special skill to pilot them. Unfortunately, Nix States has lost some good pilots to the alluring promise of wealth gained by risky trade."

"Paul told me about all those ruthless traders, many of whom frequent the bars of Doria to share their tales of adventure." She sneered with disdain. "The latest stories were about the TRA extending their borders our way once they gain control of the Telexan government."

"Is that so?" Bill's interest perked. "I haven't heard anything in that regard. But, there may be some truth to it. The TRA have become very powerful and no one quite knows where they're getting their support. It's believed they've amassed a sizable fleet with plenty of firepower. What disturbs me is that the TRA are not known for their diplomacy."

Marie shuddered. "What about the other nations, like the Blue Rift, or the Three Kingdoms?"

"They're probably too small, or too remote for the TRA to bother with at this point."

"Then it's a good thing we have this Fringe between us and Telexa. It should slow them down a bit. The area sounds lonely. And dreadful."

Bill gazed out towards the triangle of stars. "That it is. But I've heard that some of the local Fringe groups have formed a rudimentary political alliance, although I may just be spreading another rumor."

"A government?" She smiled. "I think of the inhabitants of the Fringe as being primitive bands throwing spears at each other."

Bill chuckled. "It's possible, but mostly it's occupied by a bunch of crazy merchants who prefer to live life on the edge."

He diverted her attention starboard, to another group of stars on their right. "That," he said, "is the core of Sector 12. The brightest star you see is actually quite close to us now. It's the solar system of Iggid where we'll have our stopover." He squinted, and Marie followed his gaze. "No, wait. I have something wrong. That isn't the star. It's the one over there." He directed her to another bright star close to the one he'd just indicated. He looked to be confused again. "Maybe it's been too long. I don't recall there being two stars at that location. Yet I'm sure of our coordinates." He rubbed his chin quizzically.

"Maybe it isn't a star, but the lights from another spacecraft," Marie suggested.

"Ah, you've saved me! Yes, it must be another ship." His brow furrowed in thought. "But it's too bright. Another ship wouldn't travel so close on this part of the route. It's too dangerous."

Bill stared at the misplaced star. Marie noticed him dart a look at Spencer, then Rossgar, sitting at discreet distances amongst the other observers. Marie grew mildly anxious. "What is it, Bill?"

"Nothing," he answered nonchalantly. "I'm no space man, and you're probably right. It's just another ship. This is a busy route, after all." Bill's voice trailed off. His eyes remained riveted to the prominent star that glittered brightly against the thick canopy of Sector 12. Suddenly Bill's face paled. He stiffened slowly. "Well, I'll be damned," he muttered softly.

Marie sensed an urgency in his voice. She glanced back out the view plate, her own eyes riveting to the star. She involuntarily straightened, unable to breath. Emerging from behind the light, Marie could discern a tubular shape. The next instant, a thin ruddy bolt of laser light fired from the nose of the distant gloomy structure. It sliced through the blackness and slammed against the side of the *Starquest*. Giant sparks scintillated along the ship's outer skin, just below the observation deck. Their power created an explosive display of scarlet lightening momentarily blinding those in the darkened area. Marie screamed, tossing herself into Bill's protective arms. Punching the uproar of voices was the screech of emergency sirens. The deck flew into a panic.

Bill shouted to his assistants. "Spencer. Rossgar. Get over here!" But, the two had already sprung into action.

As Bill leapt from his seat, Marie grabbed his jacket, her fingers straining to keep their hold on his lapel. "Bill, what's happening?" she demanded.

Another laser bolt rocked the side of the ship, jolting the massive, lumbering craft and extinguishing what little light they had. The observation deck flashed with the slashing sweep of search beams from the approaching craft. Marie glanced quickly over her shoulder through the transparent bubble. The long, black tubular structure was more definable now and undeniably evil. She heard

Bill's voice rise over the clamoring of the emergency sirens. "Pirates. Goddamn pirates!"

So terrified was she by the revelation that she nearly choked Bill with the strength of her grip on his collar. Bill wrenched her knuckles from his lapels and held her wrists while he shot staccato instructions at his agents. Marie threw another glance over her shoulder. *Pirates?* Paul had warned her about their existence but she hadn't really believed him. Yet, before her unbelieving eyes, a long, black ship hurled itself towards them. The *Starquest's* exterior lights ended the alien ship's camouflage as it emerged, menacing and heinous from the blackness of deep space.

Pirates! Her mind burned with thought. They would want jewels, credits, food, perhaps clothing. She scoured her brain for things that might appease a band of pirates. Suddenly, Bill handed her over to the firm control of Spencer's grip. Terror engulfed her.

"Marie. Follow the boys' orders," he shouted at her. "I'm going to secure us an ejection pod." Looking around at the frenzied deck, he swore again, "Goddamn captain! I'll have him court marshaled for this! Some warning!"

Bill left them, darting down the main isle, wrestling his way past the frantic passengers before disappearing down one of the emergency stairwells. Marie screamed after him, but to no avail. He was gone. She had no choice but to put her trust in his plan. She gave Spencer and Rossgar a worried look before muttering a silent prayer. Seconds later, they led her off in the opposite direction.

Bill swore in disbelief at the mayhem in the main companionway. The emergency lighting did little but convey the considerable damage already done to the hull. The extent could be estimated by the layer of smoke that threatened to descend and choke the panic-stricken crowd. Bill prayed that the hull would hold, that the acrid fumes would remain below critical levels.

As he struggled down the corridor, he found little to feel positive about, except that this part of the ship was separate from the economy class. Nevertheless, it seemed that all four hundred bodies of the First Class section crashed into him as he fought his way in a direct route to the bridge.

Another explosion rocked the monolith. Fear crept into Tripp's bones as he smashed into the bulkhead. He narrowly missed having his eyes gouged out by the long fingernails of Lady Phoebe as she reached for a hold on her way to the floor. He tried to dodge her but she recognized him and clung to his pant leg.

"You!" she screamed. "This is all that girl's fault. She's trouble, I tell you!"

Tripp kicked himself free and scrambled down the hall. Other things quickly dominated his thoughts as a low resounding thud rang through the cruiser. The pirate ship had coupled to the starboard side. It would take the marauders another ten minutes to board, and perhaps a few more minutes to disperse themselves. Surely he could complete his mission by then. If they *could* launch, his only chance was to keep the bulk of the *Starquest* between themselves and the pirate ship until they were out of firing range.

On the run, he pulled out his commlink. He had to warn the boys to avoid the main companionway. He received nothing but a crackle from the device. The pirates had already jammed the communication systems. Grimly, he stuffed the transmitter in his pocket. Just then, he came across a young flight crew officer being jostled by the crowd in his direction. Bill lunged for him. With a solid grip, he threw him against the bulkhead. "Why weren't we warned?" Bill demanded.

"The...the Captain negotiated a cash offer," the officer croaked. "They agreed—then went back on their word—just like that!"

Tripp clenched his jaw. "Where's the Captain?"

"St-still on the bridge."

Bill let go of the terrified officer who immediately crumpled to the floor only to be trampled by a stampeding horde with nowhere to go.

Bill finally reached the stairwell to the bridge, but stopped to calibrate his stunner before proceeding. As he suspected, the bridge had been closed off to anyone but those with security clearance. Thinking quickly, he dashed into firing range and dropped the first security guard in his path. Turning to face a scuffle behind him, he fired again, but only marked one of the two men coming towards him. A quick maneuver saved him from a white bolt that sizzled past his head. Bill quickly regretted having only a stun weapon with him. That blast came from a soft-laser, enough power to kill a man yet not pierce the hull. He threw himself into a tumbling slide around a corner. A shower of sparks cascaded on him from a second bolt that struck the bulkhead's edge.

Bill scrambled to his feet but stayed in position, hoping his pursuer would believe he had run. The officer fell for the trap. Bill felled him with a point-blank pulse from his stunner as the officer rounded the corner in full pursuit. He quickly traded weapons with the unconscious officer, gaining himself a blaster capable of maximum onboard power. He fumbled through the officer's pocket and pulled out a remote. Without hesitation, Bill dashed towards the bridge. He punched at the remote, squeezing through the security doors before they had fully opened. The bridge was virtually empty with all available help having been dispatched to the emergency, but the captain was at his post, He was twenty feet into the bridge area leaning weakly against a computer console. In seconds Bill had the blaster against the captain's graying temple.

"I thought we'd reached a workable solution," the Captain said in a defeated tone. "They agreed. Then, this. The bastards have boarded."

Bill brought his face close to the Captain's dazed features. "I want a code key for a Class A life-support pod. And, I want it off portside. Now!"

The Captain shook his head weakly. "We've suffered extensive damage. There are only a few pods still operational and everyone wants one."

"I have Marie Flechette with me," Tripp barked. "The code key!" He shoved the blunt end of the blaster hard into the man's temple.

"Ah, the Princess. But it won't…"

Bill turned with lightning speed and fired at an officer who'd entered the bridge shouting at Bill to freeze. The officer's body exploded into several large fragments. Bill turned back to the Captain, repeating his demand. The Captain swallowed. Resigned, he turned and pushed a series of buttons at the console. Tripp noticed him shake his head, discouraging the remaining staff who had their full attention on them now.

Seconds later, a small, flat disk popped out of a slot. "Pod 226, section 1-A. This will give you access, and also activate the emergency release."

Bill didn't offer his thanks. He simply released the Captain and sidestepped out of the bridge, stepping over the bloody mess on the floor on his way out. Shoving the disk into his vest, Bill tore down the hall, his mind stewing with plans.

Marie trembled uncontrollably while Spencer and Rossgar guided her down the narrow emergency stairwell off the observation deck. Another explosion rocked the ship. Marie's scream drowned in the resounding aftershock of the blast. She lost her footing. Her forearm caught a metal edge as she thudded down a dozen metal steps before landing unceremoniously on top of Spencer, also off balance on the litter covering the floor. The ceiling had crumpled under the strain of the attack and had strewn its debris along the narrow emergency passageway.

Rossgar dropped onto the landing already crowded with passengers. An operetta of whimpers and coughs filtered through the fine white powder that hung in the air. Rossgar wiped a dust-laden hand on his pant leg and got a better hold on his weapon. He discussed their next move with Spencer, and with little hesitation, each took one of Marie's arms and helped her over the pile of rubbish. Marie bit her lip, curtailing a yelp from the grip Spencer had on her bleeding forearm. To her dismay, the next corner stopped them cold. The entire passageway had been blocked with debris. Rossgar backtracked a few paces and scanned the walls and ceiling. "We'll have to go through that shaft." He pointed to a grate in the ceiling.

Marie's jaw slackened. Before she could protest, they were hoisting her up like a rag doll into a narrow metal air duct. She could not believe they could actually crawl inside such spaces, or that such spaces even existed! In panic, her arms weakened. She prayed they would support her. She wobbled in an awkward crawl as Rossgar urged her to follow him. Marie heard herself whimper as another thud resounded through the ship, vibrating the shaft until it sang.

"Shit, they've locked on!" she heard Rossgar curse.

Marie felt her stomach churn with liquefying terror. "Help...help me!" she whimpered, afraid she might faint.

"Hang on, Marie," Spencer urged quietly. "You're all right. We have to move on. Just another few yards and we can make the drop to the next level. Then we're away. Sound good?"

Pursing her lips, she nodded. Courageously, she mustered the strength to resume her crawl. The hard metal bruised her tender knees and the palms of her unaccustomed hands. Spencer had not lied about the few yards. She was not, however, prepared for the acrobatics of dropping from one man to the other into a small storage room stamped Level Five on its door. Rossgar opened the door a crack then quickly waved them out. In the hall, smoke hung noxiously in the air. Marie blinked. The acrid fumes stung her eyes and ravaged her throat but her heart leapt as she noticed the numbers on the doors. She grasped Spencer's arm. "We're close to my stateroom! Javid and the women might be there."

The two looked at each other bleakly. "We're sorry, ma'am. There's no time, but Mr. Tripp said he'd do his best to pick them up."

Dismayed, Marie nodded. One look down the disheveled hallway told her they were right. This was a war zone. Visions of Javid flashed through her mind. This must be it. Devastation. She glanced at her arm. No lasting harm.

An interminable five minutes later, they reached the crowded main lounge, the fastest route to the docking bay. Seconds after entering, Spencer crushed Marie to the wall, his body shielding hers. In one fluid motion, he slid her back along the paneling toward the entrance from which they'd come. Rossgar fired across the room, but not before Marie saw his target from around Spencer's large shoulder.

Several figures, dressed in dark camouflage space gear poured into the lounge in expert military formation. Most had flipped open their visors. Marie gasped at the sight of their hideous faces. One had removed his headgear to flaunt his gruesome features. He seemed to have lost half his head in some sort of accident and replaced the missing parts with a metal prosthesis that took up a good portion of the right side of his face and head. Another snapped open his visor and scanned the hysterical crowd with a mocking smile. His intense black eyes looked down the barrel of his weapon. With coolness and accuracy, he fired. A pale green bolt sizzled across the elegant lounge, slamming into the chest of a shrieking passenger, cutting off the voice mid-scream.

Marie was beyond reason. She tore at Spencer, trying to release the grip he had around her waist. It didn't occur to her that he was creating a human shield. He hauled her down the hall, now crushed full of passengers fleeing the peril. Spencer curtailed Marie's attempts to run while continuing to glance behind for Rossgar. Seeing his partner escape safely into the hall a few yards behind them, Spencer turned and forged ahead. Rossgar shouted and Spencer pulled Marie into a doorjamb, forcing her to wait. Rossgar reached them, panting hard. "The lounge has nearly cleared out," he said. "The raiders have split up—spread out through the other entrances. If we double back, we can get over to the port side stairwell and still rendezvous with Tripp."

"I'm not going back in there!" Marie hollered, but they held her fast. "This is crazy!" she blurted. "I didn't think they'd actually kill people!"

The two men looked at each other but said nothing, just waited more interminable seconds. Finally, Rossgar stepped away from the wall, craning his neck to see as much of the lounge as possible. "Now's as good a time as any," he declared. They moved back toward the lounge, now littered with a dozen bodies, the taupe carpets stained dark with death. Marie's hand flew to her mouth as she retched dryly. Spencer raised a palm to shield her eyes from the sight.

They moved Marie stealthily from one pillar to the next, staying as close to the bulkheads as possible. She heard Rossgar let out a sigh of relief as they approached the wide staircase to the lower levels. Rossgar raised a palm to stop Spencer and Marie, took a few steps toward the stairs, and peered down to check for danger. He gave a clearance signal with a toss of his head. They hadn't taken a single step when a hideous scream curdled their blood. The three simultaneously spun toward the source, a doorway at the opposite end of the lounge. Marie expected to witness the torturing of a passenger, but filling the doorframe was a solitary gunman, feet apart, knees slightly bent, his weapon trained on them. Behind the sleek firearm, Marie caught a glimpse of metal glinting colorfully off the ceiling lights. She instantly knew it to be the half-faced pirate. Without hesitation, the black-clad figure fired. Rossgar stiffened, and jerked uncontrollably before falling hard at her feet. His eyes remained wide open. They stared at her, glassy, hopeless. His chest lay open, singed, sputtering and oozing blood.

Paralyzed, Marie heard herself scream. Suddenly Spencer pulled at her arm and threw her down the stairs. Penetrating the shocking numbness was a searing pain that fired along her right side as she landed on her shoulder and thudded down the stairs. Above her, she could see Spencer fired his blaster in response to another attack by the pirate. A bolt narrowly missed his head. He jumped down the stairs three at a time, grabbed Marie by the waist and pulled her beyond the stairwell to safety.

Only a dozen steps farther her bruised knees gave way. She crumpled against the wall. The air filled with a distant screech from the deadly metal-faced pirate. Marie struggled to get up. She thrust herself forward but her muscles were losing control to liquefying terror. When they reached an intersection, Spencer threw out an arm to stop her reckless forward propulsion and grasped her in a protective hold. Panting against his heaving chest, she looked up at his features, full of outrage mixed with deep pain at the loss of his partner. Marie could not do as well. Her voice exploded in anguish. Tears flowed unchecked as they slumped together in exhaustion against the bulkhead.

Mourning for Rossgar would have to wait. Within seconds, Spencer was checking his directions. Without formality, he spoke. "Come on, Marie. Bill should be down on the docking bay floor by now." Spencer attempted a few words of encouragement. "He'll be there with Javid and the women."

Marie blinked. That, or they had suffered the same fate as…no, she couldn't think like that! She let Spencer take her by the hand and did her best to keep pace with him.

There was no further sign of the metal-faced pirate so he had either lost interest, or had begun to hunt them down from another direction. Suddenly, they reached the catwalk that overlooked the docking bay floor of the lifeboat bay. Marie's heart sank. The huge floor space below crawled with hoards of frightened passengers all wanting to be on the first lifeboat out.

Marie's shock grew when she noticed that over half the pods had been damaged and lay dead in their molds. Only a few of the pods were operational and it seemed like thousands of people were crushed against them praying for the hatches to open. "This is hopeless! We're going to get mutilated if we try to board one of those!"

Spencer's face was grimly set. "We'll make it," he growled with raw determination. "One of us is all these bastards are going to score."

Marie looked away to hide a new explosion of tears. Rossgar may have died honorably in service, but he had died in her service. Rossgar had given his life for her.

Bill shoved the disk into his vest pocket. Blaster raised in readiness, he moved stealthily down the hall, his senses heightened to everything around him. Something caught his eye down an adjoining hallway. A small human form was sprawled on the floor, blood pooling around the abdomen. He meant to ignore it, but there was something familiar about the form. Bill checked quickly in all directions before moving toward the body. He crouched slightly and reached to turn the body on its back when he recognized Javid. Agony tore though his soul. He reached down, then jumped back up in surprise. Javid rolled partly towards him and grimaced. "Ah, Mr. Tripp. Good to see you, sir."

"Great Creator, Javid!" Bill seethed with rage. "Those bastards are going to pay for this."

Javid raised a palm to Bill who was preparing to pick him up. "No. The injury isn't serious and I am probably better off left behind."

"No!" Bill interjected.

"Please, trust me," Javid said. "I can be of help later on. Right now, I'll only be a burden."

"You're dying!"

"No. I'll be all right. Go! You must help the lady. I will implore my gods to protect you."

The weak smile that Javid produced indicated to Bill that his injuries were probably graver than he chose to let on. "Go. Quickly," the Rashmarian implored.

Bill left him and sprinted down the hall toward the main stairwell, the fastest alternative. It was a bad move. Entering the lounge, he ran headlong into four of the black clad pirates. Then, a miracle? Had Javid's gods already come to his aid? A crowd of frantic women entered the lounge across the room, drawing the pirates' attention, but not for long.

As he turned to run, a bolt sizzled past his hip. Bill twisted and fired, his aim off as he discharged the weapon while in a full backwards run. It was of little use. The next cover was only a doorjamb. Several bolts smashed the bulkheads around him. He remained miraculously uninjured. The invaders were excellent marksmen, so why—?

A cold feeling of dread spread through his limbs with the realization that they were hunting him down. They wanted him *alive*. Which meant they would use him as bait to flush out…a figure hurled from the shadows, slamming him to the bulkhead. Not prepared for a physical attack, Bill took a vicious blow to the gut. In fury he swung back but his punch missed its mark.

The others joined in. A snapping blow to the base of his neck sent him crashing to his knees. Another punch landed on his jaw. His body sprawled against the bulkhead, sparkles bursting behind his eyelids. Bill wondered if he'd simply been hunted down for the sport, until he heard a voice bellow an order to stop. Bill slumped into a haphazard heap against the wall where he was immediately surrounded by a dozen of the ruthless savages, every one of them pointing a weapon at him. He had a mind to ask if they didn't think one shot would do.

The collection of blasters parted. Their leader stepped forward. Bill peered at the man's metal skull-plate and grimaced at the sight. Half of the pirate's face was composed of a computer prosthesis of some unrecognizable design. The wide-toothed grimace did little to soften the image. The pirate's build made up for his repulsive features. The flight suit contoured over an impressive muscular physique making Bill thankful the leader had chosen his lesser beasts to soften him up.

The leader spoke. "We meet at last, Mr. Tripp."

Bill stopped massaging his jaw and gaped at the pirate in stunned silence.

"You're reputation precedes you, Mr. Tripp. Quite a show." The alien's voice was slightly nasal with the added hindrance of a vocoder. He placed a hand mockingly at his heart. "Much as I was amused by a demonstration of your skills, the fun is over. We're in a bit of a rush, so, boys…?" He made an elegant sweep of a hand.

Bill's abdomen tightened as they hauled him to his feet. Instead of blowing off his head, they shackled his wrists behind him and brusquely patted him down. One of the captors yanked the disk from his jacket pocket. The leader took the disk and examined it carefully.

"Very good. It seems we have a rendezvous at Pod 226 in section 1-A." The pirate gave Bill a mocking smile. A dose of murderous rage surged through Bill. His only advantage now was not to furnish them with the fact that Spencer and Rossgar didn't know the pod number. He swallowed. It didn't matter much. The invaders would stay until their mission was accomplished, and Pod 226 was certainly not going anywhere.

"Let's go," the metal-faced pirate barked. With a ruthless shove, Bill was moved along with the boorish company towards the lifeboat docking bay.

Marie and Spencer wormed through the crowds, their desperate search for Bill coming up futile. The others weren't to be found, either. Marie and Spencer clung to each other as they were jostled about on the narrow catwalk that over-looked the large floor area below. It was also wall-to-wall with bodies, all frantically looking for a means of escape.

Spencer clutched Marie's hand and led her down the metal stairs to the main floor. Marie looked anxiously at the long segment of lifeboat pods that remained inert in their molds. There had to be a hundred passengers for each of the available pods capable of boarding only a few dozen each. A senior officer shouted to a deafened audience that the attack had damaged most of the pods. The captain had ordered the remainder to stay closed as boarding them would ensure death. Even if Bill did get them access to one of those pods, she wondered how he would get them past this mob alive, let alone past a crew surely as desperate as they to escape.

The situation suddenly worsened. Marie had seen only about a dozen pirates enter the lounge earlier. She'd sorely mistaken their numbers. Rapidly, through every possible entrance, came one raider after another, blocking any chance of escape back into the main ship. The crowd grew hysterical as the pirates fired soft-lasers into the air, letting the people know that they were surrounded. Spencer wrapped himself around Marie, protecting her from the crushing madness.

The staccato of weapon fire stopped abruptly. Spencer kept his arms wrapped about Marie, consoling them both in the face of the horror that lay ahead. Like a wave, the crowd began to retreat towards the hull, crushing them within its layers. "I'm sorry I can't get you out of here," Spencer groaned.

"Just stay with me," Marie whimpered, closing her eyes to those falling beneath trampling feet and praying that she, too, wouldn't be crushed to death.

Her heart nearly fractured when the sudden bellowing of a pirate echoed through the bay. They watched another dozen pirates walk along the catwalk. Frightened passengers scurried in every direction, crushing themselves in suffocating layers along the bulkheads. The raiders made their way down a grated stairway, pushing a captive along in the midst of their company. Marie wondered if the whole affair had been for the sake of one prisoner. Spencer tightened his grip the same instant that Marie realized who the captive was.

"No!" she screamed.

Spencer clamped a hand over her mouth. "Don't do it, Marie," he warned. "Just stay calm."

He kept their heads down, just below the level of the crowd, using the bodies of the people around them for cover. Peering between heads, they watched the marauding party stop not thirty feet from where they stood.

Marie whimpered, crushing her lips together so as not to scream. Spencer spoke urgently. "Don't yell. Think this out rationally."

"We believe there is a certain dignitary traveling in this man's company," the leader of the pirate band shouted. "We would like her to step forward." The alien's voice rasped against a vocoder but the volume was not dampened. The words propelled loudly across the bay. Marie and Spencer both recognized Rossgar's murderer.

She made a violent twist that spun her to face her rigid agent. His grip tightened as a look of desperation crossed his features. She agonized with what he must be feeling but there was no longer any hope. A gasp rippled through the crowd as Bill received a punch that doubled him over. Marie grew frantic. "They're going to kill him! Then maybe someone else. You can't do anything, Spencer. Don't come with me."

"I'm waiting," the metal-faced alien mocked.

"I can't let you—"

Marie pushed her fingers to his lips. "Stay out of sight and help us if you can. You're better off to us alive than dead." She watched the spirit drain from his eyes.

The crowd again reacted to an audible grunt from Bill. She tore away from Spencer's grasp and pushed through the crowd. Ruthlessly, she clawed her way between surprised fellow passengers. Realizing who she was, and her intention, they moved quickly to let her through.

Marie stopped within the small clearing the pirates were creating by the sheer force of their repulsive natures. She ignored her pounding heart and the strangling fear that restricted her breathing. Instead, she focused all of her remaining strength into a determination that suddenly filled her more powerfully than anything she had ever experienced. She faced the metal man, square shouldered and stone faced. Aware of Bill's hard glare, she kept eye contact with her foe. "I am with this man," she stated clearly.

The leader relaxed his posture, a lascivious grin growing across his wrecked features. "Well, well. You're so much lovelier in person."

"What do you want with us?"

"Marie, don't—"

She fought to control herself when one of the men guarding Bill grasped his face and crushed it to silence. Her voice came out with quivering force. "Leave him alone. What do you want?"

The leader stepped toward her. His eyes, one natural, the other slightly over-sized within the prosthesis, stared down at her until she felt she would collapse with fright. She tried to stand her ground, but his steady approach forced her backward until she bumped against the crowd. She felt hands pushing on her, thrusting her toward the alien like some sacrifice. Still, her eyes never left those of the metal man. They paralyzed her.

"You," he stated, plainly. "It's you that I want."

A deadly hush fell over the docking bay. From the enigmatic depths of Marie's core surged a courage she didn't know she possessed. Her voice spat out hoarsely. "Then take me and leave these others alone."

His reflexes hit her like the strike of a snake, his hand darting out in response to her offer. With a horrified gasp she instinctively threw herself backward but he'd latched onto her arm and pulled her swift and hard to him. She crashed against the stiff outer fabric of his flight suit. In the same fluid motion, the pirate's arm encircled her waist He swung her to face his hideous band. Her breath was crushed out of her when the metal-faced brute squeezed her with a jerking pull against him. "The prize!" he cried out to his men. "Ha! Will you look at her!"

Her fear of them nearly obliterated reason, but Marie quickly stopped fighting when she realized that her attempt to dislodge herself only excited him in his conquest.

Bill locked eyes with her, his gaze wild with fury. His captor pulled hard on Bill, choking him to silence.

"Tell me, Mr. Tripp," the metal-faced pirate asked, "is this she? Is this Marie Flechette?"

Bill burst forth with a choking curse. Marie flew into a frantic fight for their lives. She heard Bill shout at her. His cry was cut short with another punch to the gut. The pirate's grip tightened on Marie's torso until she couldn't move. Her face rasped against her captor's suit, redolent of decaying flesh and lingering sweat. Her resolve began to shatter. But she *couldn't* let them break her.

She screamed hoarsely at her assailant. "What do you want with me? Leave him alone!"

Her breath shuddered when she saw Bill doubled over. He was pulled to a standing position by his shackled arms. Sweat gleamed over his wrought features. One of the raiders brought a blaster to his temple. Marie saw Bill close his eyes in a final prayer. She screamed hysterically for them to stop while her captor shouted even louder to the gunman in a language she did not understand. Before the trigger was pulled, another of the pirates clamped a hand on the gunman's forearm, lowering the weapon forcefully. Marie dared to believe they were going to spare Bill's life. Then, to her horror, the same pirate who'd just prevented the assassination raised his own weapon—and fired.

A light blue aura enveloped Bill's body. He jerked with the powerful force of the blast before crashing to his knees. Marie could bear no more. She heard her captor yell at his men to move out, then Marie Flechette fainted in the hands of a dozen savage warriors.

CHAPTER 11

Her dry and swollen eyes opened only a crack. They wouldn't focus. She closed them again. An attempt to move shot pain through her ribs. With a low moan, Marie rolled onto her back, letting a tear wash over the dryness of her closed eyes as she realized that her whole body was a mass of aching bruises. She turned her head slowly to one side, then the other. Even her neck felt like a mass of tight cords. The tear trickled down her cheek, trailed along the angle of her jaw and down the groove of her jugular as if her soul was reaching out in caressing solace.

Eyes closed, she stretched the fingers of her hand, exploring the hard bed beneath. Her fingers closed, wrapping around the edge of a thin mattress, knuckles feeling the cold metal of a cot. She groped more, finding that her cot was adjacent to a wall on one side. Her body gave a convulsive shudder. Quickly she squeezed her eyes more tightly, but despite her resolve, the memories returned in grisly detail. She let out a cry for Rossgar, then Bill. Oh, her precious Bill! Was he really dead? She couldn't face that. And Reebe, Jessa and Kit? What had happened to them? And Javid? Her heart pounded fiercely in her chest as she remembered surrendering to the metal-faced savage. In sharp realization she knew she must be on the pirate vessel. Her eyes flew open.

Without moving a muscle, she looked at a dull beige ceiling. She stared at it a long time. She listened to the low rumble of the ship's engines far below, humming steadily, unaffected by the erratic feelings crashing about in her chest: fear, wonder, hopelessness mixed with confused thoughts of escape.

She dared not move. Closing her eyes, she thought unconsciousness might be a safer place to be, but sleep would not come. She concentrated on the ship's white noise, the fans, the engines, not daring to look around, afraid of what or whom she might see.

Questions filled her mind. Ransom? Sport? There were no answers to the questions, but she knew that the pirates had come on board for the sole purpose of her capture. It pained her beyond comprehension to think of the people who had lost their lives in the mayhem of the hunt. Had she known, she would have gladly surrendered. And her parents. Would they know yet? She wished she could cry out to them so loudly that they would hear her voice and know that she was alive. Oh Creator, the torment of her parents must be worse than her own.

Unbridled anguish erupted from deep within her, every bone in her body shuddering with cries of sorrow. She rolled onto her side, crippled with both physical and emotional pain. Without conscious volition, her body curled into the fetal position. Her hands covered her face and she wept until blackness spared her once more.

Upon awakening a second time, Marie found her soul empty, as if the weeping had drained her body of every shred of feeling, leaving her like a withered, lifeless carcass on the hard slab.

She was still curled up, lying on her side. Her eyes focused on a wall that was no different from the ceiling in texture. Blinking was the only movement she made, eyes shifting about without another muscle twitching. She gazed at the wall. There was a tiny counter and a small basin, and further into the corner, a wide-open privy bulged from the wall. She looked away in disgust. The walls were solid with no portholes. The dim lighting was unchanged giving no indication of how long she'd been here. She felt weak and famished, guessing she'd missed a meal or two.

A resounding clang stopped her heart. When the thick steel door swung open, Marie's eyes widened with apprehension. A man in a black flight suit stepped in. His features were grimly set, mouth in a frown, his black eyes looking her over curiously. She thought for a moment she recognized him as the man who killed the first passenger in the *Starquest's* lounge, but she couldn't be sure. Something silver flashed out around his waist and Marie found hidden strength. She sat bolt upright on her berth, clinging to its cold edges with a white-knuckled grip. Immediately she recognized the silver object as a lunch tray and her shoulders slumped sharply. With a clatter he dropped the tray on the counter. Then he was gone.

She stared at the tray with its three foil packets, one allowing steam to escape from a small crack along its edge. Marie wiped a hand across her brow, her lungs heaving from the exertion of the moment. How in creation would she survive this ordeal?

Erasing the hideous thoughts from her mind, she concentrated on the tray. Gingerly, she slid off the high berth and stood beside it a moment, afraid to let go in case her limbs wouldn't hold her. Without food, she'd never regain her strength and she had a feeling she would need plenty of stamina in the time to come. Taking a few steps, she felt confident she could make it to the basin. She doused her arm in the thin stream of water, scrubbing off what dried blood she could. For Marie, it was a grisly task. She moistened her face and neck, but the spacecraft's water left her skin feeling taut and dry. There would be no Flechette fresheners and creams supplied on *this* ship, although she would like to see the metal man try a few!

The metal man! There was no better name for the brute.

She rested her head in folded arms over the counter top for a moment and wondered what Javid might advise her to do in this situation. She wondered what had happened to him. She could only hope he'd survived the attack. Long ago, he told her that she would have a strong sense of knowing if he ever died, as he had connected a part of his soul to her own. She didn't feel death's void now, and she knew that if he were able to, Javid would somehow utilize his powers to help her, no matter how minuscule his contribution might be in the enormity of her situation. For the moment, she had to look at what was right in front of her. Her eye darted to the side counter. Her first foil packet meal.

At first the peculiar flavors nauseated her, but her hunger became full-blown with the second bite of the strangely textured food. To her surprise, in very little time, every foil packet lay empty and she sipped on a thick vitamin drink that tasted worse than the rest but gave her a sense of revitalization. If they'd kidnapped her for ransom, they would have to return her in decent condition if they expected to gain any satisfaction out of a financial deal. That meant she might be able to negotiate a better meal next time around. Whatever happened, these brutes would have a lot to account for, and they wouldn't get off as easily as they probably believed. Her father would have Ray Lapp and the entire National Security Forces combing the galaxy for her. She would be rescued soon, of that she was sure. With a renewed sense of hope, she settled back down on the thin mattress and promptly fell asleep.

From the depths of slumber, she recognized the clang of her door opening. Heart thundering, she sat up quickly. The little bit of hope she'd fallen asleep with instantly shattered in the presence of the metal man who strode into her cubical followed by several of his officers. The garish lighting of the small room enhanced the metal man's gruesome features. Marie had a mind to ask him if he remained horrid looking for effect. It was working. Her flame of determination flickered when he came to stand so close that his flight suit brushed her knees. His lips curled into a mocking smile, one side crinkling as it butted against the ill-fitting prosthesis that covered his right face and temple. The false eye darted about, receiving data that would be changed into usable information by the complex microprocessor embedded in front of his ear. He wore black, his musculature undulating beneath the flight suit. She stared at his bulging pectorals, gathering strength to rake her eyes up to meet his but they didn't get past his neck. Propping his hands on his hips, he announced, "The doctor is waiting."

Marie's eyes shot up. "Doctor?" A nervous twitch danced at the corner of her mouth. "I feel fine."

His smile grew wider. "That is good. We need you to have all your strength for this."

Marie swallowed and blinked in alarm. The pirate leaned forward, placing his hands on either side of her thighs. His fowl smelling features came all too close to hers; she recoiled at the sight of the skin decaying where it met the prosthesis. Despite her resolve, Marie found herself crumbling in terror before the monster.

"My orders are to have you recovered before I hand you over to the Commander. Well and untouched. Those are always his words. Pity for me. I don't think he's aware of his prize."

He reached up and traced the contour of her cheek with the back of a finger. She pressed her head against the bulkhead, twisting sideways to avoid him. Her mind swirled in confusion. The metal man was not her ultimate captor?

He gripped her upper arm, dragging her off the bunk. Her first reaction was to struggle, but she fought to control her impulses when again she noticed his men in the doorway. She convinced herself of the futility of a fight and chose not to react when she was given a shove in the direction of the door. The troops escorted her down a long narrow corridor, the metal man in the lead, while the others surrounded her as if *she* were the criminal. The poorly lit corridor was somber, conjuring earlier images of this ship, a long tubular structure emerging from the darkness like a bacterium about to attack its prey.

Her gait was erratic, her knees stiff and sore, her body shivering spasmodically. The dimness ended abruptly when they entered a room. She squinted against blazing lights. Blinking, she looked around in horror. The chamber terrified her. It looked like some sort of operating room, lined with cabinets filled with medical instruments and dominated by a central table, all gleaming in sterile silver chrome. The metal man pushed her unceremoniously to the edge of the table.

She scrambled back, but only retreated a few inches before the men stopped her. She shouted. "What are you going to do to me?"

The metal man gave a small groan. "Not what I'd like to, my sweet."

He grabbed her by the waist and threw her onto the table. She screamed and struggled with survival instincts she had no idea she possessed. Within seconds her arms were strapped by her side; her knees and ankles were strapped in the same manner. Her chest heaved painfully against the wide, restraining bands.

Then she saw the doctor. He stood over her, donned in a white lab coat, a shock of white hair intensifying the cone shaped skull and loose jowls. He held a syringe. Like a deadly conduit of evil, the long, gleaming needle carried a drop of clear liquid on its tip that showered a rainbow through the powerful overhead lights.

The metal man took her chin and turned her to face him. "The Commander is a busy man, and so to save him time, I have the honor of asking you some questions." He glanced at the doctor then back at her, a look of condescending pity crossing the natural side of his features. "I would have preferred using my own methods, but—" His fingers left her chin and trailed between her breasts to stop at her navel. "I have my orders." Then he smiled. "However, I don't suspect that my wait will be a long one. You see, once the Commander is finished with you, I will have you back."

It took all of her strength to remain conscious. Barely breathing, she rasped, "You won't get one credit from my father if you dare lay a hand on me!"

He tossed his head back in laughter. "Credits? You amuse me, Miss Flechette. Don't delude yourself, my dear. I don't believe anyone would pay to have a traitor brought back to their country. All of your secrets will soon be known, Princess, then nobody will want you!" He brought his face inches from hers. "So, relax. Enjoy the ride, because if you don't talk for me, you will talk for the Commander. I'd advise you not to resist and save yourself some grief, my pretty one."

Marie stared at the monster, completely confused by the villain's words. "*Traitor?* I don't know what you're talking about."

He straightened sharply, his mouth pulling into a frown as he barked at the doctor. "Start the injection!" He turned and walked away, vexed.

All she could do was watch the doctor roll up the sleeve of her immobile arm. He cleansed the area with an ice-cold solution and shoved the needle in. Burning pain flooded her upper arm. Heat developed and poured from her shoulder into her head and chest. She heard herself shriek before blackness overtook her.

The timeless depths of darkness gave way to an endless swirling gray, and acute pain in her knees. With shocking intensity, Marie realized she was off the operating table and on the floor. Her stomach crunched with the exertion of forceful retching, her muscles straining with the function from the bottom of her toes. A silver basin had been shoved beneath her to catch the streams of hot pungent liquid erupting from her mouth. She heaved again, then gasped for air, moaning with the agony of it. Her eyes blinked opened. She stared at white floor tiles and a basin full of frothy pink fluid. The sight brought on another bout of retching. Finally she pushed the basin away, realizing it triggered more agony. Very gently, she wiped a sleeve across her mouth, her pounding head drooping with exhaustion.

A voice drifted somewhere above her. "She's been sick since she woke up, sir. She gave us no information."

Boots clapped across the floor, stopping inches from her splayed fingers. Her eyes focused on the toes of black boots, polished to a blinding gleam. Their owner spoke. "Get up."

Marie slumped against the pedestal of the table. There was no hope of finding the strength to obey the order. She muttered that she couldn't. The man swore beneath his breath, bent down, and scooped her into his arms. She recognized the stench and closed her eyes against the reality of the metal man's intimacy. He carried her all the way back to her cabin. Her strength spent, she lay like a rag doll in the mad man's arms. One arm flailed about uselessly, her neck arched back, unsupported. He deposited her on the bunk and briskly left the room. The door closed with a resounding clang.

A different aroma overpowered the metal man's stench. It was a pleasant aroma. She opened her eyes. On the counter lay another tray. Steam slipped from one of the packets, curling innocently towards the ceiling. Marie starred at the tray, then promptly dissolved into tears. Fervently, she began to repeat Javid's words. No permanent damage…no lasting personal harm…no permanent…

CHAPTER 12

Paul scrambled down a hallway that led to Henrie Marchand's grand office. At this hour, the secretary was gone, so he punched his code into the security box and waited impatiently, hands stuck in his pockets. Finally, a languid voice came over the intercom. "What do you want, Paul?"

"Let me in, Henrie!" Paul's voice was thick with urgency. The double doors clicked open. Paul pushed his way through and rushed into the opulent office.

Henrie sauntered to the bar and calmly poured two drinks, handing one to Paul. He took a moment to assess his half-crazed partner and shook his head in disgust. "I thought you were on your way to Doria. Are you taking those pills again?"

"I haven't had one for two days," Paul lied. "My scientists still haven't come up with an antidote for this one, damn it. A month ago, they told me they'd have one in a week. Bloody imbeciles." He grabbed the drink that Henrie offered and gulped down a couple of healthy swallows.

"Take it easy. Things can't be that bad."

Paul stopped and stared at his partner. "You haven't heard?"

Henrie raised an eyebrow. "Heard what?"

"The ship! The *Starquest*, attacked! Two days out of Iggid!"

Henrie lowered the drink from his lips. "You mean...that wasn't your plan?"

"No. *No!*"

"Who's responsible then?"

"I don't know," Paul shrieked, eyes bulging.

"All right. Calm down," Henrie shot back, trying not to fall prey to panic himself. "What exactly are you telling me?"

Paul clenched his teeth. "I'm telling you that my plan is destroyed, that's what. My men—they were waiting on Iggid, ready to board the *Starquest*, kill that bloody bodyguard of hers, then get her to Doria. What am I going to do now? The damned ship was attacked! It took Iggid over fourteen hours to get a rescue team out to them."

Henrie huffed. "Surely somebody knows who attacked the *Starquest* for God's sake."

"We don't know. I don't think anybody knows. From what I've gathered it was a pirate raid, or a gang mimicking pirates. Space Navy Intelligence is trying to tell me that it was a bunch of pranksters going too far. But it was far too professional a job for them to make me believe that. The truth is, any way you look at it, we're sunk. I'm sunk!"

"Are they all dead?" Henrie asked, horrified.

"No. A hundred and thirty dead, two missing."

"And...Marie?"

"Missing." There was an ominous silence. "Aren't you going to ask who else is missing?"

Dumfounded, Henrie said nothing.

"Tripp. Bill Tripp. The man we love so much…I hope they kill the bastard!"

"Great Creator!" Henrie uttered, rubbing his eyes wearily.

"Somebody's on to us big time, my friend, and that makes me very nervous. By what I can gather this attack was no kids' play. Pranksters, my ass!"

"Don't jump to conclusions. This incident could be completely unrelated to our operation. Marie could have been kidnapped for any number of reasons," Henrie pointed out. "She did take off in a hurry, with only three guards!"

"Phoebe hasn't been able to get a scrap of information. Not a hint. Not a lead! Hell, just the look he gave me practically killed me. He's saving it. I know he's just saving it this time. He doesn't care who I am at this point."

"Don't worry. He'll cool off," Henrie grumbled, unconvincingly.

The two men looked at each other, knowing the truth stared them in the face. Their part of the plan lay like an open wound, a serious wound, one that could cripple the entire operation. Paul flung himself down on the plush leather couch, balancing his drink in the free fall. He groaned. "My teams were ready. This was all going to be rectified, smooth as silk. How could this have happened?"

"You couldn't have known about this attack, much less have prevented it. So, before you go tearing into some great 'fix it' solution, let's think it through. She'll probably show up in a day or two—and if not, Phoebe will have every available ship out raking the galaxy for her."

Paul heaved a sigh, letting his head fall back against the couch. "I spent days preparing my men to board in Sector 12, then I was up all night trying to get new teams together to track those pirates!"

"Paul," Henrie's voice was stern. "Slow down, you hear me? When we're sure Marie is missing and not dead, we'll act. Until then, there isn't much use killing ourselves over it, although Phoebe may do it for us."

"But, without Marie, the invasion can't go on as planned."

"I realize that. So we'll have to find a way to fix it," Henrie growled.

"I may as well go hang myself. I'm a freakin' dead man."

"Not if you leave this to me. You take care of Doria and I'll worry about Marie. Did you get back into the computers at Flechette Cosmetics?"

"Yeah, the old man let me have my time at closing up shop. I planted the magic seed just like you asked. I'd love to be there for the fireworks, but like a good boy, I'll be on Doria."

"Good."

Paul took the last swallow of his drink. He swished it around, savoring the powerful minty flavor before it slid down his arched throat. No matter how much they coerced him, he vowed never again to accept an assignment involving a woman to this degree. Especially one in her position. He thought he could get used to her, but he couldn't. And children? God help him! He was glad his assignment had ended before he was forced to play the father role.

Henrie rubbed the bridge of his nose. "I told you I wouldn't get involved if you screwed up again, but seeing as this isn't all your fault, I'll do what I can. I'll talk to Phoebe." Henrie looked at his partner tiredly. "Now get your sorry ass off this planet before I decide to put you out of your misery myself."

CHAPTER 13

Her agony wouldn't end. She had fallen into a fitful sleep, the meal having gone cold. Her watch was gone, her necklace stolen. She had no toiletries, no change of clothes. There was no way to know how much time had passed, but the familiar clang of her door traumatized her into a fully awaked state. She twisted her head and wished to die. Alone in the doorway stood the metal man. He closed the door, the clang resounding ominously. Adrenaline clashed with a drug-induced grogginess as she scrambled clumsily to a sitting position. He took the two steps that covered the distance between them. She didn't think he could hear the pounding of her heart, yet she swore it shook the bunk beneath her.

"You disappointed me today, Miss Flechette. Such a pretty thing, lying there on the table, thrashing about in resistance to my drugs. You are a very brave girl, but continuing to resist will only bring you more pain. Can you not see that?"

Wholly confused, Marie couldn't utter a single word in her defense. He leaned closer. She pushed so hard against the bulkhead that she swore her head would leave an impression in the wall. When he reached out to stroke her shoulder, she flung her arm back. Her wrist smashed painfully against the wall. "Get away from me," she croaked, the words rasping over her abused throat. In a flurry of movement, he had both her wrists pinned over her head. All she could do was look away and pray she could somehow empty her mind, become lifeless and unresponsive to any verbal or physical attacks she knew were coming.

"The Commander is a lucky man," he whispered in her ear. His fetor oozed through the small space between them. She breathed shallowly in an attempt to avoid inhaling the odor.

"You are incredibly lovely," he continued. "Such a pity to waste yourself in lies and deceit."

Marie turned to face him, indignation strong in her words. "I have told no lies. I have no secrets. And I do *not* know what you're talking about when you call me a trait—"

He released her. One hand flung out and slapped her solidly across the face.

In complete shock, Marie's initial response was to stiffen in utter disbelief. Her reaction was then swift and sure. With an equally fast reflex, she kicked back, her heel hitting its mark in his groin. The metal man's natural eye twisted with unexpected agony. Marie had a second to scramble out of his grasp and off the berth. In three strides she reached the door. To her horror it was locked solid. She tugged at the handle, pulling at it with her entire weight but the thick portal wouldn't budge.

Terror reigned.

Sinewy fingers gripped her shoulder. She held on, the act brutally stretching her upper arms even though she knew in her mind that a fight was futile. Her damp palms lost their grip. Her body flung back into his chest. Fiercely, she fought the alien, but with remarkable swiftness he pinned her to the bulkhead, one forearm across her throat to curb her writhing. He leaned his torso heavily against her. "You have a lot of spirit for one who's never known hardship."

Marie wheezed against the pressure on her throat. "I've been reserving it!"

His natural eye narrowed. "You? For what—your next hair appointment?" Quickly, he added pressure to her throat to curb her angry, snake-like motions. "It will do you little good, my love," he told her. "Surrender is your only option. That, or death in the struggle."

She glared at him. "Then I'll die!" She sucked in enough air to martyr herself further. "I will *never* give in to you!"

"Is that so?" His voice revealed a hint of surprise. Pleasant surprise. Marie blinked in panic. She had just agreed to fight his advances to the end! Terrified, she could feel his throbbing groin push against her. "Let's see about that."

Another swift move brought the arm that pressed across her throat down to grasp her other wrist. With both wrists clamped on either side of her head, he brought his lips to her neck. She could feel his teeth sink into her flesh. Marie gasped in horror before a loud cry bellowed from her lungs.

His body curbed any kicks she attempted to deliver. "You think you frighten me, little one?" he hissed. "I assure you, quite the opposite is happening."

His face came around to her throat. He gripped the collar of her shirt with his teeth and gave a vicious wrench. The two top buttons popped. She strained against him, keeping her part of the bargain, but abhorrence filled her as his tongue licked between her breasts, his face pushing the material out of his way, his tongue reaching for her nipple. His foul breath wafted beneath her nose. Sweat glistened on her skin; her hair clung to her forehead. Behind the curtain of hair, her mind struggled to find a means of escape.

An unexpected, misty image of Javid exploded into her mind. He was reaching out to her, his lips moving, trying to tell her something. Suddenly, a thought of brilliance exploded into her thoughts. "The Commander!" she yelled sharply. The metal man's body froze momentarily. He lifted his head, twisting his lips with rage. Her lucent blue eyes bore through his, grabbing the attention of both the natural and artificial one. She could hear the hum of the microprocessor assessing the data she'd just fed it.

A ghastly howl bellowed from deep within the pirate's chest. He hurled himself upon her, his teeth finding her neck. The power of his thrust forced her to lose her footing. Together they began to slide against the bulkhead to the floor. His abdomen pinned her hard, his legs splayed out behind him.

Marie held tenaciously to the thread of hope that Javid had sent her. "The Commander has ordered you to bring Marie Flechette to him, unharmed."

The pirate moaned deeply while dragging his lips slowly from her neck and down over her shoulder already bared by his monstrous aggression. A corner of the prosthesis caught her skin. Marie felt a searing pain along the length of his travel, followed by a hot, wet sensation. She squeezed her eyes against the torture and spoke as loudly as she could. The force of it helped her to avoid losing ground to a tremulous delivery that would betray her fear of failure. Again, she directed the message to the microprocessor. "You are to bring Marie Flechette to the Commander, alive, and...and..." In wild panic, she struggled to remember the exact words. A new image of Javid flashed through her mind; then it became clear. "well and untouched!"

The metal man instantly began to shudder, faintly, then with more vigor. Arching back like a venomous snake, he let out an eerie, primeval howl. Marie trembled against him, yet found more words to throw in her defense. "He would be very displeased with you," she admonished. "I am to be recovered and well. *Look at me!*"

She caught his full attention—then realized with sickening horror that there was a deadly loophole. She'd had no time to work it out, and now it was too late. He could simply announce his mission a failure, with the captive dead of shock, or suicide. But the next second proved that the thought had not yet crossed the pirate's mind. He stopped, momentarily immobilized. This commander he spoke of must have tremendous power to bring a brute such as this to his knees.

With a sudden, forceful shove that squeezed the air from her lungs, the madman scrambled to his feet. Shoulders humped, body poised like a wildcat, he pointed a finger at her. "The Commander does want you well, but do not forget that he is also returning you to me upon the completion of his tasks. We are not finished yet, my sweet one. Such a body shall not be cast aside without first having all its pleasures wrung from it. *That* is when you shall die!"

Marie didn't care about his threats now. All she cared for was the victory of the moment.

"You will die with me." Even the ocular prosthesis conveyed the message by darting back and forth as if to photograph her every feature for future study. Marie lay on the floor, shoulders and head propped weakly against the bulkhead, his threats unable to stir a reaction.

The pirate's black form skulked towards the door. He remained silent in his retreat and was gone as suddenly as he'd appeared.

A long time passed before Marie found the strength or the volition to move. Finally, with a trembling hand, she clutched the torn material to her throat, a moan escaping as pain seared across the top of her shoulder. Craning her neck, she could see a long gash running down the length of her shoulder, blood oozing from the wound. Her golden colored blouse was saturated with a brownish streak nearly to her elbow. She fought to control the nausea that threatened at the sight of her own blood. Just thinking of the metal man scraping her with that horrid prosthesis brought trembling upon her entire body. She sniffed sharply, wiped a tear from her eye, wiped her soiled hand on her pant leg, then clamped a hand over her mouth to prevent a cry of outrage that ached to jump from her throat.

She shook her head. She would not let this monster or this situation overwhelm her. With renewed fortitude, Marie struggled to a standing position, leaning against the wall for support. She eyed the berth only a few feet away and gave a push to propel herself in its direction. Gripping the thin metal edge of the berth, she scowled.

"My next hair appointment!" she spat hotly. "How dare he!"

She was not...*not* just a spoiled child of the well-to-do. Hours in front of a camera or millions of people was a hardship he would certainly never learn to endure. Painstaking development of products and programs that brought a greater sense of self-esteem to the people was another thing he could know nothing about. And always looking and acting your best, he certainly knew nothing about. Him! Him and all his brutes on this ship. They knew about destruction, greed and torture—and if that was the kind of hardship he felt she was so unfamiliar with, well—she would show him that she could endure that too!

With fiery determination, Marie wobbled over to the sink and splashed her face and then her chest, vigorously washing off the remnants of the metal man. She had a mind to take her shirt off and rinse it as well, but one glance toward the door changed her mind.

There was no way of counting the hours. She knew only that the hours were getting long. She sat cross-legged on the cot, attempting a meditation technique Javid had taught her. Her skills were crude, making her wish she had paid closer attention to his lessons. However, making an attempt was one way to thank him for his timely mental appearance and her subsequent recollection of the words that had halted the madman's advances. With a sigh, she emptied her mind as he'd taught, humming softly as she did so. For a few minutes it proved to be useful, until her shoulder began to ache.

She craned her head to reassess the wound. Lifting her stiffened, blood stained shirt, she was relieved to find that the laceration had stopped bleeding, but one whiff of it terrified her again. A horrible odor oozed from the wound. Infection? She'd never had an infection and had no idea how it should be treated. If this was 'well and untouched' she dreaded the encounter with a Commander who believed that torture lay within the categories of *well*. Untouched, she had managed by her own wit!

She took on the grisly task of washing off the wound as best she could and then returned to her berth. Sleepless and scared, she stared at the ceiling as she had for countless hours already, but this time she saw, with a new mental clarity, something she'd been staring at since her arrival.

"Rossgar," she breathed. Slowly, she brought herself to a precarious standing position on the berth. There, in the same color and material as the rest of the ceiling was the grating of a large air vent. She stared at it, then cast a nervous glance at the door before bringing her attention to the latticed vent once again. She gave a prayer for Rossgar's soul as she stared at the vent. It was a crazy idea, but it was something! Not a way off the ship, but perhaps to other rooms where she might find some sort of weapon in case the metal man decided to try his tricks again. Taking a deep breath, she reached up and gave the lattice a push, throwing furtive glances at the door as she did so. The grate moved a fraction, its corner lifting with an abrasive sound. Her heart pounded fiercely. She gave a shove with both hands on the edging and to her astonishment, the entire thing popped up and landed crookedly inside the duct. In alarm, she sat down on the berth, deathly afraid someone might have heard. When no one came to check on her, she cautiously stood on the berth again, blood pounding in her ears with the daring of it.

Never having done such acrobatics, other than with the help of Spencer and Rossgar, Marie spent several minutes figuring out the physics of her planned stunt. She pulled herself up, her feet scrambled against the wall until she could hook one elbow inside the duct. To her relief, the duct appeared large enough to accommodate her, and with much grunting, she hauled herself into the rectangular metal structure.

The sound of her own breathing echoed within the tubular passageway. She blinked to focus down the tunnel, helped by a shaft of light that beamed a diffuse rectangle into the dark passage. To her surprise, another haze of light filtered through another grate perhaps thirty feet away. Barely breathing, she slowly crawled towards it. She was only a few feet away when a loud cough stopped her in mid track. She heard a shuffle, a soft groan. Her breath nearly exploded in her lungs. The urge to backtrack to her cell was almost overpowering.

Javid's voice came to her again. "There is no future if one takes no risks."

As carefully as possible, she edged towards the grating, much smaller than her own. Eternity seemed to pass before she lowered to her stomach, biting her lip as the gash on her shoulder pulled against the stiffened fabric of her shirt. Gingerly, she dragged herself forward until she could peer into the room through the grate. Puzzled, she squinted at the naked back of a man whose skin had two long gashes running from shoulder to waist. The wounds appeared to be healing, but the metal man had a bad habit of treating his people ruthlessly. In a startling moment of recognition, she gasped.

The man spun in a circle, his eyes darting in every direction, looking for the author of the voice. His gaze shot to the grating when she cried out. "Bill! Oh, Great Creator, you're alive!"

"What on—" Bill's jaw dropped. "Marie? Is that you?"

Quickly, she wiggled her slender fingers through the latticework and pulled off the grating. Bill pulled over a chair and was now beneath her.

The two clasped hands in a grip that brought a film of moisture to Bill Tripp's eyes. He gave a short laugh, with both relief and amazement that the girl had actually found the fortitude to crawl through a vent, being unaware of her introduction to such escapades by virtue of his own men. Marie squished her face to the hole.

"I can't believe you're alive! What a miracle!" she whispered loudly.

"Of sorts. I hope I never have to take a stun ray at point-blank range again."

"I thought they'd killed you!"

"Well they didn't. And you, my lady," he shook a finger while trying to cover a grimace full of pride, "will never risk your life for me like that again!"

She stuck her face as far into the space as it would allow. "But they would have killed you, and probably would have kept killing until I gave myself up."

Bill frowned. "You're right, and so I thank you." He suddenly caught a full look at her face crammed into the opening. "Oh, my darling, you look awful!"

Marie grinned tightly. "They forgot to fetch my cosmetics."

Bill pursed his lips. "Not funny. How on earth did you get up there?"

"My vent is big enough for me to fit through. I can't believe I didn't think of this sooner. Spencer and Rossgar showed me how."

"They did?" He shook his head. "You'll have to explain that one later. I'm proud of you, my girl, but if you get caught you won't see another day. You seem to be all right. Are you?"

"I'm all right, I guess," she said, "but, what have they done to you?"

Bill grimaced. "It wasn't that bad, really. I passed out long before it was over by their standards. A little trick of mine. Nobody has bothered me much since."

Marie wished she could say the same.

"Darling, you have to get back before they catch us, but it is the greatest relief in my entire life to know that you're all right."

"And likewise. I thought I'd witnessed your execution, although I couldn't bring myself to believe that you were actually dead." She hesitated. "Have you ventured to guess where we're going?"

Bill grimaced. "To spare my sanity I've given up guessing. Which reminds me. Where the hell were Spencer and Rossgar when you came out of the crowd?" He cut himself off seeing the pain on Marie's soiled features.

"They'd have killed Spencer for sure. I convinced him that he would be more help to us alive than dead. Rossgar, he...ah..." But she could only shake her head.

Bill's shoulders dropped. There was a momentary silence.

"And Javid? And the women?" It was Marie's turn to ask the unthinkable.

Bill looked up at her. "I'm not sure. I can only hope they were rescued. But right now, it's you that I fear for. This little gig wasn't on my account."

A low thud, followed by another, resounded throughout the ship. The vent shaft vibrated. Marie's heart stopped. Bill reached up to grab her hand. "Marie. The ship...it's slowing down," he said with urgency, looking about the room as if he could peer right through its walls.

She found her voice. "The metal man—he said he's taking us to his Commander."

Bill's brawny chest heaved in nervous anticipation. He nodded slowly. "Well, that puts one piece of the puzzle in place. I think this is more complex than simple ransom. We'll see if I'm right." He squeezed her fingers. "Marie, listen carefully. I don't know what's going on, but my being here alive adds to the puzzle. From their questions, I think they believe that you and I are implicated in something, but I can't figure out what." Bill paused, immediately aware that sharing his suspicions might upset her. Yet, he had to give her hope. "If that's what they think, they'll keep me alive, so know that I'll be doing the Creator's best to get us out of this mess."

Overwhelmed, Marie stared at him. "Do they think we're involved in some sort of scandal?"

"I think so, but I don't know what. Now, please, get back there before they notice you're gone!"

Another rumble in the ship drove her to action. "I'm scared, Bill," she added. "But I'll do as you say."

She replaced the grate and began a snaking slither back towards her cell. Half way there a feeling of splitting apart and coming back together washed over her. Marie knew they were coming out of hyperdrive. As soon as the feeling of weakness passed, she resumed her retreat, confident that no one would be coming to her room while making the jump back to normal space. Just the same, she trembled badly and almost lost her grip while sliding back thought the vent hole. She muttered a prayer of thanks when the grating fell into place. Trembling, she sank onto the berth, spent.

Waiting for the next horrible event with no sense of time was the hardest thing Marie had ever endured. At least two or three hours passed while she sat awaiting her fate, hands folded in her lap, her mind too cluttered to try to make sense of anything. Mindlessly, she stared at the steel door, concentrating on the changing hums and groans of the engines.

A deep thud shuddered through the ship. They had landed. Before she was quite prepared, the familiar clang of her door resounded. Marie stiffened as it swung open.

CHAPTER 14

As Marie expected, the metal man himself came to fetch her from her cell. He stopped at the threshold, his men organized behind him. The natural side of his face scowled darkly as he strode brazenly into the room. Without a word he dragged her off the bunk, wrenched her arms behind her back and snapped icy clamps on her wrists. His men parted as he pushed her out the door. A short distance down the hall, Bill was brought out of his cell in the same manner.

"I see you had the decency to spare my bodyguard," Marie growled, looking squarely at Bill, who returned with a near imperceptible nod.

The metal man turned to lead the procession, sniffing as he did so. "You are both prisoners of Commander Shaw. There will be no talking!"

Shaw? A strange name. A common name for a Commander of such a pile of brutes, she thought as they were marched down the long corridor. Stepping off the ramp into a heat wave surprised Marie. Instant curiosity in her surroundings managed to take her mind off the blast of heat, although a push on her shoulder gave her a stab of pain that she couldn't relieve because of the cuffs that wrenched back her arms.

Although significantly smaller than the *Starquest*, the pirate vessel looked longer and darker than she remembered. Its matte surface absorbed the sunlight as effectively as a black hole. Numerous crewmembers crawled about the craft, darting up and down the main hold ramp, unloading the spoils. Marie's blood boiled at the sight, wondering if her parents would be receiving her belongings or if they were somewhere amid that pile.

She and Bill were pushed along within amongst an entourage of pirate beasts. The group began to walk away from the ship where the two could study a limited view of a well-equipped spaceport. The pirate vessel was berthed along one edge of a massive airfield. Behind the pirate ship, a wall of heavy tropical foliage reached loftily into the sunshine, its undergrowth inundated with blossoms of unimaginable size and color. Marie's senses were instantly invaded by an aromatic, floral scent that wafted between acrid coolant and jet fuel billowing from the ship's engines as they slowly wound down. The tangle of trees and vines rolled upward, blanketing a series of low-range mountains that encircled three sides of the landing field. The far edge of the field abutted a sheer mountain face. The rounded summit of the mountain had been partially cleared to make way for a hoard of antennae and communication towers. Otherwise, the surrounding terrain looked blue and soft in the afternoon sun of the alien planet. Two large moons crept over the sun's opposite horizon, one so close its craters were easily discernable. Marie and Bill were directed at a walk past a row of stealthy fighter jets. The words stamped in bold typeface along their aerodynamic flanks made her jaw slacken.

Fringe Federation

She cast a glance at Bill who looked as surprised as she. So! They had arrived in the ominous Fringe, but a Federation? Bill had worried that he'd been spreading rumors when he spoke of a rudimentary government here. This was no rumor. By the look on Bill's face, he was as awestruck as she. The metal man urged her along with a shove against her aching shoulder. Marie's spirits plummeted. Federation or not, the stories she'd heard about this awful place were now a stark reality. However, in contrast to the stories was the airfield itself. A gleaming tower rose loftily above the tarmac, its mushroom cap allowing a full range view of the impressive array of spacecraft on the ground. It all reeked of meticulous organization. Marie was surprised by the large hangars, warehouses and multiple rows of long-range fighter jets. Farther behind those sat a dozen large support ships. Marie wondered why they had need for such an extensive military base when no one seemed to know they existed.

The heat of this jungle planet was adding to Marie's already weakened state. The aromas from a nearby blossoming tree only made her want to close her eyes and believe she was walking amongst the greenhouses of home. This surely was all a bad dream! The sudden wafting of a gangrenous odor exuding from her outfit tore her back to reality. She noticed that Bill was holding up better, his ogle-eyed interest in their surroundings diverting his attention from the sweat streaming from his brow.

A small transport unit hummed to a stop beside them. Five of the dozen pirates stepped in with Marie and Bill. The metal man took his place beside her. Marie automatically shifted closer to the side of the unit, grateful that he made no further attempt to touch her. She relished an open window that allowed a rush of air to swirl about the small cabin. Frequently, she glanced at Bill. He remained expressionless although his shifting eyes caught her every glance.

The transport unit headed toward the sheer cliff face. Her quick survey of the area had missed a stupendous cave that marked the entrance to an underground bunker. As they made their approach, the cave could have been mistaken for the yawning mouth of a sleeping giant, the sharp rocky shards along its upper border like teeth ready to snap down on its unwary prey. Marie calculated that the orifice must be one hundred feet high. Their transport unit felt no larger than a pebble as they approached the enormous opening. As they approached, the nose of a large assault fighter emerged from the orifice, pulled on a set of huge rollers manned by powerful robotics. Marie tried not to notice the array of deadly firing canons attached like leeches to its side. As their transport edged into the cave it swung by the assault fighter, the opposing effects of size and speed created a dizzying sensation.

Dimness overcame them as they entered the cavern. Within yards of entering the cave, the rock sent its natural air-conditioning swirling about them. Marie sucked in great gulps of the cool air while blinking in her surroundings.

She gaped in awe. The raw, stone ceiling high above them was crammed with metal beams that supported bay after bay of service modules, fueling equipment, data monitors, all strung together by a series of mobile and stationary catwalks. Winches supporting space planes hovered at different levels above the ground, repair technicians swarmed about tending to the array of wiring and conduits attached to them. A multitude of floodlights directed their white beams onto the varied activities on the massive floor space. The cavern buzzed with activity: human, alien, and robotic, all snaking about, intent upon their particular tasks. The entire place came to a stop to gape curiously at them. Their arrival was obviously anticipated.

Her stomach fluttered anxiously as they ventured deeper into the bowels of this forsaken mountain hole. The cuffs pulled menacingly at her wrists, her chest crushing with panic as the claustrophobic effect of the cave took hold. The huge cavern narrowed down to tunnel-size at its deepest end. Other transport units buzzed past them creating a Doppler effect that echoed off the stone walls pressing around them. Their little trolley veered to miss others and Marie feared they would tangle in the conduits that hung in loops off the walls and ceilings. Suddenly the tunnel expanded into another stone hewn chamber where more refined activity was being carried out. Although the Flechette mansion could easily fit in this space, this second chamber was significantly smaller than the first and appeared to serve as a converging point for several other tunnels that opened into this area.

In what seemed like no place in particular, the transportation unit stopped. Marie followed Bill's intense gaze over her shoulder. A large tubular-shaped alcove fingered into the rock. It housed the most advanced computer equipment imaginable. Marie didn't possess much knowledge in this area but she did recognize the tall, wafer-thin rectangles that reached thirty feet toward the ceiling as three-dimensional galactic star maps.

Near one of the central consoles a knot of officers clustered in conversation. The group seemed to be the focus of Bill's interest but Marie wasn't given a chance to study them. The metal man ordered her off the trolley accompanied by an unnecessary yank on her sore arm. Marie's only relief was to find Bill flanking her left side. His wrists were likewise secured, thwarting his ability to protect her. Marie knew they were about to be handed over to the metal man's Commander, but any view of this enigmatic person was obscured by the hoard of captors surrounding them. Instinctively she hesitated, then lunged as yet another shove propelled her deeper into the control room.

Within the alcove, the pirates stopped abruptly. The metal man stood at attention, his back to her as he curtly addressed one Commander Shaw. He snapped a salute before stepping aside to take his place on Marie's right. Her other guard moved behind her, giving her a small push forward. Marie found herself immobilized as she locked eyes on the man who stood before her.

She gaped in total surprise, wondering momentarily if this was actually the Commander to whom the pirate had saluted. Obviously it was. He was the one who stepped forward. Marie glared at the leader, her shoulders angled in preparation for an impossible retreat.

"Good work, Captain Boro," the Commander said. He stepped closer to assess his prize. Marie wasn't sure who was doing the most assessing. She might have presumed his rank from the poise; arrogant. But she wouldn't have guessed it by his clothing, or his overall color. Bleached hair hung in loose waves that fell to a length just below his muscular shoulders. Wispy bangs angled in different directions, half pushed back, half clinging to his forehead. The chiseled jaw line was rough with growth, hiding something. What? Worry perhaps? His dark blue eyes, although alert, showed signs of fatigue. Despite the obvious physical strain, the fiery determination of a true leader exuded from his very core. Haughty, his gaze swept over her as if she were some sort of commodity. He gave a short grunt as if disappointed before turning to assess Bill.

Marie's gaze remained latched onto Commander Shaw, amazed by the worn leather boots and weary trousers. An old leather gun belt holstered a weapon she didn't recognize. A blowzy shirt of light weight cotton hung on his shoulders in a superfluous manner, sleeves rolled to the elbow, the collar open to mid chest giving hint of his powerful build. This was not the image she'd conjured for the metal man's Commander. Did he even have a uniform? He looked like he'd been wearing this same clothing for years. Suddenly the Commander startled her with an abrupt order. "Take Mr. Tripp to his cell."

Marie's heart convulsed. Someone began to tug on Bill's arm, but for a second Bill held his ground, his eyes shifting quickly to the metal man, Captain Boro.

"Yes, and keep the lovely one here," the metal man jeered, his hand grasping Marie's chin, wrenching her to face him. "She will need a bit more softening up, I'm afraid." His hand left her chin to travel down over her breasts.

Marie burst with a scream of revulsion, twisting sideways then backwards, pushing hard into the guard behind her. Both she and the guard tumbled to the floor. At the same instant, Bill's foot shot up in a kick that caught the side of the metal man's natural skull, only landing a partial blow to the beast who saw the attack coming. In seconds Bill was tackled to the floor, his shackled arms crushed beneath him.

Side arms clicked into firing position, shouts exploded, and instantly the Commander bellowed for order. Marie, oblivious to the commands, continued to scream hysterically, "Get your hands off me!"

Brusquely, she and Bill were brought to their feet, Marie was held fast by one of the guards while Bill was nearly choked with a grip on the back of his collar by another. The glint of a knife flashed at Bill's temple. He eyed the weapon with a shifting glance. The pirate Boro glared at him from behind the knife. "You are as insufferable as the girl!" he spat, his one eye blinking, letting Bill know that his kick had hit its mark.

Commander Shaw physically hauled the pirate back. "That's enough, Boro. You are dismissed. See me in the boardroom on Level Three in one hour. Captain Hollis, take Mr. Tripp to his cell. The girl comes with me."

"Don't take—" Marie held back. Desperately, she controlled her terror as they began to take Bill away. She caught his worried glance as he was pulled from her sight. The metal man marched off in another direction. Marie twisted violently within the grip of her guard to face Commander Shaw. "What do you want with me?"

"You should know." Then shouting over her head, he demanded of Captain Boro's men, "What happened to her? She looks like hell."

Before any of the pirate crew could answer, Marie screamed at the Commander. "I look like hell because your pirate-man nearly killed me!" She kicked out, landing a viciously blow on the shin of the Commander's boot. "Like he killed all those others. And if it weren't for you I'd be dead!...and it would *not* have been a pretty sight."

The Commander stepped forward, a surprised smile on his lips. "Is that so? Well I'm glad I was of service to you."

Hysterics had taken over fear. "And if you let that monster near me ever again, by Creator, I'll kill you both! That's going to happen one way or another for this atrocity. If it's credits you want, believe me, it would have been much simpler to *ask*."

"Don't think for one minute that I'm stupid, Miss Flechette." His voice was as incisive as it was mocking. He leaned forward to force his message. She recoiled sharply. "Your acting skills don't get by me. You're not that good."

Her fists bunched against the cuffs. "I don't know what you're *talking* about! I-am-not-acting!" she screamed, the shake of her head loosening the hair plastered to her forehead.

With a rigid finger, the Commander ordered the officer holding her to follow him to the boardroom. The journey wasn't far, around a few consoles jutting into the central floor of the alcove but Marie's writhing body sent the staff scrambling out of her path. Her mouth burst forth with a barrage of words she wasn't aware she possessed. The officer nearly threw her into the room before hammering on the controls located on the exterior doorjamb. A thick steel panel slid with dizzying speed across its threshold. Dead silence ensued. Marie was left to face the Commander alone. He stood at the far end of a rectangular boardroom, arms crossed, his displeasure evident. His jaw muscles knotted as his eyes silently attacked her from his end of the room. She felt paralyzed, the silence of the fortified room further crushing her collapsing courage.

Commander Shaw suddenly spoke. "You can make this easy on yourself, or you can make it difficult. The choice is yours. There is no place to go. There is no getting away. I think you know the consequences of your silence."

Marie looked at him as if hearing a different language, but his dialect was clearly Central Nixodonian. She felt so utterly confused that she wanted to just sit on the floor and cry but an appalling disbelief kept her gaping at him. Thoughtlessly, she asked, "Am I really in the *Fringe?*"

"Yes," he drawled, slowly closing the distance between them.

Her torso wavered forward, then backward. "Isss hot in here," she slurred.

Commander Shaw rolled his eyes then strode over and caught Marie before she collapsed. She whined a thank you as he removed the shackles and helped her to a chair. He leaned over the boardroom table and punched at the central panel. It bleeped to life. "Get a medic in here," he grumbled. "Oh, and bring a protein drink...and ask Lieutenant Mondiran to find out what happened to this woman." He glanced at her. "And when she was last fed. Wait. Ask Mondiran to check on Boro, too. Something's wrong with him." His voice lowered. "He looks worse than the prisoner."

As he waited for the medics, Commander Shaw found himself tapping the woman lightly on the cheeks in attempt to keep her conscious. It was worrisome how her pale blue eyes kept rolling to the back of her head. This, he didn't think, was acting.

The door snapped open. A white clad professional walked in and set to work. The Commander moved out of the way, taking a position on the opposite side of the boardroom table. Her hair hadn't been washed in a few days, he thought, and for a cosmetics queen she'd somehow forgotten to doll herself up this morning.

He fumed. Boro did his job, no doubt, but he habitually failed to remember the ethical standards of prisoner care that they'd tried to drill into that thick metal skull of his. Still, Boro had never treated a prisoner this badly. Just one glance at the pirate had assured the Commander that Boro had been neglecting his prosthesis again. Shaw hoped all this wasn't some crazed repercussion from a lack of care of that microprocessor.

Marie Flechette moaned, head resting on an arm stretched across the table. When the medic injected a mixture of sedative and pain killer, she groaned, "Not another needle, pleeease."

She was slim and obviously well toned. The jump suit of expensive lamé may have graced her beautifully days before but now it hung, tainted and torn. Richard Shaw dared not wonder how her shirt torn had gotten torn like that, or how the blouse got so extensively soaked with blood. He rubbed his eyes wearily. As long as he could get her in good enough condition to interrogate, he'd be happy. Time was of the essence.

The medic looked up. "She has a pretty mean gash down her left shoulder, sir. Infection has set in so when you're finished I'll arrange for Doctor Faulk to see her for further assessment. I'll have to give her a dose of anexet if you want to keep her awake, sir."

"Sure, go ahead."

Marie groaned with the second injection, her face remaining pressed into the crook of her arm. The medic pried open her left elbow. "The scrape on this forearm appears to be mending." The medic knit his brow. "She's quite dehydrated. We should get her a protein drink."

"Fine," Shaw grunted, livid at the situation. At least his prisoner reacted to the injection and regained full consciousness. At his insistence, she began sipping on the protein drink brought in by an aide. Then he cleared the room.

"Now—."

Her half-closed eyes snapped open with the force of the Commander's voice.

"You will tell me the name of your leader. In fact, before we're through, you will tell me the names of all the ring leaders and their base locations."

"Pardon me?" she squeaked. "What's that got to do with a ransom payment? Please, no games. I know my family will pay you. My parents will be worried sick by now."

His torso lunged forward as he slammed both fists against the table. Marie stared wide-eyed at the reflection of his fists in the table's polished surface. Less focused were the white strands of hair and a bobbing glottis. The drugs may have been dampening her reactions but doom crept unheeded through her heart. Her own throat bobbed in trepidation.

"Your Nixodonian leader, Miss Flechette."

She looked at him quizzically, "That's what you want to know? It's President Pao Knabon. You should know that!"

His spine sunk between shoulder blades. "Funny. Very funny."

"It isn't funny, it's true. I should know. I live there." She slammed the protein drink on the table. The liquid slopped noisily within the container.

"Your personal leader, Miss Flechette." His voice grew adamant, his gaze remained fixed on the table.

"What do you mean, *personal* leader?"

He lifted his head sharply. Their eyes locked. "Why are you doing this? Do you want me to resort to violence? I have no stronger truth drug than the one Captain Boro gave you. Not one that wouldn't kill you, at any rate. Just be straight with me and you'll spare us both a great deal of trouble."

Without warning, an outrage she had never experienced overpowered the dizzying effects of the drug. Through stiff jaws she stated her case as clearly as possible. "I would tell you anything you want to know, if I only knew what you wanted to hear. But I obviously don't have the answers you want." Her voice rose in crescendo as she narrated. "I was on a journey to see my aunt, Cecilia Flechette, who's an artist. Yes, that is where I was going. It wasn't that hard to figure out. It seemed everyone else knew! You didn't have to drag me over here like some sort of criminal. She lives on the satellite moon of Badar. It's in the Kutar system, in case you've never heard of it. Kutar 2 to be exact. There. Is that such a secret? My fiancé cheated on me, so I left. I last worked for Henrie Marchand. He's a film director and I'm the star in his latest movie. That's no secret either. If they had a theater in this god-forsaken part of the galaxy, maybe you and your boys would care to watch it! I don't have any personal leaders, or secrets." She threw her head back and laughed pitifully, "All you have to do is read *Celebrity Quest* or any of that other trash and you can find out everything that I do, and a lot that I don't." She snapped her head forward to lock onto his unblinking stare. "They can tell you when I last peed if you're really that interested."

"Ah, yes," he agreed, beginning a slow walk around the table. "Marie Flechette, household name in Nix States, and probably the Blue Rift, and the Three Kingdoms, and now Telexa as well. Quite a reputation. Your uniqueness is so exalted that establishments galaxy-wide plead for a chance to touch you, examine you." He kept his gaze locked on hers as he rounded the long table. "Museums want bits of your clothing, your hair. Sectors are bickering over film rights, and everyone wants to know how you live, what you eat, where you sleep, what your secrets are."

"I think you exaggerate."

"I exaggerate none, but very few know your real secrets, do they, Miss Flechette?" He was only a few feet from her now.

Fear chilled her bones. "I—I don't have any secrets."

"The military base locations, Miss Flechette. Where are they?"

Her shoulders dropped in frustration. She threw back her head, eyes focusing on the ceiling. "I don't know anything about military bases! I'm a model for a cosmetics company, and now I've done a movie. What has that got to do with bases?" Turning to look at him again she saw that he was practically on top of her. She scrambled out of the chair and backed away, edging deeper into the room. Her hands were open to him, her eyes stinging with tears. "Great Creator, I am innocent of whatever it is you accuse me of! Please give me a hint, anything. What leaders? What bases?"

His approach and her retreat brought her shoulders hard against the wall. He placed a palm on the wall by her head, the length of his powerful arm being the only distance between them. Bleached hair clung in curls about the nape of his neck. In contrast, a damp film made his muscles look deadly. Marie wilted with fright. Her heart thundered, sending jangling pulsations throughout her body. Desperate to avoid another physical attack she slapped her palms against the wall, quelling a fierce urge to push him away. Dark blue eyes glared at her but she could only gape back stupidly.

"The base locations, Miss Flechette."

Desperately, she pleaded with the gods to save her from this one too. "Oh, Javid, help me now."

"Who's Javid?"

Javid? She was suddenly afraid for him. "No...nobody."

"Who is he?"

"He's nobody important," she shouted, then stiffened in terror when he asked more forcefully, "Who is he, Miss Flechette?"

"My chief beautician," she snapped.

"Come again?"

"My beautician, I said." She pushed her head hard against the hard wall.

"Oh? And what might his duties involve?"

Her face contorted. "He does my hair, sometimes my make-up, and my nails. What else do beauticians do?"

"Who-is-he?" the Commander articulated.

She shook her head. "My beautician. Nothing more, except, well…"

"Ah, now we are getting somewhere. Go on."

She let it all out in one quick breath. "He was teaching me to communicate with the spirit world of his home planet." Her words slurred as the stimulant coursed through her system. "And thass a real secret. Please don't tell my fffather."

A smile touched his lips. "I won't. But I think I should have let Boro spare me this. Tell me. How is it that I saved you from more of Boro's wrath?"

For a moment Marie wondered where *that* had come from, then she vaguely remembered giving this awful man credit for her survival. Embarrassed, she answered, "Um, I remembered him saying that you wanted me well and untouched. That's what Javid helped me remember. And I sssaid it just in time. But now you'll probably kill me anyway."

"It's tempting. First, I need to know where Javid's base is." He traced a finger along her jaw and lifted her chin.

"He doesn't h-have a base. He has an office at our headquarters."

"And, where is that?"

"At the FC headquarters on Enderal. His department is on the eightieth floor, Main Tower, same building as mine."

Commander Shaw's finger dropped from her chin. He ran the same hand through his white mane, revealing a slightly receding hair line. "And I thought first-time actors faked it. Maybe you are good. Are you really a movie star?"

She glowered at him. "Not yet."

"A model then?" Fingers moved toward her cheek but veered to take a lock of stiff hair between his fingers. "Naw sssso much anymore, but yess." She fought off waves of dizziness.

He continued to play with her hair. "Mmm. I don't usually pay much attention to trivial nonsense such as movie stars and models, but I can see why some people do—although they may change their minds if they got a whiff of you now."

The insult brought color to her cheeks. She was about to bat his hand away but thought better of it half-way through her action. She slapped her palm back against the wall.

"Feisty? Think again. You have no power here, my love. This is a very, very secret place. No one knows where you are—nor will anyone find you. I can do whatever it takes to make you tell me what I need to know and no amount of resistance will save your lovely ass this time. Unless of course, you've chosen to be a martyr for your cause."

Marie blanched.

"Tell me. Where do these gods abide, the ones Javid is teaching you about."

"Ah, on a..." she hesitated, wondering what in creation interested him in Javid. "They're the gods of a planet called Rashmar."

She noticed him stiffen. His eyes widened, as if with astonishment.

"Is it near here?" she asked, innocently.

"The Javid you speak of is Rashmarian?" he asked, as if it were some huge shock.

"I know. Others think it's strange too, but he is surprisingly goo—"

His hand was around her throat, not tightly, but threateningly. "How long has he worked for you?"

"I—I don't know exactly. Ah, almost twenty years now."

"What is he doing in Nix States?"

"Working for me."

"I know that, but why? Rashmarians are known to be homebodies. Why did he leave his home planet?"

"I don't know." She swallowed against the grip of his hand that mockingly caressed her throat. "He never told me all the details. It was hard on him, and I didn't pry. All I know is that some bad men ran him off his land a long time ago, and—and the only way he could survive was to escape. So he came to Nixodonia and has been with us ever since. Except for his training. He went to the Cosmetology School of—"

"Never mind that. He never told you who the bad men were?"

She shook her head, lifting her chin to avoid the grip on her throat. "No. Just bad men."

"Good. Very good."

The breath squeaked from her lungs. She'd succeeded in furnishing him with one satisfactory answer. Then he daunted her again.

"If you think hard, I'm sure you could tell me the names of those bad men." His voice was both threatening and derisive.

"I have no idea who they are. You'd have to ask Javid yourself, but seeing as your pirate-man left him to the fate of the *Starquest*, I guess you'll never know, will you?"

His grip on her throat tightened. "Well, fortunately for you, I know who some of them are, but not who the Nixodonian leaders are. *You* know who the Nixodonian leaders are."

She gave him an icy glare and retorted hotly, "I said I would tell you anything you wanted to know but you keep asking me stupid questions!"

"Is that so? You seem intent on becoming a permanent missing person. But let's give you one more chance. Just one, mind you. And if you aren't a good girl about this, I'll see if you might respond to one of my more...creative methods."

Marie's bottom lip trembled. She bit it to stillness. The great gasps of air she sucked in were laced with his maleness as his face inched closer to hers. She refused to look directly at him and found her eyes riveted to the loose curls reaching out from his open shirt. In a ragged voice she dared to defend herself. "I don't think you understand, I don't know—"

She let out a throaty yelp when his hand left her throat to encircle her waist, pulling her forward in a quick crushing maneuver. The other hand twisted itself in her hair, He drew her head back, forcing her to look directly at him. Her hands had instinctively moved to his chest where they became pinned against him.

"You're wasting my time and I am not a patient man," he warned. Marie realized her naiveté. He was about to resort to his "creative" methods and there was nothing she could do to stop the madness or appease him in his quest for facts she did not possess.

"Oh, please don't," she begged, but he found the waistband of her two piece outfit and in seconds his large hand roamed over her back. Marie arched forward, unwittingly thrusting her breasts against his frame. She gave a cry of alarm and shook her head in wild defiance of his actions.

"No?" he reiterated her thoughts. "You can't have it both ways, Marie. As primal as it is, sex has remained a wonderfully persuasive tool over the millennia."

Her voice broke through. "I'll talk. Anything, anything you want to ask, I'll give you the answers. I promise!"

She trembled so badly, Richard Shaw thought she might vibrate her way out of his arms. Never had he encountered such veritable actions from a prisoner. It was sure proving to be effective. He dallied over the possibility of her innocence, but shut the thoughts out for the time being. "All right," he said. "Seeing as you claim ignorance about Rashmar, perhaps you would care to tell me the coordinates of Route 86."

To his utter surprise, she screeched at him, "Not a question like that! It doesn't even make sense!" And with a howl of distress, she grabbed and pulled at his collar as if to rattle him into believing her. Her eyes had locked onto the notch of his throat as if to diminish the embarrassment over a stream of unexpected tears. Her words came out in a torrent.

"You talk in riddles. You! You and that metal-faced man, Boro, or whatever you call him. I can't answer that question or any of those others about leaders and secrets and routes and—and traitors. If you can believe it, he, that Boro man called *me* a traitor! Paul was the traitor. I haven't done anything wrong. I don't know why I'm here. I don't know why all those people had to die because of me. My father is the one who is going to die now. He's going to be sick, and I mean *sick* when he doesn't hear from me. And my mother, and Rossgar! Oh, poor Rossgar." Her hands went limp, and the Commander found himself momentarily speechless. He found himself amazed at how captivated he was by an act that might convince him that she was innocent if he didn't know better. He studied her face, smooth and clear, almost transparent however streaked with dirt, tears, and dried blood. Even her eyebrows warped perfectly in a look of anguish that almost made him want to pull her close and comfort her, the conniving little vixen.

Her long neck arched back gracefully as she continued her emotional charade. "All I ever wanted out of life was to live as normally as I could, get married to a good man, be happy, and live in peace. Oh, it's all messed up now."

With the hand still tangled in her hair, he tilted her head forward. She looked at him with large wet eyes. She babbled on, enticing him. "I just want to be a normal person—you know, have a family with children who call you mamma and say they love you and—"

His mouth came down on hers in a hot, passionate kiss that left Marie with only a muffled squeal of shock to her defense. He pulled sharply away. "I can arrange that."

"Not like *that*!" she blurted.

"Oh? I didn't know there was any other way. Sorry. We're not up on the latest methods of conception out here in the Fringe, but I can show you a method that works just fine."

There was a second of catalepsy, eyes caught in a strangle hold, before his lips resumed their torment on her mouth. A whimper escaped Marie's throat as his lips parted hers. She smashed her eyes shut against the brazen motion of his tongue trying to push its way between her clenched teeth. A hard inrush of breath was laced with a tang of machines, musk and manhood as he threatened to devour her in a mass of muscular flesh.

Richard Shaw tasted the salt of her tears, smelled dried blood, the antibiotic cream and days of mild feminine perspiration. Deeper, he sensed a lingering perfume.

It all clashed with the taste of protein supplement.

Then, for some godforsaken reason, he was unable to carry out his intended persuasion that had somehow lost its original purpose. An annoying corner of his mind told him to open his eyes and take a look at the girl. Yet the evidence was unmistakable. Or was it?

Very suddenly, he stopped. His mouth left hers with the pop of a suction cup, his hand trailing the length of her back as it left the cocoon of her top. He pushed away from the wall and walked away as if nothing had happened.

Marie practically collapsed with the sudden release. She trembled uncontrollably, clutching at her ragged, blood crusted clothing and stuffed her top back into her slacks. Then, as if her lungs weren't full enough, she sucked them fuller, inhaling the back of her hand against her lips. She shouted at his back. "You're…you're a psychopath! You're a loathsome…seshual psychopath!"

He glanced at her, the corner of his lip curling. "Who? Me?" With obvious frustration, he punched at some buttons, flush with the table's surface. The table cut itself open and a series of panels ejected. The Commander played with their controls while eyeing the wall to the right of her head. She recoiled when the wall began to snake with patterns. She stepped further away, eyeing the forming image with dreaded skepticism.

"No, not me," he continued. Marie's gaze darted back and forth, from the Commander to the wall, the back of her hand staying frozen to her lips as she watched the bits of data race at top speed across the wall that had liquefied into a data screen.

"I was just acting. Like you. It's all part of the game." With a half smile, he added, "Wait till you get to know the real me."

She stood paralyzed, trapped. The lighting dimmed.

"Come here," he barked.

She couldn't move. Obviously not used to being disobeyed, he stalked over, grabbed her good arm and pulled her towards the end of the table. He pushed on her shoulder, sitting her forcefully in the chair that faced the racing data on the opposite wall. As her hips met the chair, her jaw dropped. Her eyes locked onto the scrolling letters that had begun to stop, one by one.

"You wanted a hint?" he said. "Here it is."

She sobered. "Those are FC computer codes!" Puzzled, she glanced quickly at the Commander who propped a boot on the chair beside her. "What are you doing with our computer codes?"

He didn't answer. She dragged her gaze back to the screen, and then her heart stopped. "Not only that, they're my codes! What is this? I use those codes for my own formulas. No one has access to these but me. In fact, all our formulas are password…protected…" Her voice trailed off. She watched the letters continue to drop into place as the Commander's own deciphering unit broke each datum down into letters, then phrases. She shook her head in confusion as she read the message.

Shipment E-2263877. route 86. Decon.

.check

fusion bomb quantity 2000.

.check

Orrilla long-range fighter jets. AA-72. unit quantity: 35.

.check

**)\\ ^^ received .check.

~~~~tts acknowledged.

.check. M. Flechette.

Marie gripped the table so hard her fingers turned white with the strain. She leaned forward as if to bring herself to a better understanding of what was transpiring before her but nothing could lift the black cloud that hung between herself and the decoded message, or her apparent name attached to it. Her voice quavered. "What is this? What does it mean, and why does it look like I turned my codes into some sort of military jargon?"

"Because you did this dozens of times. Don't you remember? Here, let me refresh your memory." He reached in front of her and manipulated the keyboard again.

"This is a very interesting one—one that ought to jog your lapsing memory."

Marie stared at his fingers as they opened the gates of hell upon the screen before her. A new message began clicking into place, each letter bringing on a wave of fresh shock.

Angel's Testing Grounds

check. acknowledge ***

Shipment A2263972

Turbo laser canon—power ZZ-287 **

Quantity 450 ~^^^##

Decon *** Route 86 .clear

^^^^^ acknowledged .clear

bases on standby .check
.check. M. Flechette.

She flung herself from the chair but he grasped her wrist.

She challenged him. "Where did this come from?"

"I have good men. Even Boro, who probably gave you what you deserved. And others, faithful to me and to our nation." He thrust his chin toward her. "We intercepted these transmissions to Telexa by you and your secret faction. Who would suspect the distinguished Flechette Cosmetics and the *Princess* of the galaxy as the corrupt arms supplier to the TRA? Well, we did. And now you will tell me where to find Route 86 because your precious arms are getting through to Decon, to Angel's Testing Ground. To get there, your shipments have to go through *my* territory. Yes, the Fringe Federation. With those arms, your TRA plans to traverse back through the Fringe to overthrow Nix States. There you are, M. Flechette. Your secret is out, but you haven't won the war yet!"

CHAPTER 15

Horror struck every cord of Marie's being as she locked eyes with Commander Shaw. His hand held her wrist in a vice grip between them "You will tell me everything you know," he ordered sharply. "There will be no secrets between us, Marie."

Her voice exploded. "There's been a mistake! I know nothing about this—"

"Who are your leaders?" he shouted.

"I have none," she yelled back. He released his grip as if her arm were hot metal. With her arm freed, both hands flew up to grasp clumps of hair into tight fists. "Those codes are for cosmetic formulas, and I don't—"

"You bet they are, and they are about to distort the features of millions of innocent victims. They won't be those of my people, I can promise you that."

"Oh, *God!*" Marie's hands trembled as she forced them through tangles of hair.

"The first transmissions were intercepted from the Enderal system. Now they are being transmitted from another location but we haven't been able to trace it. Where is that location?"

"I don't know!"

"You don't know? You left Enderal in a big hurry. Where were you going?"

"I told you that. To my aunt's estate."

"I don't believe you. You uncharacteristically traveled with a very small party, led by Bill Tripp, and too late for me to realize, Javid of Rashmar. Your pal Javid I'm not sure about, but your bodyguard, how long has he been with you?"

"Since," she cudgeled her brain for the answer, "since I was six years old."

"I mean as a TRA agent."

"*What?*"

"You heard me. What's his function?"

"He...he..."

"Tell me," the Commander pressed.

"He isn't an agent. I'm not an agent." Her hands flailed about her head. "I don't know who got those codes and used them like that."

"Well, somebody did."

"Not Bill, I can tell you that," she cried vehemently.

"Ah, so sure are you. Then, who works with you? Javid?"

"No. Nobody," she stammered.

"You work alone? Who do you answer to?"

"I don't work alone. I don't work for anybody. Except Henrie Marchand. And I don't even work for him any more. Ahh! You have me completely confused!"

"Confused? Then let me enlighten you a little. Just a few hours ago we received word that the TRA have taken over another two key planetary systems in Telexa. I suppose you expected that, but you've been out of contact for a while. So, here's your update. Bases on standby. Mission accomplished. Would you like me to compose your next transmission? Congratulations boys, we now have the lanes through to Sector 5 closed off."

"Sector 5?"

"Some of my spies confirmed the use of ZZ-287 turbo laser cannons against one of those planets. How do you explain that one, *M. Flechette*? Just a week ago, a TRA flotilla completely annihilated a planet because it harbored *one* spy."

Marie grew hysterical. "I don't even know what a turbine laser cannon is!"

"Turbo," he found himself correcting her.

"Turbo, then!" she hollered. "I don't even know what they look like."

"Nice try. Does Nix States have any idea that it's been drained of at least a quarter of its military arsenal? You must have some pretty big boys playing your game to get quantities like that shipped into Telexa unnoticed. But then a woman of your influence and beauty should have little trouble attracting followers."

"Stop it!" She swung a finger toward the screen. "I didn't do this.".

"No? I don't know of another M. Flechette who works for Flechette Cosmetics. Do you?"

She pressed her hands weakly to her temples. "Someone's blackmailing me! Someone has stolen my codes and is doing these horrible things."

"And, I love this one. *Angel's* testing grounds? Pretty coincidental, isn't it? Isn't that almost identical to the title of your new movie?"

"My *movie*?"

"Tell me about Decon. That planet is Telexa's immigration port for the Sector 5 lanes. When the war was officially announced, the Sector 5 lanes were closed off to all traffic, yet we've monitored several Nixodonian ships moving through. Did closing the lanes make your arms easier to ship, seeing as no one is supposed to be watching?"

She fired a defensive look at him. "You say it's your Fringe. Why don't you go find out for yourself?"

He straightened abruptly, glaring at her. She looked completely distraught yet wasn't giving an inch. Or was she innocent? Unsure, he pressed on. "I would if I was certain that you were using the Sector 5 lanes to move your contraband. But now we're not positive that Route 86 and the Sector 5 lanes are one and the same."

Shaw pointed an incisive finger at her. "And what about this fiancé of yours? What did he really do to make you break off the association? Getting a little too close to knowing the truth about you, perhaps? Or was he directly involved? Our sources tell us he's made recent trips to Sector 5. It's said that he normally travels with you. So?" the Commander cocked his head. "What were you two doing there? Planning a personal trip to Decon, by any chance?"

She squinted at him through swollen eyelids. "Wrong! Lots of things are *said* about me and those in my life, Commander. I would expect someone in your position to check his facts more closely. We don't always travel together. I've never been to Sector 5. Only Paul's been there. We were suppose to go together, but...but..."

"But what?"

"I told you. We broke up."

"Right," he drawled. "You told me. So, where is he now?"

With a tattered sleeve, she rubbed her dripping nose. "I don't know and I don't care. I never want to see the rat again."

"But he works for your company, doesn't he?"

"Not any more."

"What was he doing in Sector 5?"

"He was setting up a large research lab," she retorted hotly. "If you'd done any homework at all before dragging me out here, you'd know that. *So*, for the sole purpose of saving myself the extra grief, I will *tell* you. Paul was the director of the franchise division."

"Spare me the insult. I did know that. It doesn't explain his presence in Sector 5 does it? Was this some special project?"

"Sort of." Marie felt a rush of indefinable panic. "Doria has lots of unique vegetation that Paul will use in the development of new products."

The Commander's eyes narrowed. "Doria? Did you just say *Doria*?"

"Yes, I said Doria," she rebuked flatly.

"What was he doing there? You said he was the franchise director?"

"You are very inquisitive for someone not interested in the fashion industry."

His dark scowl frightened her. "*What* was he doing there?" Shaw felt a wave of frustration engulf him. They'd had only a handful of weeks to investigate the Flechette empire after breaking the codes, and Paul Lambert had not been high on their suspect list. One of his agents found Lambert on a small Sector 5 planet having a jolly good time at one of the local pub houses. But it wasn't Doria. Perhaps Lambert had been making pit stops as a diversion to his true destination. Shaw felt his jaw bunch in anger. He himself had called off further investigation of the fiancé who appeared to be nothing more than a drug dependent playboy trying to escape the pressures of a public life too lucrative to give up. The tabloids had no need to be creative in the case of Paul Lambert's exploits, but was there something more substantial behind the façade? Something they'd missed?

Marie expelled her breath. "I just told you. He was building a research lab."

"Why would a franchise director need to be there?"

"It was his pet project," she huffed. She suddenly found the mind to anticipate his next question. "He believed its success would be good for his personal image at FC."

The Commander paused. "An FC laboratory on a planet like Doria is below your company's standard, isn't it?"

She glowered. "I can't tell you what Doria is like. I've never been there. I can only say that Paul thinks it's wonderful and that the Dorians love our products."

"So," Shaw paused, studying her tormented features. "Is this new lab finished?"

"Almost. The grand opening was planned for just after our..." she swallowed bitterly, "our honeymoon."

Shaw made a quick calculation. That would have been just less than a standard month away. "You say the Dorians love the products and in the same breath you tell me the lab isn't finished?"

She sighed tiredly. "The lab is for research and production. There is an outlet, a *franchised* outlet, being stocked from Enderal."

"Really? And the outlet is doing well?"

She glared at him. "Why don't you go ask Paul? I'm sure he'd be happy to brag about its success. I was busy making a movie, remember?"

"Oh yes. I remember. Follow me—your latest appeal. Is that what Paul was doing? Following you? I don't believe a man in his position would go that distance to survey a building site. My guess is that Paul was elected to trot around Sector 5 and run your little errands in your absence."

"Don't be ridiculous!"

"Ridiculous? You'd think a fancy job like Director of Franchise would have kept your man at home unless he had bigger and better things to do on Doria."

"It seems he did." Her lip curled sardonically, her misty eyes focusing somewhere beyond the boardroom. "Then again, even if he had stayed at the headquarters, it probably wouldn't have stopped him from cheating on me." She leaned one hand against the table; the other hooded her eyes to hide fresh shame over the memories of her failure with Paul.

Something vague, yet definite was bothering the Commander. "Who else from the company went to Doria?"

"No one—" She cut herself off and swallowed bitter dread. "He hired all local staff. Said it was good for the Dorian economy."

"He hired the staff? Interesting."

"His image—"

"Yes, of course. But Doria is now in a rather dangerous location, being right on the shipping lanes to a country at war."

"You just said that those lanes were closed."

"Yes, but to whom, exactly?"

"Paul said that our navy would stop the TRA long before they reached the likes of Doria." She tried without reason to defend her ex-fiancé.

"What else did Paul say?"

With effort, Marie glanced at the Commander. His dark eyes, huge with intent, bore on her, his square jaw clenched tight. He frightened her, looking bug-eyed like that, and her brain was in overload. Something intangible about Doria had niggled her before. Whatever it was seemed eerily nebulous now. "He, ah, he said that one of the reasons he chose Doria was because of the excellent routes into the governing planets of the Central Sector." She stopped, thinking aloud. "Wait. Did he say that? Why would he say that?"

"Did Paul have access to your cosmetic codes?"

Her head snapped up, her eyes hard with anger. "Are you implying that Paul had something to do with this horror you've just showed me?" She tossed her hand weakly toward the screen. "He may have been unfaithful, but that's a far cry from arms dealing!"

"Then if not him, it has to be you; and if not you, then who? Your hairdresser? Your bodyguard?"

Marie trembled with cold dread. "No. No, not Bill, and not Javid…and certainly not me! So I don't know who could have—oh God, I can't believe Paul would do something like this."

"Then answer my question. Did he have access to your codes?"

"No. No one did! And even if he did, he would have to be a genius to figure them out."

"I did do some homework, my love," the Commander said, closing the distance between them. "Paul Lambert is no idiot. He came from nowhere and made a rapid climb up the FC executive ladder. And, he managed to seduce you. My homework tells me it would take a genius to do that."

The insult clobbered her ego. Without thought, she flung herself in his direction, slashing with ragged fingernails, feet kicking fiercely. Shaw clapped her against his chest, encircling her arms before one of those long nails hit their mark.

Marie struggled like a wild cat, feeding on her last bits of strength. "You would be far too stupid to seduce me, then, you bastard," she hissed between clenched teeth.

"Hold still you little vixen. You're going to hurt yourself."

His warning came too late. In one unnerving instant, the analgesic wore off and pain seared though Marie's deltoid like a hot knife. Richard watched his prisoner's expression change from wild fury to blanched shock. The same instant, a guttural wail escaped her throat. For a moment Richard wasn't sure what was wrong.

"Ahh, my arm!" she hollered. The next instant she collapsed.

Richard clutched at the crumbling woman. Clumsily, he lowered her to the floor, almost losing his balance in the process. She sunk to her knees, one hand reaching out to the floor for stability. Then, clutching her bad shoulder she lifted a tear stained face and confessed. "I've just remembered something awful. Paul didn't have access to my codes, but he did have access to my private lab. I suppose he could have—Oh, Great Creator what did he do!" She lowered her head, weeping in a paroxysm of gasps.

Richard stood there a moment not quite sure what to do next. "All right. Take it easy," he mumbled, unsure if he wanted to comfort her or not. "Here, let's get you to a chair." She clung to him for support and staggered to the chair he pulled out for her. Immediately, her head fell into the crook of her right elbow where she sobbed quietly. Her left arm dangled at her side.

"Let me see that," he said with more concern. She made no resistance as he peeled back the filthy garment to assess the wound. Shaw frowned. A gash zig-zagged from her mid neck down the length of a slender shoulder. It had begun to take on a nasty color. He was about to call the medic, but something stopped him.

Commander Richard Shaw found himself taken in by his lovely captive. Impulsively, he traced a finger along the edge of the wound as if to analyze it more closely. Some of the stories he'd heard about this woman were true, obvious even through days of abuse. His jaws clamped against feelings of compassion that suddenly welled up for the woman. Guilty until proven innocent in the interest of purging galactic terrorism. Was it Paul Lambert? Could this woman, looking delicate as a china doll, actually be responsible for arms dealing?

Guilty.

Innocent.

He found himself wondering about the color of her hair. The burnished copper hue, still glowing through days of neglect, looked so natural. He'd expected everything to be fake, acting skills included. His gaze moved to her torn blouse that exposed the soft roundness of her breasts. Just the right size, soft and swelling, so unlike that of Igna's muscular frame. His mind dissolved Igna faster than she materialized, and he focused once again on Marie Flechette.

Until a very short while ago, he had only a vague idea who this woman was. He'd learned a great deal about her since then, easily enough. She hadn't lied about her open book life, one he personally understood. Antithetically, his life had swung to the opposite end of the spectrum with the TRA trying to destroy the thin fabric of a nation he'd so carefully put together over the years. Now, forced into hiding, he and his troops worked from this hidden base, a base that now held captive the most celebrated woman in the galaxy. He wondered if she was really aware of her influence. Shaw found himself agitated that Boro had laid his crazed hands on her and wished he could have been there to retrieve her himself, but his presence would have risked the mission had it failed. He'd sent Boro because Boro was the best. But, the pirate was a crude man now, and Richard wished he could have been more successful when fitting that prosthesis so many years ago. At least Boro was alive, and when things worked properly, his old friend burned with intelligence and compassion. This sudden primal behavior was a matter of great concern.

Marie Flechette gave a little squeak snapping Richard back to attention. Stupidly, he'd rubbed over a raw area of her shoulder. Slumped over, the woman remained otherwise quiet, her face turned away, resigned and defeated.

With reluctance, Richard moved away from the chair. Just as he reached over to the central panel, the unit came to life. Richard straightened. Who would be disturbing him during this interrogation? Curious, he answered the call. It was First Lieutenant, Reese Mondiran. "Sorry to bother you buddy," Mondiran's voice rasped over the speaker. "The scout ship has just arrived."

Richard leaned forward quickly. He'd been waiting for this news. "Successful?"

"Took a few hits. Four of the boys are hurt but Dr. Faulk says they should all recover fully. They apparently have more information on your captive."

Richard Shaw glanced at the woman. "That's good news."

"Need any help in there?" Mondiran chirped.

Richard smiled. "Thanks, Reese, but no. I've done all I can here for now. I'll see you shortly."

While Richard waited for the medics to arrive, he took a moment to step out into the control room. He walked over and stood in front of the star maps that reached high into the cathedral ceiling. He asked the technician to bring up Sector 5 of Nixodonia. Shaw watched, shoulders tense, as the map swirled and changed its quadrant in three-dimensional format. He nodded solemnly as the geography presented itself. Doria, a tiny, almost imperceptible planet, whirled innocently around the first planetary star system in direct line with the mouth of the Sector 5 lanes. Could the backwater world of Doria actually be the Nixodonian/TRA relay point? Until now they had been sure that the arms dealing was going on in the distant, unpopulated corners of Sector 5, light years from Doria. Suddenly, a strategy used by the TRA to divert their attention from this obvious conclusion was blatantly apparent. For months now, the TRA had been executing constant skirmishes against a series of their mining planets edging the Telexan border. The TRA hadn't managed to capture one of them. Richard could now see that this wasn't the goal. The TRA didn't want to lose soldiers, they just wanted to occupy the Fringe Forces *and* shift his attention away from the Nixodonian border, away from Doria.

Doctor Faulk arrived at the control room in more of a fluster than usual.

"I'll need a stretcher for Miss Flechette," Richard told him.

"Oh dear," the doctor moaned, "I have only four, and I just sent them all out into the docking bay. I needed them for the scout ship casualties."

"Okay. How about the medical unit?"

"We have plenty of beds there, Commander, but if we are about to have a war on our hands, I'll need to make an urgent request for more stretchers."

"Sure, I'll sign for whatever you need," Shaw told him. There were distinct disadvantages to running a clandestine operation in a technically retarded piece of space.

"If you can wait, sir, I'll come for her in about twenty minutes," the doctor offered.

"She won't last that long."

"Oh dear! One of the boys can wait."

"No. You tend to the boys. I'll find a way to get her to the unit myself." Richard glanced at his watch, realizing he was already late for his appointment with Boro. Using his commlink, he sent Boro to help with the scout ship, deciding he would take care of the heiress himself. He asked one of the technicians to bring a trolley around.

She was still in the same position when Richard returned to the boardroom. With the help of an officer, he got the woman to her feet, then began a slow unsteady walk out to the control room. Richard sat her in one of the console chairs while he waited for the trolley to arrive.

He straightened, bent down to examine her, straightened again, trying not to let on to the gathering staff how inadequate he felt around the delicate thing that groaned in the chair. Nor was he sure why he'd assigned himself the job, except that she was his prisoner and it was in his interest to make sure she survived. Mostly he didn't know what to do with her. His hand reached out to console her, then withdrew. One does not console a prisoner, he scolded himself. He sighed with relief when the trolley pulled up outside the control room.

On a catwalk that hugged the stone wall at the upper level of the star maps, a tall woman stepped through a stone hewn doorway. Her boots made a resounding clang on the metal grating before stopping short. Her entire, sinewy body froze as her eyes clamped onto the scene in the crowded control room below. That blond-white hair could be spotted from a mile away, and now it cascaded over broad shoulders as her Commander bent down to examine a slip of a girl huddled in a console chair. A sinister smile crossed the woman's lips before her attention was diverted down the catwalk to someone coming towards her. She gave a quick smile of recognition, then tossed her head in the direction of the floor below.

Second-in-command, Reese Mondiran, a rather tall man himself, always felt intimidated by the too tall, too thin woman to whom Richard had found some bizarre attraction. Igna Cello, their weapons expert, was dressed in her traditional black again today, a leather flight suit two sizes too small, flaunting every angle in a grotesque fashion she believed to be flattering. Reese preferred his women plumper, or at least with legs fatter than his own wrist. Igna's inch short hair stood straight on end, amplifying high cheekbones and a sharp chin. He didn't care to run into her today. She would have some gossip that he didn't want to hear—for his ears only, of course. He had wounded men to attend to.

Naturally, she made an attempt to divert his attention to the action below. Reluctantly, he peered down at Richard and his captive. "Yup. That's her," Reese informed Igna, continuing to saunter past.

She latched onto his upper arm, bringing him to an abrupt halt. "What is she like?" Igna's voice was low and silky smooth.

"I don't know. I only saw her when she arrived. She didn't look happy, I can tell you that."

Igna lowered long lids and peered at Mondiran from below black lashes. Her voice iced over. "Is she as beautiful as they say?"

"Go see for yourself. I'm no judge on that sort of thing," he winked, "having you around to rival them all." The flush of anger that instantly arose in her cheeks told Reese he'd angered her yet again, but that was the plan. Pissing her off seemed to be the only way to get rid of her.

Reese shrugged out of her grip and continued on his way, glad she didn't call him back, or drag him back. Thin as Igna was, the woman could probably give him a run for his money. He clearly remembered watching her in the mud pits of Dohaw where she'd made a scant living at wrestling other women, sometimes men, sometimes beasts. Recruiting her had been an honorable thing for Richard to do, but even with her significant talents in armaments, Reese wished they'd left her in the pits.

Igna glared at Reese's back in which she impaled an imaginary knife. If he and Richard weren't so close, she would have rid herself of his pretty face long ago. She gripped the rail of the catwalk and stared petulantly at the scene below. A trolley pulled up as close as possible to the control area but that still left a few yards for the captive to walk. Igna realized that the girl was in no shape to stand let alone walk to the transport. An obvious infirmary case. So, what was Richard doing attending to the wench?

Igna gasped raggedly as she watched the woman try to stand, then fall limply against Richard's chest. He then had the audacity to scoop her into his arms! He should have let the bitch fall to the floor, drag her by the hair! She was faking it…the way her hand gripped his collar in feigned desperation. Igna burned with jealousy. She could barely watch as Richard carried the traitor, as if with tender care, to the trolley. Horrified, her hands fused to the railing, bony knuckles turning white with strain. She wished she could pull herself away, but she couldn't. Igna watched as Richard accepted the help of the staff caught up in the activity. Staff that should have stayed at their stations. Her eyes widened. He held the woman across his lap, head supported in the crook of his arm, the other supporting her knees as they buzzed off in the direction of the medical unit. Igna's face contorted, lips curling with distaste. Finally, she tore herself from the railing and stalked noisily down the catwalk.

CHAPTER 16

Disillusioned, Raymond Flechette stood, hand clenched to the handle of his cane. The authorities had poignantly told him that the *Starquest* case involved more people than just his daughter and therefore the whole affair had been turned over to the National Security Forces. They believed a ransom note would materialize any minute.

That minute hadn't arrived and Raymond had a dreadful feeling it never would. His only alternative to furthering the investigation was to seek help from his long time acquaintance, Commissioner Rhodes, but his news was no better.

"I'm so sorry, Ray, but I really can't help you." Rhodes said. "I'm not part of the Security Forces and therefore, I don't have any jurisdiction in this case."

"But she's been kidnapped by murdering pirates! Do you care about that?"

"Of course! But this pirate thing is getting on my nerves, Ray. Come on! There hasn't been a pirate ship around, like that, for centuries." He chose a cigar from an elegant case and lit it. "They're impostors. It's a hoax." Rhodes blew out the smoke. "Pirates? Give me the light of day! Sounds a bit like a fairytale to me."

"Well then," Raymond's voice dropped, "perhaps you should go tell a bedtime story to the families of the hundred and thirty dead."

The Commissioner blew a fat stream of smoke towards Raymond momentarily hiding the gaunt, stricken features of his old friend, a friend who wouldn't be with them much longer. He gave an added exhalation to rid the smoke deep in his chest before tapping the smoldering end in the ashtray. "I think it's a game being played by a bunch of crazed fans."

"Crazed fans, pirates? Does it matter? It doesn't change the fact that my daughter is gone. Great Creator, I need to do something more than the Security Forces are doing with nothing but a few spare ships out combing the edges of Nix States." Raymond flung a hand in the general direction of the ceiling. "You're the Central States Commissioner for God's sake! Who can help me if you can't?"

"The Forces are doing all they can."

Raymond leaned harder into his cane. "Well it isn't enough for me. Surely there's something more I can do."

Rhodes leaned forward. "Yes. You can pray." The desk acted as a fortress between himself and his long time friend. "Look, the Security Forces have complete charge of this case. They're answering directly to the senate. I'm out of the loop."

"The senate? When did the senate start worrying about kidnapping cases? What's their interest in this? This isn't a political matter."

"The *Starquest* wasn't exactly a small ship, Ray. Do you think your daughter was the only dignitary on board?"

Raymond was caught short. "No, but the only one taken away. So we should hire as many people as possible for the search."

Rhodes sighed impatiently. "Listen, maybe I can help, but it means letting you in on a sensitive matter."

Raymond hesitated. "All right."

Rhodes began carefully. "The *Starquest* case is being handled as a national terrorist threat, and therefore a top priority with the Security Forces, none of which is under my umbrella. Not withstanding the enormity of this case, as Central Commissioner, I can't go beyond the Nix borders." He relit the cigar.

"*Terrorists?*"

"That's what I've been told."

"Do they think Marie has been taken beyond our borders?"

"I'm not sure, but obviously they're not ruling it out."

Raymond felt terror liquefy his already weakened limbs.

Rhodes raised an eyebrow. "You should maybe talk to Senator Yousef Phoebe? Isn't he a friend of yours?"

"Yes. I saw him recently, at my daughter's engage…at a recent engagement."

"You should contact him. I'm sure he can tell you more than I can."

"Do you—" Raymond could barely pose the question. "Do you think my daughter is involved in some sort of conspiracy?"

"Our children sometimes surprise us," Rhodes said, fixing his eyes on the cigar. Raymond nodded, remembering that one of Rhode's sons had proved to be a less than honorable citizen.

"Remember that Phoebe's wife was aboard the *Starquest*," Rhodes added. "I'm sure he'll be anxious to find the marauders."

"Yes, I feel terrible about that," Raymond admitted.

"Don't worry. Lola is fine. Just a few scratches," Rhodes assured him. "Senator Phoebe's a big supporter of your Foundation. You know how fond he is of your daughter, and with his wife as an eye witness, he's got a genuine interest in the case." He chose another cigar from the box. "With the National Security behind him, I trust this will be solved quickly." Rhodes noted Raymond's pale features. "Take it easy, my friend. They'll find her."

The two men looked at each other gravely. Raymond tried not to show his foreboding. "I pray it won't be too late."

CHAPTER 17

At first, Marie's eyes wouldn't open. Her mind was a mess of confused thoughts. Too many bad dreams, she thought with a moan. With a grunt of exertion, she forced her eyes open, bringing a stark white ceiling into focus. White? Her eyes shifted about. She was in a hospital bed, cordoned off by heavy curtains. When her gaze landed on the soldier who stood at the foot of the bed, blaster slung over one shoulder, it brought a scream from her throat. Finding her strength, she dug in her elbows and scrambled towards the head of the bed in frantic retreat.

One arm came to a jerking stop. A clear tubing was lashed in place against her forearm by a few strips of wide tape that did little to hide the evidence of an intravenous needle. A second scream escaped her throat at the sight of the needle, a practice long ago abandoned in the Central Sectors of Nixodonia. She grasped the tube, but before she could pull it out, the soldier leapt forward and slammed his palms against her shoulders, pushing her hard against the mattress. His gruff order for her to calm down evaded all rational thought. On the ceiling, two surveillance cameras swung about like evil eyes, capturing the action and no doubt attracting more attention.

The next instant, a short man wearing a crisp lab coat burst through the partition, lunging to her bedside in two short strides. "I'm your doctor," he barked. "Please don't fight, Miss Flechette. You're going to pull out your intravenous!"

Her voice broke into a desperate plea. "Take it out! Who are you?"

The doctor didn't answer. With lightning efficiency, he prepared a solution in a fat syringe, its long needle glinting against the harsh lights. Marie's chest collapsed with fright, her hands pushing against the soldier's grip in attempt to distance herself from the menace. Foggy memories of being held captive by black-clad pirates torturing her with such a needle filled her mind. Her own words confused her. "No, please don't! I'll tell you what you want!"

The needle was punched into the I.V. line's stopper located only inches from her forearm. Marie flinched, unable to believe the sharp instrument hadn't been stabbed directly into her throbbing shoulder. Seconds later, she experienced a full-bodied limpness. Whimpering, she slumped against the mattress. She could only blink with shock.

The soldier watched her closely, hesitating to lift his weight until he was sure she had stopped fighting. He suddenly released her, snapping to attention as another authoritative figure entered the cordoned area. The sight of him fully restored Marie's memory. The Commander! Commander Shaw. The incongruous white mane fell forward as he took a quick examining glance at her. One look into his dark, scrutinizing eyes and Marie twisted away, a cry of despair choking back memories that returned with the intensity of a boxer's punch as each detail slammed back into her mind. The pirates. Bill. Rossgar. Her parents. And Paul! Oh god, Paul and the codes. It *had* to be a nightmare.

"She woke up in a bit of shock," the doctor said, "so I gave her a sedative."

"Good. I'll talk to her."

Marie saw Commander Shaw give the guard a dismissive nod. Instantly, the guard stepped out. Marie noticed his heels plant at attention directly beyond the curtain. The doctor fiddled with the many monitors at the head of the bed while Commander Shaw leaned over her. His hand rested on her forearm. Marie flinched nervously.

"Miss Flechette, we've studied your case more closely. We have reason to believe that you're not personally responsible for the arms trafficking."

She couldn't even look at him let alone respond.

"However, we'll be keeping you here until our investigation is complete."

She didn't answer.

He straightened. "I'm sorry if that isn't what you want to hear."

She twisted to face him. "I want to go home!"

He raised an eyebrow. "That's not an option."

"Then, go away. Leave me alone."

"Fine. The guard's coming back in. If you're good, he won't have to shackle you to the bed."

Marie sniffed spasmodically while her eyelids blinked heavily. "I don't need shackles."

"Good. I suggest that you leave the I.V. alone. I'll see you later." He left the area, exchanging a few words with the guard who took immediate post within the curtained area. Marie's eyes closed, pressing out tears that dampened her pillow. Seconds later, she was asleep.

She awoke to find a doctor working at her bedside. Oh yes, she groaned. The Commander and his doctor. She sneered at the physician who smiled snootily before turning his attention back to her chart. Taking a quick assessment of herself, she found the I.V. line still in place along with a few other wires, some of which snaked under the cotton hospital gown. A heart monitor? She wondered with revulsion who might have placed the leads on her chest.

A dim memory of Commander Shaw actually sticking the leads on her naked chest exploded into her mind. Was it really him, or the doctor? She had only a vague memory of her arrival here, but she remembered the Commander carrying her from the trolley to the bed. Whatever had happened, she knew her situation now. She was a prisoner. It didn't take a genius to read between Commander Shaw's lines. If she wasn't *personally* responsible for Paul's betrayal, then he would blame FC for its blindness toward a man like Paul, and that made her an accomplice.

The doctor spun to face her, his smile beaming. "Alive and well," he chirped. Marie sneered. The Commander had seen fit to scratch *untouched* from his prisoner care list.

In one masterful sweep, the doctor checked the data screens, the hook ups, her eyes, throat and coloring. Satisfied, he removed all the bio probes. Only a small pinch accompanied the removal of the intravenous needle. She gave a nurturing rub over the tiny bandage he placed on the insert site. The doctor's next move was to reach for the chest leads.

Marie clapped the gown tightly over her chest. "I'll do it myself," she growled and reached under the gown in such a manner that even the cameras wouldn't get a shred of satisfaction. The leads peeled off easily and she dragged the wires out from beneath the sheets.

He took them from her and smiled. "Very pleased. Yes, very pleased. Your bio-assessment looks excellent. We should have you out of here within the hour." He made the announcement as if she should be happy about it.

"Out to where?"

The doctor's thin brows popped up as he flipped a switch that moved her bed into a sitting position. "I'm not sure. I'm afraid that's up to Commander Shaw."

"I'm afraid too," she muttered.

The doctor patted her hand. "Just relax. We'll be back to fix you up shortly."

Relax? Here? There was little chance of that! The doctor left with an energetic parting of the curtains, exposing the guard to her view. That quelled any immediate plans of escape.

Ruefully, she folded her hands on her lap, and waited. She tried to distract herself by studying her surroundings but it took only seconds for the past events to fill her thoughts. Involuntarily, her interrogation by Commander Shaw replayed in her mind, with his constant drilling to get her to admit to things she had no idea had transpired.

Paul had set her up well, the rat. How could he have done such a thing? And it had to be him. There were no other logical suspects! She shuddered violently imagining his sneaking about and stealing her codes, then playing love games to cover it up. Why? Did he need money or something? Was he in some sort of secret power struggle with her? Perhaps he couldn't live in her shadow after all— but to commit treason? How could things have gone so drastically wrong?

A hand flew to her forehead. Now she was in this crazy predicament because she was suspected of *his* crimes. No wonder the metal man had called her a traitor. With fingers massaging her temples, she tried to ride out the mounting panic. Instead, the cubicle's cloth walls provided a symphony of baritone moans from other suffering inmates. Intermingled were the soothing voices of attendants and the constant beeping of monitors.

Changing her focus, Marie took a look at her shoulder. The zigzagging wound still oozed beneath the clear band of plastiskin but it looked better than when she'd arrived. Her hair hadn't faired so well, hanging in tatters that caught in her fingers as she pushed back her bangs. Her hand stopped at the top of her head just as the curtain parted.

Commander Shaw strode in. He stopped at her bedside, his eyes sweeping her over from head to toe in one smooth, analytical check. He'd changed out of his swashbuckling clothes into a navy-blue officer's uniform that looked more the part. But those long locks would always clash with the title, Marie thought, her hand still frozen in the mess of her own curls.

"Already?" she blurted.

"Good morning."

Her face reddened.

"Doctor Faulk said you were well enough to check out."

She cowered when he made a sudden move toward her shoulder.

He stopped as if annoyed. "I'm just going to have a look at the progress of this wound."

Reluctantly, she allowed him to loosen the tie behind her neck and peel back the gown.

"I forgot. You were out cold when I did this last. Hmm, looks good." His brow furrowed. "How did this happen to you?"

She glared at him. "Perhaps you should ask your privateer. The one with half a brain who decided I might be an easy catch while his boss wasn't around."

The Commander picked at the plastiskin, peeling a corner of it back. Marie pursed her lips preparing for pain that didn't come.

"Yes. I have an apology to make about that. Captain Boro did go slightly beyond the call of duty."

"I'll say," Marie muttered, hiding her surprise over the bit about the apology. She clamped the gown hard over her breast to make sure his "checking" didn't go any farther than necessary. The minute he was finished, she straightened the gown and reached back to fumble with two strings that were supposed to make a bow. She couldn't manage it. She'd never done such a thing. Her face grew hotter.

Doctor Faulk slipped back inside the cubicle and handed the Commander a khaki green jumpsuit along with a small white bundle. Commander Shaw tossed them at her feet. "We couldn't salvage your outfit, so get into these."

She reached down and dragged the small pile into her lap. He stared at her. She glared back. "Could I have some privacy, please?"

The clamoring of the medical unit pierced the curtains. Marie felt naked already.

"I suppose that is a reasonable request, under the circumstances."

And what circumstances would make it acceptable, she wondered? She wanted to scream at him, but wisely said, "Thank you."

The Commander gave a small nod. "Two minutes." He stepped out of the curtained area.

Marie's lip curled at the look of what must be standard military undergarments. Why would anyone willingly subject herself to wearing such rags? She huffed in disgust. He would get a request for finer lingerie in short order! Furtively she glanced around then slipped off the bed. The tiled floor was almost painful to her warm feet as she took a few seconds of her allotted time to test her equilibrium. Deciding she was steady, she tiptoed over to the curtains to pull them closer together. She should have saved her precious seconds. She could hear the Commander's voice in conversation. It was *not* far enough away for her comfort. She decided to get dressed quickly before he returned to help her out.

Stripping off the skimpy hospital gown brought chills to her naked body. She shivered nervously, envisioning Shaw pulling the curtain back to check on her progress. Then she remembered the cameras peering down at her. She gave whoever was watching a sneer and scrambled into the underwear. They did nothing for her figure, but the jumpsuit fit surprisingly well. Just as she pulled the zipper up between her breasts, the curtain parted. She made sure to pull the keeper to its maximum height. "Not a second too soon." she growled.

He looked at her dryly. "Your shoes are under the bed."

She looked at them with disdain. No one had bothered to clean them! With a flash of regret, Marie said a prayer for Reebe and her girls, and put them on.

With a swing of his arm, the Commander motioned for her to step beyond the curtain. "Let's walk. You need to move your limbs a bit." He grasped her forearm to steady her as they left the medic bay. They were followed by a gaggle of guards who fell into formation behind them.

The walk was actually limbering, but the Commander didn't release his hold on her arm. They entered a series of tunnels that burrowed through the rock like a rabbit warren, obviously constructed years before. A subtle, ancient decor gave the stony passageways an air of warmth. Every one of the evenly spaced wooden doors displayed intricately carved designs. Original wrought iron lamps, rewired for modern purposes, hung within hollowed niches between each door, providing lighting for every angle of the winding tunnel. Wall paintings of robed men, so old they were barely discernible, graced most of the walls. Woven runners, threadbare from years of use, imparted a warmth to the flagstone floors.

The history ended on a sharp note. They stopped outside a room that had Detention Control stamped in huge red letters across an everything-proof glass. The technology within the room was totally incongruous to the raw stone cave that housed it. Marie bit her lip as the Commander announced the arrival of prisoner number 347 for cell C-6. So much for her innocence.

A panel slid open and the Commander was issued a key-wedge. They proceeded down a new tunnel, obviously the jail corridor. It was barren of decor, harshly lit, and foreboding. The door at which they stopped was not original, but an impenetrable steel gray slab. The Commander pushed the hard wedge into a slot that activated a photo receptor. A quick glow emitted from the slot and the door snapped open.

"This won't be up to your cosmopolitan standards, but it's the best I can offer." He tilted his head, indicating her to enter. She looked at him askance before stepping inside.

He followed her in. His men did not.

She raised an eyebrow. "It's certainly up a few notches from my guest suite at the Pirate Inn," she countered.

She stopped a moment to analyze the room from the landing on which they stood. The landing was midway between a vaulted rock ceiling and a small living area below. She took the stairs, hewn directly into the curvature of the rock, down to the oval room that made up the entirety of the small suite. In the center of the floor, warmed by a few throw rugs, was a sitting area consisting of two armchairs and two love seats centered around a low square table. The chairs were made of dark leather, worn and unevenly stuffed. The arrangement allowed for ample walking space along the raw stone walls of the room, interrupted by the door to a lavatory along the back wall, and an alcove on the far wall large enough only for a single bed and a night stand. Long lacy curtains, stained by sun and rain, adorned the feature wall. They were slightly parted, revealing an arched patio door. They gave access to a small balcony only partly visible from where she stood. It was enough to notice that there was jungle somewhere far below that balcony. Marie silently welcomed the natural light that poured through the ancient glass, probably as old as the cave warren itself. To augment the sunlight, artificial lighting flooded down from the ceiling. The halogen lamps, hanging off a set of runners, looked newly installed, adding another dimension to the rivalry between old and new in this strange place.

Commander Shaw made his way down the stairs after her, causing the hair to rise on the back of her neck. She didn't care to have him in these intimate quarters in case he took a notion to exercise his creativity again.

"You can use the terrace but don't stick any body parts beyond the railing," he cautioned. "The force field will singe them off."

She grimaced. "Thanks for the warning."

He walked around the room as if to inspect it for himself. His voice was muffled as he peered into the lower cupboards of a sideboard at the bottom of the stairs. "So far you've managed to convince me that your lover has betrayed you."

"He's not my lover," Marie defended sharply, arms crossed as her only means of safeguard.

"Was your lover, then?" He finished rummaging about in the bowels of the sideboard and continued his inspection around the back of the couches. He peeked into the lavatory, then made his way toward the bed. Marie moved to the middle of the living area, keeping the furniture between them. She flatly refused to answer.

"Come now. I know that the Princess of Nixodonia fostered an image of purity, but a virgin?"

She fumed at his audacity. "Okay, was."

He stopped and eyed the bed thoughtfully. "So then, your *lover* may well have stolen your codes, and that means he is the arms dealer and not you."

"I have no idea. I said only that he had access to my private lab. So, I suppose it's a possibility." She watched the commander move to the terrace windows and pull back the curtains.

"And if I'm not responsible for the arms deals, I don't understand why you insist on keeping me a prisoner here. You would be wiser to let me go back to Nixodonia."

Shaw broke into a hearty laugh. Marie was all at once stunned, surprised, and disillusioned. His wide smile revealed a set of straight white teeth. His tanned features creased into fine laughter lines as if from years of fun, whatever form that might take in the Fringe. Then he said, "You don't see the seriousness of your situation, do you?"

She spread her palms. "You don't think so? Take a look around. This doesn't look like my bedroom on Enderal!"

"I wouldn't know. I've never seen your bedroom on Enderal. But think about it. If I send you back, it will be like throwing you to the wolves. I may as well keep the pleasure of killing you to myself."

Her lip quivered. The Commander dropped his shoulders. "Marie, if you are innocent, then you've been blackmailed, big time. Your chances of surviving are much better here with me than out there where your boyfriend can get a hold of you. He didn't use your name with the idea of letting you freely roam the galaxy afterwards. Not in arms dealing."

She nodded. "Okay, fine. But do you have to keep me a prisoner?"

"Yes. Until I know to what extent you and your company are involved in this mess."

"They're not! And, what about Bill?"

"He's with you, is he not?" He watched her features contort into anguish. "Ah sweetheart, don't think you're off the hook yet. This is a complex matter that's far from being resolved. I regret Captain Boro's treatment of you, but here, we'll provide for your needs." He glanced about. "I could have put you behind bars like your bodyguard, so I hope you appreciate the luxury of our only minimum security cell."

In an unsteady voice, she said, "That pirate, Boro, said you would hand me over to him once you were finished with me. He said he'd be the one to kill me. I'm innocent, Mister—I mean, Commander Shaw. Please don't give me back to that monster."

Her icy blue eyes nearly cracked his composure. "I'll think about it." His chest pocket shrieked, startling them both. He fumbled for the commlink clipped to the inside of his vest pocket. "Yes?"

Marie could hear only part of the directed message, something about a nurse named Deanna. Commander Shaw summoned her in.

A pleasant, dark haired woman scurried down the stairs, eyes darting about, drinking in all the details. She dropped a bundle of supplies on one of the chairs. "Glad to see you're looking so well, Miss Flechette," Deanna said, but Marie couldn't remember the woman. "The Commander will take care of you now." With that the nurse skipped back up the stairs and out the door.

Marie turned towards the Commander. "You will take care of me?"

"Do you think I'm such an incompetent?" he grumbled, striding over to where she stood. "I admit Boro's prosthesis needs a little tweaking, but I was pretty inexperienced when I first implanted that metal brain of his *many* years ago. Sit here." He pointed to one of the armchairs. Marie obeyed more out of wonder than will.

"I know it's been a few years since my medical studies, but old Doc Faulk keeps my fingers in it. Gives me victims to practice on."

Had he not smirked, she might have believed him. But then, it was probably true! He rummaged through the items left by the nurse and pulled out a piece of packaged plastiskin.

"I can't believe you still use that stuff!"

"We do. Let's see your shoulder."

She shook her head.

"Do it, Miss Flechette."

Marie unzipped the jumpsuit only far enough to pull the collar over her deltoid, then clutched the material in place over her breast. She turned her face away to let him do his work. Shaw peeled off the old transparent strip and gently applied an ointment. "Are you really this shy or are you acting again?"

She turned her head toward him, but not enough to catch his eye. "I'm not acting! Much as you think it's all tabloid hype, I am a decent person, unlike you Fringe people!"

"Hmm, I know. Boro can be a bit rough sometimes."

"I was talking about you! As for your pirate, perhaps you should put his 'tweaking' on your urgent list. The man is a maniac!"

"Maybe I'll do that."

He was far too meticulous at placing the thin, malleable material on her shoulder. Far too unhurried at smoothing it into place.

"Are you...Does it look okay?" She changed course in mid-sentence.

"Yes, I'm almost finished, and yes, the infection seems to be clearing up." A light, cold spray bonded the plastiskin. He covered it with another bandage, again not being too quick about the matter. She dared not ask if he had a fetish for shoulders.

"There, finished. Dinner will be served at eighteen hundred hours, planetary time."

"And what might be the name of this planet?"

"It doesn't have a name."

"Really?"

"If you still choose to be shy, I suggest you be dressed for dinner."

She watched him gather the medical supplies and plunk them on the sideboard before taking the stairs two at a time. He left without another word.

"A prisoner. Just great," Marie muttered as she gazed about the suite. Still, its ancient feel gave her an odd sense of warmth, as if many happy groups had lived in this mountain dwelling before it was occupied by the Commander and his clan.

She walked over to the archway that led to the balcony and parted the curtains. Her eyes widened in amazement. She must be on the opposite side of the mountain from the airfield. From here, there was nothing but a thick canopy of trees that stretched out from beneath her balcony. Marie opened the ancient glass doors and stepped onto a small rocky outcropping rimmed by a stone railing a foot thick. She took note of iridescent blue that emitted from a strip along the top of the railing, quietly maintaining its invisible force field. Beyond that, the view was magnificent. Twenty feet below her, the jungle tangled into a thick rolling carpet of green that stretched from the steep side of the mountain from which her balcony protruded to continue uninterrupted across the valley floor. The forest undulated over the distant rounded crests of the ancient range, only a few craggy peaks having survived centuries of erosion. Off to her left, a tall thread of water cascaded freely before disappearing below the tree tops, its final destination hidden by the impenetrable wall of foliage.

The stone walls of the inner chamber had muted a cacophony of sounds from abundant wildlife that sent a steady screech of joy echoing through the jungle air.

The humidity and floral aromas savored during her first steps on the tarmac of this nameless planet enveloped her again as if the planet was offering her a personal welcome. It was a sad time to be shown such beauty. Marie found herself expressionless as she leaned against the archway.

In the midst of her contemplative state, a thought of Javid came to her mind. She wondered if his home planet of Rashmar was near here, if it looked anything like this, and if he might use this opportunity to return home.

CHAPTER 18

Javid found it easy to check himself out of the hospital. Actually, he didn't check himself out; he just took an unauthorized pass. The Iggid City Sanitarium crawled with hoards of extra staff who'd been called in to help with the hundreds of passengers and crew from the *Starquest* who'd arrived for treatment. Most of the cases were short term—smoke inhalation, minor cuts and burns—but too many were on the critical list for Javid's liking. He, too, had been seriously injured but his own spiritual healing techniques worked far better than what the doctors could do for him. Javid wanted to escape not only the doctors but also the probing media that seemed to have one reporter for each of the injured.

Walking the streets of Iggid gave him a sense of freedom, unaccounted for and close to his home planet. Well, as close as things could be amongst the stars. He felt some regret about having to disappear this way, not telling Mr. Spencer that he would simply be vanishing for a while. He certainly had no intentions of causing the Flechettes any more agony than they were already suffering. In due course, he'd return to Enderal. For now, there was work to do.

Javid had no doubt that Marie was all right. She'd been thinking about him, asking for his help and advice. He felt sure that his lady and Mr. Tripp had been taken far away by the nature of the telepathic message he'd been receiving, and also by the unorthodox method of their kidnapping. The news agencies were reporting from "reliable sources" that she was being held somewhere near Iggid. Javid could only wonder if they were trying to spin the truth, or if they honestly didn't know.

There was something intangibly evil about the whole affair, something pervasive, like a plague about to wipe out the entire galaxy. While in his hospital bed, he'd listened to the coverage of the Telexan civil war. However distant the events, he feared there were threads twisting throughout the galaxy that were forming a tight, choking circle. Javid hoped the revolution had nothing to do with his precious Marie. Nevertheless, he kept his mind open for any messages that might clarify the absurd notions that the two were actually connected.

Javid's mind shifted to their last prayer together, recalling the omen of destruction. There had been a ray of hope amid all the doom and with that in mind, Javid lifted his weary spirits and set off on his quest.

Iggid was a diverse planet, inhabited by souls from every part of Nix States. It was a junction point for many of the major inter-sector routes inviting a chaos of business activity. Cities sprawled one after the other, not really having borders, and spaceports were spattered over the entire surface of the globe, creating almost the sole enterprise of this busy planet.

Javid had no idea where to begin. He concluded that a bit of a meditation ought to point him in the right direction. Besides, his wounded belly could use a rest after the long hours of walking that brought him from the hospital to a part of the city where officials would be less likely to track him down. Resting his weary frame on a public bench, Javid closed his eyes for a renewal of strength followed by a connection with his Rashmarian gods.

No great quest lay before him. It seemed he must start by probing the minds of the locals. He would look for anyone who might have inside information about the planetary origin of the pirate ship. The most likely place for free gossip was the local pubs, but Javid hadn't planned on investigating in these fearsome establishments without some protection.

It had been an arduous undertaking at the time. Javid's belly was bleeding badly when he had made his way back to Marie's stateroom before the ship was sealed off. There, he'd helped himself to some of the credits tucked away in Marie's bag. Over the past few hours he'd used them carefully. Javid visited areas he would normally avoid at all costs, but seedy pawnshops and black market dealers could supply him with some necessary and very illegal merchandise that could serve him well. All of the hard earned gadgets could fit into the numerous pouches of his blowzy beautician's outfit. The products and beautician's tools that normally filled his pouches had proved to be popular trade items in this gaudy part of town.

Now his clothing was weighted down with the likes of a miniature plasma torch and knives of various sorts. The best was a dual-purpose nucleic knife. Its shimmering energy darted out in the form of a laser blade that could melt anything in sight, biological or otherwise. Also in his possession was a small electronic device that could help him through the average to moderately complex lock, and a little unit that could help him break into most any computer. That item had cost him some effort and danger. He had to follow a frightful character deep into the bowels of the planet and prove his neutrality before being handed the item at great cost—in their eyes at least. Marie's unconscious monetary gift had given him some bargaining power. A few good credits could get a fellow a long way, as long as the right words followed convincingly behind them.

Javid pondered his situation, amazed to find himself resorting to the skills he'd learned while trying to save his people from those ruthless invaders so many years ago. The Rashmarians had no idea who those rebels were at the time of the invasion. Back then they had just been evil men from the stars. But today he knew that the group was the early foundation of what was now the dreaded TRA. He remembered a day, ten years after his exile, when he read in an obscure column of a news publication that the Telexan Revolutionary Army was discovered working from a permanent base on a small planet called Rashmar. The news had rattled him to his core, and he knew his waiting would go on. The TRA had the planet so well secured that no government or law-abiding organization would challenge it. That was to their chagrin now. The group had continued to thrive, evolving from a local menace into a galactic threat.

It wasn't anger that Javid felt, but twenty-one years in exile had left him bitter and lonely. His deepest resentment was that he'd had no Master to guide him through life, leaving him retarded in both his philosophical and spiritual training. It frightened him to think he had to face a crisis such as this so unprepared.

Before its invasion, Rashmar had been a neutral, self-governed planet. A lonely planet spinning around a lonely star and not of much interest to anyone. It lay outside the Telexan borders, huddling close to the unofficial borders of the Fringe. Therefore, the Rashmarians had historically allied with the Fringe Dwellers both in trade and in love of cultural diversity.

Rashmar consisted mostly of ranchers, peaceful people minding their own business, running their own affairs, until the soldiers from the stars came and ran them off their land, burned their crops and killed their families. There was only one way to spare oneself. That was to die, or join the Reptilians—receive the tattoo emblem of a dragon-like bird ceremonially branded onto one's upper left chest. As an elder in his ranching community, Javid couldn't allow such a fate to befall him. They'd killed most of his family, then hunted him down like a wild boar. He could not make it to the safety of the mountain refuges in time, so he used his cunning and stowed away on one of the Reptilian ships into Telexa before immediately defecting to Nixodonia. With melancholy, Javid remembered his Master's last prophetic insight: that the gods would call him back to Rashmar at a time when his help would be desperately needed. Javid's wait had been longer than he'd ever imagined. He admitted that his patience often grew thin.

Always, his omens were to wait, then wait some more. Still, his years in Nixodonia hadn't been bad. Although nothing could take the place of his beloved Rashmar, Nixodonia had allowed him to pursue his greatest passion, the love of beauty, over which the Rashmarians highly exulted. Although the Rashmarians were humanoid, the blue blood homo-sapiens considered them ugly by their standards. The Rashmarians' long disjointed faces were particularly unpopular with the humans. This was something Javid found hilarious, but he was more than happy to adapt to new ways. He especially found the FC way easy to learn and actually quite exciting to pursue.

So, Javid had managed to live fully in Nixodonia, knowing he would recognize the calling when the time came. Now he heard. The message pounded in his head. His soul strove to slake the insatiable urge to return to his home planet as soon as possible. Javid didn't know how this would help his beloved Marie, but he knew without doubt that helping her was part of a greater plan the gods had in store for him. And so his quest began.

For his first assignment, Javid chose a lively bistro. He entered with his ears tuned in for secret gossip about the *Starquest*. He could have been half deaf. Loud and boisterous, the entire place yapped endlessly about the *Starquest's* attack, even breaking into shouting debates from one side of the smoky room to the other, one betting his facts against those of another. Javid was appalled at how the entire story had changed—rumors of two pirate ships, then three, thousands dead, Bill Tripp dead, left on the ship to rot where he had dropped, and that Marie Flechette should be hung for the deaths of the innocent. One creature, his long snout freshly yanked out of a pitcher of frothy green beer, had the audacity to sputter that she had planned it all as a way to escape her unfaithful fiancé.

Javid found himself barely able to contain his rage. He sucked on a thick juice and fought the urge to heroically put these clowns in their place. This sort of gossip happened constantly but it was certainly easier to take when he wasn't in the direct line of fire. Javid knew that revealing the truth would only bring him ridicule, if not serious harm. Who would believe he was Marie's personal beautician? Shrewdly, he vanquished his pride and soberly resumed his pursuit for facts that would lead him to the heiress.

Another clamorous tavern paid off, not only with the delicious meal of native beans and flat bread, but also with a tip. It seemed there was a local pilots' association that carried on trade with a number of Fringe planets, several in the vicinity of Rashmar. They were apparently an arrogant breed who didn't feel themselves worthy of this establishment. Javid sensed a tangible strain between the planet dwellers and the starfarers, but he had no prejudice. The informant warned him the place was "members only," but Javid insisted that he had connections. Scowling, the informant slid the address of a nearby clubhouse across the sticky table. Javid shuffled a few Iggid credits back in exchange.

The informant had been right about the membership rules, but Javid wasn't sure why the pilots felt a step above. The establishment from outside looked shabbier than the pub he'd just left. Perhaps it was some form of camouflage and the interior would reflect the rumored panache of these traders.

There was no indication of hidden riches in the back alley, either. Javid settled himself in a nook along the filthy alley in direct view of the rear entrance of the establishment. Finally, a small delivery transport arrived manned by two worker androids not expecting an attack by a long metal rod that Javid had exhumed from a nearby scrap heap. With a few full-strength swings, he knocked both the androids down, the crunch of steel rod against foilskin making Javid cringe through the effort. Quickly, he finished the job by using his new computer decoder against the robots' utility boxes confusing their circuits until they lay there jerking spasmodically. The tiny plasma torch received its initiation by firing though the thin but strongly fused outer layer of one of the androids. As soon as he could pry the chest plate back, the electronic identification module was popped out and given a new home in Javid's chest pocket.

He stepped onto the threshold of the solid back door and held his breath. Luck. The door popped open and Javid cautiously entered a storage room. Satisfied that no one was in the vicinity, he slipped silently down a dark hallway. He was easily guided by the bellowing sounds of carousing, the smell of stale smoke and the squealing of delighted ladies. Finding the cloakroom, Javid wedged between overcoats and flight jackets that originated from all parts of Nix States. His hiding place provided a good view of the bar where he scanned the diverse crowd within the brothel. It wasn't long before he spotted a usable target.

A handsome pilot in expensive flight gear seemed to be enjoying an overdue leave. A few days of growth shadowed his chin, his civil ways had been tossed to the wind and replaced with a loud and flirtatious manner that attracted followers like flies to dung. Men and women alike crowded around him, toasted him, accepted his many gifts, both the free drinks and small trinkets he pulled from his every pocket. Skip they called him, and everyone was Skip's friend. Finally, Skip took his leave with two eager females, sent off with cheers and teasing laughter from friends as the trio stumbled out of the room.

At that moment, Javid slipped into the barroom and glanced about disapprovingly. Perhaps long ago this place had boasted enviable elegance, but today the ornate room was dulled by smoke, the wooden floors gouged, the velvet furniture worn to the thread. With profuse apologies to those crowding his way, Javid snaked towards the bar and ordered a mild drink. This was no easy task. Javid knew he needed a clear mind, but it took some persuading before the crystalline skinned bartender would hand him a drink thinned to acceptable levels. Only a moment later Javid's presence was questioned.

"Why, I came with Skip," was Javid's story. "And the fellow is already off with those two beauties." Javid tilted his head and laughed at the ceiling. "Ha, ha, what a master he is! Don't you agree?" Javid snapped his fingers. "Do you *know*, he told me that this was his favorite club. You can be assured that I will come with him again. Sorry to say, I get to visit with Skip only every few years, but I so enjoy myself…"

Javid was still talking when the employee walked away. So, now he had to find a Fringe pilot. The gods would direct him if he put his mind probe out to the ambiance of the room. He was surprised at the divine method chosen. A large, hairy hand clamped on his shoulder and twisted him around. Javid came face to face with a huge, hideous man who bent down to meet Javid at eye level. The brute's lips twisted into a grotesque smile. The man shouted to his comrades. "Hey, look what I have here!"

Javid's heart rattled beneath his ribs.

"We may have won the game after all," the man shouted with obvious delight. "A Rashmarian. A real live Rashmarian!"

Several of his burly friends gathered around, looking him over as if he were on auction. Without his consent, he was whisked out of the barroom and down a hallway where an elevator awaited a private code. All of them piled into the tiny elevator. The feel of Javid's lurching stomach was a sure indication that they were plummeting deep into the bowels of Iggid. Meekly, he asked what sort of game they needed his help with. One he'd know, they said, and if he helped win the game, he would have his choice of rewards, but he'd best play well. The stakes were high. They were presently at risk of losing their freighters. The doors snapped open and Javid was hustled through a large, bustling casino. Ah, this was the real club. Very posh. Very exclusive!

In one of the back rooms, Javid quickly realized their interest in him. There, on a large granite playing board lay a set of runes, something he hadn't seen since his childhood. A Colors game! The runes were scattered amongst the thin stone tablets that accompanied them. The game had been in progress for some time. A quick glance around the board told him that indeed these ruffians were in danger. But their freighters? What fools!

Touching a stone tablet brought on pounding waves of nostalgia. He fondly remembered many pensive hours around the community game tables after sundown where they could rest their muscles and exercise their minds. It was a guessing game to anyone who wasn't a Rashmarian. To a Rashmarian it was a game designed to increase and develop mental wit and clairvoyance. More quietly discussed was the true objective of the game, the ripening of telepathic abilities.

Even more interesting to Javid was how the game got here in the first place. It looked authentic, which meant that the owner must have acquired the set directly from Rashmar. If the space man who owned it had set foot on the planet, he'd obviously been able to get off it as well, TRA not withstanding.

Javid fingered the runes. He would win them their game, but his task lay in finding the owner. If one of these men was the original owner, there was no question about his choice of rewards.

The opponents arrived. A pilot dressed in a working flight suit entered the room followed by a half dozen unruly men. The tall and svelte pilot did not have a mood to match his appealing looks. Suddenly noticing Javid, the pilot pulled his blaster. With lightening speed, it was aimed at Javid's head. The pilot growled fiercely. "Where did you get him? This is out-right cheating!"

"Put the gun down!" the man beside Javid growled back. "We're not cheating. In fact, we're playing by the rules you taught us! We can add members to our team at any time during the game up to a maximum of ten. Right?" The man glanced at the moderator who nodded in agreement. "You put it in the rule book, Captain," the moderator agreed. "Anyone is allowed, as long as he is sentient. This Rashmarian fills only one of two places this team still has open."

The opponent dropped his hand and Javid heaved a sigh. Finally everyone settled, each group taking sides, both physically and mentally on opposite sides of the table.

Their infantile strategy allowed Javid to make quick headway, being sure to allow the opponent a few lucky guesses to avoid another argument. The game moved quickly at first, stones being dropped into place on the geometric playing board, and tablets clinking together with a sound Javid had not heard in many years. Feverishly they approached the fifth and final stage of the game. Colors. That level of the game would be difficult for this group, but here, Javid excelled while their basic degree of skill remained juvenile. It could be no other way without training in telepathy.

One by one, the shiny black runes dropped into position and Javid's team recovered their freighters. Javid made sure to stretch the game on for hours and as time passed, the weary minds of both teams lay like open books for him to read.

He knew what moves would generate hope in the opposing team, and where to tread lightly so personal losses appeared like miscalculations.

The room grew hot, the game intense. Javid restrained his own elation as he manipulated the game to suit everyone, almost everyone. The svelte leader of the opposing team cracked open his subconscious to him at the very last. Javid secretly commended the pilot for his innate skills and felt a bit sorry he had to pound on the poor fellow so badly. Through the pilot's weakening mind, Javid learned without a doubt that he was the original owner of the game pieces before them.

The man's name was Whale, or that is what he was called by his comrades around the table. Javid learned differently. The secret. His mysterious, undisclosed name.

Whale, now known to Javid as Clive Baker, wracked his brain until it nearly wore on Javid himself. Clive Baker desperately tried to find a way to make his last move, the one that would regain most of the booty he had amassed before the Rashmarian arrived to steal it all back. Javid ruled the game and Clive Baker knew that. But to Javid's fellow players, it appeared they had made a come back on his and their wit combined. By the end, however, Whale and Javid were left to finish the game alone. Javid had cunningly landed himself in a position of winner-takes-all. Intentionally, he let the beads of sweat accumulate across his upper lip.

The move was made. Whale marked his rune, shuffled the stone tablets. Javid did the same. Eyes met. Javid's remaining cool, Whale's remaining cool—on the surface. Deeper, Javid saw the panic, the trepidation, the uncertainty.

Whale made his guess.

Red.

Javid saw his fear, his red fear, fail him. He laid down his own tablets and calculated the placement of the runes with a double check by the moderator.

Blue.

No swords clashed. Eyes clashed. Minds clashed with a lashing out of unseen disappointment, weak arms of disillusionment flailing out at Javid from Clive Baker's soul.

Oppressing silence drenched the room, pulling down with it the thick smoke that had gathered at the ceiling. Clive "Whale" Baker stood slowly. He spoke incisively. "Take your winnings, Master."

Javid remained seated. There had been enough winnings amassed before the final move to satisfy his team players. He was sure they didn't care that he was solely entitled to the substantial winnings of the last move now that they had won back their precious freighters.

"What about the winnings of the last move, Rashmarian?" the moderator asked.

Javid spoke carefully. "There is another rule. The rule states that the victor may give back the winnings, in this case a great deal of Iggid land, in trade for something more suited to his needs." There was a weighted fuss over Javid's giving up prime land on Iggid, but the moderator cut in and agreed on the rule. Whale became visibly nervous. "And what might you want more than my land and all of its buildings?"

Javid held Whale's gaze. "You will take me to the planet of Rashmar."

The room exploded into verbal commotion, falling to hoarse whispering as the moderator forcefully demanded order. Whale remained quiet, his frame frozen. In turn, he spoke. "I refuse to do that! We're at war, Rashmarian."

"I call upon those in this room to be my witnesses," Javid said. "I have played by the rules, and therefore my request must be honored." He looked at the pilot askance. "And perhaps you know something that we don't, but as I understand it, we are not at war. The Telexans are at war—with themselves." Javid leaned against the back of the chair and laced his fingers together. "Besides, I think you might know someone who's been there. His name is Clive Baker."

CHAPTER 19

Richard Shaw's meeting with Boro had been delayed one time too many. He should have left Detention Control right away. Instead, he stopped in at the control room where he could see his lovely captive, relatively calm while looking about her quarters. His bandaging job on her shoulder would insure a quick healing, but he would check it again very soon. Just as he stepped up into his jeep, his commlink screeched.

"Buddy, it's Reese," the little voice said. "Bad news. *Starquest* death toll is one hundred and thirty."

Richard frowned. "What the hell did Boro do? I ordered an attack, not demolition!" Just as Richard's jeep rounded a corner he punched on the brakes to avoid slamming into several dozen of his company, apparently engaged in a full-fledged brawl.

"You'd better come to the lesser cave," he said. "Looks like we've got a problem."

Richard noticed a dozen of Boro's men struggling in a heap while officers of other regiments circled the action. It looked like Boro's men were holding someone down. The body beneath the pile howled and screeched as if possessed by a demon. Richard wondered ruefully who'd caused the commotion this time. His shoulders dropped when he realized that it was Boro himself who was pinned down by his men. Had he gone mad?

As Shaw jumped down from the jeep an officer hurried forward to explain. "Captain Boro went wild when someone taunted him about the *Starquest*, sir."

Richard stepped toward the action where Boro's men secured the pirate with shackles. Richard leaned closer to examine his friend. His natural eye was round with horror, the mechanical eye focusing nowhere in particular. As Richard suspected, the prosthesis was badly out of whack. He didn't doubt it was partly due to his own inadequacies while equipping Boro with it all those years ago when they were barely out of their teens. But Boro had let it deteriorate to a ghastly degree. A trickle of blood oozed from behind the edge where it joined his frontal bone and Richard knew the prosthesis had begun to drive him so wild that he'd been pulling at it.

Richard frowned. Ignoring its care, even for a few days, could begin a downward spiral that could lead to madness. This was madness. Richard wanted to share the blame, simply for having pushed his entire company too hard over the past months, but Boro should have been more careful.

Doctor Faulk arrived and assessed the pirate. "I'll get him to the unit and settle him down," he told the Commander, "but you'll have to contend with this metal brain of his. Micro-technology is out of my league."

"Have nurse Deanna prepare my instruments. She'll know what I need"

"Yes, sir. Give us half an hour."

"I'll be in my office."

Richard collapsed into the leather contour of his office chair. Tossing a boot onto his desk, he gave a sigh of exhaustion, but his peace didn't last. He leaned forward and punched on the buzzing intercom. "Yes?"

"Commander, It's Captain Hollis," the head of Intelligence said. "The scout ship was able to board a Nixodonian freighter on the Sector 5 lanes, sir."

"So, all the traffic hasn't been stopped."

"It seems not. But, all they found was thousands of movie disks called, *Angel's Test*. The media technicians are reviewing it now."

"Interesting. Let me know when they're done."

Angel's Test? Curious. Tilting the chair, he let his head drop against the head-rest and pushed back strands of damp hair. His gaze rested on the track lighting bolted into the raw ceiling, illuminating the tall banks of blinking computers that hid the unfinished walls. It was a strange chamber to have for such sophisticated equipment, but it lent well to his present needs. His living quarters were directly attached to this office making for expedient amalgamation of his private and leadership life, which were essentially one and the same these days.

His home looked similar to Marie's chamber, hewn out in an upside down bowl shape by his predecessors of this mountain dwelling. It also allowed fresh air and sunlight to pour in from his jut of rock, creating more of a terrace than a balcony. These quarters were near the mountain base, the terrace just clearing the treetops. His secretary had set up some outdoor furniture and took it upon herself to serve his coffee there, forcing him into a ritual for which he'd become grateful.

Shaw recalled many solitary days on this planet, his private planet, one he'd never expected to share with half the Fringe army! He wanted it back for himself one day, but for now the arrangement allowed him to stay hidden from the pesky Telexan rebels.

The visitor he was expecting came as a welcome. Reese Mondiran stepped into the office with his usual athletic stride. Although the two were the same age, Reese had somehow held on to his youth with greater success than Richard had. Reese's hair was still as black as empty space, his cheeks still smooth, eyes bright. Richard had more than likely lost his blond hair to stress, although he blamed the bleaching sun of this planet. His eyes felt dry and his lean cheeks had begun to draw into stern lines. It seemed too long ago when they were frolicking children with plans of grandeur.

Reese sat down heavily. "Finally, some good news! Captain Hollis' spy ship just picked up a transmission out of…guess where?" Reese spread his palms. "The Dorian system."

Richard straightened. "You're serious?"

"Yeah, but here's the bad news. We're too late. It seems that the arms shipments are complete." Reese shook his head. "We didn't manage to stop any of it."

"Remember my theory?" Richard asked. "I'll bet that most of the shipping went on while they diverted our attention and our troops by attacking, and if you'll notice, never capturing our mining planets. They have no interest in them. Well, not yet at any rate."

Reese pursed his lips. "Which brings me to the really bad news. According to the relay, the only move left is to mobilize their armada. They'll be moving against Nix States soon."

Richard felt his heart leap. The time was upon them. "When?"

"Don't know. That's the really bad news. The mobilization code will be sent from the base on Rashmar."

Richard's elation made a tumbling fall. "That is bad news. The Telexan Armada is sitting well within TRA territory, light years behind Rashmar."

"True, but they'll want to take down the Telexan democracy first. That should give us some time."

"They won't wait long." Richard breathed deeply, locking eyes with Reese. "We can't intercept their transmissions unless we're on the other side of Rashmar, and we certainly can't get that far into Telexan territory unnoticed. At least, not with a ship equipped well enough for that kind of beam spying."

"We could try sending someone to Rashmar again," Reese suggested cautiously.

"Be serious, Reese! They have that place under guard for a parsec in every direction."

"No, think about it. We could get another one-man ship through. I think you should discuss it with Hollis."

Captain Hollis was another with the same genes as Mondiran. With flaming red hair and ruddy skin, he looked like a teenager rather than someone heading the Intelligence Division. Hollis had himself set foot on Rashmar only months ago. Mechanical failures had doomed the mission, but he had made contact with the Rashmarian natives who'd remained safely hidden in mountain bases after all these years.

"I suppose another mission is something to consider," Richard muttered.

Reese gave a lopsided grin. "We probably don't have a choice. I've made some calculations and looking at the position of their armada, they'll zigzag across the Fringe then use at least a portion of the Sector 5 lanes to enter the Dorian system. The trouble is that we don't know how they're going to move, and from where they are now, there are a hundred possibilities. We can't cover them all."

Richard swallowed, wondering about his own flotilla. "How about the Saurian Fleet? You haven't moved them yet?"

"No, no. They're still sitting quietly on the edge of the NR-3 asteroid field. It's turning out to be a very strategic position, about half way between Rashmar and the Dorian system."

"We have twenty-five of our best ships out there, Reese," Richard said with mounting anxiety. "Five of them our biggest warships."

"And they're battle ready," Reese reminded.

They looked at each other, realizing the danger of their position, one they'd meticulously calculated, and one that was hugely risky. They had left Vesperoiy, their governing planet, virtually unprotected, hoping they'd look like arrogant loudmouths with nothing to back up their threats. At all costs, they needed to keep the Saurian Fleet hidden from the TRA until they were in striking position.

"Even with everything we've got," Richard said, "there's no way we'd win a head-on confrontation against the Telexan Armada. Surprise is our only wild card."

"I know. So," Reese persisted, "we need to send someone to Rashmar."

Richard straightened. "Oh, yes! There is something I forgot to tell you. Marie's beautician is a Rashmarian. He was on the *Starquest* with her."

Reese gave a short laugh. "Beautician?"

Richard frowned. "I'm hoping we didn't pull off a heist on the bodyguard when we should have been after the beautician!"

Reese thought a moment. "A Rashmarian as a TRA agent? That goes against all reason."

"I assume the same. According to Marie, he escaped from Rashmar before the TRA could kill him."

"Has anyone followed up on him?"

"He was treated at an Iggid hospital, then disappeared."

Reese knit his brow in thought. "I suppose he could be TRA, but I can't see a Rashmarian betraying his own, can you?"

"No. Let's hope this Javid fellow isn't the first."

Seeing as this was supposed to be a day off, Richard offered his friend a mug of beer made by the planet's aboriginal people. Other than a smattering of tribes across the globe, his base was the only civilization on this jungle planet. Although his troops enjoyed the familiar taste of alcohols shipped in from Vesperoiy, he and Reese preferred the smooth taste of real native spirit water, or some of the potent wine left for him by the original cave dwellers.

"Have we received any more information on Paul Lambert?" Richard asked.

"The detective reported a pretty vague history. Parents low profile and living a poverty existence on Ashum in Sector 7, pretty much as far from Enderal as you can get. Marie had yet to meet her future in-laws. He excelled in economics at the G1 University." Reese tisked. "My word! We missed being his fraternity brother by just a handful of years."

"If he's a mole, he's been in Nixodonia a long time.

"And I suspect those parents of his are just a cover."

"Where is he now?"

"He seems to have disappeared, but we're looking." Reese took a swallow then asked, "What are you going to do with your lovely prisoner now that you think she's innocent?"

Richard shrugged. "I'm not completely certain she's innocent, yet."

"Ah, you just want to keep her around."

"She'd get slaughtered out there, and her release would expose us in a hurry, wouldn't it?"

"You're right about that. Well then! I look forward to an addition to the female population on this ball of rock. You could have evened it out a bit better."

"Sorry buddy. It's luck of the draw that most of the women are with the Saurian Fleet. I forgot that you'd need regular pacifying."

The commlink in Richard's pocket shrieked again, giving him a jangling start. Lately, it was catching him by surprise. It was Doctor Faulk. Boro was settled and ready for treatment.

"I'd better get over there," Richard muttered before downing the last of his beer. "But first, how are your interrogations going with the bodyguard?"

"Good. I think he's innocent as well, and the more we questioned him, the more things seem to point to Lambert. He also points a finger at Henrie Marchand, something we might want to check out more closely. Tripp seems very devoted to Miss Flechette, but I suppose that can be expected after a lifetime with the girl. He's a good man. I like his disposition."

"Good. I'll see him tomorrow. Help yourself to another beer." Richard rushed out of the office and gunned his jeep toward the medical unit with hopes of resurrecting his handicapped friend one more time.

Boro thrashed around on the examining table with feverish moans. Wide, securing straps helped restrain the restless pirate. Nurse Deanna was scrubbed for the procedure and handing the Commander his tools. Donned in sterile garb, Richard straddled a stool and picked at Boro's prosthesis with the fine instruments. His nose wrinkled with the smell emanating from the tissues around the metal edges. "Regular maintenance is now mandatory, Boro. Look at this mess. You must be feeling rather wretched these days."

"It hurts," was all that expelled from Boro's white lips. The pirate squeezed his natural eye shut against the smarting caused by his master's tools.

"He's already on a heavy regime of antibiotics," Faulk offered.

"Good," Richard muttered, accepting another instrument. "Perhaps we can tweak your madness away my friend. Then again, you had a good dose of that before your accident."

Boro gave a crooked smile. "Even with all these gadgets, I'm a mean son of a bitch."

As Richard worked, he recalled the grisly hovercraft accident that Boro had suffered in his teens. They had all been shocked with their friend's sudden life-sentence to a sanitarium. For years he lay helpless, unable to speak except for guttural slurs. Whenever Richard was home from university he would visit Boro, whose garbles began to make sense. The two finally communicated in a rudimentary manner but the doctors didn't share Richard's excitement about Boro's breakthroughs. When Richard became an apprentice in genetics and bio-electronic technology at the Nixodonian University, the doctors finally agreed to let Richard use Boro as a guinea pig, not believing Shaw would have any degree of success with his experiments. To their utter surprise, Richard eventually strode out of the sanitarium with his new, unsightly, but highly intelligent friend at his side.

Richard cast a worried glance at Boro as he fiddled with the final touches that would bring the "metal man," like Marie called him, back to life. "When did you last clean this thing?"

Boro glared at him. "Does it matter?"

Richard looked up in surprise. "Yes, it does matter. We can't afford to lose you like this. I need you around here."

"Do you? Even after the havoc I caused on that starcruiser? Everybody around here is talking about it. Well, you have her! That should make you happy." Boro's voice was incisive. "I wish to put in my resignation, effective immediately."

Richard delivered his answer with equal force, "No, I will not accept your resignation."

"I am sorry if we have to part on bad terms, my Master. There is no other solution."

"Wait. Hear me out for one second. You owe me that, my friend."

"I owe you too much already, and I have failed you." His natural eye widened almost as large as the artificial one now fixed on Shaw.

"You owe me nothing, Boro. You haven't failed me." Richard trod carefully, afraid the adjustments weren't yet right.

"I have failed. I can't be certain how many more times things might go wrong. I cannot be trusted."

"Trusted?"

"I heard that the woman prisoner was in bad shape when we arrived, but I don't remember everything—I don't remember—."

"Hey," Richard cut in, "she's doing fine. And you'll be all right, too."

"I don't know. I'm mad, I think."

They both knew the prosthesis was hardly foolproof, but Richard chose not to dwell on that. Despite the risks, he needed Boro. "We're all under a lot of pressure. Like the rest of us, you probably haven't been yourself lately."

Boro sneered, "I haven't been myself since half my brain went missing, my master."

"Wait!" Richard mumbled, working feverishly. Boro never called him master unless things were still wacky with the temperamental metal brain. "You're more intelligent than most of my men, and it is not all because of this metal hunk attached to your head. Why do you think I believed in you all those years ago? Because you're not a failure. Because you're brilliant. Besides." There was a pause. "We all make mistakes. It doesn't make us all failures."

Boro shifted his eyes to look at his master stooped behind the long probes and clamps protruding painlessly from the right side of his skull. Boro tried to take his mind off the shivers that accompanied the release of horrid headaches he'd endured over the past days. As the pain diminished, his mind drifted to a time before he'd joined Shaw's fledgling forces.

After installing the prosthesis, Richard had returned to Nixodonia to finish his studies, leaving Boro lost after years in the sanitarium. He'd found companionship and acceptance of his disfigurement when he'd started pirating with a band of marauders, most of whom were still with him today. When Shaw returned to lead the nation, Boro and his band left their wayward lives to become one of the founding elements of the Fringe Forces. He'd gained respect and a reputation of being able to get the job done, although he never quite felt he deserved Richard's saving grace a second time. Still, he'd executed many successful sorties against the early TRA and had kept the peace with the Blue Rift and the Three Kingdoms. Slowly the Fringe Federation began to organize into a respectable nation. Never mind that the Nixodonians and Telexans hardly approved. The formerly neutral band of space separating the two nations was about to have an opinion.

When Richard had asked him to carry out an attack involving the kidnapping of a beautiful woman, Boro was elated. It was like taking a stab at the good old days. He ignored the intensifying headaches and put his every effort into the assignment.

Then it all went wrong. Before he quite knew it, the prosthesis degenerated beyond his ability to control it. He got a crazy notion to use his ugliness to his advantage. But the ugliness turned inward. He loathed the beauty of Marie Flechette, her popularity, her luck of the draw, while he'd had a young life of hardship. He'd turned on her. He knew he'd turned on her.

As Richard's tools wiggled about inside the metal brain, Boro realized he should remind his master that even with perfect care the prosthesis drove him to madness. But he couldn't disappoint Richard that way. For the most part, he remained on the right side of sanity, and that wasn't bad for all the years of life that would have otherwise been denied him.

Boro swallowed. He wanted to stay. Where else could he go? "All right, no resignation," he blurted, suddenly.

Richard laid down his instruments and removed the mask. "Good. Did you know that you succeeded beyond our hopes? Nobody tracked you. At present, the Nixodonian search teams are on a wild goose chase toward the Blue Rift. I have no other who could have done the job."

Boro fidgeted nervously, unsure of how to react to the compliment.

"You want to hear the funny part of this?" Richard added. "Remember I was saying how we all make mistakes? Well, I've just found out that our lovely heiress is innocent, and probably her bodyguard as well."

Boro's jaw slackened.

"But!" Richard raised a finger. "It hasn't been a total loss by any means. We've got some good leads regarding the TRA's infiltration into Nixodonia that we wouldn't otherwise have. And, with Marie Flechette in our hands, we might have some serious bargaining power." Richard paused. "We need your help desperately now, Boro. I'm glad you've decided to stay."

Boro stared at his Commander a moment, then nodded.

"However, there's a new protocol," Richard added. "It goes like this. We are nice to our own people, we gently manipulate the Nixodonians until we know who's really in charge on G2, but you can do whatever the hell you want to the TRA. How's that for compromise?"

A short laugh escaped Boro's swollen lips.

Richard unfastened the clamps that held Boro's head then leaned down for one last inspection. "I can't spare you as much leave as I'd like, but you *are* under strict orders for three days of complete rest."

Before his Commander was able to leave the room, Boro stopped him. "Richard?"

The master turned to his old friend.

"Thanks."

CHAPTER 20

Carrying a supper tray to the prisoner's quarters felt like a ridiculous thing for the Commander in Chief of the Fringe Federation to be doing. He caught the stunned looks of the guards, the trailing eyes of a maintenance man. Never mind! He needed to see his prisoner.

Richard entered the cell. His heart stopped momentarily. He couldn't see her anywhere. He glanced at the open glass doors and his heart stopped again. She came in from the terrace and froze like a statue when she saw him.

She looked radiant. She'd done something to her hair. It fell like silken skeins about her shoulders. Even the straight lines of the jumpsuit curved to her figure. Her porcelain face angled upward, accenting her slim neck. She looked up at him, her icy blue eyes firing cobalt lasers that hit him right in the forehead. He cleared his throat and made his way down the worn contours of the stairwell.

Marie watched him, fascinated. He looked so awkward carrying a tray that should have come from a trustee. He placed it on the small table and spread his palms. "Voilà."

She didn't move. He smiled crookedly and said, "Sorry, it's the only word I know from the ancient French tongue."

"Then you're doing better than me. I don't know any." She approached the sitting area, her eyes now focused on the long awaited meal. He was an hour late.

"I thought you were of French descent," he said.

She moved into the confines of the couches and sat down, trying to disguise her surprise at the items on the tray. "French descent means little in Hervos, Nixodonia's deculturalized society." She glanced at him. "However, I plan to research my genealogy when time permits." She waited, thinking that he would leave so she could start her meal. He didn't leave. Rather, he settled himself on the couch at right angles to her, looking like he was about to fix her tray.

He did!

In amazed resignation, she folded her hands and watched him lift the metal lid from the main dish. The aroma engulfed her senses, creating havoc with her salivary glands.

Richard inched the tray towards her, then nudged at the packet containing the utensils. The thought that he should let her dine in peace drifted into his mind, and then back out again. In turn, he folded his hands and let them droop between his knees.

Abashed, he noticed his own body language—leaning forward, feet planted well apart, and hands clasped as if to make sure he knew their whereabouts. He gave a little cough and leaned back some. He was surprised to find himself unnerved as she examined him from beneath a soft brow while timorously unraveling the utensils. There was little ceremony after that. She attacked the meal as if she hadn't eaten in days. The thought occurred to him that she probably hadn't. "In case Boro didn't feed you well enough," he said, "I brought you a little token."

"I didn't know jailers could be so empathetic," she said, glancing with mild amusement at the corked flask towering incongruously on the tray. She tilted her head. "Thank you."

She wondered why he stayed. When it was obvious that he wasn't about to leave, she probed. "And you? Your name and accent are distinctly Nixodonian. What made you come all the way out here?"

"I was born here."

Marie glanced at him in surprise. She found her attention quickly diverted to his square jaw line, to his hair. She still couldn't get used to that hair, especially on a Commander, although she somehow found it attractive. Her eyelids blinked heavily. Oh, yes. The Fringe. "You were born here?"

"My grandfather was a Nixodonian prospector who settled here. Opened up some of these planets. Well, not this one, but others."

"What about your medical training?"

"My mother agreed with my desire for post education, so I trained at the University of Nixodonia on your First Governing planet. The one you locals call G1. Anyway, the Fringe's educational system was not as good then as it is now."

Marie hid her smirk. Was she supposed to notice that he was responsible for its improvements?

"I wanted to study military economics with a minor in bio-electronic medicine."

"What in the Creator's name made you come back *here?*"

The Commander hesitated, but only a second. "Reactions like that one."

Embarrassed, she muttered, "I'm sorry."

He shrugged "It's exactly that attitude that made it possible for me to step onto politically fresh ground. Who would want to live in a place like this, right?"

"Perhaps too many of us are mistaken about the Fringe," she corrected.

"I have to admit, it was a stab in the dark," he confessed. "There are hundreds of cultures here, all desperate to preserve their ways. You can understand that none of them want to go the way of Nixodonia."

"I can understand that," she said, without looking at him.

"Although my military experience wasn't exactly extensive at the time, I *am* a Fringe dweller. I couldn't deny a request from my people."

"Of course not."

He shrugged. "It isn't the Nixodonian Space Navy, but it works well enough. Most of the Fringe systems have joined in and we've been able to form a strong coalition without the need for grandiose and expensive pageantry as you may have noticed. Fringe dwellers aren't partial to that sort of thing."

Marie found it difficult to concentrate both on the excellent stew and the Commander's revelations, but she could relate. "Then for the sake of the people, I'm glad there is a supporting structure here. As you know, I lost my own roots to empirical grandeur."

"Yes, it's funny that for centuries Nix States ignored this *forsaken* territory, until just six standard months ago when we announced our autonomy. Suddenly, everyone's interested. It seems that as a nation with an army, we've become a threat." Richard smirked. "Nix States should understand that we're not the threat. The Telexans are. Think about it? What better buffer than a peace-seeking nation between themselves and the TRA? No, someone in Nixodonia wants to talk to someone in Telexa. Now, who would want to do that?"

Marie rolled her eyes. "Are you here to interrogate me again?"

"No, no! But you were our prime suspect, and for good reason."

"I'm not anymore, I hope?"

He smiled. "Not at the moment. Nevertheless, it was a clever plan. You, or whoever claims to be you, and your boys on the Nixodonian side, and the rest of your gang on the Telexan side creating a nice tidy thoroughfare through the Fringe for a smooth galactic takeover."

"*Galactic*—? I thought they just wanted a few of our peripheral planets."

"That's what they want us all to think."

"What about the Telexan democracy. Surely they—"

"My love, the Telexan democracy is, for all intents and purposes, nonexistent."

Marie grew apprehensive. "The TRA are much more powerful than we care to admit, then."

"Yes. And their level of power is easily kept quiet because the Nix administration is laced with TRA moles."

She raised her chin. "So you've insinuated."

Mesmerized, he babbled on. "Lucky for us, the TRA think that the good guys in your government are the only thorns in their side. They believe that the Fringe will simply succumb after Nixodonia falls into their hands. The Three Kingdoms and the Blue Rift think they are too far away to be bothered with, but if the TRA succeed, they'll control even those dreaded outbacks. Are you going to eat all that bread?"

A smile touched her lips, "No, no, help yourself."

He reached over and retrieved a large slice from the bottom of a stack big enough to feed four. She wondered if he'd put her meal together while studying the latest article on the safe application of plastiskin. He ate surprisingly like a gentleman and she wondered if he'd learned his manners on G1. "So why aren't you declaring war?"

"Ah, good question," he muttered, swallowing. "We have good reason to believe that the TRA are siphoning off the Nixodonian Space Navy, which now makes them militarily more powerful than we are."

"That's ridiculous!" Marie spouted. "I know a lot of people—"

"Trust me," the Commander cut in. "It's all too true. However," He smiled tightly, "we have the advantage of being labeled barbarians, so although everyone is expecting a declaration of war, it's not happening."

"Why not?"

"So that the TRA think we are bluffing about our strength." He shrugged. "Technically, we are, but I don't think they're calculating on the element of surprise, and being the kind and gentle soul that I am, I'm choosing to follow the path that will leave my troops the least scathed."

Marie lay down the utensil. "Interesting. But, I must admit that I knew nothing of the Fringe except that it was a barren place not worthy of attention. As a High Court member, accepting idle chatter as hard fact makes me a disgrace to my nation, doesn't it?"

"Now hold it right there. I'm sure there are a number of High Court members whose primary job is to make sure that you didn't get too enlightened about certain facts."

She pursed her lips. "Then I won't be ashamed to admit that my education about the Fringe started with Paul going to Doria."

"Fair enough. Coming from a Central Nixodonian."

She held back a retort when she noticed his smile. She couldn't deny it. Even with spies and moles manipulating the facts, it was a fact that Central Nixodonians paid little heed to the events on the periphery. It was a fact that most folks never left their home planet, let alone knew the politics of other nations light years away. "I'm not completely ignorant," she added. "I was aware of trade going on around these parts, although I couldn't imagine what."

"Oh, there are plenty of wealthy planets here. Our advantage is their intractability. The Fringe is really a terrible place to navigate, so the strategy of the TRA is to wait until they can take over. Then they'll indenture our pilots to work for the greater glory of the new emperor." With strong teeth, he ripped off another piece of bread.

"I hope that doesn't happen," Marie said in earnest. "This *unnamed* planet seems to be full of riches. I'm sure it wouldn't evade exploitation."

"They'll have to find it first," he replied flatly.

Marie shuddered with the reminder that she was a captive on a secret planet with no name. At the same time, she involuntarily noticed the Commander's hard thighs, trim hips and wide shoulders. Living in the Fringe kept one fit. "I suppose they would," Marie agreed. "But if this planet wasn't discovered by your grandfather, someone else must know about it."

He dusted his hands lightly before throwing an arm over the backrest. "Only myself and a few officers I chose from the upper ranks. For security reasons, the troops remain ignorant of the planet's coordinates."

Her eyes grew wide. "So *you* discovered this place? You have your grandfather's talents."

"Not really. I found my way here quite by accident, and it wasn't a discovery as such. The planet was already settled. It used to belong to a priesthood."

"A priesthood?"

"Fringe dwellers have existed for eons, and monastic priests were some of the first settlers. Amazing navigators. The order I encountered here had chosen this particular planet because it was both relatively uninhabited and nearly impossible to find. In fact, it remains uncharted to this day."

Marie's heart grew cold at the thought. Her unnamed prison-planet was uncharted as well? Her fear drowned in the astonishment of watching him rise and make his way to the sideboard. He rummaged through the bottom cupboards and returned with two thick stone goblets. He dusted the wine flask and began to work the cork, all the while continuing his tale. "When I arrived, the priests believed this to be a message for them to move on—to another 'unlocatable' world. They literally handed me the prospecting claim, loaded their ships and left. It was my personal refuge for many years." His voice trailed off, then picked up with more vigor. "It came in handy when the TRA began to think we were an easy catch. For the moment, they're not interested in our economy per se, nor are they interested in our cultures. But our military arsenal? That they dearly wish to get their hands on."

"I see." Marie found herself overwhelmed with both information and uncertainty. "So you hide your military here?"

"Some of it."

"But, if they're looking for it, surely they'll find it."

"They aren't looking. They know we have a sizable army out there somewhere," he waved a hand at the domed ceiling, "which we do. When they realize that there has to be more, it will be far too late." He smiled cunningly. Then his grin fell. "Mind you, if they start to suspect we're hiding something before we have a chance to attack them, they'll try very hard to flush us out. All we can do is pray that we can hold off any brilliant prospecting from the TRA for as long as we can. If they ever find this place, it won't be pretty. You think Boro is bad? Just wait till you meet the Telexans."

She rolled her eyes. "I'm breathless."

He smiled and filled both goblets, placing one near her tray. She noticed a design carved around the bulb of the stone chalice. Totemic symbols of the monks, she supposed.

"The priests left me this entire underground maze without even a backward glance," the Commander said, "except to first introduce me to the aboriginal tribes who live close by. That was actually their greatest gift. The natives and I have become good friends. They've taught me a great deal on a variety of levels." He smiled pensively. "I'm now even more grateful because they're tolerating the presence of the troops so well."

"Yes. That is very tolerant of them." She wondered why aboriginal tribes would matter at a time like this.

"The priests were an industrious lot. When I moved the troops here we enlarged the main cave, but otherwise things have remained much the same." Richard let his gaze follow Marie's about the chamber.

"So that's how this place came to be," she murmured with appreciation. "It has a wonderful ambiance to it."

"They also left me some of their legacies." He raised his goblet, giving an angled nod of his head. "If you wish to join me, you will see that the priesthood could not have been so bad."

That produced a smile, Richard thought happily. The vid clips he'd studied recently did the woman an injustice. He found himself riveted in prepared salutation as she wrapped her slender fingers half way around a goblet the same size as the one that disappeared within his own grasp. Before the goblet reached her lips, he jolted into action. "Just as a warning, this wine is extremely potent. It's over a century old."

"Oh! Thank you." She met his gaze then followed his motions, bringing the goblet to her lips. Having been raised on finery, the thick rim was unfamiliar to her. It clanked broadly against her teeth. Marie wondered if she would be able to control the volume of wine taken, as sipping from such a broad rim seemed impossible. The question was quickly answered. A large swallow of the fiery liquid trailed across the back of her tongue and burned her throat before hitting her stomach like a white dwarf. Her eyes snapped open as a rapid expansion of heat exploded from her chest. "I see what you mean," she squeaked. "I'm sorry if I've offended your priests," she coughed while thumping her chest. With her ring finger, she dabbed at the moisture collecting at the corner of her eye.

A smile touched Richard Shaw's lips. "How did you stay so innocent for so long?"

She looked at him through blinking eyes. "*Innocent?*" She laughed. "By what I've studied of my heritage, it isn't the French in me."

He smiled, then settled himself more comfortably on the couch. "Tell me about your life."

She followed him with a second sip, this time prepared for the assault. Surprisingly, the second swallow slid less hotly down her throat. It tasted of light spice over a deep berry flavor. She contemplated for a moment while savoring the wine's warming effect. "My life's been wonderful for the most part, but," slowly she leaned back into the contour of the couch and absently traced the design on the goblet, "despite popular opinion, it isn't always easy, or fun. Sometimes I wish I had more freedom to do simple things like shop without a squadron of armed guards or swim in a lake." The smile of nostalgia never realized glistened in Marie's eyes. She looked at the Commander. "I never went to regular schools. The closest to that sort of thing was *Angel's Test*. It was really fun, but I didn't have much time to get to know anyone, except for Ekeem."

She took another swallow of the friendly liquid. "I have only a handful of close friends. You know, the kind who stay around year after year and know you better than you know yourself, but I hardly have time for them anymore." Another large swallow of the spicy wine managed to escape down her throat. "I was born to the Company. It is my life and my blood and everything I stand for. I love it to my core. But, FC is a jealous lover," she said, as if warning herself. "It didn't take lightly to my commitments at the theater and it hated me when I *squeezed* in extra duties after Papa fell ill. The guilt was crushing. My father on his deathbed, and me running off to attend to that stupid acting career! I never expected the filming of *Angel's Test* to drag on to my *own* dying day." She threw up a hand. "And now Paul is gone and I have to start over." She raised her goblet. "So, I hereby toast to the future success of Flechette Cosmetics. Did you *know*? I'm going to take over the presidency soon." She took another swallow then froze, feeling his hand wrap around hers.

He spoke quickly, "You had better watch this wine. It doesn't make a very good friend."

Embarrassed, she let her hand follow his guide to place the goblet back on the table.

"Sorry." Her fingers burned from his touch, or was it the wine? She felt warm all over, and had she really been babbling on like a fool? She'd only had—what— an ounce? Flustered, she carried on with her narrative. "Anyway, I've just started on a new personal journey. I was off to see my aunt Cecilia. Oh, I told you that. She tries very hard to teach me the tricks to self-actualization, but I'm not sure she's been at all successful." Marie frowned. "Believe it or not, my first step was to travel to Kutar 2 all by myself." She flushed again. "I mean, I was traveling with only a small entourage. That in itself was a challenge to my self-confidence." She smiled forlornly. "It got pretty low. Being a bride one day and a spinster the next is a tough blow."

"I'm sorry."

"Oh, it's not your fault, really. But I tell you, she'd be mad about these paintings." Marie waved a hand toward the ceiling.

Richard smiled. His lovely prisoner was getting drunk. "They're a bit faded, Marie."

"Oh, but Cecilia is an artist. She's studied all kinds of rare art, and these are rare indeed."

"Then, yes, she would love them."

"I'm an only child and she's the only aunt I have." Marie spoke to her loosely clasped hands before her eyes darted up to meet the Commander's steady gaze. "Do you have any siblings?"

"I have two brothers."

Her hands gripped more tightly, her eyes sparkling. "Oh, that's marvelous!"

"At times. I suppose we who have siblings don't appreciate them until conversations like this remind us of how important they are."

"Do they live here?"

"In the Fringe? Yes. One works with me on our governing planet—" He caught her questioning look. "Our governing planet does have a name. It's called

Vesperoiy. Vesperoiy One, I suppose. At the moment, the Fringe doesn't warrant two governing planets."

She laughed. "And your other brother works there as well?"

"No. He has a business on a planet near Vesperoiy. He's busy raising a family."

"Oh, you're very lucky."

"You're right. I suppose I am. Please, join me in a toast to that." He nodded to her goblet on the table.

She raised it and took another swallow. The wine warmed her limbs in a blanket of calm. She gave a relaxed giggle. "I'd like a sister just to fight with."

"You are a lonely girl."

Marie answered honestly. "Yes, sometimes I am, but who doesn't get lonely once in a while? I can tell you one thing! Once I take on the presidency I certainly won't have time to be lonely, which means I won't have time for marriage again."

"You were married once?"

She looked at him aghast. "No. My fiancé cheated on me, and never again!"

He burst into laughter. "Sorry. I'd already forgotten about the infamous Paul Lambert. With you? It doesn't seem possible. No. It was a doomed affair. You can do better than that."

"I won't have to. It won't happen again!" She crossed her legs in defiance.

"Right. No time. Aren't you also a member of the Nixodonian High Court?"

"An honorary member—courtesy of Ismal Knabon. He was a marvelous man and I miss him dearly. My membership is lifelong, so even if Pao Knabon eventually clues in to the fact that he and his lanky son are not my favorite people, they can't change my status."

"That's a lot of power for such a young and beautiful woman."

She glared at him. "Mark my words, Commander. Beauty has nothing to do with it. Unless, of course, beauty somehow begets astuteness in the Fringe?"

He raised an eyebrow. "I mark your words."

She huffed and took another calculated sip of wine. "As far as the High Court is concerned, I preside on a board that deals with ethical and moral law. It's through that organization that I'm able to promote government projects that can amalgamate with our Benefit Foundation. It's my greatest source of satisfaction." She paused a moment. "I also have these weird powers, a sort of diplomatic immunity for myself and others in my care, but I've never had to use those. I doubt that I ever will."

"Not so fast. You may need that protection once you return to Nixodonia."

The thought penetrated the foggy wall of indifference the wine had created. "Yes, I might after all."

Abruptly, the Commander stood, sweeping Marie's loose heart up with him. He went back to the sideboard, and this time collected the medical supplies. "I'd like to check your wound before the night is over."

That loose heart did a free fall in contradictory anticipation of his touch again. She bit her bottom lip and rubbed vigorously at the zipper's keeper dangling at the notch of her throat. Her face contorted. "You want to see my shoulder again?"

"I'm known to have secret powers, but dressing a wound through a jumpsuit isn't one of them."

Her chin thrust forward. With a nod of resignation, she prepared herself in the same manner as she had earlier, a hand clamped over her forearm to make sure the jumpsuit wouldn't slip.

"Still playing the virgin?" he asked, sorting the supplies.

"I thought you decided that I wasn't a virgin."

He cocked his head in agreement. "You're right. I did."

"Besides," she added, "half an ounce of wine, religious or not, isn't enough to make me wanton." Her shoulder blades squeezed together when he removed the gauze.

"Then, I should have let you finish your ration." He trailed a finger along the back of her neck to push away the bronzed tresses. Her skin felt like silk against his worked hands. He smiled when she cowered from his touch. Instead of shunning him, she only served to expose more of that long neck. Sighing, he studied the wound. "It looks good. Has there been any pain?"

"There isn't any now," she said with a short laugh. "The priests make a good analgesic."

A little hiss of coldness froze her shoulder for a moment. Her "doctor" then applied fresh gauze, again prolonging the self-assigned duty. It extended into helping her replace the shoulder piece of her jumpsuit. Marie was unsure if she should pull away, or, to her dismay, if she wanted to. She jumped slightly when his commlink shrieked. She took the opportunity to straighten herself.

Richard masked a look of regret as he pulled out the commlink. "Yes," he said, glad that Marie couldn't hear the message. It was a Code One, and Code Ones were never good. "Be right there." He shoved the link back in his pocket, collected the medical supplies and returned them to the sideboard. In attempt to change the mood, to what, he wasn't sure, he ended the visit with a curt parting.

"I hope the rest of the evening treats you well. One of the trustees will be around to bring you some evening clothes."

Marie stood by the couches and watched him dart up the stairs. He disappeared like smoke on a breezy day with only the lingering of a deep musky smell to remind her of his penetrating presence.

CHAPTER 21

Javid stayed out of Clive Baker's sight till he was summoned to the docking bay for take off. He'd hired a young lad as a liaison between himself and the pilot. Street children on Iggid were as tough as he'd ever seen. Javid paid the young lad a good sum, and without delay, Javid scurried off to the spaceport wrapped in the new cape he'd bought. Actually it was an old cape, picked up at a bargain store, showing signs of hardy wear by some outdoorsman. His mission became more frantic when he heard over the newscasts that a search was on for him by the local authorities. He prayed that Whale wouldn't hear the bulletin and find a way out of his duty.

The hood of the cape flopped annoyingly over Javid's eyes, but the curse turned out to be a benediction. Javid nearly slammed into a security officer who was asking a passerby if he'd seen the man in the holo photo-cube he held out. Peering over the stranger's shoulder, Javid recognized himself in the cube. He spun and ran off through the crowds of the spaceport.

He nearly got lost in the sprawling monolith of Iggid Spaceport # 744. He'd gotten too used to mindlessly following the Flechette party, forgetting the trials of solitary travel. Finally, he arrived at the indicated gate and showed the pass that Whale had couriered to him. Just the same, he was meticulously searched then scanned for weapons before being allowed through to the hangar area. Javid experienced his first real test at mind control. He was somewhat successful in that he did manage to keep all his gadgets, but he lost a good number of credits in the dealing.

The craft was already on the approach for the final checks when Javid scurried up towards it. The pilot clunked down to the bottom of the ramp. Javid lowered his shoulders in a huff. "Clive, you should have called me soo—"

The pilot took two lunging steps and clamped a warning hand over Javid's mouth. "Don't ever call me Clive," he hissed between clenched teeth. "Especially here! That name no longer exists, you understand?"

Javid nodded his head. The man lowered his hand. "Where have you been, Rashmarian? We need to get out of here."

"Fine. Don't ever call me Rashmarian, especially here."

Whale glared at him, then disdainfully swept a hand towards the ramp. Javid gave a dignified nod, and said, "My Captain, *Whale*."

Clive Baker gave a sardonic curl of his lip. "Old *man*," he retorted. Javid lifted his nose and walked with self-righteousness toward the ramp. The air of supremacy collapsed when high-nose met with hood-brim and he nearly fell flat on his face, having misjudged the angle of the ramp. He recovered his step but felt a glaring look drill into his back. Nonetheless, Javid was the one in control here and he'd best not let himself forget it!

Whale shoved past him. "Come on, old man. We've got to get going."

Javid sat in the passenger's seat appearing self-assured and portraying as much calm as he could while Whale worked on the preflight check. To distract himself, he looked at his hands.

Javid found that he examined his nails with indifference. They were long, cracked and rimmed with dark lines. For one who hadn't experienced squalor in twenty-one years, he seemed very unconcerned about his level of hygiene since the attack. Perhaps he was mentally preparing for a visit back to his homeland. Now that he was actually on Whale's ship destined for Rashmar, he found it easy to leave all the fuss behind. However, the black rings under his nails lent toward a desire to pick at them. Having no manicure set. Javid happily went to work at them with his teeth. While pretending to be engrossed in what he was doing, Javid kept an ear on radar alert for Whale's movements about the cabin. When he was sure that Whale was barely within earshot, he began with a dramatic sigh.

"I have taken into account that you may want to be rid of me at the first opportunity, so I have protected myself."

Javid could hear Whale thumping at the navigational console behind him. "I know of your misdeeds," Javid outright lied, but the statement made the noises stop. "And I have made note of them in an information capsule which I handed over to the authorities."

"You *what*?" Whale bellowed, taking one deck-shaking lunge over to Javid's seat.

"Oh, don't fret about it, Whale," Javid mocked. "They can't access it—"

"Then what did you give it to them for?"

Javid gave a light tug on one of the long nails and ripped it off carefully. "Like I was saying, they can't access it unless I give my consent. It can only be cracked with my own mental powers." He looked at the man and gave a tight-lipped smile. "Which, by the way, can be done from any distance. Telepathy has no law with the natural world."

"I knew you were cheating, old man!" Whale grumbled, recklessly strapping himself into the pilot's seat. He punched angrily at the instrument panel.

"I wasn't cheating. Oh darn, I tore my nail. Ouch!"

"We're taxiing out."

"That is the nature of the rune game. A refining tool for telepathic abilities."

"And yours were refined enough, I would say. Tighten that belt you old fool, we're taking off!"

Javid continued to chatter over the instructions being fired at Whale from the control tower. "So before that mind of yours figures out another way around this, I'd best tell you the rest of the story."

The ship blasted off, flattening Javid into the seat. The minute the G-forces let up, he leaned forward and yelled at the back of Whale's seat. "The capsule *will* automatically open if my mind becomes inert for a certain length of time, so don't try to make me unconscious or anything like that."

"Will you shut up for one minute?" Whale punched at the instruments as he continued to receive navigational clearance.

"Not until I make sure you understand that it will also open immediately upon my death."

There was no immediate response, but as soon as Whale had the ship into orbit, he twisted around. Only a tuft of black hair and equally black eyes could be seen above the tall back of the captain's chair. "You have every angle covered, don't you, old man?"

"Yes." Javid nodded vigorously. "So you'd best set those coordinates for Rashmar."

Whale rose until Javid could see his whole face. The handsome features scowled darkly. Javid gave a peevish huff and made another unenlightened guess. "Come now. Surely Rashmar is a better option than jail!"

"I'm not so sure," Whale drawled. "From what I recall, I don't think there'd be much difference." The pilot slunk back into his seat. Javid put a hand to his heart and expelled a great breath of relief. He absolutely had to work hard enough to find out what some of these misdeeds might be. The idea had been a complete stab in the dark, and perhaps some day he would make a healthy living on the sale of information capsules, if such a thing could be invented. Javid didn't doubt that Whale's mind was strong, but not strong enough to realize the deception. Rusty as his own skills were, he must remember that Clive was but putty in his hands. He was sure that Clive Baker would want to develop his skills, but Javid made a firm resolve that he would not be the one to teach him!

Javid let the Great Whale concentrate on his flying while his own mind raced off to his home planet. His heart mixed with both eagerness and dread. Had it become as bad as Clive had just hinted? Would anyone he once knew still be alive? Could he gain information about Marie from there, or from the Fringe dwellers who might still carry on trade with his people?

Javid closed his eyes, relaxing the hard scowl and deep lines that had furrowed themselves into his brow. He formed a smile and allowed that physical manifestation to fill him with positive energy. He would pray to his gods for a while. They were sending him home. Surely his journey would not be in vain.

CHAPTER 22

Marie found herself staring at the steel door of her cave cell as if Commander Shaw were etched into it. She dragged her gaze away from the landing and tried to put his unnerving visit out of her mind. What exactly had affected her she wasn't sure, but she felt more relaxed than she had in a long time: since before the attack on the *Starquest*; since before the final stages of *Angel's Test*; since before—certainly, since before Paul had come into her life!

It seemed now that the only further disturbance should be the trustee coming to deliver her supplies. Otherwise, she expected to be alone until morning. There was something refreshing about having an entire evening alone. Her freshly bandaged shoulder felt fine and her mood was light.

She pivoted slowly, scanning her unorthodox cell in detail. The stone walls featured faded remnants of ancient paintings that covered every wall and reached to the pinnacle of the ceiling. She could recognize robed men in ceremony, at work, at play. These must be self-portraits of the priests Commander Shaw told her about. Most of the paintings were too faint to be interpreted properly but she thought about how thrilled Cecilia would be to have an opportunity to study such rare art. While in thought, her gaze locked on the table between the couches. In his rush to leave, the Commander had forgotten to take the tray with him. Perhaps its removal was the duty of the trustee. The two goblets still sat by the tray along with the open bottle of priestly spirits. The collection beckoned her. She went over and picked up her goblet, then set it down. She picked up his goblet—to see if the design was the same as the one on her own.

Two things were different, the design, and the contents. His was still half full. There was no one around to call her a fool, and for reasons she chose not to dwell on, she brought the goblet to her lips and let a small amount of the wine slide down her throat. The wine was warm and comforting. It may not make a good friend, but she just might need an acquaintance for the evening.

Shattering her silence was a woman's voice that bellowed from the top of the stairs. "I need to ask him if he always takes such good care of his prisoners."

Marie spun around in panic, a hand clutching at her wildly beating heart. Furiously, she scanned the dimness of the landing to find the owner of the voice. Hidden in the shadows was a tall woman dressed in a black flight suit. Very cat like, the intruder made her way down the stairs. The thin woman's hair was buzzed short, her long, angled features sneering.

"Who are you?" Marie asked, putting down the goblet.

"Just a curious onlooker," the woman said, coming off the stairs to circle the outside of the couches. Marie was suddenly afraid, unsure of the woman's intentions.

"What do you want?"

"Ah, you speak as if *you're* the one who has power. You don't have that here." The woman slinked around the couches. Marie planted her feet and let her eyes do the scrutinizing. "Actually, I came to see what the most beautiful woman in Nix States looks like."

"Then you're in the wrong cell."

"Ha! Such modesty! You surprise me. Then again..." The woman did a critical inspection by means of a raking glare over every curve of Marie's body. "Just a few days out of your cocoon and the title is already being challenged."

Marie gaped at the woman. How had she gotten in? She must be of high rank to have access to the prisoner's cell bloc. The woman came into the sitting area and picked up the wine bottle. Marie felt the last swallow hit her feet, giving her a fluctuating mixture of courage and fear.

"He went to great lengths to make you welcome, didn't he?" The woman muttered mostly to herself. More directly she added, "I also came to see what Richard is so interested in."

"Who's Richard?"

The woman broke into a wide mouthed laugh. "You share a meal with a man without even knowing his name?"

"Oh—him." Her cheeks burned. "I have no choice about whom I see, as you're demonstrating. Nor am I, apparently, given specific details."

The woman put down the flask and scowled. "I guess I'll have to remind the Commander to be more courteous to the women he tries to lure."

"I hardly think that was his intention. Miss…?"

"My name is Major Igna Cello. I'm the Fringe Force's weapons specialist. Actually, you can call me Igna. I am more polite than he, and very cordial. See?" She spread her palms, but the sneer remained.

"No, I don't see," Marie replied tersely. "What can I do for you?"

The woman slunk about the room. Marie swore that one more glass of wine would have brought her to believe that the woman was purring like the tigress she strove to imitate.

"You can listen. Carefully. I'm here to bring you a message."

"Really?" Marie watched as the woman checked out the tiny bed. "A message?"

The woman took one lunging stride toward her, eyes darting out fiery warnings. "Stay away from my man."

Marie was so astonished that her feet unglued from the floor in a twist to face the woman. She burst forth in a single laugh. "*What?*"

"Just what I said, Marie Flechette. Stay…away."

Marie threw a hand on her hip, courage clambering to the top of her see-sawing emotions. "Now that really tops them all. What on earth do you think I'm doing here? Do you think I came of my own volition, and said, 'Oh, you handsome barbarian, take my body for this information.' Be serious! I've been blackmailed into taking responsibility for millions of lives. Yes, *blackmailed*," she spat. "And now that he's aware, he sent me a meal. It's the least he could do, seeing as I haven't had one in about a week!"

"You still claim you're innocent?" Igna asked with a gasp.

Marie drawled, "Well of course."

"You're crazy to think you will ever be anything but guilty! Richard will soon learn the truth. I've heard about your movie."

Marie blinked. "What has that got to do with anything?"

"Have it your way, my dear, but now that I've seen your cunning for myself, all the more reason to warn you. I will not tolerate Richard's straying."

"If you were half the woman you think you are, you wouldn't be concerned about that now, would you?" Immediately, Marie's courage imploded, but her feet held their ground.

The indignation was plain on Igna's face. To Marie's surprise, a catfight didn't ensue—one she'd have willingly, at this point, participated in! Instead, Igna slowly made her way back to the staircase. Half-way up, she turned to Marie. "I suppose I shouldn't worry. You'll be dead long before you become a threat to me."

Marie didn't take the words very seriously. In fact she suppressed a laugh. Igna opened the door and ran straight into the trustee whose eyes darted about with confusion. The tall woman bustled past him. A bit daunted, the small fellow's legs worked like little pistons as he rushed down the stairs. With a forearm, he backswept the medical supplies and placed some personal effects on the sideboard. "Soap, night dress, combs and stuff." With only a quick glance her way, he nodded. "Ma'am." Without hesitation, he darted back up the stairs. The guard on duty snapped the door shut. A second later, the lock's blue glow activated.

Marie burst out laughing while letting herself fall back on the sofa. She slapped a hand to her forehead. "Wow. Whoever she is thinks I want her man!" Her laughter filled the chamber.

*   *   *   *

Raymond Flechette entered the bedroom with a limp. Exhausted, he curled up with his wife on the large expanse of their bed. Arms entwined, they played with each other's fingers but most of their attention was riveted to the hyperwave vid-screen that Raymond had installed after the kidnapping of their daughter. Genevieve cuddled closer to her husband, her glassy eyes unable to keep from riveting on the screen. "I hope the senate knows what they're doing by not letting Commissioner Rhodes in on the case."

Raymond ran his fingers through her hair, loving its suppleness. He pressed a kiss gently on her temple. "I hope so, too. I just had a visit with Yousef Phoebe."

Genevieve sat up. "What did he say?"

Raymond sighed. "I'm afraid he was rather vague. It didn't help that Lola was on the *Starquest*. Apparently, she suffered only a few bruises but she's quite shaken by the incident."

Genevieve frowned. "Lola won't take this lightly. I'm sure we'll get her first-hand account in *Celebrity Quest* before the week's out. What else did Yousef say?"

"He told me that he has a special task force tracking the pirate ship. Apparently, there are a couple of agencies in Sector 12 that are experts at tracking lawbreakers through the outbacks of Nixodonia, whatever that means."

Genevieve's eyebrows warped with concern. "A task force? They still have the Special Forces fleet out there, I hope?"

He shrugged. "If you can call the few ships they spared a search party. The task force is supposed to augment the Special Forces' ships and that should make me feel better, but it doesn't. In fact, it was Phoebe's ambiguity that made me decide to call the President about it."

"Pao Knabon? What did he say?"

"That's it. That's his help. He personally asked Phoebe to take the assignment. He figures Phoebe's men are the ones for the job. But, I don't know. Sometimes I feel Marie is right about Pao being a bit of a puppet to his senate. I'm really not sure who asked whom."

"Well, at least they stopped the release of *Angel's Test* until this is resolved. I don't think I could bear the thought of her face being flashed on screens across the galaxy." Genevieve returned to the cocoon of Raymond's arms. "Great Creator, I pray for her safety. I just can't come to believe that she might be dead."

"And don't you start to think that way! As far as we're concerned, our daughter is alive, and she needs all the help we can give her."

They nearly missed the news flash.

"—has collapsed."

Together they sat up, eyes and ears attuned to the screen. "We repeat. The democratic government of Telexa has collapsed."

The news was so stunning; it was as if they lived in Telexa themselves.

The solemn face of the newscaster continued the monologue. "Telexa has fallen to the Telexan Revolutionary Army and is now under the dictatorship of General Angel Keem. We repeat that the Nixodonian Government has insured that these events pose no threat to our nation and that no alarm on the part of the public is necessary. The situation is being carefully monitored at the borders and diplomatic measures are already underway to establish relations with the new dictator. President Knabon has expressed his regrets that the measures implemented earlier in the year did not serve to uphold the Telexan democratic process. President Knabon has already begun peace negotiations with the new dictator..."

The Flechettes looked at each other in shock. Genevieve's bottom lip quivered, her eyes large and glassy with a wet film. "Oh, Raymond," she breathed before falling victim to a flood of tears. He clasped her in his arms, his jaw tight in grim response to the news. Genevieve lifted her eyes. "I was not born yesterday," her voice cracked. "They will cross the Fringe next, won't they?"

Raymond frowned. "Telexa is far too small to do us any damage. They're just rumors."

The newscast continued reporting various interpretations of the same story, but they remained clutched in each others arms, listening to every redundant word.

Finally, Genevieve reduced the volume and looked at Raymond. Bravely she spoke, but her composure quickly dissolved. "What if she's out there, in Telexa, or in that Fringe! What will we do if we never get Marie back? What will we have then?"

His tender smile brought a quizzical look to her contorted features. He brushed the hair from her wet cheeks. With his thumb he dabbed away her tears. "We'll have exactly what we started with, my love. We'll have each other."

✳   ✳   ✳   ✳

Marie wiped the tears from her eyes and started giggling afresh. She pointed a finger and spoke aloud to the closed door. "And for all you entertainers, be it known that I am quite finished with the performances for this evening. I wish to be alone to visit with my, um—acquaintance!" With that, she picked up the goblet she'd set down when the glorious Ig-naaa burst in upon her peaceful evening. She traced its rim before letting her finger slide down the bulb of the stone grail to examine its design.

"Richard," she murmured. "Commander Richard Shaw of the Fringe Federation." Lifting the glass in salute, Marie made a toast. "So, here's to you, He of Igna."

The swallow was much larger than she'd intended. Again it brought on a wave of heat. She tossed back her head in glee, waving a finger at the ceiling. "Stay away from my man. Ha! The nerve."

Remembering that the second nip would be less brutal, Marie took another swallow which ignored the Commander's warning. Reaching over, she took the flask in her hand and examined the bottle. The oval label had faded with the years. The inscriptions were still perceivable, although in a language she didn't understand. Marie peered at it with one eye then pointed at the words and improvised. "It says, 'Old wine. Drink with caution, unless imprisoned by Commander Richard Shaw.' There! That settles it." She set the bottle down and brought the goblet to her lips, sipping until the last drop slid down her throat. The rim felt strong and sturdy, generating an image of the Commander mindlessly blathering all the Fringe secrets. With eyelids aflutter, she let her lips linger on the rim a moment, blaming the wine for her heavy breathing.

Her gaze fell back to the wine flask. Marie picked it up to refill her glass. "A hundred years old, huh?"

Her mind raced back to her last moments with Paul. Scattered about his villa were at least a dozen crates of the hundred-year-old Dorian champagne he'd promised to bring to their engagement party *that night*. Marie's chest swelled with anger. She shook her head. "That was then. This is now."

She refilled the goblet. With both flask and goblet in hand, Marie stood, feeling like her feet were laden with lead while her head filled with helium. It was a marvelous feeling! A little swing of her hips and her voice sprang forth with the first lines of "Follow Me."

"You asked me tonight, when the moons were up," she sang, off key. "Will we ever change, might we ever unite." Her feet took her through the well rehearsed steps. "Life is a paradox." The dance moved her out of the seating area and around the couches. She sang louder, "Be who it is you're meant to be. *Follow Me!*" She caught a hip on the couch's edge and stumbled. Quickly regaining her footing, she burst into laughter when she realized that she'd managed to keep both bottle and goblet balanced without spilling a drop.

"Well, you would have liked that, Misser Paul Lamvert! I wonder if you're married off to that wench yet?" She gave a few fitful laughs, remembering how ridiculous he'd looked wrapped in that sheet. Uugh! And that woman! A disgusting creature. Hopefully she had the sense to sell that ring and get herself a haircut and some clothes!

"Yah, she needed clothes all right," Marie grumbled while making her way back inside the sitting area. She set the bottle down with an unintended thump, and then more carefully moved the supper tray to the couch Richard had occupied. Sitting down in her original place, she boldly did something she had never done outside her private quarters. The Princess of Nixodonia kicked up her feet and plunked them on top of the small table. Triumphantly, she celebrated with a swallow, until Richard Shaw materialized within her imagination, now sitting atop his supper tray. Ignoring the humor in that, she looked him over carefully in her mind. Someone thought he was worth fighting for. She didn't wonder what he might be like, remembering his *creativity* during that horrendous interrogation. The press weren't even that bad! She could smell him, pheromones. Then her gaze dropped to the bottle. To Paul.

Paul was tall, and she'd believed fairly broad shouldered until she'd been devoured by Commander Shaw's massive build. The Commander hadn't been very nice about that. But Paul's hands were always so smooth, his nails immaculate. Richard's hands were rough, but only enough to let you know he was no office boy. Feeling suddenly suffocated, Marie struggled to her feet, her gaze clamping to the bottle.

"So this is what distracted you so much, is it Paul?" She picked up the bottle and again analyzed it. "I lost you to *this*? To what? Let me see."

Another "first" dropped onto the bottom of Marie's list. While forgetting the goblet in one hand, she hoisted the bottle with the other, putting the fat round of the rim to her lips and tipping it back. The weight of the heavy flask threw her off balance as it gained momentum in its graceful ark toward the ceiling. Throwing her head forward, she pushed the bottle from her lips, but it was too late. A huge mouthful had slid down her throat, some of it burning back up her nose. She sputtered fitfully. "AAAhhhhhgh!"

Aghast, Marie looked at her chest by cramming her chin downward. Something felt awful! Carefully, she placed the goblet on the table, fighting to set the thing straight. She clamped a hand to her chest. It was soaked! She gave a laugh. Paradoxically, tears welled in her eyes. "Oh my…my goodness!" Her gaze tore around the suite then up to the door, hoping that no one had, per chance, witnessed her act. She breathed with relief.

Her head spun. The walls cocked. "Whadama-gonna-do *now*?" Her eyes were round with horror before her gaze latched onto the small stack of supplies left by the trustee. Relief! Night things. That was the answer. Maybe it was time to get into that gown, if that's what she saw there.

The trip to retrieve her provisions could have been described as that of a sidewinder but eventually Marie shook out a tube-like pajama. "Oh, stunning!" she purred and set off in the general direction of the bed. "With attractions like these it's no wonder Ign-ass has trouble keeping him." A laugh burst from her tight-lipped smile as she struggled to pull the shapeless gown over her head. A bit blowzy, but warm enough.

With a little skipping dance and a cry of "Follow Me," Marie returned to the couches and plopped herself down, planning to resume her happy celebration. Somehow, the mood had made an abrupt transformation. Marie suddenly experienced the depressant consequence of her evening's acquaintance. With her eyes focused on the bottle, every detail of the past days flooded into her mind. Mostly they were about Paul. She hadn't yet grieved his loss, and even though he'd betrayed her, cheated, and *killed*, it didn't annul the emotions she'd invested in their relationship. And then Paul introduced her to his apparent hero. Henrie Marchand. The great director! At first she'd been mesmerized by the man. Larger than life, of the same ancestry as she. Now, Henrie couldn't make an emotional impression on her if he tried!

"That was stupid. All of it!" she spat. "First, those ridiculous exercises, repeating over and over, 'Follow me, follow me,' a million, trillion times with my voice up, then down."

She stood abruptly, petulantly remembering the director. "He didn't like *this*, he didn't like *that*." Her hands swung in the air as her voice jumped in crescendo with every other word. "Then he made Bill teach me to use a gun. Bam, bam, bam," she punched a finger into the air. "All to cut the scenes in the end anyway. And Paul says, 'You have the best director in the galaxy. Listen to him.'

"Listen to *him*? I listened to *you*. I heard you say you loved me. You asked me to marry you. Then this? Arms sales to the TRA? Give me the light of day!"

Her anger flowed unbridled as she gripped the back of one of the couches and spoke to Paul's liaison, the flask upon the table. "You liar. You thief! What was it Paul? Jealousy? Fear that I'd be worth one more lousy credit than you? You lent your body to that scum, and who knows how many others, all the while sleeping with me! Ahhhgh!"

She stumbled over to the table, tears coursing down her cheeks. A salty drop ran along her lips, clashing with the spicy flavor of the wine. She wiped angrily at her cheeks before picking up the bottle with a trembling hand.

"You defiled me, you filthy swine, and no amount of bathing will ever wash that away. Worse, I don't even know if I loved you. You were my roots, Paul. You were my hope against a galaxy that tried to crush me into being just like it. We were going to give birth and instead you've been wreaking death everywhere. You're responsible for Rossgar, too. You know that, Paul? And all those people on the *Starquest*? You're responsible. And I hate you like I've never hated anybody in my life. I hate you Paul Lambert. I hate you!"

With a sudden swing of her arm, she sent the flask arcing through the air. It smashed in an explosion of dark glass and red liquid against the wall between the sideboard and the staircase. Marie stared, horrified by her own violence. The wine dripped like blood on a ragged voyage down the roughness of the stone. It pooled on the floor in a dark crimson puddle that inched out from the wall as if on a creeping journey to avenge its assailant.

Marie backed away, her whole body shivering. "Take that, Mr. Lambert! That's what I think of you, you shattered, *broken* man." Her throat constricted as her words squeaked out. "I don't need you—any—more."

Hands flew to her face. Her body convulsed with the agony of her distress. Racked with tears and wailing, she crushed her palms against her temples, fingers wrapped over her head as if to protect herself against the beating arm of guilt and betrayal.

"I hate you…" she sputtered again and again, forcing the pain from her heart as she staggered back.

Suddenly it was over. She didn't care anymore. Nothing mattered. She bumped up against the wall and used it to help her slide to the floor. She sat in a heap of despair, arms and legs wherever they settled. Slowly, she pulled her knees to her chest and languid hands made their way to her face. She lowered her grief-stricken features into them to hide her shame.

CHAPTER 23

Richard Shaw heard the news and met with Reese immediately. "Telexa has collapsed!"

"I just heard," Reese said. "Hell! That was faster than I expected."

"Let's call a general meeting, on the double." In less than ten minutes, all personnel under the dome of that mountain were gathered in the assembly hall. A murmur rippled through the crowd as Richard announced that Telexa was now under the totalitarian rule of General Angel Keem.

The meeting was brief, with a plan of action being devised as he spoke. Everyone was to remain on full alert. Their priority was to stop the TRA's armada from getting through to Nixodonia. If Nixodonia fell, and the probability was high, the Fringe and the other autonomous regions would have to succumb. Every ship was to be prepared for immediate deployment.

Richard concluded the assembly with some rousing pep talk before announcing that a meeting for the group leaders would begin immediately in the boardroom.

The eight leaders settled in the silver-lined room. Amongst them were Reese Mondiran, Igna Cello, and Captain Hollis. Boro shuffled in last, looking worn, but more rested. Richard calmed the drone of voices all chattering with strained anxiety. He began the meeting with a quick review on the expansion of the TRA.

"They now rule all four provinces of the old Telexan democracy and I'm sure it won't be long before official word of annexation of the Dorian system is announced. This will make it appear that the TRA plan a slow encroachment into Nix territory, but I think all of us agree that there will be a swift attack on Nixodonia's core in the very near future. According to our spies, the TRA suffered very few losses compared to the democrats, so we can assume that they remain as strong as they were prior to the takeover. The TRA base on Rashmar continues to hold its position as TRA headquarters and remains on high-level security status. As you know, Captain Hollis," Richard nodded toward the head of Intelligence, "made a successful landing on Rashmar a few months ago. Perhaps, Captain Hollis, you could refresh us on your expedition."

The redhead stood and nodded to his fellow leaders. "On my visit to Rashmar, I was happy to discover that our Rashmarian friends are still hiding in the highlands of their planet. It seems the TRA have given up trying to indenture them. They trust us and believe that, as allies, we'll some day be able to free them from the TRA. Unfortunately, I had to abort breeching the TRA headquarters because of an equipment malfunction. Planetary security is heavy but they don't believe there are any serious ground threats, so the base is certainly not impenetrable."

Commander Shaw interjected. "Right now, the rebel armada is behind Rashmar relative to our coordinates so we don't know if the fleet has increased in size. The last estimate was around twenty-eight ships, at least five of them destroyers. Our only hope of tracking them is from Rashmar itself. What do you think the odds are of getting back on the planet, Captain?"

The officer raised an orange eyebrow. "It is possible, sir. There is a disruptive magnetic force over the planetary north pole caused by the orbital ellipse of the moon. You can land undetected in the highlands if you calculate your window, except there are only a couple of allowable hours every day in which to do it safely. If we send a ship in approximately forty-eight hours, we'll be right on time for the best magnetic field of the lunar month, stretching the allowable safety margin by a few more hours. The landing is treacherous with only a rudimentary base constructed by the Rashmarians and some Fringe traders years ago. Just the same, they guided me down undetected with the use of an old radar system installed by our Fringe traders years ago. I couldn't give them any idea when we'd be back, but they told me they'd continue to keep a Rashmarian ear out for anyone else who might be returning to their rescue."

A mutter rippled through the small group. "Sounds dangerous," Igna voiced.

"If you keep a tight approach to the planet from behind the moon where the field cones well out into space, the rest is easy. A small ship can easily stay out of sight in the vortex. I think it's worth a try."

"If we can give the Saurian fleet the TRA armada's tactical plan, we might have a chance," the Commander added. "Do you have someone in mind who could handle the mission? Actually, make that two. We should have a relay ship well into our own territory to accept preliminary transmissions."

Hollis looked troubled. "We're pretty tight on men. There's Officer Clay, sir, but I'm afraid he's not great on solo. He'd be better on the relay."

Boro suddenly rose from his chair. "I would like to volunteer, Commander Shaw," the pirate offered confidently. "That is, if Captain Hollis will agree."

Richard looked at Boro, dumbfounded, wondering what would make him want to do a thing like that? Then it became clear. Boro was looking for a means of redemption.

Boro looked his Commander in the eye. "It wouldn't interfere with my R and R, master. There's light piloting for two days before entering the Rashmarian system. I can do the job solo. It is an opportunity I would appreciate, sir. My admiral is well capable of managing my crew and ship in my absence."

Igna stared at the pirate in surprise.

Shaw nodded his head slowly. "If Lieutenant Mondiran and Captain Hollis agree, so be it. Officer Clay can handle the relay ship."

Reese nodded thoughtfully. Boro's drive for personal success would surely profit everyone. "I have no objections, Commander," Reese stated.

"Hollis, you and Boro will stay for a briefing. The rest of you are dismissed." It took another hour to finalize the plans. Boro and a relay ship would be ready to leave within the allotted two days.

When Richard adjourned the meeting it was already getting late. He should be returning to his quarters, but there was one last thing he wanted to do; make a stop by Detention Control. He imagined Marie would be fast asleep but the technician watching her security screens gave him a crooked smile. "Mr. Tripp has had a quiet evening, sir. But the heiress..."

"The heiress, what?" Richard clamped his eyes to the screen just in time to hear her scream absurdities at a wine bottle. Oh, no! *Thee* wine bottle! She suddenly threw it violently against the wall. He involuntarily cringed when it exploded into a hundred fragments.

Then he froze. She backed away, hands on her head, unsuccessfully hiding her anguish. She fell against the wall, right at the corner of the wide open terrace doorway. He gripped the technician's shoulder and ordered calmly, "Turn off the force field on that balcony." He reached into the security box for her door's access unit. Before stepping into the hallway, he turned to the technician. "Why didn't anyone take that tray away?"

"We were under the impression that you'd left it there for her, sir. There were no orders to remove it."

Richard chided himself for his blunder. Quickly, he rummaged through the medical drawer. "Keep an eye on her for a moment. When I arrive, I won't need surveillance."

The technician nodded. Face expressionless, he flipped a few switches. Six screens converged toward Marie huddled against the door casing of the balcony. Another video bank of screens showed Bill Tripp calmly engrossed in a magazine.

Richard strode down the hall, brooding darkly. How could he have forgotten to tell the trustee to remove that tray? And who was it she so desperately hated?

CHAPTER 24

When Richard entered the cell, he heaved a sigh of relief. Marie was still inside and on the floor where he'd last seen her on the screens. He trotted down the stairs and crouched a few feet away. "Marie," he sang softly, but she jolted violently. The look of horror at being discovered was almost amusing.

Marie flung an arm at him weakly. "Oh please, not you! Go away. I want to be alone." She curled herself up into a tight ball facing away from him. Richard stood and closed the balcony doors. He looked around the room. "What were you trying to do, christen your prison cell?"

"No," she croaked.

"Then what was all the ceremony about?"

"Nothing."

"A lot of fuss for nothing."

She didn't answer.

He bent down to help her up. "Come on. Let's get you to bed."

"I can go myself," she argued, wiggling away from his grasp.

He pulled on her arm a little more firmly. "It seems that as long as you hate me so much, I may as well not worry about making you hate me a little bit more."

"I don't hate *you*."

"Oh? Then who were you screaming to the wine bottle about?"

She looked at him, horrified. "That was recorded?"

"I'm afraid so."

"Then you should know who I was angry at."

"Duties kept me from hearing all but the last juicy little bits." He slipped his hands beneath her armpits and hoisted her to her feet.

"I was angry at Paul for all the rotten things he's done, like sending those bombs and things and sleeping with that awful woman. Sleeping with any woman is a terrible thing to do, at least when you're engaged to somebody else."

Richard wasn't sure he should have opened the floodgates. Weeping, she babbled out her tale of anguish. "He used to drink gallons of stuff like that all the time." She pointed at the shattered bottle on the floor before drying her eyes with the long sleeve of the pajama. "Oh dear. Did I make that mess?"

"You sure did. Was it Mr. Lambert who taught you to toss wine bottles around like that?"

"No! I'll clean it up," she mumbled, and took a lunging step toward the staircase. The Commander quickly wrapped an arm about her waist, catching her in mid-stride. "Wait," she protested. "I just wanted to see—to see what attracted him more than me. I must have drunk too much, but it didn't seem like that much. Oh, my head hurts." She noticed that he was guiding her towards the sleeping alcove. She stiffened. "No. Not there. Not with you."

"I'm only going to help you get there. Nothing more."

"I'm not tired. Maybe I should sit up for a while? On the couch—help me over to the couch." Then gripping her stomach, she moaned. "Oh, Great Creator, I'm going to be sick!"

Richard rolled his eyes and guided her to the couch. He didn't move the tray that had migrated to the place where he'd sat during supper Instead, he sat beside her, preventing her from sprawling all over the small settee.

"I brought you a treat. Stay here."

He got up and went to the lavatory while she muttered something about not being in the mood for treats. Nevertheless, he returned with a glass of water and handed her two pills from a small vial. "I did you a favor and brought you these."

"I don't want 'em," she said, gently pushing his hand away.

He smiled. "Take 'em—or I'll make it an order."

She was gorgeous even in a drunken state, with her thick golden hair falling over her eyes.

She fell back against the cushioning of the couch and moaned, rolling her head back and forth. "Please don't make me. I'll get sick. I mean it, and I won't have time to run all the way to that cubby hole before things start to happen." Marie rolled glassy eyes up to meet his. "So, Mr. Commander, I don't want anything that might make me mess your uniform." Her eyebrows knit together. "That's a nice uniform, too. Looks official."

"It's been an official kind of night. Now take these. They're alcohol antidotes. You'll feel like yourself again in no time."

She peered at the little white balls in his palm, her head bobbing ever so slightly in the effort to focus. Suddenly, she bent down and gave them a little sniff. "Look okay, I guess, but—" She grasped his forearm. It felt hard under her grip, the smooth cloth of the uniform alluring. She released his arm as if it were hot steel. "I think I might feel better like this, than like myself."

He smiled. "Oh, come now. You're perfectly wonderful as yourself." He bit off his words, suppressing a horde of feelings he hadn't yet had a chance to analyze.

"I dunno! The real me gets herself deceived and betrayed and she drinks too much. That's not a good person. I should have seen through Paul. I should have known he was a rat. Oh, hell, look at me! What am I doing judging him?" She sat up straight, a hand covering her eyes. Blindly, she groped for the Commander. "I'm gonna be sick!"

"It's an order, then." He maneuvered her hands so they were both in front of her. He placed the glass in one hand and the pills in the other. She gave a comical grimace but did his bidding, arching her neck with the swallow. She let out a deep groan. "It's not going to work!"

He sighed. "Yes it will. If you just take some deep breaths you'll be fine in a few minutes." Then coming up with a clever idea, he made a suggestion. "Come on. Some fresh air will help."

With eyes closed, she groped for him as he hoisted her to her feet. "Where are we going? I can't go anywhere. I'm a prisoner."

"And I'm your jailer, remember?"

She opened her eyes as they reached the balcony. "We can't go out there. I might fall against that railing you had rigged to cut off my head."

He opened the doors. "I had the force field turned off. We'll be fine."

"Oh."

"But I'm glad to hear you kept some of your senses about you."

The warm air felt wonderful. She stood there, oblivious to the fact that she leaned against him and hummed delightfully while enjoying the mild fragrance of the night air. Within a few minutes the little pills worked their magic and Marie felt the fog in her head lift.

Then she stiffened. Her nerves became raw with a heightened awareness of her situation. Cautiously she shifted forward, putting the weight back on her own feet, amazed at herself for leaning against him in the first place, wine or not! Her attention immediately shifted to the noises from the black mat of jungle below, filling the air with screeching and chattering sounds. The two moons were both visible, one a deep copper orange and slightly flattened by the distortion of the horizon it lay against; the other, a bright whitish yellow, looking at them from the azimuth of a black-blue sky. The fragrance had changed, having become fuller and more intoxicating as the nocturnal blooms exuded their potent perfumes.

Even more intoxicating was the musky aroma of Commander Richard Shaw who stood directly behind her, hands cupping her elbows to support her. What kind of crazy notions had gotten into her head? In an attempt to seem unaffected by their closeness on the small balcony, she gave a sigh and reached out for the railing, indicating that she could support herself. Her hand withdrew like a recoiling snake. With embarrassment, she relaxed again. "Oh, right." She glimpsed the Commander. "You did say you turned off that beam."

"I did. The railing's quite safe as long as you don't try to jump over it."

She rolled her eyes. "I won't."

"Good."

Was he closer, or was it her imagination? She could feel his breath against her hair. She looked up into the sky to distract herself, but became disturbed by what she saw, or more accurately, what she didn't see. "I know it's late, but I see only about three stars." With a little more urgency she asked, "Where are we, that there would be no stars?

"Oh there are stars," he assured her. "You just don't see them."

"I drank that much!"

He smiled. "It's not that. We're in the middle of a nebula here. The gasses block out most of the stars, but believe me, they are there. You find out when you try to navigate out of here. The sky is quite beautiful on the other side of this mountain, with most of the spectrum of the nebula being visible to us there."

"I see," Marie said, wondering is she'd ever see the other horizon.

He leaned closer. "Your voice sounds much better. The pills must be working."

She turned to catch his eye. "Prisoners can't hide much from you, can they?"

"Not this one."

He gave her elbow a light squeeze. She didn't dare think it might be a show of affection. Suddenly, she noticed the long, ankle length pajama, or was it a nightgown? She wasn't sure what they would call this refined piece of nightwear in the Fringe, but she felt foolish being seen this way. She was glad that the darkness hid a deep flush that crept right from the base of her neck.

Wrapping her arms around herself, she collected the big sack of cloth. In two short strides, she was at the end of the balcony. She turned to face him. The light from inside the room gave him some kind of ridiculous halo as if he were a fire-throwing god from the ether! Marie found herself aware that the light also accented his athletic frame. All too soon she adjusted enough to the dimness to see the contour of his face, his hair, and a navy blue uniform that made him look much too self-assured. Or was she feeling very vulnerable? "I guess I'm not exactly dressed for company."

"Oh, don't worry about that! Fringe dwellers don't care much about appearance."

Marie gave a short laugh. "Certainly not in evening wear." A uniform, however, could look rather dashing on a man, she mused. "I'm sorry, but this lovely outfit embarrasses me no matter what the Fringe dwellers might think of appearance."

"I can leave if you wish." His words were delivered without emotion.

"No!" The word blurted ridiculously from her mouth. After a moment of indecision, she added, "I mean, you don't have to go—if you don't want to." She was glad the darkness camouflaged another flush. She shrugged. "I guess you've seen me at my worst now, anyway."

With the soft glow from the cell spilling onto the balcony, Richard witnessed his prisoner's cheeks burn with a flush. It brought a smile to his lips and he relaxed a little knowing he could stay, but only for a short while. He had no business being here this way. He watched her grasp the nightgown by the sides and stretch it taut. "Just pretend it's a beautiful, haute-couture evening gown."

"No need to pretend. I've never seen you that way."

Her hands dropped slowly. It was true. Marie's voice came softly. "Perhaps you're the only one in the whole galaxy who's ever seen me any way but meticulously groomed." She put a hand to her unkempt hair, then she realized her mistake, "Well, other than metal man—I mean Captain Boro, and Igna, and some of the others around here."

"Igna?"

Marie tore her gaze away. "Ah, yes. A woman called Igna Cello paid me a visit earlier."

"She did," he said in rhetorical drawl, a spark of interest touching his voice.

"She did."

"What did she want?"

Marie felt mortified, but the truth should be told. "She came to tell me to stay away from her man. I presume that's you."

The Commander didn't react for a moment. Marie was afraid she had really done it this time. Suddenly his face broke into a full smile that produced all those laugh lines again. He burst into laughter. "She came in here to tell you that?"

With a touch of urgency, Marie added, "I'm sure she wouldn't appreciate my informing on her. Perhaps I shouldn't have mentioned it."

"No. I'm glad you did, and I'll reprimand her for entering this room without my permission."

"Oh, please, don't'!"

"Don't worry. She doesn't need to know that I heard it from you. I'm sure the control room will give me the information I need. And, if she had them turn off the cameras while she carried on her little visit with you, she's in *real* trouble."

Marie suddenly remembered that he'd witnessed her drama with the wine bottle. Her flush increased. "You mean, *everything* that happened here tonight was on—" She slapped a hand over her eyes, "Oh, *no!*"

He smiled. "All on record. But don't worry. My detention technicians are very discreet. If it helps, I had them turn off the cameras for this visit."

Marie swallowed, uncertain if it was with dread or relief. "That's good."

He came and stood beside her, one hand resting on the railing. Seeing he'd been truthful about turning off the force field, she leaned against it herself, but remained facing the doors.

"What else did Igna want?"

Marie shrugged. "Nothing. I think she was curious about me."

"I suppose I can't blame her."

Marie looked at the Commander. He'd already lost interest in the jungle below and had turned to face her. "Is she your wife?"

Shaw gave a sharp laugh. Marie's heart jumped with the accent of it.

"Hardly." He lowered his head to look at her. "Igna thinks she should be. I think not."

"Oh." Marie found herself wrapping her arms around herself again, afraid they might stray and wrap around him. She blinked. Was she mad? The man was a ruthless leader of a savage wisp of space and all its barbaric lands and peoples. She was the definition of finesse and celebrity. He ruled with a wild heart. She ruled with order, planning and preparation. He'd had her kidnapped off her favorite starship in a heinous manner and if she allowed herself one inch on the miles of desire that had begun to pave across her heart, she'd end up lost and broken one more time.

Richard clung to the railing with one hand. The other hung on his belt to keep it where it belonged. Igna? Married! Ha! That would be the day! He fumed about the single fact that she'd called him "her man." He glanced at the woman beside him. In his own words he didn't think he could describe her beauty, even in that tacky nightshirt. He blinked. What on earth was he doing having thoughts like this about a woman—hell, any woman, at his age.

That one made his jaw clench. He wasn't old. So why did he feel so foreign to the teenage hormones that had begun to course about his system since her arrival? What would he do about her afterwards? She had an empire to run. He had people who needed him to keep their ways of life intact. Worse, he'd ordered her kidnapped off that starcruiser in an attempt to hang on to the last threads that might keep his nation tied together; staying one step ahead of the TRA. What would she want with him? They mixed like oil and water.

"I'm glad I'm not caught up in a marriage with that Paul Lambert," Marie blurted. Suddenly, her every nerve electrified. He had taken a step and closed the short distance between them. His fingers reached out and trailed across the back of her neck. Astonished, Marie kept her eyes staring straight into the room, her lips parting in amazed disbelief.

"Add a few spices, and you get a delicious dressing." A finger dipped just below the collar of the nightgown, touching the prominence of her spine while his thumb massaged the nape of her neck. Marie's breasts rose and fell with gasps that she tried hard to make less audible. Her eyes lifted to meet his steady gaze. Her words came out in a feathery sound. She scolded herself for her schoolgirl weakness. What was she doing letting him touch her like this?

"What do you mean? Spices, dressing? Did I miss something on my supper tray?" Her gaze swept about his face, to his hair, his shoulders. In the periphery of her vision, she could see his chest heave as well.

"No." His jaw bunched into tight knots. "I was talking about you and me. Oil and water. Two different people with two different lives that don't mix. Yet I'm fighting the urge to throw a little spice on it. Make the mad mixture into a wondrous delight."

"Ohhh…" Surely, it was the essence of the jungle that brought on the next line. "Thanks to your wine, I think the spice is already on my breath."

She felt his hand work its way through her hair, gently pulling her towards him. She did not, could not refuse, and when he leaned down to touch his lips to hers, she lost control of her arms and they slipped around his neck. Her fingers tangled his hair as she worked them up to caress his head, imploring his gentle kiss to linger. He massaged his lips against hers, then taking her fully in his arms, pulled her hard against his chest. He kissed her with ardor, responding to her embrace. His lips were full and soft, and she accepted them with abandon.

How different this Commander was from the time of the interrogation. Or was he? His arms were tightening about her, his hands roaming her back, seemingly right through the thick fabric of the gown, then in and out of her hair. She felt weakened by his grasp, by the same musky aroma that had become familiar in such a short time, as if she'd always known it, as if she'd always known the feel of his lips, caressing and molding to hers. His skin, peppered with a day's growth, stimulated her, mounting her desire for more.

Spice, oil and water. They mixed together in one soft swirling dance before the elements were forced into a natural separation.

He released his grip only slightly before smashing his eyes shut in defiance of what he'd just done. Yet, he couldn't let her go.

She let her head fall back, pulling in long gasps of air, maddeningly laced with his maleness. Her heart plummeted to her stomach and raced about in there, creating havoc with her gut. She slipped out of his arms as he continued to relax his hold on her. All those arms fell limply by their sides. They stood in silence a moment. "I'm sorry," he muttered before running a hand through his hair giving it a roughly combed look.

She was about to say, don't be sorry, but what came out was "Don't...do that."

"I know. I shouldn't have—"

"I mean, don't do that with your hair. It makes me want to do it for you, and I should have nothing to do with you."

"Oh, now you're enticing me," he moaned. With abandon he swallowed her up in his arms and devoured her with kisses. Marie wanted to draw him into her soul, and never let go. A whimper escaped her throat as she gently pushed away before there was no hope of doing so.

"We can't," she whispered against his mouth.

With his breath still heaving, he stopped, then slowly let her go. The regret that tore them apart was tangible in the space between them. He turned away, trying to distract himself by focusing out into the jungle, but it was of no use. "I'm so sorry," he muttered.

She lowered her eyes. "I am, too." She caught his sideways glance. "Maybe you should go this time."

He gave a rueful smile. "And pretend this never happened?"

She shook her head. "No. I can't pretend this never happened. We just need to make a vow that it won't happen again."

"All right. A vow it is. But now you can appreciate that you aren't the only one to suffer from your position in life."

"However different from yours, no."

He ran his fingers over her hair, then dropped his arm to his side. "I don't suppose you need any help getting to your bed."

She laughed lightly. "No, I don't think so."

He nodded in resignation, then strode through the balcony doors. There he stopped and turned back toward her. "At least come inside. I'll lock the doors again until morning. No antidote is without its side effects and I don't want to find you in the tree tops at daylight."

She made her way into the room and suddenly realized she was barefoot. The flagstone sent it's cooling draft through her warm feet, but she stood motionless just the same. They both stood there like dumb statues. Marie made an attempt to break the spell. "I guess you'd better not scold Igna now."

He leaned forward, took her cheeks in his hands and kissed her lightly. "I suppose not—except that I'm really not her man." With a final, lingering look, he turned and walked away, but not with the same urgency he'd had on previous occasions. She watched him mount the stairs and leave. He didn't look back.

Marie's hands flew to her cheeks. Her head felt like a billiard table with all the balls crashing and rebounding off the corners of her mind, each one a different event, a different thought. Finally she straightened and looked about the room that had become her home in less than a standard day. Her eyes fell again on the shattered bottle and its spilled contents by the staircase. Moisture filmed over her eyes.

"Good-by, Paul," she whispered.

Hello Richard, were the next words on her lips, but she couldn't bring herself to say them. She could never have him.

CHAPTER 25

The greatest atrocity of the century—that's how the attack on the Starquest *is being described. It seems beyond comprehension that such a horrific act could be executed upon our princess and the other victims of the pillage. To everyone's dismay, there is still no news of her whereabouts. The Flechette family has the entire Nixodonian Security Force on search patrol. It's true that Marie is Nixodonia's greatest icon and all reasonable efforts should be made to rescue her. But, wait, folks. Are we paying the Flechette's price of fame? Or did we, as a nation, create the debt? Should we have been more cautious when fabricating a princess in order to ease our sorrows over the many kingdoms lost to the new galactic order of Hervos Nixodonia? Will our nation now be held ransom for this oversight? Whatever the reasons for the heist, and despite the illusions we may have created for ourselves, we want our princess back. But you must know and believe, Princess Marie, that we pray for your rescue. Because, when you do come home, many of us will need a little of that comforting, which you so freely give.*

—Celebrity Quest

Henrie Marchand sat across a large desk facing General Angel Keem. The General's puckered face and narrow eyes studied the glossy publication. Henrie made a casual mental note that he'd never seen the General in anything but an olive green uniform, its many bars and stripes arranged in a fashion that would not obscure the reptilian bird pin that signified the TRA. In the shadows behind the desk stood the ever-present form of Lieutenant Page who peered down his long thin nose at the paper in General Keem's hands. The General tossed the magazine back to Henrie.

"I'm a busy man," he barked. "Why are you showing me this?"

"Because, this publication is read by most of the galaxy, Telexa included. We mustn't let the princess' image flounder! If we allow these sorts of sentiments to brew, the love for Marie Flechette could turn to resentment, or worse, apathy!"

"Well, their apathy will turn to fear when they realize that their kingdoms will never return."

Marchand leaned forward. "We have to find her, General Keem, while the chant of 'Follow Me' is still strong. Most of the population is still willing to do just that, but to where?"

"She can't have just disappeared without someone claiming responsibility!" Angel Keem shouted with frustration. "And if we can't find her, then who the hell can? This is probably the work of a bunch of crazed fans doing it for the thrill of seeing how long they can get away with it. And, if that's the case, she's probably already dead, with the evidence thrown out an airlock."

"Crazed fans? You don't really believe that?"

The General drew in a breath while eyeing the information spread before him on the desk: spy reports from G2, the latest from Commissioner Rhodes and the current position of his deployments. He filled a pipe while scanning the material. "No, I suppose I don't. So, it seems we have a silent enemy. We must step up the search. The Blue Rift, the Three Kingdoms, even the old Telexan democracy. Surely we can track a goddamned pirate ship."

"There's still no sign of a ransom note," Henrie ventured to say.

The General grunted. "That's too bad. We can track a ransom note. We can't track a ghost."

The General thought a moment, then suddenly gave a wily smile before making a blunt and surprising statement. "Marchand, I have a new job for you.

You're uncommissioned at the moment, so I'm putting you in charge of the Search Team. You know the girl well and that should give you some insights as to who may be responsible for this. It seems the officer I presently have in charge is an incompetent fool. So, Henrie, you are now officially Search Team Leader. I will make the necessary calls to Rashmar to confirm your position. I wish you luck. And," he sighed. "I agree; our armada is powerful, but firepower alone won't bend the Nixodonians. They must be emotionally manipulated, and the surest way is with the heiress."

"Then, the Fringe is first on my list, General," Henrie mused aloud. "They have a few secrets I'd like to unlock."

"You talk of them until I'm sick of it, Henrie. We know that their governing planet manages an army about the size of a pea. They're a walkover!"

"Really? Then why do they want autonomy? With all due respect, sir, I believe that they're hiding something. In fact, I am sure of it. I'll get probes searching the Fringe immediately."

"Ahhph!" The General waved a hand in the air. "Fine, send out your probes, but you will find nothing. They are windbags, that Shaw idiot and his band of ruffians."

"Perhaps, but they weren't pleased about our attacks on their mining planets, or the annexation of Rashmar, even though it belonged to no one in particular. And they won't be pleased when our Armada starts traversing their territory into Nix States."

"And what power do they have to stop us? Forget about the Fringe, Henrie. Shaw may growl a bit, but he'll soon understand who has indentured him."

"He'll have more power if he has the heiress." Marchand pointed out.

"Fine! Do as you wish," the General grunted. "I'll give you free reign."

Marchand accepted a cigar from the General, a gesture indicating that official talks were over. Henrie celebrated his promotion to head the Search Team with a long pull from the cigar, although the line about wishing him luck was hardly a blessing. Still, there was great relief in knowing that he'd just climbed a few more rungs toward the party's elite clubhouse. If he could expose the Fringe for the time bomb he believed it to be, and find Marie in the process, there'd be no telling what promotions could be in store for him.

CHAPTER 26

Javid felt a sting on his hand when Clive Baker gave it a swift slap. "Don't touch those buttons!" the pilot howled.

"I wasn't going to *push* on them! I just wanted to see how they felt. How am I going to learn about spaceships if I can't find out what things feel like?"

The towering Clive Whale Baker no longer frightened old Javid. He'd soon realized the man was a teddy bear beneath a rough, well-scoured hull. "You don't need to know what they feel like!"

"It helps. You should be able to fly this thing with your eyes closed. Literally."

"Oh yeah? And how would that help?"

"Goodness, Clive," Javid sighed, having taken to calling him Clive whether the pilot liked it or not. Where did he get a name like Whale anyway? He wasn't even fat! "Because, when you learn mind control, you must learn to do everything without your eyes. Not seeing is believing in this line of thinking, my boy."

The two scowled, more at themselves than at each other. Javid had gone against his own word. Here he was, teaching the old brute the fundamental rules of telepathy. Clive, in turn, was teaching Javid about space flight and navigation. They had plenty of time, having to make several hyperspace jumps through the Fringe with lots of sub-light tracks in between.

Javid also discovered that the freighter was this man's home. Everything he owned was here, including the game board they had used at the casino. And the place smelled like his, too! There were limits to Javid's relaxed cleanliness and Clive's habits had reached them quickly. Javid, therefore, took to cleaning some of Whale's things at the same time that he serviced his own. He chose to ignore the comments from Clive about feeling like he had a fussy wife on board rather than a hijacking passenger.

It hadn't taken long for Clive to ask for instruction in the colors game. Mostly, Clive wanted to learn secret strategies in order to trick his Nixodonian opponents. Before Javid knew it, he'd agreed, the trade-off being some instruction in space flight, one of Javid's unfulfilled passions. After all, there couldn't be any harm in sharing a little of each other's knowledge.

"I didn't need to *feel* anything when I learned about this instrument panel, and see? I'm a perfectly good pilot. In fact, I'm a damned good pilot!" Clive stuck his face out at Javid who recoiled. "And I know every dial and switch on this thing like the back of my hand."

Javid made a swift move to cover the back of Clive's hand. "Then tell me how the veins run on this hand."

Clive screwed up his face. "Old man, you are so weird! They run the same as the back of the other hand." Javid lifted his palm and Clive examined the backs of both his hands. His eyes narrowed. "You looked at my hands! When?"

"I didn't have to look at your hands. Nobody has the same vein pattern exactly the same on both hands. And if you didn't know that, you've got some practicing to do—with your eyes closed!" Javid frowned, then shook a rigid finger. "Better yet—" He ran back to his cot and pulled out the scarf that had come with the cape. He crept up behind the big lout and quickly blindfolded him. Clive howled with annoyance, but soon resigned himself to the exercise, having earlier accepted that the Rashmarian, true to his breed, was a bit of a prankster.

"Now, what's this one?" Javid guided the man's stiff arm over to a switch. Clive fingered clumsily. "Ah, ah...it's the right jet hydraulic!"

"If you were trying to avoid a black hole, you'd be dead."

Clive lifted a corner of the scarf and stared at the panel with one, wide eye. His face pulled into a frown of disbelief. "Well, I'll be darned, old man. It's the left hydraulic! Okay, then. Try me on another one," and Clive replaced the scarf himself. Javid guided his fingers to a small lever.

"Ha! That's the master switch to the navigational computer." Clive heard Javid sigh. He lifted the scarf for a second look. "So I'm one control off to the left. I failed. What's the trick?"

"There's no trick Clive," Javid said, mildly. "Here." Javid removed the scarf. "First, take some time to really study these controls, with your eyes both open and closed. See what a certain button looks like, *feel* what it looks like—then become it. Be the little charge that flies through the circuit and orders the machine at the other end to do what it's supposed to do. Become the craft. You turn, you nose up, you nose down. You become the thruster. Let your fingers become the landing pods. Let your body and the craft become one. Allow it to obey you with joy and life. I have to go check on our laundry. I hope you don't mind that I used the towrope as a clothesline."

Clive hardly heard him, so engrossed was he in the first lesson of the day. He waved a hand limply, sending Javid on his way. Javid felt enthralled that he was finally a teacher of telepathy himself. On his own planet, he would have years of study ahead of him before he could be initiated into the rank. Here it would be simple, elementary, and fun.

"Become the thruster," he repeated while on his way to the rear compartment. With a giggle, he lifted a leg and let loose a little thrust of his own. To think that Javid had been trying to teach Clive proper manners!

Beaming with excitement, Clive came rushing back to where Javid was folding one of Clive's flight suits. "We make the next jump in two hours, and I'm going to do it blindfolded!"

Javid's mouth fell open. "Now wait a minute—"

"Auf, I'm just kidding, but I'm ready for a test. And I'd like to thank you for introducing me to my ship. I always thought it was just a hunk of tin."

"Everything has its spirit, Clive. My eternal one tells me it's time to feed its mortal counterpart so I took the liberty of preparing some of that sawdust you call rations. Care to join me?"

"Thanks, old man. I will."

The two sat at the small fold-down table to share a cabin meal. Clive started to talk with a full mouth, thought better, swallowed a portion, then addressed Javid. "What's the real reason you want to go to Rashmar?"

Javid's eyebrows rose up his long forehead. "A stab in the dark I guess. Besides it's been twenty-one years since I left." His voice softened. "I've lost contact with my peers. I need to know if anyone I once knew is still alive."

"Oh, somebody's alive. Your people are still hidden up in the Cousta Highlands because all the valley lands are under the control of the rebels. Clever of the TRA to start their operation on a self-governed planet of little interest to anyone else."

"Sure, but that didn't help us any. No one cared to intervene. Besides we didn't have the technology to call up into the sky with those hyperwaves they have nowadays. If it weren't for some of those brave traders from the Fringe who snuck in and left us their outdated technology, we'd have been completely helpless. We were given most of it just before I escaped so I have no idea if my people were able to use any of the machines the traders brought us."

"Oh, they've used them all right. It's that low technology mixed with Rashmarian smarts that got me off the planet alive."

Javid chuckled, then sobered. "So—why did *you* go to Rashmar?"

Clive chewed for a while then muttered, "Well, seeing as you know about my little fling with Lola Phoebe, I may as well tell you the rest."

Javid's eyes opened wide. He stared at Clive, momentarily stunned. Then the words barreled out. "Lola? *Thee* senator's wife, Lola?"

Clive stopped chewing. In a loud voice he said, "I thought you knew that?"

Javid was caught in his own tacky mistake. He quickly recovered. "Well...well I did!" he exclaimed. "I knew you had an affair with the wife of a dignitary, but I didn't know exactly which one."

The pilot stood slowly, fists clenched. "You mean to say that capsule doesn't say who I had an affair with?"

"Clive! The proper word is whom in that—"

"So, fine! It doesn't say *whom* I had and affair with?"

Javid raised his chin, but his insides crumpled. "No."

The man fell back onto the seat with a thud, spine rod stiff.

Javid quaked. "Are you going to kill me?"

Clive scowled. "I can't. Smart as it was to protect yourself, old man, your best protection lies right with my own men. They thought it was pretty hilarious that I got beat by a skinny old fart like you, not understanding the fact that you're a Rashmarian, and I couldn't have won had I ripped my brains out trying. I didn't bother to explain it to that lousy bunch of scoundrels. So they told me if I didn't have you back in that playing room in less than three months, alive, I would lose my position as our trading bloc leader." He looked with remorse at Javid. "They're all I have now. Shame that that is."

"Oh, there's no shame in that!" Javid breathed. "I'm too nice to kill anyway. Just think, you can get into a clean flight suit before we make our next jump."

"Great. Are my gitch clean too?"

"Your what?"

"Never mind. Just pass me more of those protein crackers."

The two were quiet for a while, but Javid burned with questions. It became too difficult to contain himself. "Now, please tell me if I'm annoying you, but you still haven't told me why you went to Rashmar."

Clive chewed thoughtfully. "I wasn't going to jail over the Lola affair."

"Oh?"

"Because you see, our most honorable Senator Yousef Phoebe was thinking up ways to tear me apart, molecule by molecule. If it wasn't for Lola, I wouldn't be alive." He paused. "On the other hand, she sent me off to experience another kind of death. She sent me to Rashmar to a man who was going to give me a new identity." Clive gave a big-bellied laugh. "Yeah, he was giving me a new identity all right. I didn't realize what was going on at first. I thought I was just joining some harmless renegade band with all these weird rituals and stuff. For renegades they had a hell of an arsenal, I'll tell you."

"Not all was lost though," Clive grunted, "except for any chance at a normal life in the future! But, hey, I learned the ancient martial arts, all about modern warfare, and I got to be an excellent marksman." He pumped the biceps of his right arm, "And I got muscles like nobody's business."

Clive became pensive a moment, reflecting on frightening times. "Then I got my first assignment. I was to assassinate five members of the Telexan parliament. Before I had a chance to realize it wasn't a joke, they told me that I had earned their seal of excellence. So, before I was to go off and do my killings, they were gonna brand me with a reptilian bird. Right here, never to come off." Clive jabbed at his left chest.

Javid was paralyzed with shock. The implications were too much to comprehend all at once. "The TRA?" he asked in a hoarse whisper. "She sent you to become a member of the TRA?"

"You got it."

"Do you, ah…do you have that stamp?"

"No. I got away." Clive stood and paced about the cabin. He gazed through one of the port holes but his eyes were on his soul. "I escaped into the highlands of the planet, the ones past the Karari Plains. I'm sure you know where I mean." He didn't turn to see Javid nod slowly, a reminiscent smile crossing his features.

"I met the natives and they took me in as a fugitive for a while. That's when I got that thinking game. I asked for it when I was leaving. They were reluctant at first because they had never given one away; then they decided I had earned it with the little I'd learned in my time there. The Grand Master, old fellow by the name of Farol, taught me the basics then told me firmly that I, in fact, knew nothing about the game, but it might bring me some fun, and some memories of them."

"Farol!" Javid breathed in a remote whisper.

"Yah. You know the old fart?"

"Not well. He was the chief of a far away tribe. My tribe once farmed the land the Reptilians now occupy. Well, that's what we used to call them before they got that fancy TRA name. But Farol? Is he really still alive? And now Grand Master?"

"Last I saw him he was." Clive frowned. "That was almost two years ago, mind you, and I was only with them for about five months. The TRA got busy with some exercise and ignored us for a while. For the most part they ignored the surviving Rashmarians anyway because they believed them to be harmless. I think the real reason was because they could never find the little weasels. So, they never found out that Fringe ships were still sneaking in and out of the Cousta Highlands. Not that the Fringe folk could do the Rashmarians any good, but it helped their morale. I had a chance to escape, and so I did, on one of those Fringe ships there on secret trade. Got back to Iggid, figuring the best place to hide from the Phoebes was right under their noses."

Clive stared back out of the port again while continuing his story. "I knew the owner of the club you found me at and I took him up on an old offer to help me out if I ever needed it. I'd done a little shipping for him in the old days. I was a good shipper once. An honest, tax paying citizen of Nixodonia." Clive broke into a sorry laugh. "You wouldn't know that now. These days, I head that gang of ruffians because of my *skills*. I learned to kill and swindle and worm my way around the most dangerous parts of space imaginable. I suppose it takes the boredom out of regular hours." Clive turned swiftly to catch Javid's eye. "Mark my word, old man. I swore to myself I'd never kill unless it was in self-defense. I've kept that promise—although places like the Fringe and the Blue Rift give a man plenty of chances to kill in self-defense." He sniffed loudly, analyzing the black space beyond the port. "So now I do neck-breaking runs into this damned Fringe all the time. But, hey, credits are good. No law telling you what to do, and the demand for black market Fringe stuff is pretty steady. They got lots of nice planets in this here Fringe, if you can get to them without evaporating yourself in the attempt."

Javid nodded his head slowly. "So your cover name is Whale. What about your land? Won't the Phoebes get wind of that?"

"I don't have it in my name. Besides, I don't get to go there much. Got some friends to watch things for me. Mostly I live in this bucket of bolts and try to figure out when the Phoebes are off-planet. That's fairly often, thank the Creator."

"And Lola. Do you think she is actually a member of the TRA?"

"Think?"

"So...so, if she's a member, then...?" Javid couldn't bring himself to say it.

Clive walked over to the confectionery panel and popped out a couple of hot coffees. He handed one to Javid. "He sure is. Just before I got my assignment I heard Yousef Phoebe's name mentioned several times over some exercise going on in Nix. I don't know what they have going on there, but it scares the hell out of me. I always thought it was only Telexa they were after. So, when I kept hearing Phoebe's name, I wanted out of there real bad. Before I managed to escape the base, I got hauled into the office to hear all about that lovely assignment. What did they take me for? I didn't think I was that kind of guy. Playing with knives and blasters and kicking ass is one thing, but to be an assassin?"

Clive leaned over the small table until Javid could smell the coffee on his breath. "When I stood in that office and heard what I was supposed to do, I got scared. Real scared. But, do you know what scared me the most, old man?"

Javid shook his head.

"I knew I could do it. And I knew that I would get away with it. I'd become a TRA assassin without realizing it, and I was good. I could have done the job."

Although Clive's exterior showed nothing but hard steel, Javid saw clearly. The poor man wanted to burst into tears right in front of him. And really, he wouldn't have blamed the poor fellow.

CHAPTER 27

Spencer twisted his fingers together, anxious to finally meet with the Flechettes. It had taken him a long time to get back to Enderal, having first been hospitalized, then detained by the Iggid authorities. He was endlessly grateful to be standing in the main entrance of the Flechette mansion, a place he had truly believed he'd never see again. He followed the doorman up the grand staircase, down a wide hallway and was left to wait in the library. Hands clamped in front of him, Spencer gazed at the ancient décor, the shelves lined with volumes of ancient leather bound books. One wall featured a large portrait of Marie looking ethereally beautiful.

The regal Lady Genevieve entered the room in her familiar flowing stride, her stature tall and proud, but Spencer knew by her eyes that she was crushed inside. She took both Spencer's hands and smiled sincerely. "It's very good to see you back safely, Mr. Spencer."

"It's good to be back, my Lady," he said earnestly.

"We're hoping that you can tell us what happened in your own words. I know you've told the story a dozen times, but you were with her last, and—" She swallowed.

Leaning on a cane, Raymond entered the room. Spencer sat on a leather couch opposite them and in detail, gave the account from his perspective. When he was through, Raymond shook his head and said, "And still no word."

Genevieve sighed wearily. "I don't understand. Why haven't we received a ransom note?"

"I don't think that's what this is about," Spencer offered quietly.

"But what other reason could there be?"

"Well." Spencer focused on his feet. "It's nothing I can put my finger on."

Raymond implored, "Off the record, Spencer. Please, tell us anything that seems out of the ordinary to you, no matter how crazy might sound."

Spencer gave a crooked smile, afraid he'd brought on unnecessary suspicion, yet he had a compelling urge to get this off his chest to the Flechettes themselves, seeing as the authorities wouldn't listen to his hunches. "First, they took both Mr. Tripp and your daughter. It was a very skilled attack, and they had very little time to plan it. If the kidnappers followed the *Starquest* from Enderal like they're saying—" His brow furrowed. "It's not possible. They can't have followed the *Starquest* on the same lane through hyperspace and then make a lateral attack not twenty minutes after it entered normal space. No. They were waiting." He glanced at the distraught couple. "They could have come from anywhere, *except* for Enderal."

"Where do *you* think she is?" Raymond asked carefully.

"Me, sir? I'm not sure, but I don't think those pirates were Nixodonian."

Genevieve sank against the couch. "If she's been taken out of Nix, we're certain never to see her again."

"Don't give up yet," Spencer encouraged. "Too many things don't add up. There were no other captives. They didn't drag off any other women as you would expect pirates to do. They wanted Marie. That was clear. But what on earth did they want with Bill?"

The room grew silent and Raymond pondered the situation. Great Creator, the galaxy felt like a stupendous expanse at the moment, and his daughter just a small conglomerate of molecules lost in its sea.

Later that evening, Raymond tapped down the dimly lit halls of the Flechette headquarters, the cane easing the constant pain in his hip. He couldn't sleep. Genevieve had finally sent him off, understanding Raymond's need to search for some illusive or intangible clue.

Raymond buried himself in the mainframe suite trying to track possible enemies: someone she modeled for, someone she didn't model for. Someone at the High Court or the studios. Insane jealousy. Anyone who might have a motive.

The thought hit him like an asteroid.

Paul Lambert.

No one had heard from him since just after the attack on the *Starquest*, and although they weren't regretting that, it now struck a shaky cord. Raymond had noticed uncharacteristic changes in him over the past months, and had attributed it to a nervous twitch. Small town boy marrying cosmetics queen was no small potatoes. However, something felt peculiar.

Frantically he fired through every shred of data they held on the man.

His heart turned cold in minutes. How Paul had done it was beyond Raymond's understanding, but he instinctively knew no one else could be responsible for what transpired on the screen. Paul had wiped out all his personal data from the employee files! How could he have done that without knowing the codes to the entire confidential personnel section?

Terror jangled at Raymond's nerves as he continued his meticulous search. It led him quickly to Doria and the new plant in Sector 5.

Nothing, nothing. Then the hammer fell.

Raymond repeated the functions several times, not sure if his illness or the late hour prevented him from finding the catalogue numbers of every product shipped to Doria. They were meant to stock the off-site distribution center until the labs were up and running. The sales were recorded. Every last item gone, often in volumes of hundreds at a time.

Raymond heard himself laugh in disbelief, his voice echoing back at him in the emptiness of the mainframe suite. This was impossible. The figures had been made up. In fact they could all be just data, invisible products, not really existing. Without catalogue numbers, there was no way of tracing anything. Not a single cream could be accounted for, yet here were the profits. Here were the financial statements. With trembling fingers, Raymond punched in his confidential codes, accessing the Flechette bank accounts. Going through the front door would ensure that the deposits from Doria weren't fabricated. His eyes felt like they deceived him. But there they were, all the profits, not a credit missing.

Raymond wasted little time contacting the plant manager of the warehouse from which Paul would have ordered his stock. The night manager said that about a year ago, Paul had made a large order for Doria, then cancelled it just a few days later. The executive had explained that the Shelt plant was closer to the shipping company he was using.

After the call, Raymond sat in wonder for a few moments. Shipping company? Paul had an FC cargo ship at his disposal. In the middle of the next call, Raymond broke contact. Why bother the staff at the Shelt plant? He already knew that they would give him a similar story.

No products had ever been shipped to Doria. Raymond pondered ruefully. All local staff? Self-managed by the genius himself? Yet it wasn't embezzlement. He leaned back in the chair and stared impassively at the terminals before him bleeping the financial reports of the Flechette accounts. Marie was not the only one who would suffer at the hands of Paul Lambert.

Had Raymond been able to look deeper, or had he received a message from the gods to tear apart the terminal at which he sat, he would have detected a more insidious menace. Down at his feet, behind the metal plate and hidden within the bowels of the machine, a new heart pulsed. Black and sinister, a small package lay silent, waiting for its summon to life.

Brilliant, explosive life.

CHAPTER 28

The day had become too long for Richard Shaw. In fact, the hours were ticking into the next day and it looked like sleep would elude him once again. The drive that propelled him this time was a combination of anger, disbelief, and a touch of self-pity. He'd just watched the *Angel's Test* video, a quickly edited version of the movie's highlights, a little show that Richard was glad he'd watched alone. He wouldn't have wanted to share his reactions with anyone.

The guard at Marie's door jumped out of the way as Richard stormed forward and thrust in the access card. He snapped on the lights and stomped down the stone steps. Marie only shifted on the cot, the alcohol antidote having lapsed her into a drug induced sleep. He leaned heavily on her bed, glowering at her. Marie lifted her head, groggy with sleep. "Wha…what's the matter?"

"I'm so furious, I could kill you with my bare hands right this minute. I've just had a peek at your movie."

Confused, she asked meekly, "What's wrong with my movie?"

To her shock, he grabbed her by the arm and hauled her off the bed. Was this the man who'd kissed her so ardently only a few hours ago? Roughly, he dragged her up the stairs, nightgown clad and barefoot.

"What is the matter with you? Have you gone mad?" she screeched.

Reaching the landing, he spun to face her, a finger pointing rigidly. "You have deceived me for the last time, Marie Flechette."

She yanked at his grasp, not caring that she didn't succeed in freeing herself. She merely wanted his full attention, "I have *not* deceived you, you unscrupulous scoundrel!"

"No? A stolen kiss before the hatchet falls?" He dragged her into the hall where the guard now stood at rigid attention.

"Pardon *me*? If you recall, Commander, you kissed me first!"

Shaw barked at the guard. "Give the lady your cloak."

Pulling the cloak securely over Marie's shoulders, Shaw proceeded to drag her down the tunnel to the end of the detention corridor.

"I think you lowered the hatchet on yourself, you madman."

He stopped so fast she propelled right past him, jerking to a stop at the length of his grip. "You *were* involved in those arms deals, and now you rally an entire galaxy behind you? This is it, my love. The last hurrah against me!" He continued his march and drag.

She fought him wildly. "Rally a galaxy? What are you talking about?" She suppressed a very strong urge to slap him. "I did *not* send those arms!"

At the end of the detention corridor a trolley sat waiting, charged. He pulled on her arm violently enough to spin her to face him. "Do I have to chain you to this thing, or are you going to come willingly?"

"I don't care what you do, Commander," she said, hotly. "I don't know what the hell you're in a knot about this time, but I am sick of your accusations. Then again, it seems I have no choice. So, take me. Take me to whatever it is you'll condemn me with this time."

He nodded sharply and indicated to her to get in the trolley. In silence they whipped through a series of tunnels, a few of which Marie recognized. They stopped in a darkened area and Marie briefly wondered if night ever ended here.

He showed her into an office, turning up the lights as he did so. She got only a quick glance at the large central desk and a dozen consoles stacked haphazardly along the walls. They proceeded through one of the doorways behind the desk and entered onto the main floor of a conference room, again hewn of unfinished stone. Chairs were loosely lined along a half dozen tiers all facing a mess of video and holo equipment. Marie's heart pounded, unsure what sort of devastating surprise might jump out at her this time. Richard walked deeper into the room and turned to face her. "Now we really know your secrets, Princess."

Terrified, Marie backed towards the protection of the first row of chairs and watched him punch at one of the control boxes. A large, wall-sized screen, dropped into position at the front of the room. There was no dimming of the lights, no soft music. Instead there was instant blackness. The damping acoustics of the room threw a suffocating blanket on her.

Like the brilliance of a sun, the screen came to life, filled to all four corners with a movie title accompanied by music she knew all too well, the introductory score for *Angel's Test*. Her eyes were drawn to it with skeptical magnetism, the quality of the three-dimensional image giving her the sensation that she could walk into the scene laid out before her. In a near hypnotic trance she watched herself appear upon the screen. Her stomach knotted sickeningly. This wasn't the opening scene. Suddenly, the musical score of "Follow Me" boomed out at her. She flinched with dread. She still didn't recognize the scene, then her memory flashed back. Way back, almost two years. She had shot this particular segment in one of her endless practice sessions with Henrie Marchand. With a tremulous voice she called into the darkness. "This is a practice tape. What are you doing with this?"

There was no answer. On the screen, Marie Flechette raised her head from a bowed position and began to chant, "Follow me...follow me."

The theme song burst out in full, the one that was hitting the charts all over Nix States. She watched herself and listened in horrified fascination. Something wasn't right about the angles, or the backdrop. They were different, giving the song a different meaning.

> *"You asked me tonight, when the moons were up,*
> *Will we ever change, might we ever unite.*
> *I'll tell ya baby, listen, listen*
> *Life is a paradox,*
> *Untangle the mystery, untie the knot"*

> *"I see the cries of my people,*
> *I see your empty hearts; I see the wreckage of your past,*
> *Listen, listen to the distance in your hearts,*
> *Listen to the sadness and your heart sinks so fast."*

Then Ekeem Danderwood appeared in a scene that had been drastically altered. She wanted to cry out but her voice stopped when the next scene smashed onto the screen. Marie jolted. There she was again, this time with Ekeem sharing a drink from a red cup. That scene was supposed to have been cut. The shots were dizzying, wide angled, focused, in and out, every time bringing the cup closer into view. Finally the imprint of a green reptilian bird could be seen stamped across it.

It hadn't been like that! The monogram suddenly dredged up something sinister within her consciousness. She'd seen that monogram somewhere before. *Yes,* of course. It was the emblem of the TRA. The blood drained from her face, her skin crawled with the knowledge that Ekeem was actually a part of this conspiracy, one growing portentously deeper. He'd been her friend, touching her, kissing her, being ever so charming, when he was nothing but a member of the TRA? Her voice exploded. "You bastard! You traitor!"

> *"Untangle the mystery, untie the knot*
> *Come on, follow me—cause you know not the way,*

Don't fear for your life, I know the answers, can't you see.
Follow me…follow me…follow me!"

She hardly had time to absorb the implications before the scene changed and her voice continued its deceit. She was singing on a set that had been used in another practice session, but not with the hundreds of people who now stood behind her in this fraudulent clip. They were dressed in long, white flowing robes, the same as the ones that Ekeem had designed for her stage production of "Follow Me" at the Benefit Concert, and *surprised* her with at the Post Benefit gala at her own estate! How convenient!

Marie didn't notice her panic turn outward. Her body had become clammy, damp hands clutched into fists. Her whimpers were drowned out by the blaring soundtrack that grew more ominous as each scene flashed before her. Then the clips became completely unfamiliar to her. Marie found herself reviewing the plot, wondering if she'd gone mad.

A man named Skeeter, played by Ekeem, is Angel's attorney, and her new lover. Together they fight to prove her innocence to the new dictators of a fictitious nation. Angel is now accused of promoting the same acts of subversion for which her husband was executed. Angel's husband had been a loyal, high-ranking official until their government fell to a band of rebels in a swift coup d'état. Angel's husband had refused to accept the new dictator, and his widow is now charged with the same treasonous acts. Despite Skeeter's attempts to save her, Angel is sentenced to death. Just prior to her hanging, the rebel coup fails, a result of the work by an underground movement led by Skeeter. The original government is restored to power. Angel's life is spared. She then starts a campaign to support the return of the old government and ease the confusion of the people. Hence the slogan, "Follow Me."

But this! This on the screen before her was not the movie Marie had filmed. In this version, the coup *doesn't* fail and Marie herself is supporting what? The TRA? How could they have possibly done this to her?

The film before her continued in bits and pieces, mostly of practice tapes Henrie had asked her to do. Or had he forced her? Manipulated her? Something Richard had said penetrated the confusion of her thoughts. *The Nix government has no idea how strong the TRA is in its nation.*

Marie began to cry helplessly.

The scene changed again. This time Ekeem was with a woman who looked uncannily like herself on a set she recognized from another practice session. It was a love scene, but here, clips of herself had been intermingled with that of an impostor who played scenes that became suddenly pornographic. Marie gasped. Was this to show that Marie Flechette was not the innocent princess everyone believed her to be? Marie's own face continued to be dubbed in with the other woman's body in lecherous and ugly scenes that Marie knew she would never be capable of. The woman's naked breast was shown rubbing Ekeem's bare chest, the tattoo of the reptilian bird displayed above the left nipple of each.

Marie peered into unfamiliar darkness. She cried out in fright. "Richard, this is all wrong. Where are you?"

There was no answer. Her eyes were drawn again to the screen where Marie witnessed a completely different outcome to the original version. Angel, herself, was applauding her husband's execution, had planned it, in fact. She then announced that she would lead the movement to cleanse the nation of any loyalists to the old government. There was no court, no Skeeter to defend her. There was no need. Skeeter had been a long time member of the rebels, as was Angel. Marie then watched herself shoot to death, in a bloody execution, dozens of dissidents that she herself helped hunt down.

A hand flew to her mouth. Bill had shown her how to hold a weapon for this? Marie clearly remembered Henrie filming the target practices. There was no impostor in this scene. It was Marie herself holding that gun while the camera turned to include the dying rebels. Blood spurted everywhere as men and women, even children, jerked and convulsed on their way to the ground. The words of "Follow Me" began again, hardly in support of the old government, the Knabon administration!

Marie lost control. She ran to the screen, clawed at it, tried to cover it with her body even though the screen reached into the dome of the ceiling. She screamed at the top of her lungs, "Stop it. It's not true!" She spun to face the blackness of the room, her arms spread out, palms against the screen in a useless attempt to hide the heinous treachery. "I didn't do this! This is all wrong. It's all turned around!"

The music died. Richard's voice echoed through the darkness. "Like you didn't send those coded messages?"

Marie felt trapped. "No. I am *not* a traitor, and I'm *not* responsible for those arms deals." She yelled with such force that her voice cracked hoarsely. "This isn't me. This isn't the movie we made."

"Are you trying to tell me that's not you on that screen?"

The lights began to brighten. She could see him now, coming slowly down from the top level of the tiered seating area. Marie faced him courageously, although she shook all over when she growled at him, "They used clips from the exercise tapes that Henrie made me do. The rest is dubbed in. That woman is an impostor, and Ekeem is with them!"

"That isn't you with the gun?"

"I mean that woman with Ekeem. The gun was only practice. I was shooting at a target!"

"You do realize that rebels represented on this tape are the TRA?"

"I do now," she spat, "but that's not the movie we made. Somebody put this together without my knowledge. Commander, you've got to believe me. He made me do this without—"

"Who made you do this?"

"Henrie Marchand, the director of *Angel's*—"

"I know who he is," Shaw cut in, stepping down onto the main floor. "You tell me he forced you to do these scenes? Nobody forced you, did they, Marie?"

"They were *practice* sessions. Dozens of them because I was a new actress. There was never anyone else in those practice tapes, not like here."

"Do they always film endless practice tapes, or were you special?"

"I don't know how others are taught. Who was I to argue his methods? I run half an empire. I didn't have time to run around asking others how they learned. All I know is that they're going to use this footage against me."

"Against Marie Flechette? The most influential women in Nix States. How convenient."

"Yes, convenient, all right."

"I don't believe for one minute that you didn't suspect something, or better yet that you weren't willfully involved in this whole affair."

"You have yet to believe me, Commander." Her voice warbled, tears streamed down her face. "This is all a big lie." She flung a hand toward the screen. "I did *not* make this movie. Pieces were taken, other people filled in." She slapped a hand over her eyes. "And all the while Paul was tampering with my codes."

"And you say another woman filled in for that love scene?" he asked, almost laughing.

Her hand dropped. She shot him an icy glare. "Yes! Look at it. There is never a full shot of that woman. That's not my body."

"No? Prove it to me."

Her eyes clung to him in terror. She stood there, frozen, unable to move, the cape bearing heavily on her shoulders. She clutched the cape around her and staggered back. He stared at her as if waiting for her to bare her body to him. She couldn't. Not like this. She closed her eyes tightly, waiting for his hands to come down on her, tear off her clothing, see for himself. But he didn't touch her. Instead he gave a sinister laugh. "Do you know what this movie means, my love?"

She sucked in a hard breath. "Don't call me that, you hypocrite."

Nostrils flared. He stood taller, but endured the insult. "This means join us or die. Follow me in the ways of the new regime. You do understand that at least?"

"Do you take me for a fool?"

"It seems like a reasonable conclusion. An entire movie for TRA propaganda made without one iota of your knowledge?" He took another step closer. Marie found him looking very deadly. She trembled with fear and crushing betrayal. "That's right," she croaked. "Without one iota of my knowledge. So, I guess I am a fool."

"Who are your leaders, Miss Flechette?"

"I am not a part of this!" she screamed.

"Oh, no? You must be feeling pretty smug knowing that the whole galaxy will soon be watching this, probably under mandatory law, if the TRA gets its way."

Her chest heaved. "It's not true. That can't be true."

"So, you may as well hear the happy news. Your precious TRA has won the first leg of its battle. Telexa has fallen. It's now under totalitarian rule. Congratulations."

Marie's face became like stone.

"Surprised? You shouldn't be."

"Fallen?" She was one staggering thought behind him.

"What was the next step, my love. Support of your propaganda? Flaunt that reptilian stamp? Follow me or subject yourself to the fate of those who don't." His voice exploded. "Who are the Nixodonian leaders, Marie?"

The force of his voice lost its impact as Marie's mind began to sort the pieces of the puzzle. She became almost oblivious to his steady advance, his half-clenched hands.

"Paul never told me where we were going for our honeymoon," she muttered, her eyes lost to the floor.

"You're avoiding the question."

"No. I'm not. I am answering it, and if you'd believe me for just one second, you'd see that it does make sense. Paul was going to take me on a special honeymoon, all right. Then he and his cohorts were somehow going to force me into their propaganda movement. There wasn't going to be a honeymoon." Her shoulders trembled with the horror of the nightmare that pervaded her life like a silent, deadly cancer. They'd picked her out for this. They'd kept her completely ignorant of the conspiracy knowing that she would have fought them to the death before allowing them to use her this way. Now it was too late for her to change anything. When did it all start? How long ago?

"Of course there wouldn't be a honeymoon," Richard scoffed. "You'd be far too busy organizing your manhunt."

Marie's head fell back. "Don't start with me, Commander." Her words were biting. "So quick are you to find a scapegoat for your very serious problem! You're so damned afraid of losing your precious nation that you can't look at the facts and see them for what they are. Some ruler you are. Who am I? An innocent woman caught in a betrayal beyond her scope of understanding, and yet you stand there, hands ready to wring the life out of me. Well, go ahead, Commander. Do it! Then see if your problem goes away."

They stood there only feet apart, eyes clashing like ice and fire, bodies strained, auras flashing in an invisible battle. Marie's lungs burned, tears coursed down her cheeks, but she had to continue. Continue on her hopeless, fiery fall.

"That whole propaganda movie has been fixed, and fixed well. I've been used in the worst possible way, and they'll toss me to the dogs when they're finished with me. I don't know about your stupid Route 86. I don't know about any bases, or any leaders, and I *do not* know how they did this to me." She flung a hand toward the screen.

"And if you don't believe me, why don't you use those drugs on me. The ones you said would kill me. Perhaps I'll hold on long enough for you to see that no answers will come. Did you stop to think that I didn't talk on that pirate ship because I had nothing to say? And I won't in five minutes, or tomorrow. Thank you very much for thinking that I'm such a hard-core agent that nothing can crack my steel hull, but sorry, all you have is a puppet. I'm useless to you, Richard Shaw." She thrust her chin at him. "So, go ahead. Put me out of my misery."

She shot her arms out to either side. "Kill me Richard, if I am what you accuse me of. A whore, an agent, a traitor, TRAITOR: to Nixodonia, to Telexa, to the whole goddamned galaxy. If it isn't you, it will be someone else. You were right. You may as well keep the pleasure of killing me to yourself."

She stood with her arms out wide, shaking so badly that the cross she formed threatened to collapse. He didn't move. To her great astonishment, he didn't rush on her and kill her. She couldn't wait for death. Not like this. "Do it!" she screamed. "What are you waiting for? The last scene, the closing act? If that is what you want, then turn that machine back on. Give me one last dignifying act, one that will surely mark the end of the innocence of Marie Flechette. Do it! Put that whoring scene back on, and even if it's far too late for me, I'll prove to you that the body there isn't mine." She tore off the cape. "It's not me, Richard. I have no stamp on my chest. You want proof? Then, so be it."

She began to pull at the nightgown but before she'd gotten it past her knees, he'd clamped his arms around her. She pushed against him. "Don't deny me this," she cried hoarsely. "I need you to know I'm innocent. I need somebody to know that I'm innocent before I die."

Together they collapsed to their knees. Richard crushed the broken woman to his chest, rocking her back and forth without awareness of his acts.

"I know. I know." It was the only thing that came to his lips.

Marie ended her struggle and fell against him, unconscious of her own loud and painful cries. Richard's whole body quivered with the intensity of the drama. He pulled her head against his chest, buried his lips in her hair, smashed his eyes shut against his inner turmoil. But he knew. He'd known from the moment he'd laid eyes on her. He knew she was innocent, even before bringing her to this room.

And she'd hit him where it hurt. She was right. He wanted to lay the guilt on her, take it off himself. The bloody, selfish coward. And now she was a fugitive waiting to die at his hands because it was a better option than dying at the hands of the millions she would be forced to betray. His soul tore apart for them both. How could she love a man who had enslaved her for his own ends? How could he bear the knowledge that she could never truly give him her heart. He was a leader, she was a fugitive. Again, oil and water.

He tore the thought from his mind. They were survivors. Both of them. And fate had ways of twisting its threads in unforeseen ways. Richard held her hard while breathing raggedly. He had to grasp at the only thread that fate left dangling in front of him. He must protect her.

Suddenly, he dared not let her go lest she flit away like a butterfly beyond his hope of ever capturing again. His palm cupped the back of her head. His mouth crushed down on hers as if to devour the monsters that ravaged her life. He kissed her with more vigor than he'd intended and she clawed at him fiercely. She tore at his hair, pounded at his shoulders. Finally, she pushed away and gasped for breath. Desperately she pleaded. "Not like this. Please don't kill me like this. Not you."

The words startled him. He shook his head, but only gave her enough respite to explain in vain that he shared her pain. "*No*. I would never do that. I'll never hurt you again!"

Less harshly, his mouth was against hers. Her quivering hands clutched at his shoulders. He reacted by pulling her tighter to him. One hand clasped around her, the other still cupping the back of her head he pressed her into his kiss.

Irrationally, Marie joined in the passion.

Her mind was foggy, her faculties dim, daring her consciousness to dip deep within her soul where her sense of survival awakened, and exploded. Suddenly she was grasping for him, pulling at his hair, answering his kiss by demanding more. She felt his hardness against her. Unwillingly, the words to "Follow Me" penetrated the fog in her brain.

> *"Life is a paradox,*
> *Untangle the mystery, untie the knot."*

Even the paradox was changing. She was losing her life, yet life was the mystery itself. The paradox was the death of her own body and the pulsing life in the one who held her. His loins burst with heat against hers revealing the life that needed release from his body. But she couldn't have it. She was dying. Yet in her final, desperate moments, she pleaded with him to share his life with her, pleaded for one thread that might tie her back into the fabric of the living. The fog swirled in the horrors, in the deception of her song. Now she saw her own cries, saw her own empty heart. She saw with clarity her prayers float and drift aimlessly to a god she could not find. No one could follow her. She was lost. She heard the wreckage of her past pound inside her head. She heard the faraway cries of sadness from a soul that was sinking...sinking.

Richard clung to the woman slumping in his arms. Clumsily, he laid her down on the cape she had thrown to the floor. With waning strength, she reached for him. Slowly, he lowered his body over hers, covering her, protecting her. He kissed her face, her neck. A hand roamed about her breasts, her thighs, as if the cotton garment was not between them. She clung to him, yet with each passing moment her grip weakened.

He could feel her slipping away. "Marie. Marie, my love, stay with me."

"Give me your life...before I die." With a final effort she circled an arm around his waist, pulling his loins against hers. "Life...so I don't die."

"Marie!"

Her eyes closed. Her body sank limply against the floor as she lost consciousness. Richard tensed, watching her in appalled disbelief. He blinked. Her chest rose and fell, slowly, shallowly, but steadily. He should call Dr. Faulk. Immediately!

Instead, he stole a few precious moments, tracing her lips then moving his fingers through her hair. "I'll give you life, my love. That, I promise you."

CHAPTER 29

High in the mountains of Rashmar, tucked within a crude refuge, a native propped his elbows against a rocky outcrop and peered through a set of binoculars. The rims felt cold against his face, the temperatures having risen only minimally since the sun had reached its azimuth. He peered over jutting peaks that rose fifty thousand feet above the narrow valleys and gorges below. Scanning the skies, he waited until there was unmistakable evidence of his target before disturbing his master who'd suddenly fallen into an exhausted slumber beside him. The Master was bundled in a fur-lined cape, held together by thick scarves wrapped about his neck and middle. Embroidered moccasins poked out from beneath the cape. The fur-rimmed hood shielded all but a long nose that thrust from beneath it.

Suddenly, the young native dropped the binoculars and attended to the obsolete radar set propped on the rocks beside him. Quickly, he analyzed the auditory reading that bleeped from the cloth-covered speakers. Slapping the binoculars back against his eyes, he searched desperately. The signal indicated that an intergalactic freighter was within their range but the bleeps that accompanied that signal worried him. His friends in the sky were not alone.

A symphony of high-pitched whines jolted the old master from his slumber. Groggily, he watched his pupil search the skies.

"I've got them!" the young Selpin cried. A tight grimace stretched across Selpin's face as he watched a small speck drop at a suicide speed from the clouds. Right behind that speck were two larger dots—Reptilian gunships in hot pursuit.

The elderly master grasped his student's shoulder. "What do you see, Selpin? Do you see them?"

"I sure do, Master Farol. Your mind-link with Javid was successful, but they've got two gunships right behind them. Poor Javid must have his mind full just trying to stay alive."

The old master stood beside Selpin. "Mind full or not, the link I achieved with Javid was a feeble one. Life in Nix States has weakened his powers a great deal."

Abruptly, Selpin tossed the binoculars to his master and twisted toward the radar set. "They're coming this way," Selpin cried, "and those gunships are firing at them like mad!"

Master Farol put the lenses to his eyes. Being unaccustomed to this kind of guidance system, he found himself dizzied by wide, blurring swaths of sky before managing to focus on the action. The small ship dipped dangerously close to the craggy horizon and Farol gasped. His heart leapt wildly when he saw the ship bounce up again, still in one piece. "They're headed for the Ocar Pass!" Farol shouted as he watched the ship drop behind one of the mountains into what was the longest and deepest fissure on the planet.

"Perfect. That means they've locked onto our signal," Selpin said. "The transmitters will guide them down the pass to the Cousta Canyon Base."

"I'll warn the base that they're on their way," Farol offered.

Javid clung to the steering column with all his might as the drop in altitude left his heart somewhere up in the stratosphere. Clive's rickety trade ship was having a bad time keeping up to the demands they were putting on it, grinding and yawing on tight corners as they maneuvered in a wild escape from the enemy.

Another laser marked their ship. The craft went tumbling uncontrollably through a thick cloud layer. Breaking through the clouds, the planet appeared cockeyed and swaying in the view port. One of Javid's sweaty palms clenched the steering column as he maneuvered the ship with less finesse than he'd been recently taught. He feared he might make a mistake that would crash them nose first into the planet.

Clive scrambled back to the cockpit. The aft section had taken a hit that penetrated the rear blast shields, but Clive could do nothing but throw chemicals on smoldering wires. He didn't dare think of what his ship looked like on the outside, but if it still flew, the only thing to do was keep flying it.

Javid's reflexes had liquefied into soupy, hypnotic motions, his eyes and mind mesmerized by the bobbing and spinning planet's surface. His voice broke as Clive returned. "I'm not doing very well with this lesson, Clive!"

Clive reached for his seat, but gravity tossed him violently sideways. "Pull it up!"

"I can't remember how."

"The left lever, yeah, that one. Pull hard!"

The planet's surface disappeared as the nose cranked in an upward spiral. With brute strength, Clive clung to the back of the captain's chair and pulled himself around, throwing himself into it. The emergency harness automatically wrapped around him, securing him into place. Seconds later he took over from the much shaken Javid. "They're right on our tails," he shouted. "Two of them."

Javid glanced behind him only to see the door of the cockpit. He swallowed hard. "We could go back into space," he suggested. "Maybe our ship can make the transition faster than those gunships can, and we could lose them."

"Are you kidding? There'll be a hundred of them waiting for us out there."

Javid's face blanched. "Are you sure we're even on the right side of this planet?"

"I think so."

"I thought you knew the way into Rashmarian territory."

"And I thought you knew *whom* I had an affair with!"

"You are in unauthorized air space. Please land your craft immediately." The console blurted the message at them for the tenth time.

Clive finally found a second to smash the receiver. "Shut up!" he yelled at it. "We have to be close to the Rashmarian base now. So, we've gotta lose these fellas."

Javid thought he might faint. All the way back here to get blown to smithereens by his worst enemy. The ship took a hard blow, tossing it violently sideways. Javid let out a screech. The lights of the control panel flickered and hooted in protest.

"Jeez, we're gonna take one that this baby won't hold!" Clive hissed.

Another attack sent the two grabbing for anything they could as their chests were slammed against the harnesses. The panel shrieked with a sudden burst of staccato. Clive scanned the instruments in confusion but Javid's mouth fell open. So, he *had* heard a telepathic message from Master Farol. The Master had instructed Javid to listen for a special honing code.

"That's it!" Javid yelled. "Down there!"

He pointed at a long, narrow chasm that looked no wider than a thread from their altitude. Javid wasn't sure if Clive recognized it as well, but without hesitation, the ship dropped several thousand feet and slithered straight into the gorge. The gunships had to abort direct pursuit through the narrow canyon into which the compact freighter disappeared.

Escape lay down the long, stupendous trench that formed a tunnel at its far end. The tunnel was still several miles ahead of them, but if they could shoot out the other end and put the mountain range between themselves and the gunships—then land this freighter, they might be able to escape.

Clive knew that even one blast from those gunships could disintegrate them, so the enemy obviously wanted them alive. Clive could *not* conceive being back in the hands of the TRA.

When the gunships realized his escape plan, they volleyed a salvo of cannon blasts in one last attempt to down the trespassers. Clive poured every ounce of strength into maneuvering the ship down the gorge, his only hope against rotten odds.

Javid found himself crying out in panic, arms continually flying over his eyes to hide the onrush of rocky slabs. Then one of those last-attempt lasers hit their mark. The ship bounced like a yo-yo. The two looked at each other, amazed that it kept flying. Suddenly, a fine white powder burst from malfunctioning fire extinguisher nozzles, filling the cockpit with a cloud of opaque dust. Simultaneously, another run of staccato beeps emitted from the control panel and Javid's ears tuned into it like overcharged antennae.

"AAhhhh," was all that came from Clive.

Javid grabbed Clive's forearm. "That's it! It's them!" he yelled.

"We're on fire!" Clive roared, fighting to undo his belt.

Javid glanced behind him. "The powder's doing the trick. Fly the ship, you big lout!"

"Fly the ship?" he coughed, "I can't see a damn thing."

"The signal. It's them again. They're guiding us in, Clive. Fly the ship!"

"I can't," Clive barked, flinging his arms about in an attempt to clear the choking chemical powder.

"With your eyes closed. You can do it!"

A noise epitomizing death—the grinding of metal against stone—jolted Clive's survival instincts. Leaning low to squint at the panel, he flipped on the auxiliary deflector shields. The main shields had been annihilated in the last blast. The auxiliaries were barely powerful enough to keep the ship from pulverizing itself against the canyon walls. Clive was minutely relieved to remember that the canyon straightened soon, but the panel in front of him had vanished completely. He grabbed the scarf Javid had given him for mind practice and covered his nose and mouth. Javid had already pulled his shirt up over the bridge of his nose. The two hollered instructions at each other in total blindness for a time that seemed far too long for the Nixodonian.

A crooked grin began to form on Clive's mouth as he connected with the instruments, became the thrusters, felt the power of the deflector shields. He listened to Javid's interpretation of the ancient radar signal and followed the instructions that guided them down the canyon, nothing but a ghostly silhouette through the swirling powder.

Darkness hit instantaneously as they entered the tunnel. The brightly colored instrument panel pierced the white mist. Brows damp, they homed into the signal that became stronger with every bleep. The oppressive smell of sulfur, acid, and smoke began to penetrate the cabin followed by the distinct smell of fire, unabated.

The ship burst out of the canyon, billowing smoke in its wake as the wounded craft hurled forward into the next valley. The glen below had a smooth cup-shaped bottom lined with evergreens in striking contrast to the semi circle of gray snow-capped peaks jutting majestically into a deep blue sky.

All the majesty was lost on Clive. There wasn't a single place to land! Yet the signal was at its peak strength. It was too late. The two had begun to suffocate from the fumes and were barely conscious when the ship gave out and dropped to the level of the treetops. Clive did his best to slow the crate down so that they could perhaps land with the trees as a buffer; and that's exactly what happened.

Javid's chest was crushed against the harness, his eyes wide open as huge branches, then entire trees slammed against the canopy before snapping in two like sticks. The snow-covered ground loomed, then the ship's bottom hit with an ear-shattering boom. It continued on a screeching grate as it toppled more trees and flattened boulders on its sliding journey to a violent halt.

Silence.

Only one emergency signal beeped feebly from the tired console as the two broke into fits of ragged coughing. The smell of fire overcame the hazard of the chemical powder and, without discussion, they untangled themselves from their seats. Javid's strength was nearly spent but he struggled with frantic urgency to get behind the captain's chair where he retrieved his cape from the utility locker. Clive strained against the manual handles of the emergency airlock. With a pop that caused a sharp pain in Javid's ears, the lock crashed open, the incline of the ship tilting in its favor. Javid sucked in the icy mountain air that rushed into the cabin. He then coughed sharply, expelling more of the corrosive powder. With renewed strength, he pulled out one of Clive's bulkier spacesuits from the adjoining locker. Javid may have been away a long time, but he knew survival would not be possible against the freezing temperatures of the high mountains without these. He tossed both overcoats to Clive.

"Thanks buddy. Now let's clear this thing." Clive helped Javid out of the airlock where Javid gave immediate, reverent praise to his gods. Raising his countenance toward the towering peaks, he stretched his arms in thanksgiving. A radiant smile beamed from his sooty features as he closed his eyes against the blinding Rashmarian sun. He was alive! And he was home.

"Come on, save the litany for later," Clive rebuked, shoving the cape against Javid's chest.

As Javid donned the cloak, his gaze trailed down the length of the ship. Black smoke billowed from the rear quarter. Large licks of flame propelled the smoke on a rushing, upward journey. The craft had sculpted a wide swath through the virgin forest and Javid knew it was years of litanies that had invoked the protection that allowed them to inspect the carnage of this crash. He turned and followed Clive who was stumbling toward the trees that were thickest at the nose of the craft.

The force of the explosion that happened a second later came on like a power hose against Javid's back, driving him to the ground by a voluminous spray of expanding debris. Large shards of steel flew past him, followed by the tonnage of a shredding interior. Javid was pummeled to the frozen earth until the roaring noise was muted by the sheer volume of debris burying him. He tried calling out to Clive but his voice was muffled against the ground. He couldn't move. He couldn't open his eyes. He could only clutch with fright at the cold ground beneath him.

Seconds later, Javid's other senses failed him.

*   *   *   *

Dawn broke on the planet of Enderal. Along the horizon, a crescent of soft red hues feathered with shades of yellow introduced the arrival of the sun as it poked its shimmering face blindingly through a cloudless sky.

Enderal City had only begun to stir with its usual morning bustle. Sections of the city under the protection of envirobubbles still glowed with night lights, enhancing the reflection of the colorful morning sky.

Many buildings were not under the protection of the domes. One sprawling empire, the dozen buildings composing the nucleus of Flechette Cosmetics, reflected the ruddy sunrise off its ebony windows. The night staff neared the end of their vigil and awaited the shift change, marking a new day of business at the hub of the intergalactic cosmetics center.

But today would not be like any other.

Without warning, half-way up the tall, black crystalline main tower, an explosion erupted blowing out one floor of the building. Deafening, earth shattering, and crippling, a tiny black box set for detonation had reached zero. The second of silence that immediately followed was as deafening as the blast itself. Then alarms began to clang throughout the complex. In the heart of the city, disaster station consoles shrieked, sirens began yelping, and the city awoke to grieve the second great misfortune of Flechette Cosmetics.

CHAPTER 30

Marie had not expected a second visit to the medic unit. She lay on her side, gazing listlessly at the familiar medical cabinet alongside the heavy drapes surrounding her cubicle. Her soul felt empty but her mind was overcrowded with ramifications over the events of her betrayal.

Before she had time to think about him, he stood at her bedside. She stared first at the belt that secured well-pressed trousers. Through the corner of her eye she watched long white strands fall forward as he bent down to look at her. He spoke in a whisper, even though her eyes were open. "Marie?"

She didn't answer. She felt paralyzed, unable to rid herself of the tear that rolled off the bridge of her nose. He did it for her, gently wiping away the moisture before turning her chin to face him. She rolled onto her back but could only give him a look of anguish.

"The doctor says you'll be fine," he told her. "How are you feeling?"

She shrugged her shoulders. Suddenly, her anguish burst forth. "They've ruined me! They've ruined my family. Everyone will suffer because of me. Oh, I wish you had killed me. I want to die."

He pushed the hair from her eyes. "You don't want to die, Marie. Everything will be fine. You'll stay here with me, and when this mess is over, you'll be able to return home. They can't win, Marie." His voice lacked conviction.

"They will win! What can I do against that kind of manipulation?"

"You can fight back."

She shook her head vigorously. "No. For months I've been telling them to *follow me*. To where? To hell, that's where! No one will believe that I'm innocent of these atrocities."

"Yes, they will, Marie. What you need now is to get some rest. You're safe here. No one will find you."

"Safe?" she retorted in a hollow tone. "No, I'm not." She fought the onrush of delirium. "You'll hand me over to the metal man now, and he'll kill me so that you can wash your hands of my blood. That's the plan, isn't it?"

Metal man? Did she mean Boro? He was unable to suppress a smile. "No, I'm not handing you over to Captain Boro, or to anyone. I promise you that."

She glared hotly at him, her eyes glassy with frustration and uncertainty.

Dr. Faulk burst into the cordoned area and shared a glance with the Commander. With his usual hasty manner, the doctor used some of his instruments to check on her overall condition. Speaking to the Commander, he said, "She is doing much better now, but she needs more rest. He looked down at Marie and smiled. "You're doing just fine. You'll be completely recovered in no time."

Marie looked away as the doctor injected a solution into her upper arm. Richard frowned. Perhaps she'd recuperate physically, but he wasn't sure that her emotional recovery would be so quick. The doctor rummaged through the medical cabinet. "I'll do a few more tests."

"Sure, doc. I'll get out of your way." Without thinking, he bent down and pressed a kiss on Marie's forehead just as Dr. Faulk spun back towards the bed. Richard straightened quickly, an exploding blush evident. He patted Marie's hand. "I'll see you later."

Ignoring the doctor's wide eyes, the Commander parted the curtains and left.

A coffee mug clutched in one hand, a boot flung up on the desk, Richard slumped with exhaustion in his office chair. Across from him sat Reese Mondiran who tapped the end of his commlink against the scuffed surface of Richard's desk. "I've questioned Tripp several times now, and so has Hollis. We think he's innocent, so we proved it by doing a little psychological test. We showed him the *Angel's Test* clips this morning."

"And?"

"I had only a few minutes with him before being called away, but my guess is that he'll have the place torn apart by now. He's a good man. I like him. But don't say anything nasty about his boss-lady!"

Richard had received most of Reese's reports on Tripp while on the run. The narratives spanned from Tripp's mental attitude, to the size of his eyeballs. Reese rarely missed a detail but Richard wished he'd find a way to shorten his accounts a shade. Nevertheless, he would be well prepared to officially meet the man. He shared his tactics with Reese. "I'll soften him up by telling him Marie's all right."

Reese raised his eyebrows. "Marie? No Miss Flechette, or heiress?"

Richard grinned. "Jealous? I gave you authority over Bill Tripp who also came off the same starcruiser. You should consider yourself fortunate."

Reese laughed. "You drag me out to this ball of rock where we outnumber the women ten to one, and then steal the Princess of Nixodonia for your sole pleasure. Some friend."

"Just doing my job," Richard grinned. "But seeing as I'm the Commander, here," he jabbed a finger into his chest, "I get to see your prisoner, but you don't necessarily get to see mine."

"Then you'd better get your ass over to see mine, ya selfish bastard," Reed laughed.

Richard stood and rounded the desk. Just as he stepped through the door he heard Reese shout, "Don't forget who takes your place if anything happens to you."

Bill Tripp stood when Richard entered the interrogation room. Richard looked the man over carefully. He was in tremendous physical condition for his age, perhaps five or ten years older than himself. Tripp wasn't tall, but the muscular frame exuded brute strength. His balding head glinted in the brightness of the small chamber, his jaw tense. Tripp's stance looked like that of a madman ready to attack anything that might threaten his charge.

"I am Commander Shaw," the Fringe leader offered.

Tripp nodded slowly. "I know."

"I understand that you watched the *Angel's Test* clips this morning."

Tripp's chest heaved with controlled rage. "Commander Shaw, Marie Flechette had nothing to do with the changes in that movie, nor has she had any involvement with those arms deals, or any other aspect of the Telexan rebellion. I know that a lot of raw footage was taken of her during her acting lessons, and I worried about foul play, but I didn't expect anything of this magnitude. And, you don't have to explain the implications of this to me!"

"You're quite concerned, for a bodyguard."

"You bet I am. I've been her primary agent for twenty-seven years. You were right about one thing. If Marie was involved with the TRA, I would more than likely be privy to that knowledge. It's why you brought me here, isn't it?"

Richard looked askance at Tripp. "Are you telling me that you were with Miss Flechette during her acting lessons, yet you weren't *concerned* enough to act on your suspicions?"

"That was the problem. I was always in the building, but Marchand refused to let me into the inner studios saying his own security would take over from there. Unfortunately, Raymond Flechette didn't think this was unusual. That must have been when all of this came together. And no doubt, all of Marie's time at the studio gave Paul the opportunity to mess about in her lab."

Tripp had it all figured out, Richard scoffed to himself. "How well did you know her fiancé?"

"Well enough to know that I didn't trust the man. Fortunately for him, most of his time with Marie was spent inside the Flechette mansion. Much as I would have liked to dissuade Marie from her involvement with him, I'm in no position to advise her in her personal affairs."

"What didn't you like about him."

"He's a slimy operator. I escorted them on a few early engagements and realized right way that he had every line practiced. I had to convince myself that it was just my suspicious nature, but I see now that I was right. The Flechettes didn't see that in him, but I think they'd waited so long to find a suitable mate for Marie that a company man seemed too good to be true."

"Yes, how do you marry off Marie Flechette?"

"I'm afraid she'll never get a chance to find out if that movie gets out."

"Oh, I'm sure it already has. In Telexa at least. I don't yet know about Nixodonia."

Bill's voice rose. "This is extremely damaging material. Do you know what this will mean to the young and malleable population of Nixodonia?"

"I believe I do, Mr. Tripp. And not just Nixodonia. This is the Fringe, if no one has let you in on that yet. We confiscated the disk off one of *your* government vessels on its way to Telexa, and what Telexa gets, often our population gets, as well as the Kingdoms and the Blue Rift. I'm sure that's a calculated part of the plan."

After a long minute in a staring match with the Commander, Tripp gave an audible huff. "I suppose I can't blame you for the attack on the *Starquest* then, although I can't say I applaud your methods."

"We didn't have much time, so I sent out my best man. The fact that Captain Boro was a shade demented by his handicap turned out to be in our favor."

"Well, bravo. You probably fooled everyone. I certainly wouldn't have guessed that a pirate might be on government business."

Shaw smirked. "My advantage, then."

"What are you going to do with Marie now? They'll kill her the instant she sets foot in Nixodonia, if not by the jackasses who are responsible for this, then by the public who won't believe that she's innocent."

"It seems those jackasses are well infiltrated into your government."

"So you'll dispose of her for them?"

Richard was afraid his own eyes might deceive him. His gaze was clamped on Tripp's, and Shaw suddenly understood his long-term employment with the Flechettes. "No." Richard assured him. "I won't kill her. It would serve no purpose."

The bodyguard visibly released the tension locked in his shoulders. "Then you believe that she's been exploited on both counts?"

"Perhaps. But I won't release her, nor you. Not at this time anyway."

"I didn't expect that. In fact, in light of all this information, I would hope that you wouldn't release Marie, for her sake."

"Your loyalty astounds me."

"I have children of her age, with families of their own. They deserve to live in peace and freedom and it's up to us to provide that future for them."

Richard did not answer.

"Commander Shaw. I know you had good reason to bring Marie here. I also know that Marie would have been forced to promote that propaganda, and therefore you've inadvertently saved her from that for the time being. I don't know how well protected she is here because I don't know exactly where we are, but they'll be looking for her. Extensively. Lieutenant Mondiran told me that Telexa has fallen. They'll want to find Marie very soon, and if they find her in your possession, you'll be at risk for some serious pounding from both your borders."

Tripp stopped suddenly, as if to gather his thoughts. Richard, who was rather surprised at who was running this interview, decided to let Tripp blow himself out.

"If the TRA is as strong as it appears, the entire galaxy is at risk of losing its freedom. You. Me. All of us. There are only two sides to this war now, Commander, and the Fringe is one of them. My guess is that Telexa is planning a swift move into Nix States and they'll simply engulf you in the process. Is that accurate enough?"

"Accurate enough."

"And Nix States doesn't think this can happen. I think it can, and I think it will. We aren't prepared, and I doubt that you're strong enough to face the TRA alone. I don't know what we can do to save ourselves but we have to do something!"

Richard eyed him coolly. Tripp was a smart man, a devoted man. He was almost afraid that he might give in immediately to what Tripp was about to suggest. He needed extra men, that was for sure.

"Commander Shaw. This is ludicrous coming from a prisoner, but I think that the innocence of Marie and myself is clear to you. We have been no less manipulated than the billions of other Nixodonians who are about to have martial law slammed in their faces. I'm an experienced agent. I know the Flechettes, their associates, their connections, right up to the High Court. Surely, sifting through these people will give us clues as to who might be involved on a government level. Henrie Marchand and Paul Lambert are hardly in this conspiracy alone, although finding them might quickly lead us to the rest of them."

"Possibly."

"There's no hope if we don't fight back as allies, Commander. I want you to consider letting me join in the struggle from here, from the Fringe."

Richard Shaw clamped his jaw, his mind overwhelmed with the proposal. Tripp was right. He could be an important spy with access to critical areas his own spies could never hope to access in time.

"I'll discuss it with my committee," Shaw said. He spun and left the chamber. Walking to his jeep, he muddled over Tripp's words. *There are only two sides to this war now.* Perhaps he hadn't pillaged the wrong man off the *Starquest* after all.

CHAPTER 31

Mayhem erupted at the Flechette mansion. Raymond and Genevieve had been asleep when the call came through on the emergency line. The two immediately thought it was news about Marie. Instead, this? An explosion in the mainframe suite? Raymond was beside himself. He had been in the computer suite only hours before, unraveling the first threads of Paul Lambert's mystery.

A helicopter whisked them across the city toward the complex where black smoke tainted the early morning sky. As soon as they landed, a shuttle took them as close as it could to the site. The couple gaped at the inferno blasting out of the side of their main office building. The lurid silhouette of the ebony tower reflected in Raymond's horror-filled eyes. At least there'd been no casualties.

FC's finance director approached the couple. "It's the mainframes!" he needlessly informed. "I'm not sure we'll be able to save any of them."

"Probably not," Raymond shouted over the roar of the blaze. They weren't meant to be saved, he thought to himself. His gaze returned to the scene where emergency aircraft attempted to contain the fire to the three floors it now engulfed.

"What a mess. It'll take weeks to recover the data from the back-ups," the director said.

"That lousy bastard!" Raymond growled beneath his breath.

Genevieve heard him. She didn't have to ask of whom he spoke as she wondered about Paul's motives. The Fire Commissioner approached them. Not a word about Paul escaped Raymond's lips. He told the Commissioner that he had no idea what could have happened, so they were to carry on with their investigation. Genevieve held her tongue.

The Flechettes experienced a sense of hopeless relief when the flames were finally extinguished and the black smoke dwindled to a few thin funnels. Chilled to the bone, Raymond ordered hot drinks and snacks to be served in his office in the adjoining tower.

"Why didn't you tell the Fire Commissioner that you suspect foul play?" Genevieve asked over her coffee cup.

Raymond sighed and leaned against his desk. "Because, we need to see what they come up with first. Besides, sharing my suspicions about Paul with just anyone might cause yet another scandal we don't need."

"The Fire Commissioner isn't just anyone, Raymond."

"Well, I thought it best to inform Rhodes or Phoebe first." He threw his hands up in exasperation. "Maybe I won't even tell them. They don't seem to want to help us."

"They're doing the best they can, and this may have nothing to do with Marie. Maybe it was a simple malfunction."

Raymond grunted. "There's been no malfunction, Gen. After what I discovered last night, it's quite clear that Paul needs to cover his tracks, but for what reason? Do you realize that we're now out of contact with almost every one of our off-planet outlets, Doria included? What's happening on Doria that we're not supposed to know about? I'll just bet that when we contact them about the fire, they'll insist they're fine. Don't bother sending anyone all the way out here, they'll say!" Raymond was shouting.

"Then, I'll make the call myself." Genevieve slammed her cup down.

It took several hours for the Dorian outlet to reply to the hyperwave relay. Raymond dug his fingers into Genevieve's shoulder as the message began to come through.

"*We send our greatest regrets about the problems with the mainframes,*" a female voice echoed from the speakers while the conversation printed out on the screen before of them. "*There is no need to send immediate support. We are well equipped here and will take measures to accommodate for this situation.*"

Genevieve heard Raymond expel his breath. "I'm going to Doria."

She spun around to see his eyes intent on the screen. Panic-stricken, she took him by the arm and led him back to the office.

"What do you mean, you're going to Doria?" she asked, slamming the door shut.

"Just what I said." He looked at his wife hollowly. "Not today." he added.

"Not ever! You're not well, Raymond. I don't think it's in our best interest for you to go traipsing across the galaxy on some wild goose chase. For what?"

"I don't know," he bellowed. "The same thing that drove me here last night to find out all those things about Paul in the very computers he just destroyed. But he doesn't know that his secrets are not altogether safe. He thinks no one is on to him. Especially me! I need to know what's really going on. Maybe he's even holding Marie there."

Genevieve gave a huff. "I highly doubt that."

"Why? It might be the best guess we've had yet. Not a word for nearly two weeks. Doesn't that strike you as being rather peculiar? It's not like she just disappeared. We all know how it happened. And now, nothing? Senator Phoebe gives me these pitiful looks when he comes up with one dead end after another."

"He's doing the best he can."

Raymond shot his wife a glance, "For whom, I wonder. Certainly not for us. Personally, I've come to distrust the man."

"You don't trust him? So, now what? Are you going to become a vigilante in a personal campaign to find Marie?"

He nodded vigorously. "Yes, Marie *and* Bill Tripp."

"Tripp! A fine job he did of protecting our daughter," Genevieve stopped short, realizing her blunder. A hand flew to her forehead. "I didn't mean that."

Raymond heaved with exasperation. "Maybe not, but you said it. And if you can say that, I'm going to say how absolutely sick I am of the thousands of fans stuck, it seems permanently, outside our estate gates. Don't any of them ever go home?"

"Those fans are a direct result of *your* cosmetics, and what you made of Marie. And, those fans are now here to support us!" she defended.

"Well, we don't need that kind of support. Great Creator, we can't even breathe anymore. Is this what we've become?" He flung a hand through the air. "Have I created a monster?"

"Yes, and it's eating us up." Genevieve croaked.

Raymond looked at his wife, aghast. The truth slapped him hard in the face. Devastation ripped through his core as Genevieve began to cry. "Then I'd better make it right again," he said with tender urgency.

Genevieve walked over to him and leaned into his embrace. "I didn't mean that about Bill," she said, weeping. "And now they're both gone."

"So, we'll find them," Raymond muttered into her hair. "Both of them."

Pain shot through his hip and down his leg. He was dying and he knew it, but be damned if he would let the likes of Paul Lambert ruin them. Paul was about to find out how much fortitude Raymond Flechette still had.

"Darling, I need to go to Doria, even though I can't explain what's pulling me there."

She looked at him with tear-filled eyes. "I know. But I can't go with you. Someone has to be here for Marie, in case she comes home."

"Ah, my love. Thank you." He looked at her and made a promise they both knew he couldn't keep. "I'll come back to you." He cupped her face in his hands. "And when I do, I'll find a way to bring peace into our lives once again."

CHAPTER 32

Marie was sitting in the hospital bed, just finishing her meal when Richard checked on her again. She'd brushed her hair, the black rims under her eyes were less evident, but the underlying despair was betraying itself by a stiff posture and hollow stare.

"Hi," he chirped, wondering how such a wisp of a girl could manage to kick his confidence completely off balance. "I didn't know you were still eating."

"You've watched me eat before," she reminded.

He smiled. "I spoke with Doctor Faulk. He said you should get up and around. It will help your circulation. You look awfully pale." It was an excuse to touch her cheek.

"I am ready to go back to my room if the doctor says I can."

"Good. I'll send Deanna in to help you."

"That would be nice," she whispered.

He stood awkwardly then smiled stiffly before disappearing through the partition. Nurse Deanna bustled in moments later, her carefree manner and lack of deference refreshing to Marie. She gladly accepted Deanna's help to get back into those hideous undergarments and the marginally more acceptable jumpsuit.

Marie found herself enjoying the walk back to Detention where she could compare the ancient paintings on the tunnel walls to those inside her suite. The sightseeing detracted her from Richard's presence at her elbow. At least there were fewer guards trailing behind them this time.

Worn-out, she was glad to settle on the couch facing the patio doors. It was late afternoon according to Deanna, but the skies were already dark as night, laden with heavy clouds. Marie felt that the planet again perceived her emotions. A brewing storm shrouded the ancient mountaintops, the inky, churning clouds sending blankets of mist on wispy journeys to the bottom of the valley.

She smiled as Richard inspected the suite, pretending it was his job to make sure everything was in order for her. It seemed long ago since he'd kissed her on the balcony, when she felt like her life would change forever if she didn't get a grip on herself. Yet it had been only two days, and already they had bridged another tumultuous river in the course of their short time together. Marie shivered. With an inflexible hand she reached up to push the hair from her eyes. Hopelessness filled her heart like molten lead. The images she'd witnessed on the screen popped back into her mind, bringing on a barrage of horror. She blinked to erase the memories but there was no hope of their going away.

Richard sat down beside her. He reached over and touched her cold hands, further chilled by the rush of air blowing in from the open terrace doors as the storm gained momentum. "Just a minute," he said, and strode over to the terrace, pulling the old glass doors closed. Returning, he laid a hand softly at the nape of her neck. She turned and gave him a thin, haunted smile. Her eyes were swollen, her porcelain features stained by recent tears. Still, her natural beauty poured through. She was shockingly beautiful to him.

She whispered in the same haunted voice that possessed her smile. "Paul lived at the estate most of the time. He knows everything about us, our routines, our security procedures. When they release that movie, it's going to destroy me, and my family."

His hand reached up to stroke her hair. "They'll have to find you first."

She smiled thinly. "I suppose as long as I'm here, they can't use me, can they?"

"Now you're getting it."

She trembled with self-disgust. "Hoping to connect with our roots seems ridiculous now, doesn't it? I'm sure Paul has no French roots. There wasn't going to be a honeymoon, let alone an expedition to find our forgotten pasts." Anger and disappointment ravaged her features. "I just want to know who I really am, find some past record that would help me know where I belong. I don't want to belong to everybody like I do now."

"Then your life's journey isn't about FC. It's about finding yourself. It might help you to know that first you belong to Mother Universe simply by default of your existence. Another fact is that we have only the moment, whether you're Marie Flechette or a pauper on the poorest of the Blue Rift planets."

"That's easy for you to say. You have roots here."

"Not really. It was my grandfather who settled here from Nixodonia. Beyond that, I suffer the same fate as every other Nixodonian. I know very little about my roots. But, what does it take to belong somewhere? Does one generation make me a true Fringe dweller? If not, how many does it take. Five? Ten? I'm a Fringe man because I choose to be one. It's not a birthright that makes me one of them. Think about this. If you were forced to live and give birth in Telexa, would your child be Telexan, automatically absorbing its ways and customs? I wish I knew the answer, Marie, but my belief is that you belong where your heart is. And seeing as you feel lost at the moment, make this your little piece of the universe for now."

She glanced at him flatly. "I'd better not have a baby here, then. That would really confuse the issue. A Nixodonian traitor with a Fringe child. Humph!"

He smiled, and held his tongue. "You're not a traitor! In fact, the way I see things, you'll return to Nix States quite a hero."

She gave a sharp laugh. "Hero? I doubt that." Her eyes shifted sideways. "Do you really think Nixodonia will fall? They're not so weak, are they?"

He unconsciously stroked her temple. "No government is without its weaknesses. And I'm sure Angel Keem is ready to exploit every last one of them."

"Then you need to stop him."

He smiled forlornly. "I wish it was that easy. They're an oppressive force. But if they do win, I suppose our hope would lay in the fact that self-appointed rulers tend to rot quickly."

"Then why not just let it happen and save ourselves the casualties of the fight?"

Richard smiled crookedly. "I suppose that's a logical solution, but I don't think it's right. These guys are evil, Marie." Richard pushed a lock of burnished hair behind her ear. "Change is good, and often necessary, but never change driven by a madman."

She frowned. "And if you win, what will happen to the Fringe?"

"We will continue our efforts to structure our nation."

"But once you're a nation, will not the same thing happen here as it did in Nix States? I mean, there was nothing but one war after another between the sectors before Hervos Nixodonia came along to unify us. His solutions have worked, but in the event, we lost our customs and languages. So, what about the Fringe? As long as you have so much diversity, isn't there a danger that the same thing will happen here? Then someone like Angel Keem would simply do like Hervos and come and hand you his particular solution."

"Ah, but remember your history. What Hervos Nixodonia united was a group of sectors with too much tribal ego to understand compromise and not enough nationalism to govern themselves. So, unification under an entirely new set of rules was welcomed by that bunch of war weary souls."

"Yes, I suppose you're right."

"And our problem is altogether different. It isn't warfare that's urged the Fringe tribes to unite. It's the Telexan threat. So far it's working well, and it helps that we respect each other's differences."

She nodded slowly. "And Angel Keem doesn't intend to compromise."

"Nor is the word respect in his vocabulary. The difference between Hervos Nixodonia and Angel Keem is that Keem is a tyrant!"

She glanced at him again, "Richard?"

"When did you learn my name?" he asked, laughing lightly.

"Oops!" A light flush evened the stains on her cheeks. "I'm sorry, Commander, your woman, ah, what's her name? Igna. Igna told me your name."

"She's not my woman. And please, call me Richard. I've never kissed anyone who's continued to call me Commander."

She dropped her gaze and swallowed, trying very hard to ignore the tingling where he massaged the back of her neck. "I was just going to ask about Bill. Is he still okay?"

"Yes, he's fine. In fact, I'm going to send him down here to visit with you."

"Bill's coming to see me?"

She said it with such enthusiasm that it was hard for Richard to believe there was nothing but a good working relationship between the two. It was stupid to feel jealous when the woman between him and Tripp would remain in Tripp's life and not in his. "He'll be here in the morning."

"That's wonderful. Thank you." Her breath was a whisper, her eyes a pool of gratitude.

"I have to go now. Is your shoulder okay?" He leaned toward her, his fingers trailing down her deltoid.

"Yes, it's fine. Dr. Faulk took the last of the bandages off this morning."

"That's good—" His mouth clamped onto hers.

She closed her eyes, drinking in his touch. Unwillingly, she remembered the vow they'd made. Had that vow been annulled in the aftermath of *Angel's Test*? Memories of passion on the conference room floor burst through in vivid detail as his arms gathered her close to him.

They tightened their grips when the thunder pealed loudly overhead. The old, thin windows rattled and became tear-stained as the skies opened their vaults.

Strong winds whistled through the cracks of the ill-fitting windows creating a stir in the lacy curtains. Richard feared it was not the wind that moved the curtains but rather the spirit of an old priest hidden back there, peering out at him with a look of mortification.

Another crash of thunder gave Marie justification to grip him more tightly. His lips crushed hers with hungry desire, yet the tension in his body told a different story. Was he struggling with their vow as well? His lips moved down her neck, but stopped at the top of the zipper, again pulled up to its limit. He breathed heavily against the notch in her throat. Marie ardently wished she had some of Javid's powers now. She would use them to lower that zipper, but that wouldn't help. She knew why he had stopped, and she knew that she should as well.

"We don't keep vows to each other for long," she murmured, suddenly realizing her breathing matched his. His head shot up, and Marie was shaken by how attracted she was to him. It seemed impossible to suppress the ache in her loins. She suddenly remembered her last words to him before fainting on the conference room floor. *Give me your life....*

"It was a silly vow," he blurted, then cut himself off. "I'm sorry. No it wasn't. Oh, hell. I don't know. Do you have to be so damned beautiful?"

She nearly laughed. "I, ah—"

Richard kissed her again, but stopped seconds later. He gave a deep sigh while fighting to control his thoughts. They spilled from between his lips still brushing against hers. "Deanna will be in to check on you in a couple of hours. I really need to go."

"You'd best go, then." Her voice was maddeningly silky, her fists unable to let go of the crisp uniform. Was it she who pulled him closer, or he who suddenly enveloped her body with his? It didn't matter. He pressed his chest against her, pushing her down on the armrest of the couch. She clung to him, almost ready to ask aloud for some of that life pulsating through his torso.

Richard let his fingers trail across her cheek and drop to find the metal tab of the zipper's keeper. She had asked for his life force, but that had been in a moment of mindless passion. As he searched her eyes, the doubts switched off as fast as they'd plagued him. She was his prisoner, and Doctor Faulk had just filled her with sedatives. He gave a low moan. "This is ridiculous. I'm so sorry."

Marie let her head fall back, catching her breath while trying to believe the same. "You're right. For our own sakes, we should keep that vow."

He sat up straight and ran a hand through his hair. Somehow Marie found the strength to ignore the gesture, one she was finding increasingly alluring. His voice found its authority again as he stood and straightened his uniform. "I'll check on you later. Do you have everything you need?"

She nearly blurted *no*, but instead said something even more stupid. "Yes, and thank you for the antidepressant treatment."

He gave a short laugh and headed up the stone-hewn stairway. This time he stopped when he reached the landing. She noticed a glint in his eye before he opened the door and left.

It took a long time for Marie to steady her gaze which continually dragged from the rain-streaked windows to the solid door at the top of the landing. She wondered how long she would be hiding here under the care of Richard Shaw, and how long she could resist him.

There was no use thinking about it. Finally she curled up on the couch where the drumming rainfall on the windows could be her visual mantra.

Javid came to her mind. She thought perhaps that his spirit had turned into the rain and he played his drum for her, bringing her hope and courage. She began to hum little songs he'd taught her, the ones passed on to him from his ancestors. Was it that Javid was thinking of her, or was it that she was closer to Rashmar? She didn't know, but she felt his presence. And whether Javid was alive or not, she knew he would rejoice in knowing that she now found refuge with his spirit and in the prayers of his gods.

CHAPTER 33

Javid believed he was in his grave. Cold, damp darkness surrounded him. He couldn't feel his limbs yet there was warmth about his face. It felt like his eyes were open, but there was only darkness. Perhaps he was in a cocoon of death, with only a panorama of blackness to hold vigil with him till the brightness of the gods appeared.

He couldn't remember what had killed him. There was only calmness with him now. Images of Marie entered his thoughts. He felt a mixture of turmoil and resignation all at once. He fervently asked the gods to protect her now that he was no longer alive to do so. The idea that he'd failed to help her plagued at the pit of his stomach, or where his stomach had been. How was it that the gods wanted him to help the lady now that he was dead?

It wasn't long before the gods appeared. He heard crashing and muttering. The animal spirits perhaps? With a clatter and a whoosh, the brightness appeared, blinding and warm on his face.

Wait! He recognized the voice that called to him. It sounded like that of his brother! Perhaps he had joined his brother in the heavens. How comforting to hear his brother's voice.

"Javid, are you alive?" the voice cried out.

Alive? A surge of energy coursed through his frozen limbs. Yes, he was! He was alive. Javid experienced a flash of regret at not being able to see his gods at last, but the sadness quickly vanished as the rush of life lifted him from the crushing grave before his body began to stir against the cold ground beneath. He was on Rashmar! Yes, home! Bits of gravel and debris showered against his face. He really was alive! Thank the Great Creator!

"Javid, speak to us if you can."

There was that familiar voice again. Javid tried to answer but his voice was an inaudible whisper. When enough debris was cleared away, several hands took hold of him and pulled him from the rubble. The hands quickly began to sweep off his face and clothing. Javid blinked the dirt from his eyes. Soon the blotches cleared. The sight before him made his long lungs pull in great gasps of cold mountain air. His eyes went awash with moisture. "Dowlar!" he gasped. "Is it really you? My own brother, Dowlar?"

"It is I," said the near identical Rashmarian who spread his arms and clasped his disheveled brother in his arms. The two held each other a long time. Javid did not think he had cried since childhood, but now tears flowed unchecked down his cheeks. The two then clasped hands and looked at each from arms length.

"You look magnificent, my brother," Dowlar exclaimed, "Not a day older than the one that chased you away. I never doubted that you'd return to us, but the wait has been a long one." Dowlar beamed with the same long face as his brother.

Javid finally took a moment to see the other five with Dowlar. Only one could he remember, and it was like paging through the scrapbook of his mind. It was Old Man Ness, a neighbor of his parents. Javid greeted him in the traditional Rashmarian way, hands clasped, foreheads touching. Javid then greeted the others who had also come to his rescue. Suddenly, his attention turned to their surroundings. *Clive!*

"Have you found the pilot?" Javid asked with urgency. They looked at each other, aghast. With long sticks, they began to prod and poke the ground in the same manner that had produced Javid. Soon, the big lug stirred beneath the mess of debris. From the rubble, loud grunts accompanied the rise of the great Clive Whale Baker. Even in a hunched posture, weaving about trying to regain his senses, Whale towered over the Rashmarians by a foot. Everyone fussed over him, straightening the pilot's clothing, dusting him off until Dowlar let out a sudden howl. "I knew it! I knew my spell would work!"

Clive rubbed at his dirt-smeared eyes, and opened them, blinking at the fellow who had called him out. "Dowlar?"

Javid looked at his brother, then at Clive. Could it be these two had met during Clive's earlier expedition?

"Ha! you big oaf." Dowlar cried. "I knew you would come back. Remember I said that when you did come back, you'd bring my brother with you?"

Clive scowled, wanting to reach out and grab the Rashmarian by his skinny neck. That whole memory had evaporated until this very minute. But there he was, that clown Dowlar, here to heckle him again. He looked at Dowlar, then at Javid. A groan of disbelief surged from his gut. He wondered if the great Rashmarian gods had planned this whole mess as some sort of outlandish joke. "You had better not be responsible for my ship, you wily old fart," Clive grumbled, glancing back at his crumpled freighter. The rear quarter had cracked wide open and the whole thing was charred right up to the cabin. Before further comment was made, Rashmarian ears picked up the sound of approaching aircraft.

"A search ship," Dowlar said dryly. "Come on. Let's get going."

Javid glanced about the sky. "Oh dear."

"They're after us already?" Clive whined.

Dowlar gave a despondent look. "The TRA have been a bit antsy since they took over Telexa. Your arrival will definitely attract attention."

Javid gasped. "Telexa has fallen?"

"We were flying clandestine," Clive explained. "We didn't hear the news. When?"

"Just a few days ago."

Clive whistled as a hush fell over the group. They claimed to hear the buzz of two search ships in the distance. Clive could only believe them. He recalled their keen sense of hearing, and didn't care to embarrass himself by admitting he didn't hear anything. A search ship was the least of his concerns right now. He looked at the wrecked freighter and watched his entire livelihood finish off with a few coughing sputters. The twang of loss that wrung his heart came as a surprise. Ironic that he'd always cursed this hunk of tin until Javid came along to show him a new appreciation for it. Now he wished he could get this particular ship back. Never mind that he'd spent a lifetime feeling that spacecraft were simply a means to an end.

Not only that. They were stranded!

The thought hit Clive like a nuclear bomb. His voice rocketed from his mouth. "I'm stuck in TRA infested territory, and I'm stranded!"

Dowlar gave him an exasperated look. "You still have to learn about faith do you, Whale? You've been stranded in TRA territory before and survived. So will you again, unless you manage to *think* your way back into trouble."

"Think? Dowlar, do you really still believe that you can think your way in and out of things?"

"You bet, Whale."

Javid suppressed a great fit of hilarity. Whale? Is this how Clive had come to choose his code name? How he loved the jesting gods of Rashmar!

"Well you'd better *think* me my ship back, then." Suddenly, Whale did hear the buzz in the distance. Okay, I hear 'em. Let's get out of here."

The eight of them started a rushed journey down a steep, slippery path. Clive was the clumsiest of them, but as the ships approached, his feet pattered along the snow-covered trails with more urgency.

"That scout ship will be looking for any signs of life," Dowlar warned as they scurried down the narrow mountain path. "They started to hunt us down again before Telexa fell to them. Our spies have told us that they're expanding the base again. We think they want to use us as slaves or something. Your wreck will be the point of interest on this excursion, but they'll be keeping an eye out for us as well."

Clive and Javid looked at each other, questions filling their minds.

Dowlar led the small party alongside a narrow ravine sheltered by towering evergreens. Not half a mile down the side of the half-frozen gurgling brook, he led them into a small cave. Clive shivered, his damp clothing absorbing the icy chill from the rocky cavern. Iggid never got this cold! Every bone ached, his head hurt, and his shoulder had received an angry blow. No one even asked him if he was all right. Then again, the little monsters probably looked right through him and saw that he was all right. In self-disgust, he realized that what he really needed was a little pity.

Groping about, they lit torches that had been left propped along the walls. Flickering and puffing, the blazing torches revealed the cave's interior. Clive grew despondent. There was nothing here! Just a round, hopeless hole. Some hideout! Then, with a seemingly magic touch of Dowlar's hand, the back wall of the cave slid away, exposing a narrow passageway that burrowed into the bowels of the mountain. Once inside, Dowlar touched what looked like a smooth patch of rock and the door slid shut.

"Hmm," Clive mused aloud. "Your gadgets have improved."

Dowlar grinned at him. "Yup. But not yet to the point where we can regain our land from those Reptilians, although we're making progress. A little noggin, a little help from our gods, and no worries." Torch in hand, Dowlar began to lead the party down the tunnel. "In fact, to worsen your fears, my friend," Dowlar's voice echoed back to Clive, "we are in what's considered TRA territory now. Master Farol called you down to this location, rather than the one farther up the Ocar Pass."

"*What*? What for? What are we doing here?"

"We were sort of forced here. When they tried to recolonize us a few months ago we were ordered to move down from the highlands. Naturally we obeyed because, half-way down the mountain, we disappeared again. Our highland base is only about fifteen miles from here, up on that mountain." Dowlar pointed to the ceiling of the cave. Clive figured the Rashmarian thought he could see through the stupid rock, forgetting that he did not possess their powers—yet!

"All they did was move us right back to the labyrinth home of our ancestors. This cave system has been out of reach to us since the Reptilians first came."

"So, this is even *closer* to the TRA base? Didn't you have some secret hidey-hole any farther away?"

Dowlar stopped abruptly, causing the procession of bodies to pile into him. He looked back at Clive, who trailed the pack. "I gave you a tip once, Whale," Dowlar said, and Javid suppressed another giggle. "I said that often the best place to hide from your enemies is right under their noses."

Clive visibly reddened. The humor was too much for Javid, who burst into gut wrenching laughter. Had Clive not said that the best place to hide from the Phoebes was right under their noses? Getting a hold of himself, Javid turned to Clive, who looked ready to kill him.

"I think I'm just too happy to be home, Clive." Javid squealed in uncontrolled laughter.

Clive stood his ground. "You brought me down in TRA territory with no place to land!" he argued loudly, wrenching one more resentment off his chest.

"I did not." Dowlar defended. "It was you. You overshot the underground hangar by two miles. I don't argue that I was amazed the doors even opened after all these years, but they were wide open when we watched your ship fly right by with all that black smoke saying, 'We're here, we're here!'"

Dowlar frowned with regret when the group giggled. "Sorry, Whale. You couldn't have seen us by that time, especially with the hangar doors being flush with the ground, which requires a vertical landing. With this being TRA territory, we only dared open the hangar doors once we had visual contact with you, and by that time your ship was in real trouble. We were pretty scared when we heard that explosion. We closed the doors and came immediately to your rescue."

Clive grunted, not sure if he felt indebted or not.

Dowlar tossed his head. "Come on everybody. The others are waiting in the central cave."

Clive sauntered along at the rear of the pack but Javid kept pace with Dowlar. "I was so excited to learn that Mister Farol is Grand Master now."

"He is, Javid, and oh, how happy he will be to see you. He and Selpin sent you the signals from the Ocar Pass."

"My old friend, Selpin? What a blessing this is." Javid said softly, shaking his head. He could hardly believe his providence; he was back on Rashmar after all these years with some of his family and friends here to greet him despite all odds.

Clive marveled at the intricacy and consistency of the passages, although the fifteen-minute walk gave him plenty of reminders that the ceilings were not built with Nixodonians in mind. During the times he wasn't watching his head, he listened to Old Man Ness tell him how these particular tunnels had been built nearly a millennium ago. They'd been used as a secondary base and also as a refuge. They had now come into use as a refuge for the second time. The first time had been during a great volcanic eruption nearly five hundred years ago when many families had lost their lands to the lava flows. However, no livelihoods were lost because they were prepared. The eruption had been predicted through an omen, and during that time, a new omen of evil had been predicted. Now that evil was upon them. The leaders at the helm directed with unshakable faith, believing that peace would be restored, as promised.

Clive wanted to tell them that their omens were trash. Didn't they just say that Telexa had fallen to the TRA? Peace might not ensue for decades! With sudden tremulous clarity, he remembered that the Rashmarians did not consider time into the workings of their gods. Clive would have lost faith in the first six months. These folks had held out with the same zeal for over twenty years.

Clive continued to listen, trying not to get emotionally involved with their way of life and beliefs. These were not his troubles and the minute he could find a way off this block of ice, he would leave them to fight their own war. In one way, he wanted to laugh with disdain at these scrawny, long limbed short-bodied humanoids who wore their pants too short, but something told him to keep his big mouth shut.

They arrived at the central cave, a place large enough that Clive didn't feel he had to watch his head every minute. At least a hundred others greeted their group with exuberant celebration. Clive was still too irked by the situation to be very happy about anything, but he did recognize several of them from his stay two years before. Did they never die, or separate, or anything?

Thick carpets covered the floor area where they feasted, and after filling his shriveled belly, Clive promptly fell asleep.

It was a sudden lack of chatter that awoke Whale Baker. He sat up and followed the gaze of the crowd that watched the arrival of Master Farol. A smile touched his lips. It had been a long time. Clive stood, forgetting that he would tower over everyone, and of course the Master noticed him immediately. Clive had no choice but to go to him. He felt sheepish to admit that there was great honor in taking the Master's hands and bowing to touch the Great One's forehead.

"You return to us as the omen predicted," the Master said with a tender smile. "And you brought back our loved one. You will be greatly blessed for this, Mr. Baker."

Javid was in rapture at seeing the Master and followed Clive in paying his respects. The old Master looked warmly upon Javid. "Welcome home, my neighbor and my friend."

Javid's joy radiated despite the solemnity of the reunion. "I wish it were peace that brought me home, Master, but other things concern us all. My Nixodonian employer has been kidnapped, and it was that event which allowed me to return. I fear for her life, Master, because I believe this incident is somehow connected with the Telexan menace we all suffer. My powers are weak and I've been unable to see clearly the messages the gods have sent me, except to return at the first opportunity."

Clive raised an eyebrow at Javid. Nixodonian employer? He made note to ask the rascal about that later.

"You have done well," said the Master. "It is a long awaited opportunity and together we will find solutions. Later tonight, the General Council will meet in prayer, and the gods will surely direct us more clearly then."

Javid spent a long while with hands clasped and forehead touching that of Selpin's. The two had been close friends, sharing grazing and farmlands. The mountains lacked the sense of home he felt with Selpin, but it mattered little. They were together again.

The entire congregation sat themselves down facing the Master. Clive joined the brothers against the back wall of the cavern. A hush fell over the congregation, disturbed only by the central fire that crackled hotly, its fiery fingers leaping and dancing, ignorant of the Master's words.

"Many months ago, Captain Hollis of the Fringe Federation said he would try to send more help in a joint effort to regain our freedom. We must continue to keep a watchman at the lookout point day and night to guide any incoming ships to our new base location."

"How many months since this Hollis fellow came?" Clive asked Javid. "And who's your employer? Coming here was a stab in the dark, eh? What's really going on, old man?"

"Shah. Later, Clive."

"We could be here for years before anybody comes!"

"Shhhh!"

Grudgingly, Clive held his tongue.

"Meanwhile," the Master continued, "we must do what we can while the TRA are occupied with the restructuring of Telexa. If they try to resume their colonization efforts, we will have to come out of hiding to protect the other clans still up in the mountains. Only then can we begin to negotiate our freedom with the new Telexan government."

"There will be no negotiating with the Telexans, I tell you." Clive's baritone voice caterwauled over the congregation. The attention he drew to himself brought a near purple color up the Nixodonian's neck. "B-but we can maybe find ways to deal with the situation. I'll need to get back to my ship and salvage what I can, Master Farol. I have some useful caches hidden in the cockpit that the rebels hopefully won't find."

"I remind you that we do not advocate violence." The Master said.

"Fine! But I see clearly now that this isn't just your problem. This is a galactic problem, and you are not going to stop them alone. Look around. Without some sort of intervention, your personal freedom is not possible. We need galactic freedom." He glanced at the blank faces staring at him. "Well...I don't know! You guys have the noggins. I'm sure that together we can *think* up a solution of some sort, a way to get help from the other nations...or something!" Mostly Clive Baker wanted off Rashmar before he was condemned to exile here until the day he died. These were not bad folks, but they weren't Nixodonian! The women especially!

"As you wish, Mr. Baker. The control room tells us that there are scout ships scanning the area as we speak. As soon as the danger passes, I can send you out with a party."

Clive wanted to argue that he was perfectly capable of handling the expedition on his own. At the most he would need one, two—well, maybe three others to carry out his planned salvage operation. Wisely, he chose to leave the argument alone. He turned to Dowlar. "What control room? I thought the only one you had was at the upper mountain base, and that isn't anywhere near here." Clive screwed up his face. "You guys were going to land me in the trees with your radar brains, weren't you?"

Dowlar sneered. "No! Remember that we've been landing Fringe ships for years. Can't do that with your brain alone when pilots like you think that electronic waves are superior."

"You're right. I do. Now show me this control room."

Dowlar took him at a trot down another maze of tunnels more complex than the first. They emerged into a huge cavern that rendered Clive speechless. The tunnel expanded very quickly into a cave large enough for a healthy-sized landing pad. Although outmoded, it was equipped with all the support equipment and guiding mechanisms necessary to dock a spacecraft, vertically! The landing pad was cordoned off by thick transparent-steel partitions that would prevent the thrust of the landing gear from cooking the technicians to a crisp. The consoles were positioned haphazardly against any jut of rock that served the purpose, but a kind of organized chaos prevailed.

Clive wandered about the area, calculating and judging the hangar and its capacity. He peered up at the long slit in the ceiling above the pad. He wasn't sure if his ship would have fit through those doors, but as he made his way more deeply into the hangar, he realized that they were much larger than they appeared from afar. He supposed he could have squeezed through.

After his self-guided tour, Clive met with Dowlar at one of the rudimentary consoles. He screwed up his face. "You guys still use this stuff? I feel like I'm on a museum tour."

"It's all we have besides our minds, and believe me, that makes up for a lot of your fancy equipment. One of the search ships has already gone back."

Clive grunted and bent down to examine the screen. It took a moment to remember Basic, but he soon noted that one ship had indeed left. "As soon as that second ship is out of range, I want to know," Clive told the technician who nodded a head laden with an oversized headset. "I'm sure they've already sniffed out the ruins, but hopefully they haven't discovered my secret compartments."

"The team that Master Farol organized to lay false trails is already out there."

"Good. I guess Farol is right then. We'll just have to wait a little longer."

The two returned to the main cave and Clive could see that the Rashmarians were not held to despondency for long. The food tables were now laden with desserts, the fire rekindled, and the women adorned in their festive jewelry and dress.

Clive resigned himself to a little more waiting. And, he could use some of that dessert. Hell, he might be stranded on this ball of rock for a long time, so he might as well stretch out on his mat and enjoy the dancing and carrying on. He helped himself to the food and wine brought to him by some of his old acquaintances who came to welcome him back. He had a hard time admitting that it was nice to see them, but he managed to come out with it anyway. On his first encounter with this race he'd believed all the fuss to be an ostentatious display of caricature. Now that he'd become acquainted with Javid, and things were quite unchanged here, he had to believe that this was simply the genuine nature of the Rashmarians. His theory was instantly established when Dowlar plunked down beside him.

"So, Whale," Dowlar said rhetorically as he filled Clive's mug with a squeeze from his wineskin before aiming a long squirt directly down his throat. Dowlar felt Whale's gloating stare. He gloated right back while giving the wine a swish before swallowing. "What? Do you think your attempts at refining me worked?"

"There's an irony here." Clive drawled.

"And what's that?"

"You're brother. He tried refining me on our way over here."

Dowlar broke into howling laughter. "Yes, I noticed that Nixodonia has softened the lad up a bit. I guess that's what working for the Flechette family did to him. But he tried refining you? That is a funny one."

"Flechette?" Clive asked with curiosity. "Not the Flechette cosmetics company with the daughter, Marie?"

Dowlar's hands stopped just before the next squeeze. "You know her?"

"Everybody knows her. Javid told you he actually worked for the Flechettes?"

"For many years already."

"I don't believe it! So, did he tell you how he found me, then?" Clive was thunderstruck with the revelation of how Javid had gotten to Iggid.

"We're not that far along with our stories yet, but he can tell us both. Here he comes now."

This was all Clive Baker needed. These two pranksters together on his mat! He made Javid explain how he'd gotten to Iggid, even though he'd already guessed. "So, why didn't you tell me?" Clive asked.

Javid smirked and gestured with open palms. "Would you have believed that I'm Marie's primary beautician? No. You would have laughed me right off the planet. That, or handed me over to the authorities and destroyed any chance I had of coming home. Better to beat you at a game of Colors."

"So if you were so anxious to get back here, why did you leave in the first place?"

Javid explained the horrific events that had forced him from his home. His face grew emotional with the memories. Clive felt that he was watching the events unfold on the windows of Javid's eyes. The story both amazed and angered him. As compassion crept into Clive's heart, he found a way to crush it. The old man was a sissy, plain and simple! "Sounds like a cowardly thing to do? Jump on a rebel ship to save your ass."

Dowlar came to his brother's defense. "We do not believe in martyrdom," he stated imperatively.

Clive's goblet stopped at his lips. The seriousness of a Rashmarian rarely showed through.

"Martyrs are revered by some races," Dowlar continued, "but we feel that they fail to understand the truths, and therefore die in an attempt to further a cause that they never truly came to understand."

Clive glanced from one solemn brother to the other. "Sorry if I misunderstood."

"My brother is more what you'd call a hero in your land, although we don't revere heroes either, and he certainly isn't a coward. If Javid had given his life in a useless fight to save our planet, would he be here to help us today? To share laughter, and wine? No."

Javid interjected "And you think that we'll not save our planet now, either. True, we have no way of knowing how it will unfold, but recent events certainly point in our favor."

"Favor?"

"You see," Dowlar explained, "often the best thing to do in times of trouble is to wait for the next crisis. Then, if you are mentally prepared, manipulation of the events becomes much easier while your opponent is too confused, too frightened...or too sure."

Clive began eating again. "You guys are so weird."

Both the brothers laughed, having been subjected separately to Clive's peculiar way of telling them he accepted, although grudgingly, their philosophy.

"And now, you big oaf, tell me about this Colors game you lost to my brother."

CHAPTER 34

Marie thought it was Bill coming to see her. The door on the landing opened a crack, allowing a shard of light to illuminate a strip on the domed ceiling, bringing life to the paintings of the priests. Marie sat up, noticing that the early morning light had begun to penetrate the patio windows. She'd been on the couch all night! Pushing thick bangs off her forehead, Marie rubbed her temples, hastening her grip on reality.

"Bill?" she called out, desperately anxious to see him.

"No. It is I."

Marie's heart stopped. She recognized the nasal sound of the vocoder. As the lights turned up, a glint off the prosthesis of the metal man's skull confirmed her fears. He came down the stairs, stopping at the bottom.

"What are you doing here?" she cried hollowly. "Get out!"

"Commander Shaw knows that I am here, Miss Flechette. I do not have much time. Please, if you could listen, just for a moment?"

Trembling, Marie stood. "You had best not be here to carry out your threat!"

"I will not harm you. I am here to tell you that I leave for Rashmar in just a few hours."

The sound of his artificial voice brought on a torrent of warnings. At the same time, her mind swirled with confusion.

"Rashmar? Why are you going there?" Her voice quavered in panic as she developed images of the metal man slaughtering innocent Rashmarians.

Captain Boro moved closer to the couches. Marie scrambled behind the protection of the farthest one. Her eyes were now wide open and clamped on the monster. But he looked different. His head was cleaner. He smelled cleaner.

"This will sound insincere," he told her, "but for what it's worth, I must apologize for my mistreatment of you and your people."

"How kind!"

"You do not have to believe me, Miss Flechette." He put his fingers lightly against the prosthesis, his natural eye giving way to a touch of sentiment. "The Master saved me with this, when we were just boys. The doctors gave up on me, but Richard never lost faith. One day he came home with this strange gadget, and he gave me back my life. I'll always be indebted to him. Unfortunately, he knows only of his accomplishments. I must live with the monster within."

Marie hardly breathed as she listened to him. He hesitated. She stared, unable to move or react.

"I do not expect your forgiveness, nor am I seeking pity. I have heard the Commander speak highly of you, and one thing this metal hunk does give me is perception." Boro rapped against the metal plate with his knuckle. "The Commander is my master, my life-giver and I will therefore bestow the same respect upon those whom he loves."

Marie's fingers clutched to the back of the chair.

His natural eye softened. "I cannot change the past. In my own way I did what was asked of me. Now I will go again on a mission in an attempt to preserve the ways of the Fringe."

He walked closer, coming into the area between the couches. When he reached into his pocket, Marie's voice blared, "What are you doing?"

He stopped short, then smiled sorrowfully. "I have something that belongs to you." He pulled out her Duval wristwatch and laid it on the table. "I'm sorry. I don't know what happened to your necklace."

She swallowed and shook her head. "It doesn't matter."

"I must go now."

"Wait! What's so important about Rashmar?" she demanded, fearing for Javid's people.

"I must access the TRA base located there."

Marie's face fell. Had the ones who chased Javid off his land been the TRA? Why hadn't he told her?

"I wish you well, my lady," was all he said before turning toward the stairs.

Marie's mind filled with a hundred facts all at once. It was a good thing he wasn't looking for pity, because he certainly wouldn't get it from her! Despite this little charade, she loathed what he'd done—but was her predicament any better? That vid clip would be shown as a warning to those now under the dictatorship of Angel Keem, and there she was, in full-blown reality, killing dissidents. Everyone would believe she was one of them.

She was a victim of her own blindness, he of a horrible disfigurement. She would be blamed for the lives of millions because she fell for the empty promises of one who would fulfill her selfish needs. Billions! Not just the few who had fallen at the hands of Captain Boro on the *Starquest*. She would be made responsible for both the arms trafficking to Telexa and the propaganda movement that revealed her as a monster. It was no wonder that Boro had called her a traitor.

Suddenly, she found herself striding with urgency toward the base of the stairs. Just as the door was opening, she called up to the metal man. He turned to look at her, his natural eye betraying his surprise.

"For, for what it's worth, from me," she stuttered, "I wish you success on Rashmar. The natives there will help you, I am sure of it."

He smiled crookedly and only nodded an acknowledgment before he left.

Marie stood there a long time, first in awe, then in doubt. Suddenly she began a feverish pacing around the room. She went out to the balcony and tapped her toe while ruminating over Captain Boro's visit. Suddenly a horrific thought hit her. What if he was after Javid, and she had just encouraged him! She tore back into the room, and screamed.

Standing at the bottom of the stairs was Richard, looking as frightened as she.

"Oh God, you scared me!" she breathed.

"Sorry." He looked at her wide-eyed then pointed to the landing. "I called, but—are you okay?"

Marie patted her chest hoping to slow her heart. "No! Captain Boro was just here."

He sucked in a breath. "Already? How did it go?"

Her voice was stern. "Is he after Javid?"

Richard looked confused for a minute before his countenance softened. "Oh, I see. He told you he's going to Rashmar."

"Yes. He also told me that the TRA base is there. I don't know what his mission is but," her voice was tremulous, "I swear to you that Javid is not involved with the enemy."

Richard's stark blue eyes stared at her. "Well, it would have been a perfect connection, but you can relax. Boro isn't after Javid. In fact, he's not even aware of him. As far as we know, a Rashmarian has never betrayed his own."

Marie released a long breath. "Oh, thank the Great Creator."

"Besides, we don't know where Javid is. He escaped the sanitarium on Iggid and no one has been able to locate him since. Do you know where he might have gone?"

Marie swallowed. "Javid once told me that his people believed he would return to help them one day, but he's probably just off to do medicine his own way. He hates modern medicine."

"Rashmar isn't an easy place to get to these days. Even for a Rashmarian."

"I don't doubt that," she frowned, "but Javid can be very resourceful."

"And I for one, want to believe that your faith in him is not ill placed, which means your friend Javid is innocent until proven guilty."

She smiled thinly. "That's reassuring."

Richard shuffled about nervously. "I just came in to see how you were doing this morning."

"I'm fine, thank you."

He nodded, then looked at her in a manner that tested her resolve to remain neutral.

"That's good. Right now I have to get to the launch fields. I just dropped in to tell you that I'm sending Mr. Tripp down to join you for breakfast. He's got a few things to tell you. I can't stay right now, but I'll see you later in the day."

She nodded, containing her excitement.

"So," he added, clamping his hands behind his back, "I'll see you later."

The waiting nearly drove Marie mad, yet not more than ten minutes later, breakfast for two arrived. Just as she was sorting the tray, Bill opened the door and called her name. Marie dropped the utensils and dashed to the bottom of the stairs. Bill bound down, two at a time and grasped her in a tight hug, swinging her in a circle before giving her a solid kiss on the lips. "Great Creator, it is good to see you, Marie."

"Oh, Bill!" She clasped her arms around his neck.

"I've been worried sick about you," Bill breathed. "I really lost it when they told me about the codes. Then, I thought I was going to kill somebody when I saw the clips of *Angel's Test*."

"You could have vented your anger on me. Finding a way to commit suicide was too grisly a task!"

"Oh, come now! You're not one to be defeated so easily. In fact, you're looking quite well. How are you feeling?"

"I'm all right. They've been taking pretty good care of me."

"They'd better be."

"Richard just told me you have some news for me."

"Richard?"

Her face exploded into a rosy hue. "I mean, Commander Shaw."

"Ah, yes. Richard the Commander," Bill groaned.

"I've had a lot to do with him lately," she defended. "It's been an interesting few days."

"I'll bet it has. I was going crazy wondering what was happening to you."

"If you'll join me for breakfast, I can tell you about it."

"Great. I'm starved."

She poured them each a coffee and slathered jam on a scone. "New skill," she jested.

"Cheers," he said, tapping his tin mug against hers.

"Tell me the news! What did Rich—Commander Shaw mean when he said he'd kept you busy lately?" Marie sat perched on the edge of the couch.

His lips pressed into a thin line. "Well, this will come as a shock to you, but I asked if I could join the Fringe Forces. After accepting my proposal, they put me together with a carrot-head by the name of Hollis who's in charge of Intelligence."

Her jaw slackened. "You did? You have?" She paused, contemplating the implications. "Well, that's wonderful! That means that they believe us to be completely innocent? Why hasn't the Commander told me this?"

"I asked if I could tell you myself, because…there's more." He touched her arm. "I've volunteered for some work away from here."

Her shoulders dropped slightly. "Oh. Well, that's good news, I think."

"I wouldn't have agreed to the assignment if I didn't trust in your safety. This planet is enshrouded in a nebula and is literally impossible to detect from the outside. A very clever hiding spot, except it's almost as impossible to pilot in as out of here."

"I know."

He looked at her curiously.

Marie waved a hand. "Never mind, go on."

Smiling, he continued, "So far no casualties. These Fringe folks seem to be born with navigational computers in their brains."

"Yes I kno—yes, they must."

"But you're my first concern. I need to know if you're all right with—"

"Bill, I want you to join them. Anything! Anything to help us."

"I double checked with the Commander. He promises to keep you under strict surveillance. I'm confident that he's serious because it's in his interest to do so."

"So, what are you going to do?"

"I'm going to do some spying." He took a sip of coffee.

"Spying! Where?"

"Nixodonia."

Her spine stiffened. "You're going *home?*"

"Strictly under cover. I'm going to dig up the culprits responsible for this." He pointed to his chest. "I'm the man for the job, you know. The TRA will hardly suspect me on their tails."

"Will you see Maman and Papa?" She leaned forward swiftly, clamping a hand to his forearm. "Oh please, tell them I'm alive."

He frowned. "I'm afraid that unless circumstances bring me to reveal myself to them, I cannot blow my cover."

She nodded slowly. The disappointment was numbing.

"I'm sorry, Marie."

"I'm just crazy with thoughts of my parents finally hearing from me, but I understand." She straightened suddenly. "Are you going after Paul? Because if you find him, I give you permission to mutilate the man."

Bill laughed. "My pleasure. And Henrie Marchand?"

"String him up by the family jewels. He threatened to do that to Paul once but claimed not to know him well enough. Ha! That's fairly unlikely."

"I believe they're involved together."

She expelled her breath. "I'm sure you're right."

"And you," Bill said. "I heard you weren't so well after seeing those clips."

"True." Her throat tightened at the very thought of it. "It was really awful. I just got out of the medic bay yesterday afternoon—for the second time!' She flung a hand through the air. "Ah! I'm going the way of my father! I swear I've had more drugs this past week than in my whole life. Unfortunately some of the pain was self-inflicted with a little over indulgence in the good priests' wine."

"Wine?"

"Yes, Richard brought me…oh, wait—"

"Ah. The good Commander Richard brought you some wine? Well. That was noble of him."

"No, wait, you don't understand. It was just—"

"It's okay, Marie. You don't have to explain it to me." He suppressed a giggle. "But I'm jealous. No one brought me wine."

"I'll send Igna your way."

"Igna Cello? The weapons specialist? You have been busy!"

It was Marie's turn to laugh. "Yes. She's the woman who wants to be his woman, and now thinks I'm going to steal her man, but he claims not to be her man anyway."

Bill raised both palms. "Sorry I asked. But am I missing something here?"

"No," she giggled, feeling her tragedy liquefy into comedy.

"Maybe I shouldn't be leaving you in the protection of that warlord. I'm not altogether sure I trust the man."

She looked at him solemnly. "You can trust him. He won't harm me. Besides, I'm a big girl now. I have to start looking out for myself one of these days." A melancholy smile touched the corners of her mouth. "I'll miss knowing that you're watching my every move."

"So will I."

"I'll be fine." She slapped a hand to her heart. "I promise."

He looked at her steadfastly before letting his gaze roam the ceiling. "I don't know. Fragrant jungles and ancient priests with potent wines make for a rather adventurous setting. Perhaps these paintings were meant to help keep one chaste and pure."

Marie followed Bill's gaze to the ceiling. "Ah, but look at them. They're so in love with life, with what they're doing. The wine I had was from a goblet hand-crafted by the priests themselves, so they weren't as chaste and pure as they seem."

His gaze lowered and locked onto hers. "Maybe that's the secret. Trust in your Creator, then live fully the life that you've been granted."

She looked deeply into his eyes. "I think the Commander is giving you the power to give us that option."

It was late in the evening when Marie heard her door open. He must have checked on the cameras to see if she was awake. Having slept most of the afternoon, there was little danger of sleep taking over for a while yet. However, with no entertainment, no one to talk to, she'd regressed to pacing the uneven floor around the rectangle of couches, stopping each time to check on the jungle activity outside the open terrace doors while contemplating the latest turn of events. She was standing there when he came down the stairs. He was out of uniform and Marie briefly imagined a wardrobe of about two personal items. It wasn't surprising to see a pair of boots, britches, and that same blowzy shirt he'd been wearing on the day of her arrival.

"How was your visit with Mr. Tripp?"

She nodded. "Wonderful, thank you." She felt awkward under his intense gaze. "I'm glad you've taken him on your team. If anyone wants to crush these bastards more than you do, it's him. He won't disappoint you."

"He's a skilled man. And you? How are you feeling?"

"Much better."

"That's good." He strode about the room, checking things again. "I came to tell you that this is no longer designated as a prison cell."

"Oh?" she said with surprise. "Well, thank you!" She clenched her fists and suppressed an urge to hug him.

"You're free to come and go. Mr. Tripp will be quite busy in the coming days, so I'll assign another agent to your personal care."

Marie's mind assessed the possibilities, and consequences. "Oh that's great. But—" She stopped, formulating her plan.

"But what?"

"Well, if this planet is home to no one but yourselves and the natives, maybe I could be without a personal escort." Her heart leapt with the daring of it. "It would be the first time in my life."

He thought about it for a moment. "I can only partially agree to that."

She smiled. "Am I about to partake in a Fringe-style compromise?"

He suppressed a smile and paused, formulating his own plan. "Yes. And here it is. Some of the cameras in this room will stay on. I'll have certain officers watch you with as much distance as they can allow. You're a key figure in this mess and I need to make sure that nothing happens to you." He pointed a finger at her. "You are not to go off this base. If you ever want to visit the jungle, then you must have an escort." He put a hand on his hip and tossed back his mane. "In fact, no one knows the jungle better than I do, so I'll take you myself if you ever want to go. After Tripp and his relay ship are gone, I should be able to find a few spare moments. Until then, the base is plenty big enough for you to roam. Stay on it."

Marie could hardly breathe. "Compromise accepted."

"Good. Then here's tomorrow's itinerary. I'll have someone escort you to the mess hall for breakfast. After that, you can be shown around the base. During that time, nurse Deanna will catch up with you and take you for a check-up with Doctor Faulk."

She furiously calculated the details in her mind.

"Breakfast is at oh-six hundred hours. You can have it ordered here if that's too early?"

"Oh, no! I'm sure I'll be ready to explore by sunrise." They stood, smiling awkwardly at each other for a few interminable minutes. Marie broke the silence. "I'll take you up on that offer for a jungle excursion later on. I've never been to a jungle before."

"All right. It's a date." He swiftly clamped his hands behind his back. "I'll see you around in the morning. Have a good evening."

"I will. Thank you."

She waited until he'd gone before clenching her fists in a suppressed cry of joy. She ran out to the balcony to check that there was no blue emitting from the railing's strip. None. She drew in a full breath of the jungle air before dashing about her suite in exuberance. She skipped up the stairs and tested the door. It was unlocked. She opened it just a crack. The powerful lights of the detention corridor had been dimmed for the night, but not enough for her to miss the trailing white mane of her Commander as he rounded the corner out to the shadowy caves beyond.

CHAPTER 35

The next morning, Marie joined Bill, along with Captain Hollis and nurse Deanna, for her first experience in a mess hall. She quickly concluded that this was the best party she'd ever attended. Only Igna avoided her, throwing her scowling glances from several tables away. After breakfast, the promised grand tour was conducted by one of Richard's officers. Later in the day, Marie was left to move about on her own. There were hundreds of things to explore while learning the workings of a military base. She tried a bit of everything, from stepping inside the bowels of a turbo hyperdrive engine to trying her hand at finding Enderal on the three-dimensional star maps.

Marie's exploration of the base gave her an awareness of freedoms fulfilled. By the time Bill was scheduled to leave, she'd experienced more liberty than she'd relished in a lifetime.

Just before sunrise, the inevitable time arrived. Marie found herself standing in the safety zone of the launching sites to witness Bill's ship leave. Dozens of others were present to orchestrate the liftoff of two state-of-the-art ships, on the inside at least. One looked like a battered freighter. That was Bill's ship. The second was an even more archaic looking craft, acting as Bill's relay ship. The two ships rumbled in anticipation, bursts of steam hissing from release valves. Even with the sun still hidden behind the rounds of the ancient mountains, the breeze was hot against Marie's face, and redolent of nighttime fragrance oozing from the blossoms that bordered the spaceport. Had the delicate scents not been mingling with the pungent fumes of jet fuels and ozone, the whole idea of war would have been unimaginable.

Marie looked anxiously upon the activity of Bill's receiving his last briefings from and Captain Hollis. Richard and Lieutenant Mondiran also had their last words with Bill before he was allowed to come to her. They grasped each other in a tight embrace. With mixed emotion, she wished Bill luck and added, "Please, be careful!"

He smiled ruefully. "Don't worry. We're going to win this thing."

Richard was suddenly at her side. "The pilots are giving the signal, Tripp. Ships are ready."

Captain Hollis accompanied Bill to the ship where Bill received his final instructions. Bill ran halfway up the ramp before turning toward her. With a wide arc of an arm, he waved, and disappeared into the cockpit of the freighter.

The two ships blasted into the atmosphere, shooting toward a bank of gray clouds touched with the silver of a sun just creeping over the horizon. She waved at the two dots as they disappeared into the forlorn gray of another pending storm. How quickly the weather changed here, perhaps this time as a token of Bill's departure. Eyes downcast, she turned back toward the base and followed the others. She found Richard beside her again. He looked exhausted, the uniform hanging stiffly on his slumped shoulders. "Well, I'm about three hours late for breakfast. How about you? Have you eaten yet?"

"Actually, no, I haven't."

"So, then. Seeing as your bodyguard is gone, may I take the first watch by asking you to join me in my suite for breakfast?"

Marie smiled. "You could."

They passed through his office where Marie had a grim reminder of her encounter with that hideous remake of *Angel's Test* in the conference hall beyond. This time they took the second door. It led to his private quarters. The suite stretched into three distinct rooms: a large sitting area with patio doors twice the size of her own, a roomy kitchenette with latticed cupboards and an attached dining room with a sturdy wooden table that would seat a party of eight. Beyond the living area, she caught a glimpse of the bedroom. Marie imagined it would be as lovely as the rest of the suite. She meandered over to the patio and watched the building of the dark stormy skies that had sent Bill on his way. As she watched, the torrent started, streaking the windows and obscuring her view with huge droplets that splashed on the terrace with such volume that puddles immediately appeared. She liked storms. They encouraged a natural form of meditation.

A moment later one of the kitchen personnel arrived with breakfast for two. She grinned, realizing that Richard had placed his order before asking her to join him.

"Your confidence was high."

He smiled while pouring them each a coffee. "I decided that if you refused my offer, I could probably devour both portions myself."

They ate their fill while Marie made nonsensical conversation in response to the knot in her belly that had arrived as a third party to this private affair. "Bill off to Doria, of all places."

"He thought that would be the best place to start."

"Sure." She laughed. "He'll find out what it looks like before I do. And Captain Boro gone to Rashmar. Unbelievable!"

"Tell me, what sort of things did your Rashmarian beautician teach you?"

Marie shrugged. "Just tools for sane living, really. Relaxation, stress management, that sort of thing. He would ask for omens from his gods for me, and you know, I don't ever remember his being wrong."

Richard watched her, wondering if she knew that her latest hardships had done nothing to diminish her beauty.

"In fact," she continued, "when he predicted destruction, I had no idea anything could be as brutal as the *Starquest* attack."

"I'm sorry about that," Richard mumbled.

Marie glanced at him. "He also said there'd be a bright light in my life, and that I would find peace." She chuckled. "I've certainly known peace these last few days. It's really been fun getting to know everyone. They just treat me like one of the gang!"

Richard watched her with burning intent. Marie deflected the energy by continuing. "Then Javid said that despite the destruction, I would suffer no lasting personal harm. And look!" She nearly peeled the jumpsuit off her shoulder, then chose to pat it brusquely. "I'm all healed." She rubbed her shoulder while giving him a tight smile. "It makes me feel marked somehow. Another step to normalcy for Marie Flechette."

"And the bright light?"

She looked at him. He stared right back. His features were all so perfectly balanced. Maybe Paul had been too tall, his features too drawn, his hair too styled. Richard's hair cascaded in a mess past the collar of the uniform, its pearly color continually drawing her attention. Thin wisps fell across his broad forehead, accenting his tanned features. The angles of his jaw bulged slightly as he looked at her, and when he swallowed, his throat bobbed, bringing her eyes to rest on the light curls escaping his loosened collar. She followed the crisp angles of the jacket down the length of his arms. The veins stood out on the back of his bronzed hands and she remembered them roaming about her back. She felt their imprint burn her as she recalled the incident with vivid sensations. Perhaps he anticipated her thoughts. One of his hands crept across the table, seemingly ignorant of its own travels. She shrugged, almost imperceptibly.

"I don't know what the light is supposed to mean."

His fingers reached hers. "It's a positive light, I'm sure. You deserve that. When I researched your file, I couldn't believe that all the goody-goody stuff was for real. No one in your position could possibly be that genuine. Yet, all those billions across Nix States couldn't be wrong. And, they aren't."

She flushed while finding herself accepting the will of his fingers to intertwine with hers. "I'm a product of my parents," she stated. "They're the ones responsible for who I am."

"I could say that of mine, too, but our parents aren't the ones who make the choices that keep us discovering our own paths. It's *you* in those advertising campaigns, you on the stage to benefit millions of impoverished souls. I like that about you. A winner."

Marie felt completely abashed. "Well, my mother is a strong force behind the benefit concerts, and I didn't exactly win where Paul was concerned."

"You haven't lost yet." Richard's hand tightened on hers. "Besides, Lambert is a professional, connected with many other professionals. An unsuspecting cosmetics company is no match for that. In fact, the presidency may be no match for it."

Marie smiled crookedly. "So, we fight on?"

"Yes we do. And therefore, Javid's light will come to pass."

She smiled. "You speak as if you know him."

"I know his people. We've supported the Rashmarians a long time. They're a good lot."

Marie pulled her free hand through her hair. "Well, I could sure use Javid's wizardry right now!"

Richard laughed. She was again drawn to his straight teeth, those laugh lines. He was beautiful! "You look beautiful to me."

Marie straightened. Did he say that? Did she?

"One of these days," she warned, "I'll show you what I normally look like. But you've provided me with another first." She pulled out the loose inch from the waistband of the jumpsuit. "This is the first time in my life that I've ever worn the same thing two days in a row. Or, is it three now?"

They both laughed. It was so unique not to worry endlessly about her hair or dress. Her nails were now a ratty mess, yet she couldn't bring herself to care.

"I could get you some civilian clothes if you like?" he offered, mesmerized by her smiling eyes. How innocent she was for one so scrutinized by everyone she came into contact with. Her hair was the softest he'd ever seen on a woman. Her face was again blemish-free, her long slim hands as if coated with silk. He eyed the iridescent polish that graced their tips, still disclosing the latest manicure, polish hard and intact, every cuticle in meticulous condition. Her voice drew him back. "No, don't bother with that. It's actually fun to conform to the dress code and not worry that one strand of hair might be out of place."

Suddenly he reached across the table and fingered her tresses. "You wouldn't mind if I fuss with it a bit?"

Her heart handed in its resignation. She could not begin to resist him. Her hand involuntarily tightened in his, and she whispered, "No, I wouldn't."

"I haven't slept much these past few days." He spoke with mild urgency. "Reese offered to take over for a while. You can go if you have other plans." He paused a few seconds. "But, I'd like you to stay."

Her breath quickened. Her eyes darted about his face, drinking in the features that asked her to be with him. There would be no one to appraise her courtiers here. This was her decision, but on the surface she read big caution signs. What was he after? How would she handle this later? And what about their vow? More quickly than she could assimilate the possible dangers, she abandoned all caution, erased the vow. Here, she was just Marie. No titles, no responsibilities. She wanted to be free, to be herself, to choose for herself.

"I would like to stay," she told him.

Still clutching her hand, he rose from his chair and circled the table. She stood to meet him. Instantly his lips were upon hers, his hands roaming about her back and into her hair in that already familiar manner. She circled his neck and joined in the embrace. When he released her long enough to begin the journey towards his room, she sputtered, "It seems that a Commander's work is never done."

"No?"

"May I obey *my* orders and prove to you that there's no stamp on my chest?"

He moaned and directed her in the direction of his bed. "You could, if you wanted."

His lips devoured hers, explored her eyelids, her cheeks, her ears, all the while moving back, step by step, deeper into his sanctuary. His breath, hot on her face, left her burning with passion. He picked her up in powerful arms and laid her across the bed ever so gently. Marie marveled at his ability to make her feel as light as a feather while surrounding her in his muscular mass. She remembered an ancient proverb Javid had once told her. "There is nothing as strong as gentleness, and nothing as gentle as real strength."

Gone was her ability to judge every move a suitor made, calculating, scheming—is this right, is that right? Is this good enough for Marie Flechette! Here was someone who could erase all that. When she heard the zipper of her jumpsuit zing away toward her navel, she arched back, needing to pour her body and soul out to him, to have him devour her, and she to consume his gift.

His voice muffled against the thin fabric of the chemise between her breasts. Her eyes opened, bringing a painted ceiling into focus. There, on the azimuth of the stone dome, in old, ruddy paint, a priest stood in his vineyard with arms raised toward the heavens, praising the world about him, a smile of thanksgiving across his worn features.

"I'm afraid you're too late to carry out my order," Richard's throaty voice croaked with repentance.

Her mouth fell open, but her eyes smiled. "Oh? What do you mean?"

He pulled himself up to meet her eyes while his hand found a space between the undergarments that failed to embarrass her now. He had given them to her.

"I stand guilty. I already know that you have no Reptilian stamp...here." His fingers touched the skin above her hardened nipple.

Her eyes grew wide. "How? When?"

"The medical unit. I'm afraid that I stayed and help the nurses put you to bed. After all, you were my prisoner, and I am the Commander here." His mouth fell on hers, stifling a giggle. So, she hadn't imagined that! His hand lowered onto her breast. He left it there, unmoving, allowing the cup of his hand to feel the nipple protrude into his palm as he kissed her deeply, his tongue touching and exploring her lips, then deeper.

"That's not fair," she protested hoarsely when his lips left hers to move down her neck.

"You're right. But don't forget, I'm supposed to be a barbarian."

"You make a lousy barbarian," Marie laughed.

"We'll see about that."

She couldn't wait long. She needed to see for herself and began her own exploration. His chest was hard, the curls like soft fur. Her hands trailed about his torso. She was captivated by the taut skin, the hardness of his muscles. She believed it would take a long time to explore all these crevices, shadowed and cupped as if a sculptor had masterfully crafted his perfect vision of manhood. The sculptor must have foretold this event. Richard's arms wrapped around her as if designed to her specifications.

Her chest rose and fell against his. His breathing matched hers. Suddenly, a nauseating fear ripped through the pit of her stomach. She looked at him, desperately. "Richard?"

"Mmm?"

"Richard, I need you to know something."

He stopped, giving her his complete attention. She looked as if some terrible secret was about to erupt from her, but rather, she said, "I know that everything you've read about me isn't so innocent. I'm not what people think. I haven't," she looked at the ceiling, "how would your priests say it—*known* a lot of men." She trailed the sentence off quickly, regretting her confession. He looked at her lovingly, tracing her warped eyebrows with a finger. She felt strangely emotional. "You're bringing things out in me I didn't know I had. On one hand it's frightening. On the other, you make me feel more beautiful than ever before." She bit her lip.

"Shhh." He touched a finger to her mouth, his expression sobering. "The truth of the matter is that you make me feel beautiful, too. I was warned that this would happen, if I were ever with the right person."

"It would? By whom?" Her voice was barely audible.

"A wise man I know. But that's for later. Do you remember asking me to give you my life?"

It was a long time before he spoke again. A long time before she wished to. When she removed the last of his clothing, her breath caught in her throat. She liked the look of her barbarian, the feel of his arms wrapped about the small of her back, pulling her into his manhood until she could stand it no longer.

He waited eagerly, molding her, centering her until she thought her middle would explode. In all her years, she'd never experienced her womanhood contracting within her, asking to be caressed, achingly so. With abandon, she asked for his life, with her hands, her eyes, with her hips. He obliged, moaning and shivering with the triumphant release she brought to him. Moments later, she couldn't quell the cry that escaped from her throat as she joined him in a bonding ceremony that flooded through her, body and soul, ultimately consuming. She whimpered, and laughed, unable to explain the tear that escaped from the corner of her eye as her body shivered and slumped with exhaustion.

They made love again, more slowly. Marie discovered herself by the touch of his hand, and him by the touch of hers. She opened like a flower after years of being closed against fears of rape from a galaxy that wanted her every fiber.

A rumble rattled the windows, deep, omnipotent, as if the planet granted its approval to their new-found love. The gusting wind drove the rain in soft blankets against the windowpanes of the bedroom. The drops were smaller now, as if the storm had released its passion as well.

Richard and Marie entwined themselves about each other. His fingers stroked her shoulder, tracing the scar that had nearly disappeared. His nostrils breathed in her feminine scent as he buried his face in the copper silk strands that draped across his pillow. Marie lay exhausted, her fingers entangled in his mane, her lips parted to accommodate the deep relaxing breaths.

In settling closer to him, her gaze trailed across the ceiling, bringing the glorifying priest into her field of vision. "Ah, yes," she whispered. "Glory to the Great Creator."

They awoke with the sun streaming onto the chamber floor. Marie blinked, but chose not to move. The bedside clock indicated that it was already mid-afternoon on this mysterious planet. She felt Richard stretch, and settle again.

Her eyes wandered about his quarters. The bed had four large posts reaching above the mattress. They'd been ornately carved in thick vines with leaves and grape clusters. She wasn't sure what the mattress was made of, perhaps some sort of fiber, but it was comfortable, whatever it was. She glanced up at the benevolent priest and wondered why he'd had need for such a wide bed. She smiled, and thanked him for it anyway.

The floor was strewn with intricate carpets of varying designs and sizes, hiding large portions of the smooth stone floor beneath. All the furniture appeared to be hand-made. She admired the bowed willow branches that made up the frames of the love seat and chairs padded with thick, colorful cushions. A large trunk with its curved lid securely padlocked stood along one wall, its design incongruous with the rest of the furniture. Marie thought it must be one of Richard's personal artifacts. A trunk. She dreamed about what secrets it might hold and hoped he would divulge them to her some day.

Her smile widened as she turned to welcome her stirring barbarian.

He blinked at her. "How can you look so gorgeous after a long sleep like that?"

"It's all fake. Don't tell my fans, but I'm actually a genetics junky."

"Can't fool me." His voice was low and throaty. Marie's breath immediately quickened. To desire him again must be the result of some mad drug lacing the perfumed jungle air. It settled right in her loins. She found him to be affected as well and giving in to this strange intoxication, they made love again.

The sun blanketed their bodies during the course of satisfying their hunger for each other. Spent, she let the sun heat her skin, remembering an accusation she now proved corrected. "Shy no more, my love." She touched his nose with her finger. "Here I am with you in broad daylight."

"You have led a sheltered life!" he laughed. "Which brings me to the fact that we need a shower. But we'll have to get dressed first."

Her eyes widened. "You don't have a private bath?"

"More than one," he smiled mischievously. "Come on, I'll show you my favorite."

As they pulled on their clothes, he took a knapsack from one of the tall cupboards. Without checking its contents, he grasped her hand and led the way. They left his quarters by a side door and jumped into one of the small jeeps parked outside his private entrance. Marie relished the breeze through her hair and had to crush the urge to wave at everyone they passed. He parked the jeep near the end of a dim tunnel where a damp and deserted staircase descended. He threw the pack over his shoulder and led her down the stairs. Small lights secured at the base of each step illuminated their way as they followed the twisting stairway into the bowels of the mountain.

Richard's voice was muted by the moss-covered walls. "These stairs aren't used much, except by me." They reached the bottom, and Marie noticed that he still kept all the entrances covered. A guard saluted as they walked into the exploding sunshine of the moist steamy jungle.

"Your room is right up there." Richard pointed up the cliff face where she recognized the small semi-circular balcony, and others as well. Richard explained that each balcony was strategically placed so that protrusions of rock shielded one balcony from the other, allowing the priests their necessary privacy.

They continued down a well-worn path that narrowed slightly as it entered the thick of the jungle. Marie studied the unique flowers responsible for the fragrances that had enticed her since her arrival. Blossoms from pin-point size to a foot across painted the forest. The larger ones drooped heavily off the vines, and inundated the many plant species of the underbrush. Most of the varieties Marie couldn't even identify. Wouldn't her father love this place! The branches above sprinkled them with glistening drops of moisture as the breeze stirred the ancient giants that towered above them. Marie lifted her face and laughed, her voice mingling with the chatter of monkeys and the cackling of birds. Suddenly, she became aware of a deep rumbling sound that conjured the view from her balcony. "The waterfall?"

He nodded. "It feeds a pool. Do they teach Nixodonians how to swim?"

"Well, yes, but is it safe?"

He laughed. "It's safe, except for the currents on the far side."

"Currents?"

"Most of the pool is plenty shallow enough with lots of bathing spots."

She didn't disclose that she'd never bathed in anything but facilities designed for such things. Her apprehension radiated to him with the tightening of her hand in his.

Richard smiled as they rounded a hairpin turn that brought them into full view of a sparkling azure pool. She drew in a breath of awe. A tall thin ribbon of water hit the rocky cliffs just below the canopy, exploding into several fans of water that undulated over boulders and rocks on its relentless journey. The cascading streams pooled and overflowed within smooth gouges of rock until it plunged over a final jutting plateau. The thin, clear sheets rippled the pool's surface just enough to make its bottom look alive with movement. The edges of the pool were lined with large boulders mostly smothered with moss and creeping jungle foliage. Around the rocky edges, the jungle made a solid, green wall that opened into a sunny oval above. The only access seemed to be the small beach on which they stood. Looking up through the break in the canopy, Marie squinted against the brilliant sunlight. It shimmered against the falls where a misty halo painted small rainbows up its entire length. "It's magnificent!"

"Even more so if you get in."

She watched in awe as Richard stripped off his clothing. He strode into the water, white buttocks winking at her. He dove in elegant form then surfaced, shaking his mane. The droplets burst into a halo of tiny rainbows around his head. He flashed her a wide smile and called her to join him. She stood there as if she were being asked to jump into a vat of boiling oil.

"I'm scared," she stated simply.

A few powerful strokes brought him back to the shallower area where he rose and walked towards her. The water dripped off his hair, raced down his chest and cascaded off his manhood. It beckoned her to join him with its swaying motion as he waded toward her. "Come on, take my hand and we'll go slowly." He grinned at her. "You can't bathe fully dressed."

"What if someone comes?"

"No one will come. Well, I shouldn't say that. The natives sometimes come and join me."

"*What?*" She stared at him in shock. "What kind of natives?"

"The planet's native tribes. Remember? I told you about them. Some of them live right around the base of this mountain."

"Like real wild natives?"

"Yup. Barbarians, like myself."

"Will they throw spears at me?"

He suppressed a burst of laughter. "No. I'm a friend of theirs. They help us; we help them."

"How can aboriginal people help you?"

"Ah, the natives have tremendous secrets, secrets a computer could never know or learn. They'll introduce themselves to you if you come here often enough."

"Then, no way. I'm not taking off my clothes."

"The natives think it's silly that we wear anything more than a loin cloth as it is. They'll think you're crazy if you stand on the bank, dressed"

She thought about it for an uncertain moment then became acutely aware of the heat building up in her jumpsuit. She finally decided that the pool and its adventure enticed her more than the wild natives scared her. Here was her chance to swim in open waters. Besides, the mysterious Planet of Shaw might be her home for some time. To miss this because of some childish fear was absurd.

The raw sunlight on her breasts, then her hips and legs felt wonderfully strange. She stepped into the water and instantly recoiled. Richard chuckled softly while holding out his hand. He stood only knee deep, so she tried again. The water was not as cold as she'd first thought yet she held a wary breath as she made her way to him. The shimmering water felt strangely like silk against her legs, the pebbles massaging the soles of her feet. Grasping his hand, they continued to where Richard said the bottom would be sandier. As they ventured, the water reached up between her legs, letting her know that her sensitive parts would not be as tolerant as others. To lessen the shock, she dipped to her navel, crying out as she did so.

She gave him the most ridiculous grimace imaginable. Richard burst into gut wrenching laughter. "You may as well get it over with, and wet the rest of yourself too."

"Don't dunk me!" she warned with fiery eyes.

"I won't. I want you to come back here with me again."

She looked at him from beneath lowered lashes, her jaw clamping against cold that really wasn't. "Oh, I don't know."

He knelt and the water closed to his armpits. "Come here. It really feels better once you're wet and moving about."

Teeth gritting against the unfamiliarity, she dropped into his arms.

"Better?"

Shivering, she nodded while taking a moment to marvel at the water that felt like a satin blanket wrapped about them. The water smelled so clean, so pure, unlike the chemical laden waters of her covered pool at home.

As Richard urged her to swim about, Marie found that every stroke brought a new discovery. She saw weeds growing on the bottom, rocks of every shape and size glisten in the depths, and the surface dance with the sparkle of a thousand tiny diamonds. Suddenly she let out an unexpected scream. Richard was at her side in seconds. She clamped one hand over her mouth to suppress involuntary hysterics. Fear and excitement mixed in the pit of her stomach until she thought she might cry with the strength of it.

"What happened?"

She removed her hand only long enough to disgorge a quick burst of words. "I think I saw a fish!"

He looked at her in blank surprise, then remembered that the Princess of Nixodonia was really a sheltered nymph, at least compared to the way he'd experienced life. He suppressed the urge to laugh aloud. "You did?" he asked in earnest. "What did it look like?" He gathered her slowly in his arms and pulled her to more shallow waters.

"About this long." She indicated a length with her hands. "And I think it touched my leg. Maybe it bit me. You should have a look."

He gazed into the water and saw that she'd raised her leg for him to inspect. His hand reached down and ran along its length. "There's no wound. There are fish that live in this pond, but none have ever hurt me."

"Maybe I should get out."

"Hey, this is nature. You're a part of it, so enjoy the encounter. Really, they won't hurt you. Maybe you're just getting too brave too soon. Let's stick to the shallows for today."

She had no trouble with that. He asked her to sit in an area only bathtub deep, supposedly clear of any pond-living members while he waded out to retrieve the knapsack from the bank. Marie leaned back on her elbows and wondered how it was that the water had become so warm. It felt like bath water now so it was appropriate that Richard arrived with a bar of soap and a small tube of shampoo. They cleaned and splashed, teased and caressed. The play-fight lasted until the suds had vanished and she shivered once more.

"I don't think it's the water," she told him when he suggested they get out and dry off.

"Good," he moaned, "but the sun's getting low and when it dips behind those mountains—poof, darkness!"

"Can we come back tomorrow?"

"I hope so, but right now, it's pretty hard for me to get away."

"Well, soon then."

The sun had nearly set behind the mountains by the time they reached the entrance to the stairway where the guard again saluted them. At the top of the staircase they jumped into the jeep and purred off down the tunnels. He dropped her off at Detention where they chatted idly for a few minutes. Finally, he gunned the engine. Regretfully, he could do nothing but acknowledge her wave with a smile and a nod of his head before squealing away.

The remainder of the day took Richard all over the base, from the control room to the landing fields. As the evening wore on, he buried himself at his desk to tend to loose ends. By midnight, he'd been undisturbed for several hours, so when the door buzzer rang, it jolted him from his concentration. He punched on the receiver. "Who is it?"

"It's Igna. I need to speak to you about the weapons drill tomorrow."

Mechanically, he pushed the button that opened the thick door. Igna's tall, lank figure slid into the room. Richard asked her to go ahead and brief him without even looking up from the data screen that preoccupied his attention.

Suddenly, his eyes darted sideways. Right by his nose were Igna's long black-clad legs. He leaned back in the chair and looked at her with annoyance. "There's no problem with the weapons drill, is there, Igna?"

She smiled and leaned forward, one arm on the desk, the other on the high back of his chair. Unconsciously, Richard leaned farther back. "You're right, everything's fine, but I've been worried about you lately."

"Me? There is no need to worry about me."

"Oh, yes there is." Splayed fingers bolted toward him and ran themselves through his hair.

He grasped her wrist. "Igna, I know we saw each other a while back—but it's over."

She looked at him, disheartened. A false smile curled her lips. "It's not over, it's just a little delayed. With a war on our doorstep, we've had no time for each other. I understand your responsibilities and wouldn't think of interfering with your work. Not everyone can appreciate the life of a leader so you ought to be grateful that I do."

He again stopped her wandering hands. "Igna, you're a lovely lady and a good friend, but you don't mean more to me than that." He wasn't sure how he could be more direct, but she didn't get the hint. Suddenly, she pushed the chair back on its rollers, raised a leg and straddled him. He was so surprised that he didn't instantly respond. When her lips smashed against his, he reacted. Grasping her shoulders, he pushed her back. "Igna! Off!"

"Oh, come now. You're tired and you need a little loving," she cooed, her hands roaming over his head.

More gently, he took hold of both her wrists. "It's over, Igna. In fact, we never really got started, and that is because I don't feel that way about you. I thought I might, but I don't, and I'm sorry if I didn't make that clear."

"It's the heiress, isn't it?" she said flatly.

"What do you mean?" It was a stupid response, but she'd caught him off guard.

"Marie Flechette. Funny how you've found time for her already."

"You're in charge of weapons, Igna, so leave the spy work alone."

"I don't need to spy, Commander. The way you look at her—everybody already knows."

"Everybody? You, Igna. That's who everybody is. And you're right, you don't need to spy. You just walk into Detention Control and interrogate my prisoners for yourself."

Her face blanched. "Who told you that? Did your innocent little *Princess* tattle on me?"

"She hardly needed to do that, Igna."

"I hope you are not taking advantage of a woman in your captivity."

He gave her a boost and pushed her off his lap. He stood and faced her. "I resent that, Igna. Besides, what I do is none of your business."

She blinked moisture from her eyes and said quietly. "You really don't want me, do you?"

He was surprised to see her this way. Even he hadn't witnessed emotions from the woman they nicknamed the Iron Lady. "Igna, please, don't do this to yourself, or to me. I told you months ago it had to stop. Please accept that."

Igna's sorrow quickly twisted into anger. "Fine. I accept it." She stormed out of the office, slamming her palm against the door's controls. It snapped shut behind her. Richard rubbed his eyes wearily, sorry that he'd started anything in the first place. Or had she? Oh, hell, it didn't matter. Blame it on seclusion. Space fever. That's what it was.

But, had the staff really noticed? How did he look at Marie? He looked at her like he looked at everybody else, didn't he?

∗   ∗   ∗   ∗

Igna thought she was alone in the shadows of the tunnel. Just a short distance from Richard's office, she let her shoulder fall against the wall in defeat. She straightened a little when she heard footsteps. She knew it couldn't be Richard who'd changed his mind, but she didn't expect Reese Mondiran with a look of concern in his eyes. Reese glanced at her, glanced at the Commanding Office door, then back to her. "Did you and Richard have a fight?"

"What are you doing here? It's the middle of the night." The normal venom in her voice was diluted with sadness.

"Day, night. Doesn't much matter in times like these. I just received the first relay from Boro. Things are going well. The relay ship is in position and Boro should be in the Rashmar system right on schedule."

"Good."

"He asked me to say hello to you."

Her eyes narrowed. "That's nice."

There was a long pause. Igna felt ashamed about being seen in such a depressed state, in front of Reese, no less. It surprised her even more that she didn't want him to leave. The soothing manner he'd often tried to impart, to no avail, was welcomed right now. Then he made her angry again despite the softness of his voice. "Forget about Richard."

She averted hate filled eyes. "So, it's Richard you're trying to protect. Do you think I am harassing your precious Commander? Even if I was, it's none of your business."

"I care about both of you—believe it or not—and I know it won't work for either of you."

"That's easy for you to say. I am the one who loves him."

He sighed. "That's right, you love him. I never doubted that. But you are not *in* love with him, and that's the difference. We both love him, but I'm not *in* love with him either."

A smile cracked the corner of her lip. "It's amazing there aren't rumors about the two of you. I wish I could spend half as much time with the man as you do."

Reese laughed. "I'm about as attracted to him as I am to you, Igna."

She smirked. "Well, at least we're clear on that."

He put a hand on her bony shoulder and nudged her down the hall. "You feel indebted to him. He saved you from a life in the wrestling pits. He gave you a chance to lead the Weapons Division. And, you feel indebted. Think about that."

She dabbed at the moisture in her eyes. "I suppose that's an easier way to look at it."

"Come on, girl, let's see some of that spirit you're so famous for."

"Well, I guess I have to put this loss behind me. It seems he's *in love* with Marie Flechette."

Reese chuckled. "Yeah, he's got his popularity match there, I would say. You can laugh at him when he's nursing his broken heart."

"And she goes back to where she belongs."

Reese grinned as they slowly strolled down the hall. The iciness in her voice warmed as she asked, "Did Boro really ask about me? He's been a good friend, you know."

*   *   *   *

It was two in the morning. He'd called it quits at his desk an hour ago because he was exhausted, notwithstanding Igna's little outburst. Now, he was wide awake and slumped on the settee that gave him a view of the nebula which tonight, was dazzling. The storm had left the skies clear, providing a grand view of the icy nebular spectrum that graced the eastern skyline. He regretted that the nebulous gasses were so thick on the west side of the mountain that they obscured all but a few lonely stars. But, she had seen both moons the night he first kissed her.

Richard's hands dangled between his knees. He fiddled with his nails, thought of those two moons, then her lips, her hair. Abruptly, he stood, swearing as he did so. Stomping across the room, he pulled on his boots and stormed out of his quarters.

He arrived at Detention Control in a fluster, having no idea how to tell the technicians to stop their hourly surveillance at this time of the night. A look of serious determination and a simple demand did the trick. Commander or not, he felt completely embarrassed to be found out by his men. He felt as if he was the guilty one as he strode down the detention hall corridor.

The door slid open. Everything was dead still, including the lump under the covers illuminated by the moonlight that streamed past the open curtains. He crept down the stairs, worrying that he might frighten her. Reaching the bed, he leaned over and admired her porcelain features, partially covered by a thick skein of golden hair. He bent down, listening for her breathing. Should he even bother her? This was ridiculous! But her name escaped his lips anyway. "Marie?" It was hardly audible. He firmly resolved that if she didn't awaken immediately, he would let her sleep. But her name slipped out again, louder. She opened her eyes, squinting and blinking. She rolled over quickly, then seeing who her visitor was, rubbed him into focus with a brisk turn of a fist against her eye.

"Richard, my goodness! Is—is everything all right? What time is it? Are you still working?"

"It's very late, and I'm very sorry." He paused, watching her lips creep into a smile, then he added, "No I'm not."

A little ghost thumped its fists against the walls of Marie's heart as she watched him tear off his cotton shirt.

"I couldn't stand it over there all by myself. Can I just hold you?"

"Of course. You must be exhausted." She moved closer to the wall, making room for him.

He gave her a long, sensuous kiss, then sunk against the pillow. "That I am, my love."

She settled into the cocoon of his arms, her back nestled against his chest. He held her a few minutes, gently caressing her hair. He sighed loudly and relaxed, but she doubted that his attempt at sleep was genuine. Her own attempts were useless as her body sensitized to his presence.

Her body twisted, their lips met, and his relaxed torso came alive.

CHAPTER 36

Clive Whale Baker was a nervous man. Selpin had just brought word that the second scout ship had landed and was still there. Clive worried that they would check his ship too meticulously. Into the bargain, the clans hadn't yet slowed down with their merry making. Just as Clive thought it was all coming to an end and he could get a team together, somebody piped up about the latest clan birth and everyone jumped up to fetch more food and wine.

Before Javid could join the throngs, Clive grabbed him by the collar. "How long do we have to wait after that last search plane leaves the area?"

"I don't know. You'll have to ask Dowlar."

Clive grunted. "That joker brother of yours never takes me seriously."

"What are you serious about this time?"

"My ship! It may be just a charred wreck to you guys, but I did notice that the front cabin remained intact. There'll be lots of things I can salvage if your snoopy neighbors haven't already helped themselves."

"Dowlar's at the control center. Go talk to him. I'm hungry."

Sure enough, Clive found Dowlar at one of the control center consoles.

"Hey, buddy," Dowlar chirped, "I hope you've chosen me for your salvage team."

Clive looked at him with cynical suspicion. "Why?"

"Because it'll be dangerous," Dowlar smiled. "Things can get a little routine around here. Besides, I'm very interested in your secret cache."

"Well, let's hope we're not too late." Clive's eyes raked up the wall of the cave that reflected the same endless degree of flickering illumination. "How the hell are you suppose to know if it's day or night in this burial chamber?"

Dowlar stuck a wristwatch up to Clive's face, bringing on a giggle from the console technicians. Clive smirked and set his own chronometer to local Rashmarian time.

"Good news," one of the technicians called out. "The scout ship is leaving."

"Good. I need two more volunteers, then you can show me outta this worm hole."

Clive ended up with three of them. His leach, Dowlar, and Javid and Selpin. He knew that Selpin wanted to spend more time with Javid, and that was fine with Clive. He knew that Selpin could hold his own.

The trip back out the cave system seemed much shorter than the trip in. Their pace had quickened, and familiarity lent to an air of speed. They reached the raw outdoors where a brisk hike up the mountain trail warmed them. Clive's heart chilled as they peered through the darkness over a snow-covered boulder at his ghostly craft. Signs of a touchdown by a scout ship were apparent, but the ruins appeared abandoned now.

"Let's go."

Dowlar's hand clamped firmly on Clive's forearm. "Two of us go. The other two wait here."

Clive saw no reason for that, but didn't argue. Suddenly, he slumped against the rock as repugnant memories of his previous visit to this planet came flooding back. Dowlar was right. All of his hair-raising expeditions through the galactic outbacks were nothing compared to the horrors he'd learned to execute here, horrors that would be meted on them if they were caught. He reached inside the jacket of his flight suit and pulled out a small blaster. He handed the weapon to Dowlar. "You know how to use this thing?"

Dowlar nodded sheepishly. "Yeah, and don't tell Master Farol."

"Old man Javid will come with me. The ship will have our bio-assessments and hopefully they won't look for any more of you guys if there's trouble."

Javid and Clive scuttled through the underbrush. As they approached, they were surprised to find the ship's hind end still smoldering. Sputters and coughs emitted from the rear quarter of the ship before bursts of sparks escaped into the atmosphere.

The rear quarter had blown apart except for a contiguous attachment along the base fuselage. Clive thought it resembled a big cracked egg. His nervous system took him on a quick tour of his bruises, reminding him of the power of that blast. A quick peek inside the open portside airlock revealed only the cockpit's black interior.

"Most of what we need is here," Clive whispered, then pushed his friend up into the ship. Javid in turn gave a surprisingly strong pull to the back of Clive's collar as the Nixodonian fought to scramble up the incline of the floor to secure his footing. They stopped and listened a moment. A baleful creak emitted from the back of the ship. Then silence, except for the wind that cued Clive's sensory system into high alert. His hackles were up and every nerve would play its little harmonics if danced upon. He looked over the instrument panel, squinting against the blackness.

"A little mind work and…" Clive fingered the panel blindly, landing on a switch that would hopefully still function, "…and…" It was a disappointing display. Three red emergency lights glowed dimly in different areas of the cockpit. It wasn't much, but in a few moments their eyes adjusted and the cockpit gave them a gloomy welcome.

They immediately noticed that parts of the control panel had been ripped out. The communications terminal had been destroyed, as were the radar sensors. Several of the communication screens had been shattered. "They thought we might want to call on our friends."

Javid expelled a breath. "Good thing we didn't need these to find them."

Clive's fingers dragged along the edges of the ceiling. Javid squinted at him curiously. "What are you doing?"

Without warning, a compartment door popped open, narrowly missing Javid's head. "They didn't find these." Clive put one boot on the captain's chair, anchored the other against the bulkhead and poked his head inside the secret cavity. He began to hand Javid a series of weapons; a blaster, grenades, a soft-laser.

"What are you doing with all this stuff hidden up there?"

Clive bounced a little to secure his footing. "I trade with the outbacks, remember? They're not always the friendliest lot, especially those Blue Rift merchants. Wow. Those guys will demolish your ship for one lousy bottle of Iggid hard bitter."

"Wait, wait. I can't carry all this."

Clive dropped to the deck. "Don't worry, I'll help you get this load out, then we're out of here. Something's giving me the creeps."

Clive equipped himself with a small but powerful hand blaster before helping Javid out of the freighter with the goods. Dowlar and Selpin darted out to accept the weapons before disappearing like shadows into the bush.

Back in the cabin, Javid had accepted only two blasters from the second load when he heard a thud from the rear quarter. "Clive!" he whispered sharply. Clive stopped, his head still stuffed into his secret compartment. The sound of shuffling feet had Clive dropping down instantly. The rear door of the cockpit flew open, smashing Clive on the side of the head, leaving an open-mouthed Javid to face the intruder. Javid had no idea how a blaster worked, but he hoped that simply pulling the trigger would stop the huge man who was about to enter the cockpit in one giant stride. The blaster only clicked. Javid shook it vigorously and squeezed again. Nothing.

Clive hadn't lost much ground. He pushed back against the door, catching the man mid-chest. The intruder let out a howl, and shoved back.

The battle had begun.

Javid watched in horror as Clive mounted the man's back and tried to strangle him. The huge man flailed about, once whacking Javid across the shoulder. Javid's blaster clattered to the floor. He jumped onto the captain's chair to clear himself from the brawl.

"Up there. The knives," Clive shouted at him.

Javid didn't know that he was capable of acrobatics until he found himself swinging from the edges of the secret compartment, legs scrambling to find footholds against the bulkhead. He pulled himself high enough into the crawlspace to get one hand groping madly for the weapons stash. Stretched to his limit, Javid fingered a gun and knives. Yes, they felt like knives. The racket below urged him to toss things below with lightening speed. No longer able to suspend himself, Javid dropped, landing on a mass of writhing legs. In the dimness he witnessed the flicker of a blade pound in and out of the body beneath. The wet blade was darkened by the reflection of the ruddy emergency lights. Javid swallowed bitter bile.

Clive struggled to his feet, taking a moment to assess his kill. He rolled the body over to retrieve Javid's blaster. Before handing it over, he gave Javid a wiry look and flipped the safety. "Now don't point this thing at me!"

They climbed out of the air lock, but not before two new enemies found their way out of the rear quarter through the large mid-ship fissure. The enemies cleared the undercarriage of the wreckage in order to gain a better firing angle. Javid took partial cover behind the round of the airlock. Trembling, he fired, but only managed to singe a tree behind the two men. Javid let out a blood-curdling scream, partially in fright, and partially to warn the others. The foe stopped for a second, wondering what unruly alien they might be facing. In their moment of uncertainty, they didn't see Clive crawl atop his ship. Seconds later, Clive took one of them out from above. The survivor quickly slid under the curvature of the ship for protection. The man fired at Javid who was escaping around the protective tree trunks towards the nose of the ship. Missed. In the same arcing movement, the rebel discharged a thin, deadly bolt up at Clive. Javid gasped, but there was no killing Clive with that one. From his vantage point, Javid marveled at Clive's agility and marksmanship. The pilot prowled like a big cat, blaster pointing toward the moon that profiled him. With great swiftness he moved along the top of his leviathan ship to where the rear quarter had split in two. Clive peered down over the ragged edge into the exposed interior below. Javid's heart thudded as he watched Clive deliberately toss a chunk of debris several yards to his left. It clunked loudly on the surface and stopped just short of a fall into the belly of the ship. An orange blast streaked skyward from the interior of the ship.

A fourth one.

There was nothing Javid could do militarily. His hotrod curling iron would be useless with his lousy aim. So, he did what Rashmarians do. He squeezed his thin body far beneath the nose of the craft and concentrated, keeping his eyes open but not focusing on anything but his inner self. With a few simple techniques, he thought himself into invisibility—not in the true sense of the word, but his aura would be undetectable to his hunters. Footsteps came his way, stopped, shuffled, fired at Clive, and carried on.

Clive had his hands full and hoped that Dowlar had been serious about his ability to handle a weapon. He hoped that Javid was hiding and not dead. It was a long slide off the side of the ship, but a strip of spared exterior allowed Clive to hit the ground unscathed. He dashed to the nearest multiplex receiver dish, now sadly grounded from its original lofty position. Just as he crouched behind it, a barrage of lasers scintillated off the side of the craft, showering up and over the dish. A dozen sizzling sparks landed on the thin mesh of the dish. It exploded into flames.

Clive threw a hand over his head to save his hair from scorching, and backtracked, covering himself with his own shots. A large crumple in the ship's hull gave him a moments reprieve. With only a second to think about it, he dashed for the nearby forest. The two remaining pursuers spotted him, but not before Clive dove behind the cover of a large bolder that cracked with the impact of a poor aim. A long, spiny branch sizzled off overhead and crashed down on Clive. He struggled to free himself, unable to quell a growing panic. Clive often wondered how he would die, but a trap in the form of a thorny branch seemed like an unusual and sad ending. With riotous thrashing Clive freed himself only to face a blaster leveled at him in the moonlight. He froze, then watched the man keel over, smoke spiraling from his chest. The enemy's partner, standing directly behind the downed man, dropped to a crouch. Arms outstretched, weapon pointing in front of him, the man quickly twisted toward the rear of the ship

where the deadly blast had originated. It was a second too long. Clive had time to
raise his own blaster. The rebel flew into gory bits as he was hit from both angles
at once. Dowlar had a fair aim, Clive mused.

Silence.

Only the wind.

These Rashmarians were not stupid, Clive thought. They waited to make sure
the great, inanimate crate didn't give birth to any more surprises. Finally, the cold
helped Clive decide that they'd waited long enough and he crept out of hiding.
He was silently joined mid-ship by the others, all unscathed.

"We disturbed their sleep," Dowlar commented dryly.

"Yeah. Well, the boys from the valley aren't going to be happy! Four dead soldiers will bring the whole fucking army up here. They'll find us for sure, now."

"Don't worry," Dowlar said. "The wolves will smell a free meal and be here to
clean up the evidence long before a rescue team arrives."

"Wolves aren't about to cover our tracks, Dowlar," argued Clive.

Dowlar grinned crookedly. "These aren't exactly wolves. Not like the Nixodonians know wolves. These creatures will cover our tracks plenty well enough."
He giggled. "And the TRA are scared to death of them. They won't hang around
long if they know the wolves have been here."

Clive peered beyond the shadowy trunks. The murky woods brought shivers
up his spine as he imagined some giant hyena-type monster leaping into the
clearing and lunging directly for his throat. "Let's get out of here, then. I don't
feel like being part of something's lunch"

"Have we got everything?" Javid asked, his own gaze peering through the forest for signs of the beasts growing vivid in his memory.

Clive eyed the monolith, his gaze settling on its broken back. "Everything
except whatever goodies our friends might have left for us at their camp. I'm
really tempted to take a look—except for those wolves."

"They won't be here yet, and even if they come we know how to deal with
them. They don't take well to certain mental manipulations."

Clive rolled his eyes. "Great. Then get your radar brain in repel-mode and let's
check out the hold."

They made their way in a slow, cautious procession through the gaping
wound of the ship where they found a comfortable little hide-out; thermal winter
sleeping bags, a food unit, a few personal supplies. A small fire crackled in the
middle of the makeshift camp, burning a hole through what used to be Clive's
rear corridor. He felt great loss for the pathetic derelict.

Clive kicked at the hood of one of the bags, face string still pulled tight. "This must be why they didn't hear us right away. You'd think one of them would have been standing guard. It looks like the cold got to the little wimps."

"TRA search components!" Dowlar whispered excitedly, looking over a stack of electronics equipment. "Quite a find if we can get these back to the cave."

"My bag expands," Selpin said. Clive nodded and Selpin began to fill his bag with the square, awkward objects.

"Good news, Whale," Dowlar said while fiddling with the equipment. "First, the sleepy goons weren't fast enough to send an alert, and second, there's no way that this equipment could detect our old radio codes. It's too sophisticated. Who knows what they have downstairs," Dowlar jerked a thumb toward the valley, "but I imagine it's even more sophisticated than this stuff. And check this out." He tapped at a small screen. "We may be able to monitor *their* meanderings with this baby. Sure turns the tables on who's watching who, doesn't it?"

"Whom," Clive corrected.

Dowlar scowled. "Whatever. This might help us land our Fringe allies with greater ease—if they dare send anyone to our rescue now."

*   *   *   *

When Boro found the deep space magnetic field of the Rashmar moon, it did exactly what Hollis said it would do: throw his electronics system right out of whack. Except for unverifiable outgoing transmissions, he would now be out of touch with the relay ship until he made his way back out of the system.

His piloting prowess came in handy. Boro managed to catch not only the field, but also the precise gravitational corridor that would pull him right to the moon's surface. He shut down everything but emergency power and settled for a long wait in the captain's chair. He was tired after all those hours of feverish calculating while dangling precariously in space, looking to connect with this acclaimed magnetic field. It was nothing but a death trap if not calculated properly, but then, not everyone would make a free fall. Hollis had recommended a controlled inward flight, which would have been much easier, but if the images of the security ships that circled this planet were really what he thought they were, he needed to remain invisible.

Several hours later, the scanner's buzzer jolted him from a sprawled doze in the captain's chair. The Rashmarian moon had filled the view port. Rubbing the sleep out of his natural eye, Boro analyzed the screens before him. The long-range screen had pulled in clear images of the ships he had in question. Muttering an oath, he settled in to study the information. Boro fingered the scanner controls to expand the segments of Rashmar's upper orbits. He magnified portions of the ships that most attracted his interest. It was somehow shocking, yet no great surprise. There, protecting the TRA stronghold was half a dozen KM-223 Security Cruisers, fully armed, recent models, and built exclusively for the Nixodonian Space Navy. In addition, the scanners picked up the presence of at least six headhunters. No one would dare attack this planet.

That wasn't the biggest surprise. The bastards hadn't even bothered to paint over the make and model of their booty, yet they had the audacity to smear emblems of their reptilian bird in huge murals across the bodies of the stolen vessels. Boro transmitted the information on a spy beam, feeling anxious about the inability to confirm the success of the transmission through the distortions of the magnetic field. Putting aside his foreboding, he calculated his lunar landing.

Alone in the cold darkness, the little ship hid amid the boulders of the barren moon, camouflaged and waiting. The moon rotated silently until the white and blue crescent of Rashmar came into view. Meanwhile, Boro reviewed the geographic charts. Hitting the mountainous region wouldn't be a problem. Mountains covered eighty percent of the planet. Hitting the right mountain would be the trick. He clenched his jaw, wary about sending out a radar code no one would believe still existed. Nevertheless, Boro punched in the code stored in his electronic brain, one that should warn the Rashmarians of his presence. Then he waited, dubiously.

CHAPTER 37

Marie spent her days in near bliss, the activities on the base creating endless diversions. For the most part, she had abandoned her lovely cave home in lieu of another. Her nights were spent where the nebula cast its mauve illumination across her lover's bed. Her days were spent wandering about the caves, making herself popular as an avid student of military procedures and logistics. Her joy was enhanced by Richard himself. He quickly gave up making a secret of their relationship. Before long the rumor was accepted as truth, and no one argued the Commander's whims. He allowed Marie to join him whenever possible and today Marie included herself in the group that gathered in the control room for an impromptu meeting. She took the liberty of standing near him in order to better understand what was transpiring at the console. Only Igna resented Marie's presence. Tall and cat-like she kept her distance, standing only within earshot of the work station.

The technician at the station looked up. "Captain Boro has successfully relayed a transmission from inside the magnetic corridor, Commander. You might want to see this, sir."

Richard leaned forward for a closer look. His breath drew inward forcefully. "Those are Nixodonian KM-223 battleships!"

"That's correct, sir. Look, here, in the magnified view." The technician punched a series of commands to give them a broadside view of the cruisers. Marie's skin crawled when she recognized the reptilian bird mounted across the body of her nation's stolen vessels.

"They don't deny a claim on these ships, do they?" Richard alleged.

"This looks bad," Hollis muttered. "And look. They've also got a half dozen headhunters."

"What's the latest from Bill Tripp?" Richard asked.

"He's just entered the Dorian system, sir."

After a short discussion, the group broke up. Richard guided Marie's shoulders toward his office where he surprised her with an announcement that he was sneaking away with her for another swim. He was desperate for a break. Now!

With his approval, Marie had gone to the pool twice on her own. It had been an exhilarating experience, alone in the wilderness, but she much preferred Richard's company. It wasn't long before Marie curled her arms around Richard's neck in shoulder-deep water.

"You know, I'm already addicted to this. Swim until you're exhausted, then sun on the rocks until you roast. It's marvelous!"

His gaze raked across her naked flesh. "I hope you haven't been giving my guards too much of a show?"

She laughed. "If they're hoping for that, they'll be sorely disappointed."

"Why? What have you been wearing?"

She grinned. "Those sexy undergarments you so kindly supplied me with."

Suddenly, Marie heard laughter that wasn't her own. She stopped abruptly, cocking an ear toward the sound. Richard wondered what was wrong, and then heard the tittering voices. "Ah, the natives have come to meet you at last."

Marie created a vortex in the water with the sudden swirl to check all 360 degrees of the shoreline. "Where?"

Richard let out a soft whistle, and a little brown face poked out of the underbrush. Marie gasped excitedly. The face was beautiful. White teeth contrasted against a chocolate milk complexion rimmed with straight black hair. The child looked so young! Another face appeared. The two children giggled, hands covering mouths shyly, eyes a-sparkle. As suddenly as they appeared, the faces vanished back into the underbrush.

"Wait, little ones," Marie called quietly. She glanced at Richard. "Can you bring them back? Whistle like that again."

"No need."

She followed his gaze to the tiny beach where a total of five children came quietly from the underbrush to stand on the sandy crescent, hands clasped, grins wide. Marie figured they were anywhere from five to ten, or twelve years of age. It was difficult to tell. Their only clothes were in the form of small loincloths low on their hips. Decorative thongs wrapped about their arms, waists or ankles. A hand-crafted pendant hung from the neck of one, a leather pouch hung, full of lumpy objects from the youngest boy's neck. Three had colored paint smeared across their faces while the others displayed color in the dangling pieces of cloth about their groins. The youngest stood naked.

"Hello," she breathed, then dragged her gaze away to meet Richard's. "Can they understand me?"

"Say 'Yawka.' That's hello in their language."

"Yawka."

The children burst into uncontrollable laughter, their bodies writhing with embarrassed hysteria. Marie found herself caught in their joy, and laughed with them. "Yawka," she said again. In chorus, they answered back. The young boy was the bravest, wading out to his knees, then his waist. Marie was afraid the child would wander too deeply. She sloshed through the water to meet him. Marie stopped short, her cheeks flaring with embarrassment. She shot a glance at Richard. "I'm naked!"

Richard smiled. "So is he."

She swallowed and talked softly to the little boy as he approached. His pudgy cheeks nearly occluded his stern little mouth. His black eyes had no visible pupils, but she knew he inspected her in detail. Marie crouched in the water beside him. Instantly his hands reached up to explore her hair. Suddenly, he showed her the pouch around his neck and fingered the hard contents. Marie was relieved when the little boy didn't care to share his treasures with her. Suddenly he looked deep into her eyes. As if they were already long-time friends, he began to chatter in a clear, small voice.

Perplexed, Marie turned to Richard. "What is he saying?"

"I don't know the language well, but he's talking about his tree house. I think he wants you to join him there."

"Oh…great!" she laughed.

Suddenly the boy was in her arms. Marie nearly dropped the child, being completely foreign to the feel of a child's bare skin against her own. He settled himself comfortably on her hip, totally oblivious to her nakedness. Marie's mind flashed back to her last doomed Benefit Concert tour. She would have visited the sick children on G2, but they would have been carefully selected, dressed in their best clothes and meticulously screened for communicable diseases. Just for the media's sake, she would have been allowed to hold one or two. Others she would have been allowed to see only through crib bars or behind glass plates. This! This was heaven. She turned to Richard, smiling until her cheeks cramped. She wondered if he understood the uniqueness of this experience.

The beaming face that turned to share her excitement with Richard was one he'd not soon forget. Her full smile and brilliant eyes radiated her immeasurable content at the opportunity to hold the young boy. After a few moments, the child lost interest and wiggled in her grasp. She set him back into the water and he waded out to his companions. When he reached the shore, the whole bunch disappeared into the tattered foliage without even a backward glance.

"They'll need some time to get to know you. Their first visits are often short."

Marie waded out to him and grasped him in an exuberant hug. "He let me hold him!"

He held her tightly, unable to avoid visions of Marie's belly swollen with their own child, perhaps as a way to trap her here forever? Quickly erasing the thought he said, "I think that little one would like to be your friend."

CHAPTER 38

Clive and the others each hauled a sack of confiscated goods away from the broken freighter and down the path toward the ravine bed. He'd thought to dispose of the bodies himself until an eerie howl from the deep forests quickly changed his mind. The group glanced at each other in relief as they reached the entrance of the cave. Icy breaths steamed about their frozen faces but no one spoke. Their shared glances expressed gratitude to the Rashmarian gods who were about to protect them yet again. Outside, a heavy snowfall had begun—huge, white, blessed flakes. Clive peered out at the slate gray sky. This snow would adequately cover their tracks to the cave before the new search teams arrived. And they would come!

The main hall brought a disappointing welcome. There were only a few folk warming by the fire. "We've received a message from a Fringe ship," one of them said excitedly. "It's made a safe landing on the moon. Its captain is waiting for us to guide him down."

"Are you sure?" Clive asked, shocked at the possibility.

"Yes. The space teams are already preparing the underground hangar for his landing."

The control room crawled with nearly every member present in that mountain dwelling. Clive wished the curious crowds would thin until he noticed that everyone had his particular job to carry out. Master Farol called Clive to the terminal at which he stood.

"A Fringe officer sent by Captain Hollis has arrived, Mr. Baker, but there is a problem. There are too many security ships in the area to guide him down. He seems safe enough on the moon for the moment, and seeing as he's missed the magnetic window for today, it gives us another day to come up with a solution. Do you have any advice on how to proceed?"

Dowlar wormed his way between the knot of people at the radio terminal and grinned up at Whale. "We could do it with that confiscated equipment, old friend."

"What! Somehow trick TRA away from the moon's magnetic field?" The wide-eyed Clive looked into the mischievous eyes of Dowlar. Clive gave an irritated huff. "Tell the pilot to hold tight. He's my only way off this block of ice, so I'm gonna get him down if it takes me a week!" Moments later, Clive tapped at the screen displaying a detailed description of the Fringe Dweller's space rig. "This is only a T-38 so he should fit through that hole well enough." Clive glanced at the rusty slit of the hangar doors. He looked at Dowlar. "Come on radar-brain. Let's get to work."

Clive and Dowlar toiled late into the night, selecting pieces that might work to send those security ships on a snipe hunt. By midnight, they'd rigged a tap into the hangar's antennae, giving them a visual display of nearly every ship in orbit. They also picked up the arrival of a scout ship. The TRA boys were already here to find out why their comrades hadn't called in.

There were tense moments, with everyone sitting as still as mice. Clive tried telling them that it wasn't their voices that would give them away. No one listened. Then Javid whispered that they were protecting the hideout and the hangar doors by means of a meditative cloak because physical camouflage alone wouldn't be enough. A befuddled Clive chose not to ask, but later he'd beg Master Farol to teach him more about this weird religion of theirs. A meditative cloak? Did he mean a cloaking device, but one spiritually created? Hokey. But anything would help, in his line of work.

An hour later, the search ship most graciously moved on, leaving the skies barren all the way to the Ocar Pass. "Now we just have to clear the lower orbits," Dowlar said. "Wait, here's an idea. A satellite." Dowlar pointed to the small screen. "We'll wait until just before the window opens, then send a distress signal that will look like it's being emitted from this satellite. That should distract the ship long enough for our friend to drop into the magnetic funnel undetected."

"Better than a good game of Colors," Clive muttered, admiring the power of the portable equipment they'd pilfered. "Still," he added with foreboding, "it's hard to believe we can track all of their moves with this stuff."

"Yes," Dowlar hesitated. "Let's just hope they can't lock onto us in return." The two glanced at each other, and silently decided to let the gods take care of that one.

It took only one distress relay to attract the rebel ship, which was no doubt confused. However, curiosity got the best of them, and the most troublesome security cruiser blipped across the screen, away from the narrow funnel of the moon's magnetic core.

With a sharp nod, Dowlar signaled to the technicians beside him. They began to punch in the message that would call the Fringe ship home.

*   *   *   *

Boro watched in amazement as his worst menace suddenly took off in a backtracking motion across his screens. Moments later, his console bleeped. It was Rashmarian ground control. They were giving him the go. With a deep breath, he fired up his thrusters and sprang off the moon, dropping head first toward the growing emerald crescent of Rashmar.

*   *   *   *

The entire clan was mesmerized by the screen before them. The moon's invisible funnel hid the Fringe ship for the entirety of its journey. Suddenly, the headset-clad technician thrust his thumbs upward. The hangar doors could be opened.

Each one scrambled to his station. The great panels separated with a grinding screech. Clive found himself gritting his teeth against the noise and feared the aperture would fail halfway through its rusty function. Brilliant light from the descending ship's thrusters blinded them as chunks of white snow fell inward to melt instantly on the pad below. The T-38 lowered through the aperture with an ear-splitting hiss. Its landing gear fingered downward, the howling thrust allowing the ship to alight softly. The thrusters dropped in volume as the pilot shut down the engines. The hangar doors scraped shut and the natives were left with a moment to readjust to the artificial lighting.

Javid waited eagerly for the pilot to disembark. He squeezed his way around Clive's lumbering frame to catch a glimpse of their savior. The misty shroud was now settling at the base of the ship and the Fringe man emerged into view. Javid's pounding heart stopped, painfully. The pilot shook hands with the technicians who greeted him on the pad, but Javid could not join in the excitement. Rather, he grasped Clive's arm in a steel grip.

"What is it?"

Javid stared at the mutilated pilot with the anomalous half-metal face glinting under the bright ceiling lights. His mind ricocheted madly from the sight before him to images of the murderous pirate who took away his precious Marie.

"Clive, we've got trouble!"

CHAPTER 39

Boro didn't have time to react to the punch he took in the gut while shaking hands with the Nixodonian. Nor did he expect the shove at the back of his knees by no less than a dozen of the little Rashmarians. They were on him like a swarm of ants. His latent reactions couldn't prevent his wrists being pinned behind his back and his legs bound. He could do nothing but howl in sheer surprise when he was thrown onto a makeshift gurney by a dozen of the little weasels. They carried him at a run down a tunnel, his arms crushed beneath his body as he bounced against the wooden slats of a gurney. They took him to a small prison chamber where they dropped the gurney to the stone floor. The Rashmarians shouted orders at each other and managed to chain him to a wall, his arms stretched out to either side. Boro seethed. Had Hollis set a trap for him? Was this how they were going to be rid of their infamous pirate?

Boro hung on the chains and watched the natives step back against the opposite wall. A long-nosed native, draped in a colorfully woven cape, stepped into the cell. Boro guessed this was the leader. With him came several others carrying extra oil torches, giving Boro a better look at his captors. One little fellow stepped closer than the others dared. He vibrated with anger. Again, Boro was astounded.

Hollis had said nothing but good things about these natives. At the top of his list had been their excellent disposition. Lies! All lies. The angry fellow came closer, thrusting his face forward.

"What did you do with her?"

Boro's eye narrowed. His microprocessor sifted through recognition patterns, but nothing positive came up. Curious, Boro hung forward from his shackles. The flames danced eerie shadows across his face. "Do with whom?"

"Marie Flechette," the native yelled.

Boro was completely stumped. "Who the hell are you?"

"You ought to know!" the Rashmarian spat. "It's a splinter from your laser that landed in my gut when you attacked the *Starquest*."

Boro's natural eye narrowed. "You must be joking!"

"It's no joke, you fiend."

"Now, Javid. Give the captain a chance to tell us his side of the story." It was the Master's voice, steady and calm. Javid waved a hand at the Master without taking his eyes from the half-faced brute. "I can tell you all the story. He killed more than a hundred people before kidnapping my employer and her bodyguard. It's because of him that I'm here now."

"Then you should be grateful."

Javid's body remained rigid. Inside, he crumbled. Had he been away so long that he'd lost his soul to anger and mistrust? He wanted to personally strangle the brute, here and now, while the villain was powerless. Clive was right. He was a coward. The Master came and stood beside his servant. Javid made an urgent plea to the pirate, even though it was disrespectful to do so.

"Just tell me if she is alive or dead."

Beads of moisture were forming along the pirate's forehead. The taut muscles in his neck glistened. The artificial eye clicked back and forth between the master and the servant, but the natural eye stayed focused on Javid. "Oh, she's alive all right. And very safe."

Clive Baker dipped below the low cell door and propped himself against the back wall, towering over the group. He'd checked out the man's ship. It seemed friendly enough. The pilot, on the other hand, looked like some sort of warlord who'd lost his fleet. He wondered if the pirate had really followed Javid here, or if he was on other business. The coincidences were definitely uncanny.

"Tell us who sent you, and the reason you came here," Farol said.

"Like I said, Captain Hollis of the Fringe Federation sent me. But how did this little weasel get here?" He tossed his head toward Javid.

"I am not a weasel, you brute, and I want you to tell me where my Lady is!" He lunged forward and kicked the prisoner in the shin. Farol had to physically haul Javid back. The prisoner fought against the chains, his bound feet slipping out from under him, causing his arms to strain painfully from the shackles.

"Enough, Javid! I will speak to our prisoner."

Javid shook himself to straighten his clothing, insolently holding his ground while glaring at the Fringe man. Farol put a warning arm across Javid's chest and asked the prisoner, "Is it true that you are the same one who attacked the space cruiser called the *Starquest*?

"Unfortunately, I am," he admitted. "I was doing the duty asked of me by the leader of the Fringe Federation. Trust me, it was in your best interest as well."

"How is that?"

Boro explained about the misuse of the heiress's cosmetics codes for the purpose of arms dealing, and the propaganda movie that would now be in the theater houses of Telexa.

Javid slowly stepped back toward the wall. His face registered pain, humiliation, and disbelief. As he reached the wall, he felt a reassuring grip from a large hand he knew to be Clive's. Javid became only vaguely aware that he remained glued to Clive's tall frame. His eyes stayed locked on the Fringe man.

Javid wanted to hate the pirate. He didn't want to believe what he was hearing. But the pirate mentioned Paul Lambert, then Henrie Marchand and *Angel's Test*. He even said something about Senator Phoebe who was now in charge of a useless search for the ship that had taken Marie away. He felt Clive's frame stiffen with the mention of the senator's wife, Lola Phoebe, who'd also been aboard the *Starquest*. How could the pirate know all these things? Then he made reference to Bill Tripp, saying that Bill had joined the Fringe Security Forces after he and Marie were deemed innocent. That finished Javid off. He crumpled to a squat and took in great gulps of air, unsuccessful in his attempt to ease his clamoring mind. He'd known there was a thread tying Marie to the galactic crisis. But this? If Captain Boro told the truth, Marie faced a future that could lead only to exile or death. Oh, how he wished he could comfort her now, tell her how sorry he was that his powers had become so weak that he hadn't suspected anything until it was too late.

The Fringe man continued his account in crescendo. "And the security ships guarding this planet? They are all Nixodonian, with their original marking still on them. That's because very soon it won't matter. Every bit of military equipment in this galaxy will be under the control of Angel Keem."

Farol sighed. "It seems there is little hope for a quick resolution, then."

The artificial eye snapped images of the room while the other stayed focused on the Master. "There's certainly no hope if you keep me chained up. My mission is to find out when the Telexans plan to move their armada into Nix States. We need to know their flight path through the Fringe. Our only hope is to ambush them. We have very little time, and I need your help. All of you."

There was a grave silence. Paradoxically, Javid found himself smiling when he heard Clive drawl, "I don't believe this." For a man whose only crime was to have loved the wrong woman, he'd paid dearly. Javid was sure Clive would soon be asked to face his worst enemy.

It was quickly decided by Master Farol that the Fringe man could be released. Javid found his wit and scrambled to his Master's side, cowering behind him as he watched the pirate massage his wrists. "Please, Master, may I say something?"

The Master nodded. Javid swallowed then spoke. "To me, you are guilty of many crimes, but I now understand why you did those things. We must somehow forgive each other, and work together if we can."

"To be fair, they could be called misfortunes of war. I cannot blame you for your anger, but it is because of my actions that your lady is safe."

"Where is she now?"

"I cannot tell you," Captain Boro said. "I say that for your protection. If things fail here, you would die passing the information on to the Telexans."

Javid nodded. "Then, if you won't tell me," he took a stab at a sudden, crazy proposal, "perhaps when you leave here, you can take me to her. I've spent almost twenty years with Miss Flechette. As you can imagine, I fear for her life."

The metal man grunted. "Fear not. She is well protected."

Javid sighed with relief.

"As for taking you to the princess, perhaps I would consider your request in exchange for helping me find my way to the TRA base."

Javid smiled. "You hardly need bribery for that. If you are here for our greater good, we are all willing to help. Our ways are not as technically advanced as yours, so be prepared to do things in an ancient, but effective kind of way."

"Yes, its seems I've been introduced to your level of technology already."

"Transportation may be a problem. Yours is the only ship in our service. Clive and I arrived only a few days ago but our ship was destroyed in a crash landing."

"Great! Two refugees!"

Clive stepped forward. "Good to have you on board, Captain." He shook hands with the pirate. "But if you're short on space, I'm Nixodonian, so I get a ride out of here before this weasel does."

CHAPTER 40

One would have expected a welcoming delegation when Raymond Flechette set foot on the tarmac of the Dorian spaceport. Instead, he walked alone. Even the crew had been ordered to remain within the craft until he returned. He planned to stay only a few days, during which time Raymond hoped to remain incognito despite the FC monogram on the side of his ship. Sunglasses, a long gray coat and wide brimmed hat kept onlookers searching for something more titillating as Raymond slipped into the terminal unnoticed.

Raymond found lodging at a third rate hotel. An overpowering fatigue changed his focus from the unsightly room to his duffel bag in search of his pills. These were supposed to be the latest miracle drug? Some miracle. He could hardly walk and his insides felt like they were about to explode. He stuck his nose close to the mirror and blinked his bloodshot eyes. With a sigh, he decided that if his only hope of lasting even a little longer was to take these pills, then he'd best take them.

It wasn't until the next morning that Raymond felt strong enough to venture from his hotel. It took a long time to find a cab driver who had even an inkling of what FC was, let alone its location. Finally a hovercab arrived with such a blur of speed that Raymond feared it might crash into the tacky front columns of the hotel. The cab came to a nose-plunging stop, setting it rocking as the buffers fought to stabilize the craft. A short man, dressed in riotous clothing, jumped out of the cab and extended a hand in greeting. Raymond nearly choked when he heard the price needed to hire the only cabby who knew the location of the FC laboratory.

"Come wid me, sir. You berry special. I take good care. Take you where you like."

Right! At that price, everyone was berry special.

Believing at his age that he was through with surprises, Raymond found himself surprised time and again. This, according to Paul Lambert, was a city that long-awaited the prestige and economic advantage of an intergalactic company. But there was obviously no interest in popular fashion here. The people who walked the streets certainly didn't look like the type to care. How gullible had he been? The crowds were of endless cultural diversity. He couldn't tell which might actually be Dorian. One race he couldn't identify. Humanoid, for sure, but hair covered to a great degree, with long noses, and ears that would rival the radar on his own spaceship. He spotted a few blue-skins from the Blue Rift, but who could guess from which sector any of these other ruffians might have come!

The cab hummed on and on. The suburbs came and went.

In mild alarm, Raymond tried communicating with the driver. The cabby seemed completely mistaken about his desired destination, yet the cabby just kept flapping a hand loosely while saying, "No Prrroblem. Eeez berry far."

Raymond became apprehensive when no logic would change the cabby's mind. Perhaps he did know where he was going and the distance was the reason behind the exorbitant cab fare. As the cabby ventured north, far into a barren and rugged countryside, Raymond grew more concerned. He'd been in the cab almost an hour and another of those damned fevers was attacking him again.

Feverishly, he watched the flats give way to boulder-ridden hills. The range achieved little height, but it was scarred by deep ravines that plummeted to narrow fertile creek beds below. As they followed the snaking patterns of the ravines, Raymond suddenly noticed a tall, fortified fence. Its dimensions alone warned that it would fulfill its purpose with deadly intent. The fence stretched beyond the hills and out of sight.

"What are we doing here? This isn't where I asked you to take me," Raymond argued.

"Sure it is," The cabby pointed a finger. "I think you wish to go here. See?"

Raymond thought his eyes deceived him, but as they drew closer, a set of buildings came into view. His heart plummeted. On the side of a massive, metal-sided warehouse, and so small that they were within a quarter mile before it was noticeable, was the FC logo in its full and correct colors. It was the only visible marking anywhere. Behind this warehouse was a second stupendous structure that covered an area at least the size of his estate. Raymond wasn't sure what he'd expected to find, but it wasn't this. He could only speculate on the actual purpose of this fortress, but whatever this space-occupying lesion was, it had no doubt been financed with FC money. His body convulsed with a nervous shiver, the fever provoking a fresh onslaught of sweating. Raymond urged the cabby to approach the gate where a military guard stood. The guard seemed prepared enough to talk to them, but no sign of emotion encroached the stone cold features. This was no ordinary guard. This was a trained military killer. According to this guard, entering the premises required special identification, and that stalled Raymond right there. His mouth curled. Why hadn't he thought to forge himself a few identification papers to hand to a military guard at the gate of what was supposed to be his own damned plant! Raymond stared at the soldier and fell silent. He no longer kidded himself. The guard asked how else he could help. Raymond smiled stiffly "I was told that this was the best place to buy some creams for my wife. Ah, perhaps at a factory discount?"

"The plant isn't open for business, sir."

"I was afraid of that," Raymond muttered while memorizing the property's details.

"Pardon me, sir?"

"Do you know when it will be open?" Raymond said. "I was told it was already."

"I'm not sure where you got your information, sir. This is not a public area. If you wish to buy some products you'll have to go back to the city. There is an outlet at the City Center Promenade. Your cabby will know where that is."

Raymond looked at the guard in hysterical disbelief. Was this bullet-laden character really telling him where to find a cosmetics outlet? What a joke!

The cabby innocently turned around and told Raymond that there was "no prrroblem" taking him to the Promenade. Raymond gave his cabby a weak smile and ordered the cabby to turn around. They sped off in the direction of the city—vaguely. The hovercab bounced and skipped over boulder-littered terrain on what the cabby said was a "short cup" back to town. The happy fellow glanced over his shoulder, grinning stupidly. Raymond wished the cabby would keep his eyes on where they were going. Another surprise.

"Why you not go in? Your plant, no?"

Raymond felt the blood drain from his face. "Who are you?"

The cabby gave him a look of injured pride. "You, me friend. You berry special. You Mr. Flecheeet, no?"

Raymond's heart pounded. "How do you know who I am?"

The cabby laughed, throwing the craft sideways with a jolt on the steering. "Me smart cabby! You no be scared, Mr. Flecheeet. Me take good care."

"How do you know who I am?" Raymond grasped the back of the cabby's collar.

"Eeeesy, Mr. Flecheeet. Me see you at spaceport yesterday. Me look for you because me know where you want to go. Me no tell others. Stupid that!"

"You tell no one?" He caught himself falling into the cabby's slang.

"Me tell no one. Me take you where you want to go. You berry special."

Raymond glanced about the desolate landscape. "Is this a dangerous planet? I mean, do factories or businesses have a tendency to put up that kind of security?"

"Naw," he grunted. "That too much, don't you think? Such big fence for cream…ohhhhh! Me and friends wonder why."

"Do you know why?"

The cabby shook his thick hair and stuck out his bottom lip. "Nope! But, me like to know."

Raymond leaned forward. "I'd like to know, too."

"I know you okay. We love princess. But them FC boys?" he thumbed over his shoulder. "They bad ones, no?"

Raymond sighed in relief. The cabby didn't believe he was a part of the conspiracy, part of the obvious military base that invaded their countryside.

"How much? How much to keep you quiet? To tell no one of my presence here."

The cabby glanced back again, mouth frowning, eyes large. "No special price. My name is Dee, and Dee do special for you." He burst into laughter then reached a hand back to give Raymond a friendly, but solid slap on the cheek. "Da wife like sample. I get for her from Promenade and they make her look nice. You berry special. Me take you there."

They had strange ways these Dorians!

"Instead of going to the Promenade," Raymond ventured, "could you take me to an electronics distributor?"

"Oh, yes, yes. You want things to help you into your proberty? I got place for you, but you tell no one. Special friend this. Give you hot goods. Guard dead— *boom!*" The cabby jolted a finger into the air.

Raymond frowned. "Not that special. I just need a commlink—for you and me, you understand? I pay you well. You be available for me day and night."

"Ohhh," he turned with big eyes, "No prrroblem. Dee work for you." The cabby suddenly laughed deviously. "Soon we have secrets, eh? So what you say. Me no tell—you no tell, eh?"

In an unhealthy part of town, the cab came to a bouncing halt. They entered a small, obscure shop, that crawled with sentients from every part of the galaxy. Every one of them seemed to be a "berry special" friend of his driver. Looking over the tough group, Raymond ventured that there would be lots of "me no tell—you no tell" going on here.

While looking over an impressive array of links, Raymond remained surrounded by several weapons-laden cronies who scrutinized his every move. Finally, a tall humanoid gray-skin showed him a more useful commlink after Raymond argued that he really didn't need the high security model with the built-in dart gun.

The affair ended on a sharp note. Dee had to help Raymond to the cab after a fit of coughing doubled Raymond over. The storeowner waggled his head as if giving his permission for them to carry on. Dee waved and cut in full thrust leaving Raymond plastered weakly against the back of the seat. Dee twisted back, again ignoring the road. "You berry sick, no? Why you be sick?"

"I don't know. I just am." Raymond coughed painfully. Dee brought the cab to a sudden rocking halt and poured himself over the backrest to examine his passenger. "You take drug. Why you take drug? They make you berry bad."

Raymond rolled his red streaked eyes. "No. I take medication for my illness."

"Bad medicine. You die soon. Why? You good man, no?"

"Yes! I am a good man. But, drive. I need to get some rest."

The cabby obeyed, and then helped him out of the cab at the hotel. "I stay nearby. I berry worry."

"No, you go home," Raymond said weakly. "I'll call you."

The cabby didn't look like he was going to obey, but Raymond didn't care. The fool could stay all night if he wished. Raymond made it only as far as the reception couch before having to sit down. He looked at the bistro across the lobby and decided that slaking his hunger would solve the problem. Slowly, he made his way into the darkened atmosphere and settled on a stool at the bar. It was clean, but certainly not the kind of place he'd grown accustomed to over the years. When he saw the bartender, he knew he'd never get used to places like this. The man looked down a wide pug nose shadowed by superfluous eyebrows all drawing attention to his large fleshy pout. Raymond ordered a sandwich and a glass of water to take his pills. Just as the first capsule slid down his throat a familiar voice had him choking.

"Are you still taking those pills, you stupid old man?"

Raymond slowly lowered the glass from his lips. He hadn't been prepared for *this* surprise. There, in all his demented glory, stood Paul Lambert. The image before him swam in a blur. He wasn't sure if it was the worsening fever, or blinding rage. The tall, dark-haired Lambert was smirking at him with an impish grin. Paul's body contorted as he snaked closer.

"You're so naive, Ray. Here you are, still taking these damned pills. Haven't your grossly overpaid doctors figured it out yet?"

Raymond's lips barely moved. "How did you find me?"

"It wasn't me who came in that FC freighter," Paul laughed childishly. Raymond stared in horror at Paul. The man was drunk, or stoned, or something! Raymond's voice finally broke.

"What have you done with my daughter?"

Lambert stopped laughing. "I don't know. Nobody knows. I thought you might know."

"You liar. You have my daughter hidden somewhere." Raymond smashed the glass against the bar's surface.

Paul made an exaggerated shake of his head. "Nope. This time…this time, I'm not lying. Believe me, I'd like to have her. I'm supposed to have her, but I don't. So if you don't know where she is, and I don't know where she is, I guess the pirates really do have her." Paul sat himself on the stool next to Raymond. "The rich bitch gets what she deserves, after all."

"I resent that." Raymond spat.

Paul fought to control another fit of laughter, elbows spreading across the bar. "There are lots of things you should be resenting, Ray. That's the least of them."

Raymond quivered with anger. "Where's my daughter?"

"Listen, I came to find you because you're a really nice guy, Ray. I actually feel pretty bad about all this, but really, I was hoping you would be able to tell me where Marie is. I need the lady real bad. As for you—? Oh, never mind. You're half dead, anyway. You may as well finish my plan. Give me a little satisfaction, seeing as your daughter managed to escape me."

"Your plan?"

"Yes, my *plan*. And it worked. I made you sick enough to keep you away from here all this time. What brought you here at a time like this, anyway? You can barely stand. Checking up on your *plant*?" The word launched a glob of phlegm to the bar's surface.

"Yes, in fact, I just came from there. What is going on, *Paul*?" Raymond experienced a renewal of energy and slid off the stool. Paul's mouth dropped open as he shook his head "Oh, you frighten me, Ray."

"You're drunk!"

Paul laughed, remorse lacing his voice. "How I wish I were, old pal, but you see, I got stuck with the same disease as you. Well, almost." He frowned, pointing to the vial on the bar. "Those drugs'll kill you while failing to give you even the tiniest little thrill. Shame. Mine are much more fun, but one needs more and more to sustain the fun. This planet's full of little treasures like these and I should have kept looking for something better, but—too late. They keep calling out to me in their tiny little voices, so I may as well oblige them. Like you, I'll be dead soon anyway." He let a palm drop to the bar. "And here you are, all the way out from Enderal in your condition. Amazing. Should have saved yourself the trouble, Ray. It's all over for you and me. Hell! It's over for everybody. They're coming soon, you know." He imparted the news in a hoarse whisper.

Cold fear rippled through Raymond's limbs. The galactic war he'd been dreading was on their doorsteps, and he wouldn't be around to help what was left of his family, through it.

Paul laughed sorrowfully. "Ironic, isn't it. I was looking for a slow killer for you, and found a slow killer for me. Ah, you poor fool. You let me into your house, into your daughter's underpants, into your medical unit…! It was pretty easy to switch your pills, you know, even right at the end. You ought to teach your medical people more about security."

"You bastard!"

"Ohh, nice words, Ray. You're a class act, you know. You've got—"

In roiling anger Raymond lunged at Paul's throat. Paul let out a childish shriek. They both fell to the floor and thrashed at each other in a clumsy brawl. The bartender peered over the bar to watch the druggy and the invalid squirm on the floor, neither able to land a significant punch. He thought he'd wait a few minutes before calling security. It didn't look like this one would last very long.

He guessed right. The younger fellow won—sort of. The druggy wiggled his way out from under the nearly comatose old man, then scrambled out into the lobby before weaving out the main entrance. He decided to wait a few more minutes, see if the old man would get up on his own. It seemed not. Just as he was about to call for help, someone dashed into the bistro to the old man's side.

"Do you need help with him?" the bartender asked.

A balding man, who appeared to be of Central States descent, looked up. "Yes, please call an ambulance."

Bill Tripp carefully turned Raymond over, lifting his head and shoulders off the floor. Raymond breathed through colorless lips. He blinked red eyes, taking a moment to focus on the man holding him. His hot breath expelled in disbelief. "Bill? Bill Tripp? Great Creator, is that you?"

"Yes it is, Raymond. Take it easy. You'll be all right now. Do you know where Paul went?" From the elevator bank, Bill had seen Paul dash across the street, but priority brought him to his employer's side.

Raymond shook his head weakly. "No, but quickly, go after him. I'm sure he has Marie. Go! I'm going to die anyway. Tell Genevieve I love her."

"You're not going to die! And, Paul doesn't have Marie. She was with me. She's alive and in good hands. Don't you die on her."

The open mouth formed a smile. "My Marie is all right?"

"She sure is." Bill clenched his jaw against the emotion that threatened to engulf him. Suddenly a colorfully dressed Dorian knelt at his side. "Oh! Mr. Flecheeet berry sick."

"Who are you?"

The fellow looked offended. "Ebreebody ask me! The name is Dee. I work for Mr. Flecheeet. See?" Dee pulled out his half of the commlink. "He gib me this. I take care. He need help now."

Raymond rolled his head feverishly within the crook of Bill's arm. "Our lab— it's been turned into a military base." Laboring for breath he added, "He poisoned me! Damn the man, he poisoned me."

"I must hurry. I take him to Healer." The cabby pushed on Bill's shoulder, indicating he release Flechette to his care, but Bill resisted.

Raymond spoke in an anxious whisper. "Bill. Go! Dee will take care of me."

Feeling highly skeptical about the proposal, Bill clutched Raymond a few seconds longer. When the cabby grabbed his collar, Bill expected a punch in the head. Instead, the cabby brought his large lips to Bill's ear. "Me hab friend on street. Got straw hat. He watch where bad man go. Hurry. Berry sick. I take Mr. Flecheeet to Healer."

Bill vacillated between compelling responsibilities, then nodded. Putting Raymond in the care of this stranger, Bill strode out of the bar, but left the hotel at a dead run.

Dee pulled a small flask from his shirt pocket and twisted with vigor at the cork. He propped Raymond up to a sitting position and forced some of the milky liquid down his employer's throat. Raymond coughed on the sour taste before feeling incredible heat burst from his core and blast through his system. He sat bolt upright, gasping and clutching at his chest, his eyes bulging from their sockets.

"Sorree. Bad taste. But you awake now. See?"

CHAPTER 41

Marie watched the shadows on Richard's features flicker in the candlelight that blazed between them on the wooden dining table. He hadn't surprised her totally. She'd suspected something special when she received a hand delivered card requesting her presence at his quarters for dinner that evening. Deanna had come to her rescue by offering a simple cotton dress, perfect for the jungle heat. Richard was wearing that blowzy cotton shirt again. He had on a newer pair of trousers, but those boots…She swore they were a part of him.

He'd asked one of the mechanics, a known expert at the eight string Zeeta, to play some serenading background music for them. As the Zeeta tinkled its lofty tones, they shared more of the priests' wine, for which Marie showed greater respect. The meal arrived, hidden under the regular silver domes they saw every day, but the apartment was adorned with bowls of fresh fruit and bouquets of jungle blossoms making the dented domes shine along with the rest of Richard's efforts. He reached over and touched his goblet to hers. "You look wonderful tonight. Did you do your hair up like that?"

She gave a little laugh. "No. Deanna gets all the credit for the vogue look." She watched him remove the lid from a hot steaming dish. "What's the occasion?"

"No occasion. Just a celebration of life. I'm grateful that I've been blessed with your presence for a small part of my journey."

"I'm glad too, even though it seems like I've been here forever." She caught his eye and noticed a flinch. She'd been caught in the timelessness of this planet with no name, but Richard wasn't in the same frame of mind. He would see the time pass much more swiftly.

As they began to eat, Marie suddenly remembered her afternoon adventure. "I was at the pool this afternoon. "The children came to see me again."

"Ah, you have some new friends."

"It seems so, and I love them all, the little boy in particular. Remember? The one who let me hold him?"

"I remember well," he murmured.

"I love him to death, even though I can't understand a word he says."

"At his age, the others probably don't either."

She laughed. "After the swim, they pulled on my arms until I thought they'd fall off. I think they wanted me to go to their village." She raised an eyebrow. "But I know the village is off bounds." She tasted the root vegetables and wondered what the aborigines would have on their plates this evening. Wild boar? Exotic plants and spices? Did they eat any of those big beetles that she'd seen roaming the forest floor?

"An invitation to their village is a great honor, and with the situation the way it is, I can't guarantee that I'll get away long enough to go with you. I think you should accept."

She looked at him in astonishment. "You do? But, I don't know how far it is, or how I would get back. I'd have to take a guard."

He smiled. "Believe me, the natives are much safer to be with in the jungle than my guards. I'll tell the guard to wait at the stairs for you, and the children will return you safely."

She looked at him, thunderstruck.

"Marie, the village isn't far, less than a mile from the pool. The natives will insist on accompanying you wherever you go, unless you ask then not to." He leaned forward, latching onto her gaze like a tractor beam. "Please don't go anywhere without them."

She shook her head. "I wouldn't think of it."

"Good. Then, if you do go without me, the Chief's name is Ungu."

"Ungu."

"He speaks pretty good Galactic taught to him by the priests, and a little more by myself. He'll know who you are, and take good care of you."

"He'll know who I am?"

"The children will have told him that you're a guest of mine, but he'll have known that anyway."

"Oh," she said, wondering about the power of these jungle people.

He looked at her somberly. "Don't thwart a chance to visit the village. I would hate to see you leave here without the experience."

"Do you think I'm leaving so soon?"

He raised an eyebrow. "Things are about to change; there's no doubt about that."

They stared at each other in silence. She did want go home, but something was happening to her here, something that would take time to discover. And now, there might not be time.

Richard interrupted her thoughts. "Don't worry about it now. Things will work out, as long as we believe in the ultimate goodness of the universe."

She grinned. "You're so philosophical."

"It helps. We all get caught up in the paranoia these days. Then again, if it weren't for my paranoia, you wouldn't be here with me tonight."

She smiled and raised her goblet. "To the ultimate goodness."

Marie listened to the music, loving the casual way in which the unlikely musician entertained them. It was refreshing not to have a formal orchestra—all gussied up yet not able to produce a note any more beautiful than the ones strummed by the mechanic dressed in civilian clothing.

"He really is very good," she whispered, "I've just realized that I've had some cultural deprivation over the past weeks."

Richard laughed. "When we're not trying to save our asses, there's a lot of merry-making that goes on around here. Your cultural deprivation would be short-lived in better times."

When the mechanic finished, he wiped the Zeeta with a cloth and placed it in its case. With a nod, he let himself out.

Richard turned to her. "I have something for you."

She took his outstretched hand and followed him to the bedroom. She knelt with him before the large wooden chest that had so piqued her interest. The wrought iron key clanked about inside a huge engraved pad lock. The chest lid creaked open. There were books, bound boxes, a colorful quilt wrapped in plastic, folders: an endless supply of treasures.

"Are these your things?" she asked, peering into the chest.

"Yes, and don't laugh. I keep this stuff because our mother gave us each one to keep the special things we've collected over our lifetimes. I think it was a way of expressing her wish for a daughter. So, I've obliged her."

He dug through the articles carefully. With his arm buried to the elbow, he laid his fingers upon the thing he sought. "Here it is."

"What is it?"

He placed a very old, palm-sized box in her hand. "This belonged to my grandmother. She told me to pass it on to someone special in my life. I believe that person to be you, Marie. However short our journey together might be, I want you to have this."

She looked at him, finding moisture blurring her vision.

"Go on, open it."

She did so, carefully, afraid the old cardboard might disintegrate in her palm. She wiggled the top off and pulled out the protective batting. Her eyes grew large at the sight of a gold chain from which hung a large, round pendant. Her eyes darted back and forth, from the gift, to Richard's intense gaze. Slowly, she pulled its length from the box.

"It's beautiful," she gasped, fingering the pendant. One side showed a caricature of a sun carved in relief. The sun's face had large eyes fanned by long lashes and a smile buried within pudgy cheeks. The sun looked down upon a tiny orb representing a planet. On the orb stood exaggerated figures with arms raised in veneration to their sun. Marie turned the pendant over. In ornately carved letters intertwined with vines and leaves was something written in a language she didn't recognize.

"It's our local dialect," Richard offered. "The one my grandfather adopted when he married into a Fringe clan."

"What does it say?"

"Well, first, you must know that my grandmother's people are some of the original Fringe Dwellers. They are great believers in the universe as a vital organism, and my grandfather adopted these beliefs. To us, the truths are simple, without a lot of ritual clutter. These doctrines are followed by most of the clans, even though the cultures themselves are quite different. It's this unity that enticed my grandfather to settle here, and the same thing that's allowed the Fringe Federation to be so successful." He cupped her hand that held the pendant and pointed to the words. "In any event, this reads: *We Glorify You, Oh Resplendent, Oh Loving, Oh Bountiful Universe.*"

Marie swallowed. "It's beautiful. Is she still alive? Your grandmother?"

Richard shook his head.

"I'm sorry. She must have been a wonderful person."

"Yes she was, and my mother is much like her." He took the pendant from her hands and slipped the chain over her neck. The pendant settled between her breasts. "When I researched your company, I was surprised to find out that you have core beliefs similar to ours."

She smiled, straining to hold back tears. "It's a feeble attempt. Nixodonia killed all its cultures for some hedonistic and devastatingly empty way of life. No wonder 'Follow Me' is such a hit."

"It's not your movie that attracts your followers. It's you, and the FC creed. So, perhaps you could redirect them," he suggested.

She shook her head. "I don't even know where I'm going."

"You'll find what you're looking for."

Putting a hand to his cheek, she said softly, "Oh how I love you, Richard Shaw." She wasn't immediately conscious of her words. She gasped, but couldn't retract what she'd said.

His hand reached out to cup the back of her neck. He pulled her to his shoulder. "God, woman. You torture me."

"I didn't mean it that way." Her voice muffled in his collar. "But, it's true, and wrong as it may be to say it, I must. I do love you, Richard."

He rocked her back and forth, his neck arching, his eyes unwillingly focusing on the saintly paintings she loved so much. "And how dearly I love you. That's the torture. Loving you, yet not being able to have you."

He didn't give her a chance to respond. His lips crushed hers with passionate force. She responded with equal hunger, making him wish he could devour her, draw her into his soul by osmosis where she could stay forever. He pulled her onto the bed and covered her body with his. His lips took her face, her shoulders. One arm slid around the small of her back and he gripped her tightly. His lips came to rest by her cheek. He took in a ragged breath. "I know I can't ask you to stay. That wouldn't be fair, but I need you to know that if things were different, I would ask."

Her mouth opened but no words came out.

"Don't say anything," he said with urgency. "There was no question, really."

Marie stared at the ceiling, at the priests, doing what they believed to be the will of their god despite all the other pulls and attractions from the outside worlds. Tears coursed down her temples, dampening the quilt beneath her head. Her hands wrapped themselves protectively around his head, pulling him close against her shoulder. There had been a question.

She couldn't say yes—or no.

Her parents, Bill, Javid, the Benefit Foundation, the entire FC complex, everything! Her mind flooded with thoughts that drowned her with their onrush.

In a tangled haze of memories she remembered telling her father that FC was her life, her blood, everything she'd ever known, loved, or represented. Every corner of FC felt like a part of her extended self, from the greenhouses to the banquet rooms. She was Flechette Cosmetics.

But now. Now?

In a matter of weeks, all of it had begun to change. She clung to the man who could challenge it all. He felt like home. His taste, his smell, his feel, his words when he spoke, and when he said nothing. These crude stone walls were an extension of him, yet they were not his life force. He had a power within himself, and the Universe was the all-powerful force that drove him to preserve those truths. These walls and the tunnels, the waterfall and the aborigines, the jungle with its magnificent collection of life; these things made up his home.

Had they become a part of her home, too?

Suddenly she felt split, like an atom undergoing fission, but with rivaling forces not quite strong enough to break the gravitational pull back to its nucleus. Her anguish imploded with the whimpering of an indrawn cry.

Richard's grip tightened. "Please don't answer now."

CHAPTER 42

The decision was an easy one. There was room for only four passengers aboard Captain Boro's ship. There'd been no need to delegate appointments. Javid and Clive, along with Dowlar had volunteered to be Boro's squadron each having his own contribution for the party's total skill and knowledge.

The T-38 took off vertically through the open hangar doors into a clear night. They followed their flight plan, hovering just above the treetops in the direction of the Ocar Pass. Clive exchanged a glance with Javid. Each recalled his own terror when they'd last passed through here, ship aflame, fire-extinguishing dust choking the life from them. Clive suddenly recalled Dowlar's words about not believing in martyrdom. He had no trouble adopting that particular belief!

Javid patted the pockets of his garments that still contained the compact weapons he'd so arduously acquired on Iggid. Being back amongst his comrades made him painfully aware that time had weakened his mental powers to the point that Clive Baker was a serious rival. He may have to rely heavily on his gadgets and felt better knowing they were right in his pockets, good and handy.

Dowlar sat in the copilot seat, his mind focused on the Cousta Canyon with it's fissure-like valley plummeting as deep as forty thousand feet. The few space-faring ships in their possession had slowly been lost to the rebels over the years, the last one gone before he'd fully mastered space flight. Still, his sub-light flying skills were excellent and his piloting knowledge came back quickly. He felt freedom with the craft, out of hiding and into action. Although hiding was a necessary thing to do, his patience had often run thin. Now with his brother and his friends at his side, his confidence soared.

Captain Boro fed on Dowlar's self-assured poise. This little Rashmarian knew his flying techniques surprisingly well. Boro wasn't sure if Javid would be much help, but he sort of liked the big Nixodonian, a man nearly as big as himself and thwarted in similar ways. With his own scores to settle, Clive Baker would surely be an asset.

An hour later, the craft settled among a mess of boulders on the mountainous perimeter surrounding the base. Clive had a problem keeping his composure as he peered down at the TRA base, now sprawled over several more acres than it had when he'd graced its premises only two years earlier. At least the core of the facility remained the same and from their vantage point, he analyzed the layout.

"What do you say, Clive?" Boro asked, his mechanical eye swirling back, using its extended periphery to bring the freighter pilot into focus. Clive leaned forward, as if nosing closer to the canopy would yield more detail. "Lots'a changes. But the core is still how I remember it, and that's where we need to go. I can't tell you what that huge structure might be, that one to the right of the main building."

"I think I know," said Dowlar, fiddling madly with the scanners. He glanced at Boro. "Nice features on this craft. You Fringe folks aren't suffering too badly in the toy department."

A smile grew on Boro's face, crinkling the corner of his lip against the prosthesis. "That's my invention you're playing with. What does it tell you?"

"The internal details are a bit obscure," Dowlar muttered, "but it looks like some sort of hangar. I believe those are fighter jets inside."

"Can we guess the make and model?" Clive rolled his eyes.

"What else can we scan?"

"Here," Clive tapped on the screen. "This is the control nucleus."

Dowlar hummed, "Lots of computers: mainframes, hyperwave channels."

Javid pulled a small black box from deep within the layers of his clothing. "I've got a gadget here that could help us access those computers."

Clive grinned as he fingered the box. "Great. We can make the control center our first stop."

"Not only that." Javid produced his laboriously-acquired door jigger. "This should help us get in there."

Dowlar laughed. "Well, my brother, you have a sense for gadgetry after all."

"Clive and I have blasters from each of our crafts," Boro said. "Would you boys care to take your pick?"

Javid grimaced. "I can't aim at the side of a starcruiser. I'll be the gadgets man."

"I'll have one," Dowlar murmured, knowing he should be using his mind control rather than relying on weapons. Master Farol had given him a long lecture after hearing about the display of military might back at Clive's ship. Just the same, he accepted two weapons, one from each of the humans.

"Come on, you grandmothers." Clive retorted. "Let's get going."

A tubular land craft dropped neatly out of the back of Boro's ship. It nearly perished beneath the weight of the four allies. Javid teased Clive about possibly losing some weight. Clive's eyes widened. "I am not fat, you lousy, skinny Rashmarian!"

Boro broke up the tussle by offering a plan. "We'll head down to the level of the plain, then we'll have to walk through those tall grasses to the fence line—about half a mile."

Clinging to each other, Boro guided the craft down the rocky mountainside. The terrain was littered with huge boulders and scrub brush, but that was barely enough to conceal them. There was tangible relief as they reached the lower altitudes and into the protective shield of the mighty firs of Rashmar. Javid's heart bled for the land that used to be his, its soft curves now a disarray of geometric cubes that pierced their glaring lights obtrusively into the velvety night sky.

Once on the grassy plain, Boro expressed his concerns of being detected before they reached the outer fence line.

"Wait!" Javid's hoarse whisper brought the creeping party to a halt. "I have a nucleic knife, and if I recall correctly..." He patted at his clothing and dug out the high-powered knife. "The salesman told me this could be used as a personal shield unit. I didn't pay much attention at the time. Protection wasn't on my mind." He gave Boro's shoulder a clap. "Sorry buddy, but I had an urge to melt your metal brain."

"Javid!" his brother scolded with a giggle.

"Let's see that thing."

Boro and Clive simultaneously reached for the knife. Clive was the first to grab it. He turned it over a few times then handed it to Boro.

"Here, you figure it out."

Dowlar swore that accompanying the hum of the nucleic knife was an iridescent blue film that enveloped them in a small bubble just big enough to accommodate the four of them as long as they clung together. With renewed hope, they scuttled across the plain with no signs of being detected. The huge fence yielded under the power of the knife's dual function and the four stepped gingerly over the molten metal that had been thick fencing only moments before.

"Where did you *get* this thing?" Boro asked, amazed at Javid's find.

"From some unscrupulous Fringe trader."

Boro spun to catch Javid's grin. He returned with a petulant smirk, then glanced about nervously. "Why don't they have this fence hooked up to a force field? Getting in here was too easy."

"Because," said Clive, whose memory of the complex began to flood back in horrendous detail, "they don't consider anything on the ground to be a threat, except for the wildlife, so they don't bother wasting the huge amounts of energy it would take to fortify a boundary like this."

"Makes sense. So, seeing as you know the way, Baker, you take the knife."

Back under the protection of the knife's shield, the small party traversed the rocky terrain directly toward the main building. Getting inside was made possible by Javid's door jigger and the party was soon deep within the bowels of the massive control center. They slunk from room to room, glad that most operations in this part of the complex were shut down for the night. The halls were dimly lit and virtually empty in these lower levels. Clive made a sudden stop.

"I remember this now!" he whispered. "There's a laundry service right down the hall. We should get ourselves some proper attire."

It was a good plan, but before they had found uniforms for everyone, a voice bellowed out from behind them.

"What are you fellows doing?" In surprise, the whole group spun toward the voice. A stoutly-built guard stood rigidly at the door, looking them over curiously. His eyes widened as he recognized the two shorter members of the party. "Rashmarians?"

Before he could pull out his commlink, Boro and Clive were on him. The guard's laser sliced into Boro's deltoid before Clive was able to retaliate with a guillotine slash to the guard's neck with the nucleic knife. Severed cleanly through, the head thumped to the floor and rolled against the lockers before the body followed in collapse. Clive raised his eyebrows at Javid, whose face had markedly blanched.

"Who said I wasn't neat!"

Javid regained his composure and rifled through the metal lockers. He tore up the first piece of material he could find and wrapped Boro's arm right over the sleeve.

"I'll be okay," Boro hissed. "It didn't hit the bone."

The four wasted little time stuffing the body parts into an empty locker and pulling TRA uniforms over their clothing. The end result was one that looked suspiciously bulky but the effort concealed their identities long enough to get them safely to the third level. Javid's door jigger gave them access to the mainframe complex, also quiet in the dead of night. They were all nervously aware that the control room, two levels above, would be buzzing with round-the-clock activity.

Clive's prayers were answered as a secondary console came to life. Certain access codes had remained unchanged from two years before and lists of information spilled down a screen. The luminescence of the screen was the only light they allowed themselves in the bowels of the huge room that hummed with the low drone of ever-functioning machines.

"What does all this mean?" Dowlar asked in a whisper.

Clive shook his head. Boro leaned forward.

"Clive, slow down that data. I might be able to commission my microcomputer to decipher the information."

He exchanged places with Clive. They all gathered around, amazed at the intensity of Boro's focus. His mechanical eye locked onto the scrolling information. A second later, the embedded microcomputer began a high-pitched whine. Boro muttered unintelligibly, unable to verbalize at the same speed as his synthetic brain simulated the data. Suddenly, he sat bolt upright.

"No, this won't help. Dowlar, can you fiddle with this thing? See if you can find something about flight paths, anything military. This is just all policies."

Another exchange took place. Dowlar thrilled at the chance to play with such advanced equipment. Clive shuffled about nervously.

"Hurry up Dowlar."

For several more minutes there was dead silence, save the anxious breathing and clicking of computer keys.

"Got something," Dowlar said.

They exchanged places again.

The pirate smiled. "Yes, this is better. We might be onto something."

As the pirate began to concentrate, Clive got annoyingly nervous. Dowlar gave him a kick on his boot.

"Don't get so worked up, Whale! You're going to attract attention with all that negative energy."

Clive gave an exasperated look. "I've already done my time in this joint. The sooner we get out of here, the better."

"Got it." Boro said. "Dowlar, expand this segment for me."

Moments later, Boro whispered excitedly, "This is it! The time *and* coordinates for the Nixodonian attack. The whole flight plan across the Fringe is right here. I'll store this in my microcomputer's memory, but let's have a backup. Javid, get that black box of yours over here. Let's see if the price you paid was worth your effort."

Javid fumbled about his clothing, now one menacing layer thicker. He and Boro then sprawled on the floor under the work station and managed to tap it into an access port. It was not easy work, especially with Dowlar right over top trying to make sure the right information was recorded. Five minutes later, the two wiggled out from under the console and Javid secured the black box into an inside pocket. Boro scanned the screen, his mechanical eye snapping as it strained under its master's will. "That armada is going to move very soon. Too soon. We have to get this information back to the Fringe right away or we're going to miss our chance at an ambush. Let's move."

The four crept back into the dimly lit hallway. A ghastly clang made them all jump.

The clang continued. Rhythmic, loud, and deadly.

"Alarms!" Dowlar cried.

The group took off at a run in the direction from which they'd come. They managed to scramble down only one level before coming across a contingent of guards. The guards immediately attacked with a salvo of lasers that lit the dim hallway like a lightning storm. Boro, Clive and Dowlar returned fire. Javid's job was to pray. The guards were unprepared for such heavy artillery. The had to retreat down the hall that was quickly filling with smoke.

The four dashed into the first available room: a laboratory, empty in the dead of night. They locked the sliding door permanently by blowing out its electronic circuits. Dowlar looked frantically about for an escape route.

"Shit!" Clive muttered.

"Get over to the windows everyone," Dowlar ordered.

The others turned to find a long row of windows barely noticeable behind an array of glass tubing and lab equipment scattered along the work benches. Boro ran to the windows and peered out. "We're on level two. We can jump."

Dowlar had already started collecting every flammable object he could find and was piling them up against the door. As he worked, the rebels could be heard hammering on the other side of the thick steel panel. A hissing sound marked the forced release of the door lock. Making sure they were all under cover behind the work benches, Dowlar waited until the door began to inch open, then let a bolt erupt from his laser. He dropped just in time to protect himself from the violent explosion he'd created.

Seconds later, the others joined Dowlar in firing through the thick glass windows. They kicked away the shards, climbed over the window sill and dropped to the soft earth below, Boro was the last to climb onto the window's ledge. Javid noticed Boro clench his teeth while using his wounded arm to pivot himself out the window. He landed hard, crumbling to the ground. Boro wheezed, catching his breath, but Javid knew he was trying to overcome the pain in his arm. Boro recovered quickly and urged the group to run in the direction from which they'd come.

Their path back to the fence had been cut off by two security vehicles. That forced their next decision. Search lights snaked white beams back and forth over the terrain, some coming from fixed locations on top of buildings, others coming from oncoming vehicles. They headed at a dead run towards the big bubbled building, earlier discerned as a hangar. The four entered deep into its mechanical bays before being fired upon again. Clive scanned for escape routes as the others fired back trying to destroy whatever security instruments they could within the enclosure.

Clive shouted to his comrades, "The best way out will be the exits near the hangar doors."

"Lead the way," cried Boro, twisting his body around a crate to fire deadly shots out the barrel of his blaster. "We're road kill here."

"Let's keep the faith, boys," Dowlar encouraged.

"Go. We're getting surrounded." Boro yelled.

They created a billowy smoke screen by shooting at any flammable object they could locate. The four dashed into the open area of the hangar, and stopped dead in their tracks.

"Shiiit!"

"This place looks even bigger from the inside!" Boro gasped. The hangar could easily service a hundred or more fighter jets under a single roof.

"All the more places to hide," Dowlar shouted, leading the way amongst a forest of landing struts. There was still some staff running about, but with alarms screeching overhead, they were not about their usual business. Rather than taking cover, they could be seen scuttling around the periphery of the hangar.

"Don't be fooled." Clive yelled. "These guys are trained soldiers. They can drop their wrenches and kick ass as well as anyone else. So, anybody got any bright ideas about what we do next?"

"Look!" Everyone followed Javid's finger. "The hangar doors are open at the far end."

Clive grabbed Boro's arm. Boro yelped and tugged away. "Ah, sorry buddy," Clive apologized, "but take a look at that ship, second row, third down."

With fingers wrapped around his upper arm, Boro's eyes followed Clive's direction.

"That's an Orrilla fighter jet," Clive said. "A 248, at that! It's the only deep-space, long-range fighter in existence. I can fly that baby, compliments of the excellent training I received at this very astute training facility."

"Is it Nixodonian as well?" Dowlar asked.

"No, everybody has them. The Orrillas don't care who they sell to."

"That's a ridiculous idea!" Javid spat nervously. "They'll shoot us down in seconds."

"I know these guys. They'll try to save their jet first. And this may come as a surprise to you, old man, but I'm not just some washed-out freighter junky." He fired at a skulking mechanic. "I'm a highly skilled fighter pilot, again compliments of this very astute—"

"Save the modesty for later, Clive" Boro retorted. "Get us boarded and I'll give you the coordinates that'll get us out of here."

The thick landing protuberance they were using for cover splintered, sending the four scrambling.

"I don't care where that bolt came from. Follow Clive," Boro ordered a protesting Javid.

As they ran, the flooring around them fractured under the impact of repeated salvos. An ambush hit them from the opposite direction just as one of Boro's random shots hit an unexpected target. The overhead lights shut off completely in their half of the hangar. The building shook with the resounding boom of crashing generators. They continued running, taking only seconds to adjust to the sudden dimness.

Dowlar stopped only yards from the jet. Javid came to a stop, too, watching his brother scan the area around him, both floor and ceiling. Javid was sure the rebels would be trying to restore the lighting, so why was his brother wasting time?

"Come on!" Javid yelled frantically.

Further encouragement was thwarted by a barrage of lasers, all firing in their general direction. Javid noticed, true to Clive's word, that the TRA was trying not to damage its own planes. Javid ran and joined the other two behind the service vehicle that sat idle beside the Orrilla 248.

"He won't come!"

"We're surrounded!"

Seconds later, Dowlar arrived, face ashen. "Go. I'll cover for you. Fire up the jet, but don't lift-off until you know that I've diverted their attention."

Javid gaped at him. "But—"

"Go. The hangar doors are still open. We still have a chance."

"I thought you didn't believe in martyrdom!" Clive shouted angrily, firing randomly toward the back of the hangar.

"I don't, Whale. So promise me you'll come back some day."

Javid clasped his brother tightly. The heat of a combusting oil slick licked up their ankles, tearing them apart. The brothers used their coats and boots to put out the blaze that raced toward the Orrilla. Dowlar then grasped his brother's arm. "I've got to go."

"No!"

"Javid, trust me. I'll think my way out of this."

The brothers looked desperately into each other's eyes. Dowlar shook his paralyzed brother. "Don't you think I worried about you? I had no idea what happened to you, and twenty-one years later you show up, just like I believed you would. You'll be back, Javid, and I'll be waiting."

Javid could not comprehend being separated from his brother again, but he knew it must be. He fumbled through his pockets and handed Dowlar all his special gadgets. "Take these. They will help you escape, and—"

Boro suddenly let out a sharp howl. The brothers spun to see him collapse. A black hole smoldered straight through his calf.

"Go!" cried Dowlar. "It was a fluke. They're shooting blindly. Hide in the craft until I divert their attention. Good-bye my friends, and good courage." Dowlar dashed between the rows of space jets without a backward glance.

Javid stood, riveted to the spot, staring in disbelief at the shadowy landing strut that had swallowed his brother. Clive gave a hard tug on his arm, propelling him toward the Orrilla. Gripping the ladder, Boro pulled himself to his feet. With excruciating effort, he began to climb. Clive helped with a steady push on his buttock. He and Javid followed right behind but had to crawl over the pirate who'd collapsed on the deck as soon as he'd entered the hold.

"Is he all right?" Javid squeaked, afraid that they'd be left to escape with no indication of where to take the vital information tucked inside his chest pocket. Getting a hold of himself, he searched the craft for medical supplies. A shot of stimulant spay revitalized Boro enough for Javid to help him into the copilot's seat.

Clive fired up the engines, with only terrifying darkness to greet him beyond the canopy. He shuddered, then concentrated on the preflight check.

"Is this thing going to fly?" Boro asked while clutching at his wounded arm.

"We're in luck. She's been fully serviced."

"Then punch this in. It'll take us back to the nebula."

"Where's that?" Clive asked quickly, afraid the Fringe man was losing consciousness.

Boro whined between clenched teeth. "It's the secret Fringe stronghold. They're the ones who need this information. Ahhh." He grabbed at his lower leg.

Clive swallowed. Now a secret base? What next! Boro started giving him a long series of numbers which Clive punched in, fingers working like a sewing machine. Javid showed up with some liquid and drained it down the pirate's throat. Boro revived enough to continue his litany of navigational data. Clive typed while watching closely for any magic from Dowlar. Suddenly, a massive explosion rocked the far end of the building opposite the open hangar doors.

Clive raised his arms. "Dowlar lives!"

"Fire up. Let's clear this place!"

Javid strapped into the passenger seat behind Clive and lowered his head. "Goodbye, my brother. *Ohh*...." His throat throbbed painfully. "May our gods be with you."

The ship wobbled as it rose. Clive nervously maneuvered the craft, afraid to nick the wings of the other ships parked in an environment not exactly designed for liftoff. As he hoped, the enemy didn't fire directly at the craft. That would be too risky, but he punched in full-thrust when he saw the huge doors begin to close. The Telexans had been too slow at realizing the deception and Clive burst outdoors with plenty of clearance.

"Put on the speed, my friend," Boro advised. "We have the advantage for only a few minutes. I need to tell you that those coordinates will help us only once we are back behind the moon and into the outgoing magnetic field."

Clive shot him a glance. "And how the hell do I get there from here?"

"I don't know. Just fly. We'll figure something out."

Javid moaned. What had happened to the comfort of space flight aboard the luxury cruisers he'd become so accustomed to? This was madness! He felt sickened with the massive acceleration of the craft, fearing the thing would tear apart, even if it *was* designed for such maneuvers. He dared to peek out the canopy but was dizzied by the spinning of a million stars. The craft punched through the stratosphere then burst into deep space. Clive's heart plummeted as he saw that they were heading directly towards two security vessels positioned in geosynchronous orbit. "Now what?"

"Stay as close as you can to the stratosphere and head northbound," Boro yelled, again looking perilously close to fainting. It was only then that Javid noticed the large dark stain soaking down Boro's sleeve. There was nothing he could do for the calf, singed and bloodless. Javid thumped on Clive's shoulder.

"Not now, Buddy."

"We're losing Boro!"

Clive shot a sideways glance at the pirate sitting cockeyed in the copilot's seat.

"I'm all right," grunted Boro who then sputtered another set of coordinates at Clive that shot them in the direction of the moon. The craft jolted.

"Shiiiit!" Clive roared. The craft shuddered again. The emergency screens exploded with warning lights. Boro found enough energy to flip on deflector shields before rising from his seat. He stumbled toward the back of the craft, informing them he would not let the rebels thwart their only chance of escape.

"What does he think he's doing?" Javid screeched.

"I don't know, but I need you here. Remember any of this stuff?"

Javid moved quickly to the copilot's seat. "It looks awfully different."

"Don't let that fool you."

The two of them did what they could to evade fire from the massive, stationary security vessels seemingly unprepared for a planetary menace. The guns firing on the Orrilla were weak, with the ships' heavier cannons facing out toward the stars.

The instrument panel revealed that Boro was managing the aft gun turret. He discharged a blast that connected with its target. The impact caused severe damage to the security vessel closest to them and the Telexans delayed for a second too long while dealing with their loss. The small Orrilla 248 zipped away just above the atmosphere. The enemy could only watch as their stolen craft kicked in full thrust before vanishing into the magnetic funnel of the moon.

Like osmosis, the craft fell toward the moon's dull gray surface. Boro limped back to the cockpit and leaned over the back of Javid's seat while instructing Clive on a safe maneuver through the magnetic field by using the moon's gravity to swing them around to its back side.

"Thank your Creator that I've been this way before, my friends. While I was waiting on the moon for my descent, I made the calculations for a hyperdrive jump even before clearing the magnetic field."

Boro fired off a set of numbers retrieved from his microcomputer's memory. Clive punched them in, hardly able to keep up to Boro's rapid dictation. Just as the flow of data came to an end, Boro's head dropped forward. The pirate quickly jerked his head back up and rapped a knuckle against his metal prosthesis. "Now, Cliiive, "he slurred, "unless there is a dire emergency, you *must* first contact my relay ship that is stationed…" He swayed slightly. "…that is stationed…at the coordinates…" Boro moaned. "Clive, here's the coordin—" The pirate slapped his hands around his head and dropped like a stone. The metal skull clunked loudly against the deck.

"Aw, shit!"

Javid's hands flailed at a loss. "Quick. Let's get him to a cot."

Clumsily, they dragged Boro to the rear cabin where Javid administered what he could from the medic hatch. Javid then waited a few interminable moments while monitoring Boro's steadying pulse. As soon as he could hear Boro's regular breathing, he returned to help Clive.

The great Whale looked hopelessly at Javid. "I guess this is an emergency then, isn't it?"

Javid nodded. "Unless there's a miracle. I don't think that Boro will be able to tell us more about that relay point before we have to make the hyperspace jump to the nebula. That must be where the Fringe leaders are hiding."

"Yeah, well I don't like it very much, but I suppose we have to give it a try. Are you ready?"

"Ready as I'll ever be." Javid took one last longing glance at the bejeweled crescent of his beloved Rashmar. His heart wrung with anguish at the thought of his brother still caught within the TRA stronghold. He sent out a silent prayer, not only for Dowlar's safety, but also for his own safe return.

CHAPTER 43

Richard was standing behind the chair of a hyperwave station when Marie entered the control room. His sagging posture betrayed fatigue as he eyed the screens before him. Marie sauntered among the technicians who greeted her as they would an old friend. She said hello to Reese, who gave her a friendly smile while directing military operations. Finally she arrived at Richard's side. He put an arm around her shoulder and pulled her to him.

"Hello my love," he murmured, giving her a kiss on the temple.

The technician seated at the console raised an open palm. As she'd been taught, she returned the greeting with a gentle slap. The tech glanced up. "I'm keeping your Commander busy, Marie. Sorry."

She smiled. "Good. It will keep him youthful."

Richard's fatigue was accented by the bluish glow of the star maps. "Great. I'll stay up one more night!"

Her attention was drawn to a shift on the star map above them. A cluster of dots appeared near the center. "Is that the Saurian Fleet?" Marie ventured.

Richard looked at her with pleasant surprise. "Very good."

"Twenty-five ships?"

"Are you boys giving away our military secrets?"

"I can count," she jested. "Are they moving?"

"Slowly. This asteroid field is very dynamic. They'll stay camouflaged if they move in conjunction with the belt."

She watched the map rotate, presenting a new angle while new coordinates ripped across the statistics screen at the bottom of the map's field.

"Any word from Boro?" Richard asked.

The officer immediately shook his head. Igna arrived in a burst of commotion. "Commander Shaw," she spat formally, eyes briefly clashing with Marie's.

"Yes, Major Cello."

"The Section-A laser cannon on the mother ship is still faulty and the technicians don't agree with my solution! I need your authorization to have parts ordered from Vesperoiy."

"Igna! I've already given you personal authority over the weapons maintenance."

She gave an audible huff. "I know. But I need your signature for that as well."

Richard expelled his breath. His arm slipped from Marie's shoulder and he trudged off to see to Igna's problems. Igna managed to keep him busy in the conference room for nearly twenty minutes. When they exited, there was a terse exchange of words. Richard stomped back to the workstation, looking first for Marie.

"I wish you two weren't such enemies, now," Marie said in earnest.

"It's a love-hate relationship. She thrives on it." His smile was so genuine that Marie was inclined to believe him.

"I still think I'm the greatest cause of her misery."

"No one can make her miserable but herself," he said poignantly. "Come on. Let's get out of here for a few minutes."

Richard excused himself and promptly led Marie to his quarters. He grasped her in a tight embrace before the door had even closed. The roundness of the pendant pressed into her flesh beneath the jumpsuit. He found it, fondled it. A frustrated groan escaped his throat. She had recently discarded the chemise, finding the heat too oppressive with the extra layer. In reality, there was nothing in space sexy about regular military issue.

"I wish I could go to the pool with you today," he muttered. "Or better yet, why don't you just stay here where it's hot."

She looked up and smiled. "Will I get to see you later?"

"Of course, but I'm afraid it will be much later. So, before you die of heat, get yourself into those cool waters and we'll make a date for say, midnight?"

"Midnight?"

"Ah, but what a midnight it will be."

"I'll hold you to that."

"Just hold me right now, before the lands and peoples call me back to duty."

"You mean Reese!"

CHAPTER 44

Bill Tripp left the hotel with Raymond in the hands of the stranger and chased after Paul. Raymond's cabby had not lied. Across the street waited another driver with the promised straw hat shading observant eyes. Those eyes didn't miss Bill. The cabby signaled as Bill approached. The man whispered surreptitious information into Bill's ear. Bill then dashed on foot down the street and spun into the alley Paul had taken. Alarmed, he found himself in a maze of alleyways. Three and four story adobe dwellings lined endless narrow streets, all looking identical. A flash of Paul's yellow shirt winked at him through the thick crowd before it disappeared around a corner. Bill headed at a full run through the mob that grudgingly made way for a second intruder. Bill failed to catch up to the fleeing agent who jumped into a parked vehicle stationed at the other end of the alley's maze. The vehicle swerved down the wider fairway, nearly crashing into a storefront before disappearing amongst a throng of vehicles and pedestrians.

Frustrated, Bill stopped, not sure how to proceed. He was only half surprised at the opportunity that presented itself. From around the city block the informant's cab screamed toward him, nose-diving to a halt. The cabby waved frantically to Bill who rushed toward the open door. "Hurry, get in!" the cabbie exclaimed. "I can take you to the FC plant. No need to follow him."

Where Raymond managed to find his collection of helpers, Bill could not guess, but he didn't waste time wondering. He slammed the door shut just as the engine cut to full throttle. "How is it that you know where to take me?" Bill ventured, glancing out the cab window at the strange assortment people walking the streets. The cabby shrugged. "I work for Dee. Dee knows everything. The only thing I know better than Dee is how to speak Standard Galactic."

"That's good," he remarked. "So, how does *Dee* know these things?"

"Dee has a good eye. And even better ears."

"And?"

"Dee doesn't like those FC people. He checked out Mr. Paul. Dee says Mr. Paul has found criminals here to help him. Dee knows these people. Greedy bunch."

"Really?" The hackles rose on Bill's neck as his eyes fell on an array of weaponry strewn across the dashboard of the cab.

"They took land that doesn't belong to them, land that belonged to Dee's relatives. Then they made space pads with lots of different ships coming in and out. They make too much racket where there used to be peace."

Bill clamped his teeth. "If he doesn't like the FC people, why is he helping Mr. Flechette?"

"Oh, Dee is not stupid. He knows those army ships do not belong to FC because he checked out FC. I think mostly because he loves *Princess Marie*." The cabby craned his neck to catch Bill's eye, "At first, he was careful, but soon he was satisfied that Mr. Flecheeet is not involved."

Bill swallowed. "I'm glad he realized that. I work for directly Mr. Flechette, and I'm not bad, either."

"Then we go to FC, eh?"

"Yes, I would appreciate that."

Miles out in the country and in no place in particular, the cab came to a screeching halt, throwing Bill against the padding in front of him. He scowled.

The cabby turned to face him. "You want to go in the front gate? No? I think not. I know a back entrance that would suit you better. Is that better?"

"Yes, sure. Whatever you think."

Ten minutes later, they arrived at the designated area. In detouring to the back entrance, Bill inadvertently received a tour of the site via the surrounding hills. Raymond's report had been accurate. This was a highly barricaded military installation topped off with an FC logo! Bill checked his weapons.

"How long can you wait?" he asked the cabby, noticing that the sun would soon set.

"As long as you need, but I'll wait down in that ravine, over there."

Bill made note of a deep fissure between rugged hills. Although the area was short on camouflage, the crag was littered with recesses and caves. Bill nodded and slipped out of the cab. He crept down a hillside toward a small portal in the tall fortified fence guarded by one unwary sentry. The guard lowered his eyes while he causally lit a cigarette. The next instant, the guard crumbled and Bill crept towards the body. He dug through the guard's uniform and found the automatic gate release. Seconds later, he ran at full speed toward the closest building site.

From a vantage point near the protection of the buildings, Bill noticed a security vehicle meandering slowly in the direction of the gate he'd just accessed. It wouldn't take them long to realize that things were not quite right. Without delay, he worked his way into the enormous shed. His astonishment was immediate.

Before him, tucked securely under the protection of a domed roof was an impressive array of Nixodonian fighter jets being prepared for combat. Bill swore under his breath when he noticed the TRA reptilian emblem painted across the bodies of every visible craft. He blinked away the feelings of dread. He couldn't let himself waste time in awe, or suffocate in surging waves of defeat. He took cover, and then hammered an unwary worker about his own size. He dragged the body behind a crate, donned the man's clothing, took the identification and continued on, head down, winding amongst crates and support equipment more poorly lit than the functional sections of the hangar. He entered an empty office and rummaged about the desks covered with half-filled coffee mugs and dried pastries.

Negative. It was the daytime foreman's office. He carried on.

The next building brought both pay dirt and danger. Hiding was difficult in the modern complex, with its smooth crisp hallways and flush doorframes. Bill soon found himself in an area sprawling with what he believed were the commanding offices. Not a minute after he managed a stealthy ingress into the largest of the offices did the hallway fill with people. Bill jumped behind the tall mainframe units that lined one wall, squeezing himself as far behind the structure as the narrow space would allow. Like a ballerina, his toes pointed uncomfortably into the wiring that snaked along the floor while his chest crushed against the hot power boards.

The office filled with voices already discussing a suspected intruder. When it was suggested that the entire complex be put on alert, a gruff voice retorted, "I'll bet those damned locals are looking to steal munitions again."

"We have reason to think otherwise, General Keem."

Bill's breathing nearly stopped. Beads of sweat formed on his brow.

"We think the guard was killed with a P-72, sir. As far as we know, the locals aren't in possession of that particular weapon."

"As far as we *know*? What's the matter with this goddamn place? Everything seems to be an unknown entity. Thank God that our time in this insufferable, sneak-around base has nearly come to an end. Alert, but no Red Alert. It's just the locals, I'm sure of it."

"But, General—"

"No Red Alert!" the General bellowed. "I need the men to stay focused on getting those fighters commissioned, and my own fleet must be ready to return to Enderal immediately. The summit has been rescheduled for the last time. I am not delaying it again! Is that clear?"

What kind of summit? Where on Enderal, Bill asked himself in desperation.

"Yes, sir."

Bill heard the soldier leave the room. The General spoke words that summoned his top officers and a new set of heels clicked into the office. The room filled with noises of clearing throats and scraping chairs. The General called for order. The first few minutes of the meeting were related to topics regarding the preparatory phase of the fighting arsenal, then someone burst into the room. It must have been someone of importance, as the General didn't protest. The voice was slightly slurred, piquing Bill's interest.

"Rashmar thinks they found them, sir."

A short pause. "Found whom?"

"The secret base of the Fringe Federation."

"Is that so?" the General said with obvious patience.

"Yup."

Bill's body experienced a tremulous weakening.

"Are they sure?"

"Mmm, nope."

"Who's in charge over there?"

"Williams. But Marchand—who, by the way, is still gloating over his new appointment—just arrived on Rashmar and analyzed the data for himself. The tapes showed a big shoot-out. It seems..." The narrator wheezed. "It seems the cameras got poor images of the intruders, but two were definitely Rashmarian and one—who knows? However, the fourth one has a close description to that pirate who stole my fiancée."

"Really," the General crooned. "Well, if that's true, perhaps Marchand is on the right track."

Bill pinched his lips. *Paul!* It took everything he possessed to keep from jumping out from his hiding place to strangle the bastard.

"Anyway, they took off in one of our Orrilla 248 jets, and so far the fools haven't taken into account that an army will have trackers on all its planes. Delightfully, our boys are following them into the Fringe towards a nebula that we suspect to be the Fringe army's hidey-hole." Paul began to giggle. The room otherwise remained silent.

Paul continued. "So, that means Division 8 needs your approval to search this particular nebula, sir."

There was a shuffle amongst the members in the room. "Well," the General huffed, "as long as Marchand can guarantee that we won't sustain any significant losses, I will grant the approval. You are dismissed Agent Lambert."

Bill's muscles liquefied. He pushed his upper arms harder against the back of the mainframe to keep himself from sinking to the floor. *The base was going to be flushed out!* He had to warn Richard. He barely noticed that the room was clearing, except for a few members.

"Do you think the heiress is there with them?" someone asked.

"We haven't found her anywhere else, have we?"

Another voice spoke. "Yousef Phoebe will be happy if she is. He's lost two ships in the Blue Rift already."

"If she is found, have her brought to me at once." The General grunted. "If she will not sit at Paul's side, then she will sit at mine."

There was a soft chuckle. The General dismissed all of the officers except one who asked for a private audience. The mighty Angel Keem may well have chosen otherwise had he known who the interrogator would be.

"Why the hell do you let Agent Lambert get away with this behavior, Angel?"

"That's my business, Page."

"I must warn you," the voice softened, "his habits are creating dissention among the troops."

"The troops can mind their own business!" Keem grunted. "We must remember that this wasn't all Paul's fault. The Flechette relationship could have ended for a number of reasons. You know women."

"That's not what I meant."

There was a pause. "Page, my decision is not negotiable."

There was a pause from Page. "I know he's been one of our best. But he's through! Don't you see that?"

"This is not negotiable," the General repeated as if with remorse. "Once his assignment is over, he'll get some leave. I'm seeing to it myself."

"If that's how you feel, perhaps you shouldn't wait. I've heard threats."

"If anything happens to Paul," the General muttered spitefully, "I will find and kill the offender myself!"

The subordinate's tone softened. "I'm not sure I can guarantee his safety."

"Then extend him protection."

Page sighed "Why? He might be an A-class agent, but he's still just an agent."

"Maybe to everyone else he is."

There was a hesitation. "What do you mean?"

The General answered flatly, "He is my son, Page."

There was a stifled gasp from the subordinate.

The General's voice sounded weak and tired. "Yes, it's true, Page. Paul Lambert is my son."

*   *   *   *

If the disease didn't kill Raymond Flechette, the ride in Dee's cab through the savanna-type terrain of Doria would. Pain seared through his hip, radiating to all parts of his body as he was jostled about the back seat of the cab.

"Can't you slow down?" he screamed.

"Sorree. But look behind you. It's the Bakfins."

Raymond craned his neck to look out the rear window. They were being chased by five gigantic birds, swooping through the air, diving dangerously close to the cab. Raymond blinked, wondering if Dee's healing potent caused him to see things that weren't really there. When a great claw scrapped along the roof of the cab, Raymond screamed. "Great Creator! They're going to pick the cab up in their claws!"

"Can't. Cab too big for bird claw to fit. If we slow down, beaks poke through top."

"Then drive!"

Raymond closed his eyes and wished that Dee had saved his wonder drug for later. He would have preferred unconsciousness to this. He opened his eyes when he sensed the cab slowing down. The savanna had turned into thick jungle.

"Why are you slowing down?"

Raymond could no longer spot the flying creatures. That wasn't to say they weren't overhead.

"Eeeasy. We out of Bakfin country now. Soon we see the Healer."

Raymond's shoulders stooped with relief. He peered wearily out the front only to find a new fear grip him. Their new enemy was a gnarled mass of vines. The tendrils reached out to wrap their deadly creepers around the cab in a vice grip of death.

"*Ohh,*" he whimpered, "the vines are going to trap us!"

Dee laughed. "You be too worry, Mr. Flecheeet. I come often with no prrroblem."

"Good. Let's not break your record."

Any supreme intelligence on the part of the vines proved inferior to Dee's cab. Articulated mechanical arms reached out to chop off the vines at their base, felling them neatly off either side as the cab pressed on, deeper into the heart of a dense jungle. Raymond momentarily wondered if it was all in vain as he faced primitive medicine that surely couldn't help him. But what other hope did he have, save gleaning information from this Healer who would apparently know the properties of the drug he'd been administered?

They reached a jungle clearing where the sunlight barely filtered through the high canopy. This was home to a small native village. Raymond noticed a male figure emerge from one of the huts wearing only a colorful loincloth and a matching headdress. The breath caught in Raymond's throat as he watched the native walk towards a monstrous worm-like creature basking lazily amongst the trees at the edge of the clearing. The creature's slug-like body squashed the underbrush to either side for a length of at least sixty feet. Had it not been for the worm-thing's complacent expression, Raymond would have found it hideously frightening. Yet the native interacted peacefully with the creature. Raymond found himself staring. The great slug's yellow eye-slits locked onto his.

"*What,* is that?" Raymond asked, gutturally.

Dee swung an elbow over the backrest. "That," he informed, "is the Healer."

CHAPTER 45

Alone, Marie trod the crystal waters of the azure pool. She raised her bronzed cheeks to the high afternoon sun and floated lazily, her hair drifting in Medusa-like tendrils about her head. The sunlight pierced the treetops with shafts of shifting light that broke into tiny rainbows beneath her lowered lashes.

The small cries were familiar to her now. Little laughs and giggles meant the children had arrived. She turned to greet them. "Yawka."

They didn't waste a moment running into the welcoming waters. The little boy waddled out to her. She grasped him by the armpits, dunking his legs in and out of the water until he giggled hysterically. Today the older children felt adventurous. Somehow, in their garbled chatter she understood that they wanted to take her to the other side of the pool where the currents rushed swiftly over the smooth boulders below.

The best way to the other side was to take the path behind the waterfall. Marie found herself amazed that these young children possessed the knowledge to guide her along a moss-layered trail tucked beneath a series of jutting ledges. The water poured over the ledges in thin sheets, making the pool beyond look like a vision undulating through a frosty window. The opposite bank provided depths that allowed them to dive off the high boulders. The dangerous currents Richard had warned her about swept them down into a little eddy at the far end of the pool. In knee-deep water, the clay bottom squished between their toes as they scampered to the bank. Marie dared not tell Richard she'd mastered the entire pool, afraid he might put an end to her growing adventurous nature. But now, having graduated from Princess of the Galaxy to Queen of the Currents, she made a dozen dive-and-glide runs until they all crumpled in a giddy heap of bodies on the sandy shore.

The oldest girl drew their attention to the position of the sun. It had begun to arc over the tall jungle foliage and she knew it was time for the children to return home. The children waited patiently for Marie to dress before tugging at her arms. She knew they wanted her to go to their village. Both hands captured by the children, she let out an ungodly whoop in acquiescence to their offer. In chorus, the children began teaching her their jungle cries as they led her in the direction of their tropical home.

CHAPTER 46

It didn't seem long before the stolen Orrilla 248 dropped out of hyperdrive and floated, seemingly motionless, before an expansive splash of marbling colors. Thin strips of impenetrable galactic dust created a colorful mosaic, spattered with the ice-blue of budding stars that boasted their existence by brilliantly outshining the duller death throws of their parent supernova.

"Now what am I suppose to do?" Clive bellowed. "Request to land? Request to land where?"

Javid gave an exasperated huff. "If you would just send a signal that says we're here with Captain Boro, I'm sure they will respond in kind."

Clive fell back into his seat and flung a hand toward the canopy. "Well. It's a nebula, at least."

"So the coordinates that Captain Boro gave us must be correct."

"I hope so. The Fringe is full of these nebulae. They're a pain in the ass to freighter pilots like me." As he spoke, he punched in a crude signal asking for assistance and telling whoever might be down there that they had one Captain Boro on board in need of medical assistance.

They waited nearly an hour without receiving even a crackle of response on the receiver.

"Hell, I don't even know if I am on the right frequency!" Clive groaned, running splayed fingers through his dark hair. "They're probably sending out a fleet to annihilate us this very minute."

"Don't say things like that!" Javid exclaimed, thrusting his nose toward the canopy, afraid he might see specks of enemy ships bursting from the nebula.

Clive sighed. "Then again, maybe there's nobody down there. Who the hell would live in a nebula?"

*   *   *   *

Richard sat alone at the console that was in direct and continuous contact with Boro's relay ship. He'd sent the technicians off for their supper break, feeling he wanted some time just to sit alone and review the situation. The relay ship checked in every hour as required, but there'd been no word from Boro yet. Richard knew his level of anxiety was ridiculous. Boro hadn't been on Rashmar more than a few days. Still, something foreboding hung in the air. He wished he could foresee it, prepare for it. At least the Saurian Fleet was battle ready, but he still had no idea where to position them.

"Commander!"

Richard sprung from the chair and strode across the isle. It took only a second to see that the screens revealed a solitary visitor speeding toward the nebular gasses at a dangerous pace. "Who the hell is that?" Richard asked.

"They claim to be Nixodonian. A pilot by the name of Clive Baker says he has Captain Boro with him. He's requesting urgent medical assistance for the captain, sir."

"*What?*" Richard muttered. "Who is this joker? What kind of ship is that?"

"It's an Orrilla 248, Commander."

"Clive Baker? Ever heard of him?"

"No sir."

"That's a common enough ship he's flying," Richard noted. "Perhaps too common. Get more information on that craft before you do anything else." Richard paused. "And, what do we know about Boro?"

"They don't have the captain hooked up to any biosensors, so I don't know what kind of condition he's in, sir."

"Or if he's really there. Boro may simply be bait. Then again, unless things went terribly wrong, he wouldn't have given away our position. He would have erased his memory first." A beeping summoned Richard back to the main console. It was Boro's relay ship with nothing to report.

*   *   *   *

Javid slumped in the copilot's seat. "Maybe they do think we're hostile. We can't let them think that. Maybe we should send a distress signal. After all, I *am* feeling rather distressed."

Clive glanced at Javid's pallid features. So, the old man was scared, too. Flustered, Clive began to key in a distress signal. "Do you think they'll believe us?"

"I don't know," Javid said, "but there's a sort of a secret code you could try."

"Oh, yeah? What's that?"

"Add my name to the message. If Marie Flechette is there, they'll have heard of me."

"You are an arrogant bastard, aren't you! What makes you think she's there?"

"Remember? Captain Boro told us that he came from the place where she was being held." Javid raised an eyebrow. "This seems as likely a place as any."

The two looked at each other and chuckled nervously.

"And say something about Captain Boro's mission being accomplished." Javid added.

"Smart ass."

Clive coded Javid's suggestions into the distress signal. Again they waited. Only minutes passed before Clive began to lose his nerve. Maybe they should just forget this whole nonsense and go to Plan B, calculating how far this ship could take them in the direction of Nix States.

*   *   *   *

The technician called Richard a second time. "Another transmission, sir,"

Richard returned to the station. "Well, well," he muttered. Javid of Rashmar? Now this was a surprise. And, mission accomplished? Boro may have lucked on to some interesting allies. "Acknowledge their message," Richard ordered.

"Sir?" The technician twisted to catch the Commander's eye. "We're still waiting for the data on that ship."

"I'll see it as soon as it comes through. In the meantime, call down the ship. Boro will be with them."

The officer nodded and punched in a message of acknowledgment.

Marie would be happy about this one, Richard thought excitedly. He wondered where she was. The sun had set an hour ago. Reese arrived and together they went to the landing field to supervise the homing of the Orrilla through the thick nebular gasses. Once the ship entered the planet's system, Richard was able to converse personally with the crew. He welcomed a tired Clive Bake and an anxious Javid of Rashmar, whose cryptic description of the information Boro had acquired sounded exactly like what they needed. Richard stretched his spine and ran a hand through his hair. Finally! The flight plans for the Telexan Armada's attack. He could barely contain his excitement. A few hours later, the solitary craft's orange plumes punctured the high cloud layer.

Touchdown.

The hissing engines groaned in decrescendo, the mist dissipated, the landing lights dimmed. A tall Nixodonian stepped out, followed by his shorter Rashmarian counterpart. Javid bowed deeply to Commander Shaw, then to Lieutenant Mondiran. Clive gave Javid a flustered glance, then figured he'd better follow the Rashmarian's example. He'd dealt only with the merchants of this Federation, never giving a thought to how the leaders should be greeted. He gave a quick and clumsy bow, then clasped his hands embarrassingly in front of him. He was eye to eye with the unlikely-looking Commander, and stood an inch taller than the dark-haired Lieutenant who looked far too pretty for such an intrepid position. Nonetheless, he had respect for the way these boys handled their affairs. Not too many frills and trimmings. He looked steadily at the two. Perhaps no frills and trimmings at all!

As the group moved towards a ground transport, the two refugees gave a short account of who they were and how they had arrived with Captain Boro in tow. Reese stopped in his tracks. "Are you telling us that this ship isn't yours? That you stole it?"

"That's right. My ship crash landed on Rashmar, sadly enough."

The two leaders glanced at each other. Richard gave an almost imperceptible shake of his head, indicating that he hadn't yet reviewed the stats on the ship. They now had a confiscated TRA jet fighter in their possession.

"Let's discuss this further in my office," Richard said as Boro was being lowered from the craft.

"He's going to be all right," Dr. Faulk assured him, "but there would have been trouble had he been on that ship much longer."

"Let me know when he's conscious, Doc," Richard said before joining the others on the trip back to base. The transport had just begun to move when Javid fumbled through his pockets for the black box.

"Here you are, sir. I would be most grateful if you'd take this."

Richard fondled the box carefully. Inside this black wedge was information he hoped would change the course of galactic history.

"Excuse me again, sir?" the Rashmarian said. "I didn't want to ask you over the hyperwave, sir, but, is she here? You know, my boss, sir."

Richard smiled and nodded.

"And Bill Tripp, sir. Is he all right?"

"Yes. He's on duty with us now. He's off-planet."

"Ohhh." Javid breathed, amazed at the favorable outcome of this major mishap. Captain Boro had told the truth. Javid leaned back and smiled in peaceful satisfaction.

CHAPTER 47

Marie reached the aboriginal village in the dark. Had she not been surrounded by her little friends, she would have run very fast in the opposite direction. Several dozen natives of all ages crept from behind shacks and trees to check out their strange visitor. It helped only marginally that the brood of frightful people cooed gently as they approached. She quickly realized that this was a form of acceptance, as well as one of meticulous inspection. Suddenly the crowd parted and a tall, majestic man strode toward her. His decorative accessories were an instant indication that he was the chief. Hoping a bow was universally accepted, she lowered her head and said, "Yawka, Chief Ungu."

The chief smiled gently. "Welcome, Lady of Shaw."

She nearly laughed aloud at the title. "You may call me Marie," she offered.

He gave an angled nod of his head. "As you wish, Lady Marie. Come, share our meal."

Surrounded by the native people, Marie was shown to a large, central clearing. Chief Ungu told her that this was where the community gathered for special meals and ceremonies, both of which she would experience tonight. Marie admired the artistically designed shelters made of jungle materials that encircled the area. Most of the huts had smoke puffing up from a hole in the roof while pleasant aromas of food wafted from the arched doorways. Glancing around, Marie noticed that the trees glowed dimly with what seemed to be large glass bubbles suspended at varying heights throughout the canopy. Was this where they lived? She must ask later.

Standing on the raw earth, Marie sensed a grounding of spirit and family. A multitude of straw mats had been laid out in preparation for the meal. They were placed in a circle a respectful distance from the large, stone-ringed fire that crackled merrily in the center of the clearing. Marie sat on the ground with the others. Four of the children were allowed to sit with her but the youngest sat with his parents. Marie looked longingly beyond the flames at her little boy, now comfortable with his mother.

Another first dropped onto Marie's list. She ate a tasty stew of wild meat and vegetables out of wooden bowls, then licked sweet, raw honey directly from the combs. By the time the meal was finished, Marie was surrounded by her young friends who had happily sprawled around her. She made herself comfortable, supporting the head of one on her shoulder, an arm about another. Love poured from her like she'd never experienced. These children were healthy, robust and pure, so unlike the poor souls who could do nothing but gawk at her from behind crib bars as she gawked back during her ridiculously sterile hospital tours. To her great joy, her little boy scuttled across the dusty circle to plunk himself on her lap. His mother, a beautiful young woman who seemed no more than a child herself, came running after him, apologizing profusely. Marie gestured with urgency that the child was more than welcome. The woman seemed to understand, and indicated that she felt honored that their guest accepted her child. So, the little one stayed with Marie as the men of the village gathered around the fire to begin a dance. The children pointed to the small round opening in the canopy above the clearing where the planet's two moons encroached upon the opposite edges of the leafy hole.

Marie watched, mesmerized, as the men began a rhythmic dance accompanied by harmonic chanting and the jingling of silver jewelry. As the dance progressed, the details of the men in all their raw and savage splendor captivated her; their glistening bodies writhing sensuously in the firelight, their chants rhythmic and unhurried, feet stamping in time with deep guttural rhythms. When all their arms rose in unison, Marie lifted her eyes following the reach of their arms to the heavens. Captured within the black silhouette of the jungle's canopy, the two full moons had come together, edges touching before an eclipse was about to take place. Marie found herself swallowing down emotions. She clung tightly to the children as her eyes drank in the beauty.

"So Richard," she whispered, "now I understand what it is that you love so much."

CHAPTER 48

It took Bill Tripp hours to escape the Dorian TRA complex. He was exhausted by the time he stole another uniform and bribed his way off the complex. After crossing the fence line, he jogged for ten minutes before reaching the ravine where the cabby was supposedly still waiting for him. His doubts that the fellow would have waited all night grew, as did his hunger, his fatigue, and his despair.

The morning sun was creeping over the hills, creating deep shadows in the ravine winding below. Stopping to catch his breath, Bill analyzed his options while trying to clear his mind of anxious thoughts. His effort was short lived. The tranquil morning relinquished a warning sign. The rotor blades of a search vehicle began to echo nerve-jangling pulses from the direction of the complex. Bill lunged down the steep angle of the gorge, cursing as he spun and slid on loose rocks. Right along the creek bed, he spotted a small cave. With reckless abandon he scrambled towards it. If he didn't find cover, their bio-scanners would pick him off before they even cleared the fence. He reached the cave and experienced terrifying disappointment. It was hardly big enough to shelter him. There was no time to search for an alternative, so he cramped himself into the crevice.

Bill's foot jerked when a sharp pain penetrated his toe. He was shocked to find a large striated rodent sinking its teeth into the leather of his shoe. He howled, shaking the creature loose with a violent kick of his leg, but the animal scrambled back for a counter attack. Bill had little choice but to end the rodent's life with a quick blast from his gun. Quickly, he surveyed the cave and realized that a tunnel continued deep into the rock. The creature's lair. Peering up the rift, he prayed the blast hadn't revealed his position. Scanning the ravine with a new enemy in mind, he became aware of a multitude of other life forms teeming about the ravine. Cover? Moments later, the aircraft flew over, the twap of rotors booming within Bill's rocky cavern. He closed his eyes and prayed that the numerous life-forms in the ravine would mask his presence.

The aircraft had gone, yet Bill remained crouched, eyes squeezed shut, half with fatigue, half with disbelief that the enemy had actually missed him. Something bright throbbed against his eyelids compelling him to open them. He strained his eyes to discern its source. Could it be? Again, a single pulse. Blinking, he made out the cab, tucked into a much more carefully chosen spot than the one he'd found. Bill made a mad dash across the gully, splashed across the small ravine and threw himself into the cab already venturing out to meet him. "You didn't take long," the cabby yelled over his shoulder.

Bill looked at him, stunned. "I didn't take long?"

"Big place. Did you have any luck?"

Bill blinked. "Ah, yes. I did. Thanks for waiting."

"No problem. Here." The driver tossed him a protein bar. "You must be hungry. Where to now?"

Bill tore at the wrapper. "Ah, to the spaceport. I have to send an urgent message. After that, we'll go to the hotel. Maybe Dee will be back with Mr. Flechette."

"Mmm. Maybe not. The Healer is a long way off."

Bill let out a ragged breath. He had to get to Enderal before the arrival of General Keem, but there was no way he'd leave without Raymond. Putting his boss second on the agenda, Bill chewed on the bar and formulated his Fringe-bound message.

*   *   *   *

The Fringe headquarters bustled with activity as the Commander's vehicle crossed the lesser cave. The craft decelerated and entered the well-lit tunnels that marked the executive offices, such as they were. Richard had planned refreshments for his special guests, followed by a debriefing of the Rashmarian activities. The secretary offered the new arrivals a coffee. Richard accepted his own hot brew, then nearly flung it across the room when his commlink shrieked a Red One Alert.

Richard glanced suspiciously at Javid and Clive. The leaders' eyes met.

"Go check it out," Reese offered, knowingly. "I'll entertain our guests."

Richard tore out of the office and ran the short distance to the lesser cave. The staff stepped aside as he strode with intention toward the station that monitored Bill Tripp's communications. His heart grappled with cold fear when he saw the technician's ashen face.

"Sir," the officer's voice warbled. "We're in trouble."

"Commander!" another voice screamed at him.

Richard spun to answer the second call. The technician bounced out of his chair, eyes glued in horror to his monitor.

Richard had the sensation that everything was in slow motion as he heard, "Sir, an entire enemy fleet has pulled out of hyperspace, just two hours' flight from the edge of the nebula!"

The entire room fell to a hush. Richard had not previously noticed how loudly the machines hummed.

The officer monitoring Bill Tripp's messages swore in outrage. He then gave his report to the horror stricken crowd, and to the back of his paralyzed Commander. "Bill Tripp sends an urgent warning, sir. The escape vehicle used by Captain Boro is equipped with a military tracker." The technician paused. "And also, General Angel Keem is to meet with the entire TRA delegation on Enderal in one standard galactic week, sir!"

CHAPTER 49

Dee clutched his belly and howled with laughter, pointing a finger at the great slug in the grasses. "You thought *that* was the Healer?"

Raymond stood with Dee in the middle of the village clearing, fists clutched indignantly. "That's what you told me!"

"No. I said *that* was the Healer." Dee's pointed finger moved a fraction, toward the native who attended the slug. "Well, wait. That is sort of Healer, too." He indicated toward the beast. "That is where the man-Healer gets antidotee."

"Just lovely!" Raymond huffed, wishing he'd never been talked into this crazy expedition. He had to mask his surprise when the man-Healer walked up to them. The Healer's creased face and leathered skin indicated that the man was probably ancient, yet his body was in excellent physical condition. As for the costume, the Healer's feathered headdress differed only in color and variety from that of the rest of the tribe. A thin beaded belt secured a simple loincloth, his upper arms showing off a few gold armlets. Not much for a Healer, Raymond thought.

The Healer had a begrudging look on his face, eyebrows knitting together as he peered at Raymond. He grunted something to Dee who handed him Raymond's pills. The Healer tasted one, snapping it on his tongue as if to analyze its intrinsic makeup. Making a grimace, he spoke directly to Dee, who translated back to Raymond.

"The Healer says you can relax. He knows what kind of poison you take. Trust him, and healing will be easier."

Another exchange took place and Dee spoke again. "He say you are bad, but not too bad for good healing. They will prepare potions if you wish."

Raymond thought he would cry. He wasn't ready for death, no matter how much he'd prepared for it, yet he vacillated. Should he remain sick or let this wild man have his way with him.

"You wish the healing?" Dee asked.

Raymond clenched his teeth. "Yes. Yes, I do."

"Very good. Come. The ceremony is a big long one."

Raymond meekly obeyed the orders to remove all his clothing and donned the loincloth that was apparently the only attire appropriate for the sacred mat. He thought he was beyond caring, but cold fear coursed through his veins. Were these people about to torture him in some religious sacrifice? A glance down his emaciated frame made him suddenly more frightened of his deterioration than of what this Healer might do to him.

"Come now, Mr. Flecheeet. Healer is ready."

Raymond lay on a mat. A whimper escaped his throat as the coarse fibers dug into his thinning skin. Dee knelt beside him. "The Healer tells me that you might see things. Do not be afraid. You talk to the spirits if you wish."

Raymond stared in disbelief at Dee who calmly took his place with the remainder of the tribe encircling the mat.

The Healer gave instructions to an assistant who went to the great slug and scraped oozing jelly off its pliant epidermis. The animal, obviously aware of its role, gazed at Raymond with benevolent yellow eyes. The assistant put the jelly in a small pot and gave it to the Healer. The Healer added other ingredients and lit the contents. He fanned the billows of sweet smoke over Raymond's face. The sedative effect was instant.

Time became meaningless. Gradually, he noticed there was no longer any sensation in his body. He was free of pain. It didn't seem to matter that the Healer began to poke and prod all over, as if to find the unhealthiest areas. It didn't matter that a woman lifted his head to pour a bitter liquid down his throat. He smiled and slumped against the mat, engrossed in the chanting of the men and women. Their voices grew in crescendo with a pulsing rhythm that seemed to match the beat of his heart. The Healer's hands hovered just above Raymond's navel. Eyes closed, the Healer moaned with every exhalation of Raymond's ˙ breath creating an illusion that the Healer was drawing the sickness out of Raymond's belly with every exhalation. In and out. In and out. The chanting increased in volume.

The sun dropped below the horizon.

With a downward movement of his eyes, Raymond could see the Healer's hands, endlessly holding their position. The sensation of pulling became more powerful as time passed. With each exhalation, Raymond felt as if he were giving up the poison imbued in every cell of his body. It became an excruciating effort accompanied by his own loud moans.

Dee remained huddled in his place, watching with a tremulous smile as Raymond's body glistened in the firelight, arching with the efforts. Oozing from the patient's navel was a greenish liquid that trickled off the patient's waist.

Deep in the heart of the jungle, animals scurried about in their nocturnal business; the moons of Doria rose; the steamy, humid air cooled and stilled. A great bellowing cry was heard, piercing the blackness of the canopy before echoing amongst the hills. The bellow caught the attention of every jungle creature. They stopped; they listened; they understood; and then they carried on about their business.

CHAPTER 50

Hands visibly trembling, Richard looked anxiously at Reese who arrived moments after he was paged. "Did you send them to Detention?"

"Absolutely. Do you think…decoys?"

"If not, they would have looked for a tracker! Have Dr. Faulk wake up Boro, and," Richard could barely come out with the words, "start the evacuation. The mothership first."

Reese ran splayed fingers through his black hair. "Great Creator, Richard."

"It was my bad judgment. I called them in before getting a check on that ship. Better get the Rashmarian's recorder on the flagship and start analyzing it right away."

"I've already started on it in security control. We'll have the results any moment."

"Sir," a First Officer called, "we've located the tracker. It's a regular military unit, sir."

Richard nodded. "Disengage it and put the ship in our service. Then get the defense forces prepared for liftoff. We need to spare as much of the mountain as possible. Tell the Saurian fleet to prepare for a hyperspace jump. We'll get those coordinates to them as soon as we can…if that's really what's on that recorder."

Richard walked back to the station to analyze the movement of the Telexan fleet, now fully out of hyperspace and showing up like bacterium on his star maps.

"They're moving in fast, Commander," the technician warned. "They tracked the exact movements of the Orrilla through the nebula. It won't take them but four or five hours, sir."

Richard bit his lip. "We must hold them off, at least until the majority of this headquarters is made airborne. I don't think we can prevent them from landing, but we are *not* going to leave a welcoming party."

"Richard!" Reese shouted, commlink still at his ear. "We've got it! All the information is here, and intact. The Saurian fleet can move into position in time."

Richard rubbed the bridge of his nose. "Thank the Creator." He looked up. "Let's get the first fighter unit out to its defensive position."

"I'll start the evacuation out toward the north gravitational field," Reese said. "I know it's dangerous, but they're already too close. And, if we can get everyone safely to the rendezvous point, we'll have won half the battle."

Richard nodded. "Agreed."

"By the way," Reese quickly added. "I talked to Boro. He vouched for Clive Baker and the Rashmarian so I had them released." He paused. "Boro's doing well."

Richard slapped his friend on the shoulder. "That's great news."

Richard left the control room feeling satisfied that the endless evacuation drills they'd practiced would be carried out with expediency. He tried to console himself with the fact that they'd expected to be flushed out from here sooner than this, but the thought did little to abate his crushing disappointment. Within the hour, the control room was nearly dismantled.

Leaning over the only terminal left intact, Richard was briefed on the preparation and takeoff times of the fighter units and the boarding of the support staff on the mothership. Suddenly, a horrifying though struck him. "Marie!" he blurted aloud. Quickly he summoned her assigned guard.

"I'm sorry, sir. She went to the village. When the alarms went off, I went to look for her, but I wasn't properly equipped for a jungle venture."

"Get what you need and go find her," Richard ordered. Simultaneously, he caught sight of a bewildered pair wandering aimlessly amidst the confusion of staff. Richard clapped the guard on the shoulder. "Never mind. I've just found someone I can spare."

Richard was not well received. Clive skewered the Commander with an evil glare. "First you lock us up, then release us without any explanation. What's going on, *Commander?*"

"Your ship had a military tracking device."

Two mouths dropped opened.

"There is now an entire enemy fleet coming toward us as we speak. They'll be in firing range in three hours."

Clive's chest expanded. "Ah shit! I'm not much of a military man, sir. I didn't think to check for a bloody tracker!"

Javid's eyes grew wide. "Oh…and you suspected we were TRA people."

"Boro has vouched for both of you, and your recorder has its information intact. You boys did your work."

Clive huffed. "That's why Boro wanted us to go to the relay point first, but the wimp passed out too early! Now you tell us that we've led them to you? Aw, I don't believe it!"

"I'm hoping they won't realize what information you stole, but I'm sure they know you weren't on their base for the fun of it." Richard stalled. "And now I have a problem that I need your help with."

"What about Marie Flechette sir? I haven't seen her yet."

"That's what I need your help for," Richard admitted, quickly explaining that the local tribespeople were friends and that Marie was presently visiting their village. He simultaneously spoke into his commlink to order a hovercraft, but the best he could do was to have it waiting for them at the large cave entrance. An assistant brought a mapper and handed it to Clive. Javid stared aghast at Commander Shaw. He didn't have anyone taking Bill's *place?*

The Commander's name was called innumerable times, making the instructions choppy, but finally Javid and Clive were off down a maze of tunnels while holding a wedged mapping computer in front of them. They walked quickly, Clive's eyes darting between the mapper and the actual path his feet took. "Goddamn aliens tracked us," he muttered angrily.

Javid voiced his own concerns. "I can't believe he let her go out into a jungle by herself. To visit aboriginals, no less! Boro told me that she was in good hands!"

"Didn't you tell me she was a capable young woman?"

"Well, yes! But she shouldn't go anywhere alone. Especially into a jungle!"

Clive stopped abruptly. "What is she? An invalid or something?"

"No."

Clive gave the Rashmarian an exasperated look. "Then she should be able to take care of herself, shouldn't she? If anyone tried tagging along behind me I'd punch him in the face in five minutes flat." Clive resumed his long stride, which forced Javid into a run.

"But she's the *Heiress*."

"So?"

"She's never been alone. She always has guards. She's not allowed to…go…" Javid's voice trailed off with the sudden, powerful realization that Marie had been a prisoner her entire life. It was a simple fact that the heiress was to be supervised at all times, as if she were some sort of commodity rather than a living, human being. Javid glanced behind him to make telepathic contact with the white-haired Commander. What had this man done to make her want to go off into a jungle at night?

His eyes fell upon his immediate surroundings: the caves, the intricacy of their layout, their modernization blended with an ancient décor. Old paintings could be seen everywhere, livening up walls and ceilings in natural dyes that threatened to grow dim. Strategically placed lamps brought the masterpieces to life, not by their creators, but by the modern men who understood their value. In many ways it reminded Javid of the caves of Rashmar, and those made raw and primitive emotion ooze from him. Of freedom and adventure. Of curiosity and of invincibility. Suddenly he began to grasp an inkling of what Marie must be experiencing here.

The hovercraft was hardly big enough for the two of them. Clive's big frame bent over the steering column while Javid clung to him from behind. Clive cut in the thrusters that shot them through the massive, gaping hole of the main cave entrance.

"You're in a hurry," Javid shouted over the wind rushing down his throat.

"We have a princess to save before the bad guys come and blow us all to shit."

"She's not officially a princess."

"She is from what I've heard. But, I never trust hearsay. I want to see this for myself."

"Whale Baker, you keep your hands off my boss, you hear?"

Clive laughed and cut in more speed.

From the landmark of the staircase entrance, the path widened.

"Should be easy now." Clive bellowed, the mapper right up to his nose in the darkness.

He abruptly passed the mapper back to Javid then zipped recklessly down the well-trodden trail. The screen suddenly popped into the next division, which included a pool of water and its source. The map indicated a hairpin turn on the path just prior to reaching the pool. Javid yelled at Clive. "Watch for the curve!"

Too late. Clive hit a pack of vines along the edge of the path that suddenly narrowed and twisted. The creepers seemed to wrap their tendrils around the hovercraft and consciously hurl it sideways. An icy chill exploded over Javid's skin. The next instant he found his head underwater. Unable to swim more than a few strokes in favorable conditions, Javid immediately panicked. Clive's large hand grabbed his clothing, still one layer too thick—a forgotten token of the Telexan laundry—and hauled him to his feet. Only then was it apparent that he was in water only knee deep. Despite himself, he let out a cry, immediately mocked by Clive. Nonetheless, they both stood in the water, panting. Clive's ears tuned in to a steady roar. "A waterfall? Well that's just ducky!"

"I was about to tell you that, Clive."

"Well, you were too late. We're sure in a fix now, old man. How strong are you?"

Javid swallowed. "Not very." He looked forlornly at the hovercraft lying on its side, half immersed. "Will it start?"

"Yeah, sure, but not in there."

They pushed and shoved, grunted and groaned. The craft moved slowly, but the job was going to be a long and arduous one.

Marie delighted in the native dance, feeling like she'd connected with them in their prayers of gratitude. Suddenly, she was called to Chief Ungu's hut. Inside, the sapling walls rippled with the flickering dance of a small fire that vented through the roof. One of the elders indicated that she sit on a carpet opposite the chief's throne. The fire burned low between them, giving the chief's features a somber look as he leaned forward to speak to her.

"You appear full of joy," he said, as if he were surprised.

Marie smiled. "Yes, Chief Ungu. This evening brings me much joy."

"But there is evil coming to you. You feel joy, even when evil comes?"

Marie sobered. Was he somehow aware of a change in the galactic situation? It seemed ludicrous. Her thoughts shifted to the glass bubbles in the forest, and

Richard's words. *The natives have tremendous secrets—secrets a computer could never know or learn.*

"There are bad men trying to control us all," she explained quickly, "but they can't win."

The chief sat back in his throne. "At this very moment I sense evil coming."

Bewildered, Marie stared at him. "I believe that I'm safe. No one knows that I'm here."

He looked at her quizzically. "I know that you are here."

Her smile stiffened. She ignored the unnerving possibility of a new danger and answered on the principal that the knowledge he possessed came from Richard, and Richard hadn't been here since her arrival. "It's not like that. I'm not sure I can explain, but for now, I'm safe."

"Do you wish to pray to our gods for personal protection? We will smoke the pipe of peace, then you may dance. Your participation will protect you from this danger."

No lasting personal harm...She straightened. "I would be honored to dance with your people, and seek protection from your gods."

The chief smiled. "The gods honor your sincerity. They invite you to be a student of clarity. This means becoming connected to all things through the vehicle of your own soul. Once you learn these skills, you, too, can hear from the stars as we do and you will not need honorary protection from us. The tribe welcomes you to stay and learn from our elders."

Marie stared at him, shaken by his offer. Instinctively, she glanced down at her chest. She saw her soul as an empty cavern, its complex mysteries visible only if she were to make a searching discovery by means of her conscious will. The vision frightened her and she looked back at Chief Ungu. An intangible fear stormed her pale blue eyes. Could he really hear something from the stars? Could she? She sensed a new awakening, but it was well out of context with what she normally understood. Yet, something familiar struck a harmonic cord that resounded deep inside that empty cavern, and for a moment she felt completely alone.

The revelations were too much to cope with. An obstinate shake of her head rejected the feelings until she could think them through. "Thank you," she said. "I will remember your offer, but I can't stay now. Perhaps another time."

The chief tilted his head. "As you wish. When you are ready, you will know."

No, she'd never have time for such self-indulgences. Suddenly, that formidable cavern sent an echo like the remnant of a primordial song. Along with it came a puff of inner peace to her trembling hands and they calmed themselves. She clasped them together. Unwittingly, her voice escaped her lips. "When I am called, I will come."

The chief moaned, nodding slowly as if peacefully satisfied. "Come now, then," he invited. "The dance is waiting."

She followed the chief and his elders in a procession back to the celebration. The moons had eclipsed, sending a single shaft of brilliant light through the opening in the canopy. On the ground, the illuminated bodies of both men and women stamped their feet on the gray dust of a well-trodden circle around the roaring fire. They all wore heavy silver bracelets laden with tinkling chimes and noise-making artifacts. One of the children tapped her on the shoulder. She was surprised to see that they'd brought her a set of chime bracelets as well. One of the girls painstakingly adorned Marie's wrists and ankles. Balancing on her buttocks, Marie shook her arms and legs, bringing the children to hysterical laughter.

The chief summoned her again. Bejeweled with the special gifts, she walked over and sat before him on an outdoor mat. Chief Ungu took a couple of hefty drags from a long, slender pipe with a white bone bowl before passing it to her. Marie pushed the usual sanitation requirements from her mind and pinched the pipe between her lips. This was not Enderal. This was adventure. Pure, unadulterated adventure.

She sucked gently but was surprised by the intensity of heat that singed her throat. Eyes bulging, she resisted the urge to cough. Impossible! Her lungs collapsed with a sharp giddy exhalation. It was immediately apparent that the contents of this bowl were not ordinary. She tried again, finding it easier to hold the sacred smoke in her lungs a few seconds before expelling it slowly. She wanted to squeal with delight. Instead, she remained calm and kept her jungle etiquette to what she ventured to be proper, which was to accept a few more pulls from the pipe of peace. She returned the pipe just as the psychotropic effects enveloped her in a feeling of woozy, wholesome joy.

The Chief indicated that she could now dance with the others. With a gracious bow, Marie stepped cautiously to the edge of the dance formation. She was watched closely by the children not yet of age to join in the prayer dance. She smiled at them, then began following the steps of the others. She felt clumsy at first, but within minutes she was stamping her feet, mesmerized by the clinking of her own bracelets that she shook in time with the drums. As the dance went on, Marie became more involved. She shook back her head, flung herself in circles, stomped until the dust mushroomed about her ankles. Her voice rumbled in a loud hum as the singing around her increased in volume. She didn't understand their language but her heart joined in a universal understanding of the prayer, undoubtedly the same universality of which Richard spoke. Here, with the help of the smoke, no spoken word was needed. She communed with the spirits of those around her, with her heart, her mind, and then with her voice. Impetuously, Marie cried out with all the substance of her soul: the pain, the joys, the frustrations and sovereignty of her life, and the utterly pure love she had for Richard, his people, his lands, and his gods.

*   *   *   *

Richard slammed the jeep into high gear and sped through the lesser cave, through the tunnels now stripped of all necessary components, and on toward the great cave. With his control room dismantled, running the show proved to be difficult. On his way, he stopped to supervise the evacuation of equipment, supplies, and staff. The mother ship and two support vehicle fleets had gotten away safely. Another squadron of fighters was ready for liftoff. All that would be left was his flagship, one fighter squadron and its skeleton ground crew. Everything was in order, except for Marie who still wasn't back with the two newcomers he'd sent after her. Damn it anyway. Why had he entrusted that task to two complete strangers?

An officer ran diagonally across the expanse of the cave toward the jeep. "Commander!"

Richard slowed the vehicle. The officer gave a quick salute.

"Commander, your ship is ready, sir You should board now."

"The heiress is still missing. Hold the ship."

The officer shifted anxiously. "Lieutenant Mondiran warns that the Telexans are nearly within firing range, sir."

Richard pointed an imperative finger at the weary officer. "I'll deal with Mondiran. Get that last fleet out of here. My ship waits."

Richard drove deeper into the greater cave where the temporary command post had been erected. It was the only operating structure left in the gigantic cavity that only hours ago had buzzed with activity. Now, tucked in a protective recess near the entrance of the cave, a small makeshift control station bleeped out the latest reports, leaving the rest of the cave a stupendous foreboding black hole. The space plane winches hung silent, mechanical bays lay empty. Only the floodlights shone against the floor, their bright circles showing nothing but trampled, grease-smeared concrete. Richard coughed on the remnants of ionizing jet fuel hanging noxiously in the air. His voice echoed back from the ghostly cave. Peering out of the cave entrance he could see the bright flare of thrusters as the last squad sprang from the surface of the planet. Otherwise, the place he considered home was empty once again.

But the ships could be gone, his staff could be gone, and although he felt a loss, something deeper was missing. She wasn't by his side now, and the minute she arrived he would take her away from here forever, with none of the ceremony he had hoped to organize for her departure. No. They would tear off in the middle of the night with no good-byes save a backward glance.

The soldier at the temporary console stood and saluted as Richard disembarked from his jeep. The officer looked tired.

"Sir," the soldier said, "the enemy will be within firing range in twenty minutes."

Chapter 51

Raymond's breath heaved in and out. The excruciating effort of the final drawing of the poison by the Healer's hands made him cry out, and when his lungs were empty, they collapsed. A ghastly feeling of suffocation gripped him. He suddenly felt the Healer put his mouth to his and blow gently. It was as if the air flowed right into his legs. With a great infusion of energy, Raymond's life returned to him. Only moments later, he was able to breathe on his own. The Healer murmured quietly while passing his hand over Raymond's whole body just inches above it, as if sensing the success of the healing. Finally, the Healer rose, bowed and left the circle.

Raymond felt a tear trickle down his temple, a result of both exhaustion and the sheer joy of knowing that he would no longer experience the pain of his disease. It no longer plagued him. As he lay there regaining his strength, things became unexpectedly clear. With alacrity, his mind raced through his life's events, from childhood to the creation of Flechette Cosmetics.

In a vision so real he could taste it, Genevieve was in his arms, right here on the jungle mat. She was swollen with child. He felt the exhilaration of watching his little girl being born, with her wet body writhing in his hands just moments after she emerged from her mother's womb.

Then, Marie at her debutante ball. She was dancing. He could hear her chanting as if she were near-by. And now she was in the hands of monsters. The guilt he bore ground at the pit of his stomach. Her predicament was due to the figurehead he'd created with her name.

His eyes snapped open. He saw her. He saw her clearly, but she danced in the dust with strange things around her wrists and ankles. Her body moved in step to some strange drumming in a physical exaltation of the joy that coursed through her soul. Yet something was wrong. Raymond found himself straining to lift his head, calling out to her.

Dee rushed to his boss's side and placed a hand on his forehead. "Eeezy, Mr. Flecheeet."

He saw her again. She was still dancing, even as the danger approached. His body was physically exhausted, yet he found his mind to be energetic. Never had he known the ability to communicate with the mind, but somehow, that very instant, it came to him. From somewhere in the depth of his soul, he cried out her name. His lips did not part.

*   *   *   *

Marie's dance came to an abrupt halt. Her eyes flew open. She gaped into the dust. Somewhere in that roiling powder she could see clearly her father's face. He looked at her desperately. Bewildered, she called out, "Papa?"

*   *   *   *

Raymond put all of his energy into the pit of his stomach. "Run, my little one, run!"

*   *   *   *

Marie blinked at the dust. The drums continued, the dance continued, but Chief Ungu had noticed a change in his guest's demeanor. He rose from his chair and walked purposefully toward her. He stood majestically tall. "You are very powerful, Lady of Shaw."

Marie remained frozen in the pose of her last step.

"You have received a message," he said. "Quickly, you must act on it."

Marie had taken only two long strides toward the bordering jungle when a thick orange bolt sizzled down from the sky and pounded a hole in the exact spot where she'd been standing. The powerful laser exploded the circle into a massive dust cloud. The bolt caught the edge of the fire sending out deadly projectiles of splintered logs and hot gravel. The impact threw Marie to the ground. Women cried out, children screamed, men roared.

Marie scrambled to her feet, first seeing the large saucer-shaped hole the laser had created. The Chief had been spared but the elders had to help the shaken leader to safety. She looked up to the sky but the canopy obscured much of the view. Then, she witnessed another attack, this time directed toward the mountain.

"*No*," she cried aloud. They were being attacked! Then she saw the red glowing thrusters of jets mounting with great speed toward the heavens. "Oh God, no," she whimpered.

Her eyes fell back on the devastated village. Her little boy waddled aimlessly through the destruction of the sacred circle, screaming with confusion and fright. She took a few steps toward him, and stopped. Her eyes were drawn to a group of men and women on the other side of the circle. Through the settling dust she could see that someone had been hurt. She saw one of the men close the eyes of the woman she recognized as the little boy's mother. Marie began to cry, but her mind screamed out, "*Oh Papa, where are you? How is it that you warned me?*"

An obtrusive noise, like that of a feral jungle beast, rumbled in the jungle underbrush. The people of the village panicked. Marie scooped up the orphaned child, determined to protect him. She joined the others in running toward the far end of the clearing, but before any of them could escape, a white sausage-like structure burst from the trees and came to a screeching halt before tipping on its side just a few feet away from the scattered remains of the fire.

Two human figures tumbled off the hovercraft. Marie opened her eyes in horror. Had the TRA come for her? Paralyzed, she watched the intruders pick themselves up and dust off in a solemn fashion. They didn't act like TRA. She naturally focused on the larger of the two, but didn't recognize him. Marie was about to run headlong into the bush with the child when she recognized the other. With a gasp she took a step towards the men. The woman beside her took the child and Marie broke into run. "*Javid!*"

The Rashmarian peered in her direction, his small frame slumping in thanksgiving as he watched his dear Marie run towards him. She reached him and fell on her knees. She grasped his hands and pressed them against her tear stained cheeks.

"Ah, my Lady, it *is* good to see you!" Javid breathed, bending to put his head against hers. She looked up, laughing and crying before reaching up to clasp her arms around his neck.

Clive Baker stood rigid, watching the scene with astonishment. Was this copper haired goddess, with eyes that shimmered like translucent jewels, really on her knees before *Javid*? So, the little weasel hadn't lied. And look at her!

Clive blinked once and croaked, "Whoa!"

*   *   *   *

Richard stood squarely on the tarmac beside the huge bulk of his flagship, its motors roaring, liftoff lights flashing with impatience. The wind whipped white strands about his face, stinging his cheeks with tiny lashings as he scanned the darkness. The access ramp lay open, flooding a square of harsh light against the black tarmac. Otherwise all ground lighting had been extinguished, marking the end of the evacuation.

Reese ran down the ramp. "Any sign of them?" he asked Richard. "We can't pick up anything definite on the bioscanners." Reese peered into the darkness. "We can't wait much longer. I'm told that the fighters can't keep the Telexans from landing. They're already coming back in to pick up their ground crew."

Richard shook his head in defeat. "Let's give them one more minute, but organize a rescue to hide her in the bunker, just in case."

Reese let out a worried breath and returned to the ship. A minute came and went. Nothing could be detected save the swaying of the jungle foliage in the strengthening winds. Finally, the engines increased in power and Richard knew he'd run out of time. He looked skyward and witnessed a short burst of light coming from low orbit, then another, followed by a long blue fusion trail. Was that one of his ships? One of theirs? His heart sank. The ship's lights blinked again. Before making the heart-wrenching decision, his eyes scanned the darkness one more time.

A blessing perhaps? His boys in space could no longer hold off enemy fire. A thick blast streaked downward, slashing through the bordering jungle. The trees instantly burst into flame. It was then that he saw them, illuminated by the fire that ravaged the trees. The flames delineated three figures speeding towards them. Richard whipped out his commlink to call for assistance as he ran out to meet the hovercraft that screeched to a tilting halt. Marie fell into his arms. He grasped her, one hand pressing her head hard against his chest for the only second he had to give thanks that she was alive.

Clive Baker let the hovercraft clatter to the tarmac and ran up behind the Commander and the Princess who were making a stumbling run toward the flagship. "Wait. Can I help?"

The leader either didn't hear him, or chose not to. Plan C. He feigned a limp and accepted the help of one of the female staff while casting a perturbed glance at the royal couple. Just his luck!

Javid felt awful. Their mad, clinging trip back to base had left him exhausted and horribly scratched up. Simply too much had happened. There was no emotion left. Everything canceled out everything else. He swallowed hard as several officers rushed out to help him. Embarrassed, he found himself collapsing into their arms. He had to be carried to the ship!

The group had barely entered the main hold when the iris portal closed with a resounding zing. Richard hustled Marie to a row of jumpseats and strapped her in. The ship had already left the ground. The sudden jolt that rocked the ship sent Marie's heart to her throat. Richard squeezed her hand. "Hang on," he shouted. Marie watched him make a zigzagging dash toward the bridge as the craft twisted and turned in its escape. Seconds later, Clive Baker slammed into the jumpseat beside her.

"Well, I'm glad somebody finally showed me to my seat so I don't get pulverized in this death trap!" He glanced about the elegant flagship. "Nice death trap, too. I'm glad I'll be dying in style!"

Marie shot him an angry look. "A little confidence would be appreciated, Mister whoever-you-are."

Clive grinned. "Your savior, remember? The name's Baker. Clive Whale Baker."

"Fine. May I remind you that Javid was also my savior?"

"Whoa! How does that little weasel get so much respect from the Princess herself?"

The ship rocked and Marie found herself clinging to the forearm of Clive Whale Baker. Two crew members dashed by, each reminding them to stay put. "I'm not going anywhere," Clive insisted with a fling of a hand. Javid suddenly plunked into the seat on her left. "If we don't make it, at least I'll have done my duty," he cried with remorse. "But, my Lady, I pray for your safety."

"What duty?" Marie demanded. "Where have you been? How did you get here?" Marie hadn't had time to ask questions because Clive Whale Baker had thrown her onto the hovercraft and torn back to base, all while yelping that his last ride home was *not* going to leave without him. Both Javid and Clive began to unravel a most amazing tale, interrupted by arguments about *whom* should take credit for what.

"Wait a minute!" Marie cried. "Javid, are you telling me that you made it to Rashmar?" A little laugh wedged its way into her anguish.

Clive clasped Marie's forearm. "Him? I was on Rashmar too, you know. And not just once, but twice!"

"Yes," Javid shot back. "And remember how you got there the first time? It was because of your sick passions for women like Lola Phoebe, a breed quite different from the one you hold so tenaciously to now."

Clive threw both hands into the air. "I'm not after your boss!"

Javid glared at Clive. "Look into my eyes and say that again, Whale."

"Lola? *Thee* Lola Phoebe?" Marie squeaked.

Clive's face began to redden. "You promised you wouldn't tell!" An accusing finger pointed across Marie's face toward Javid's nose.

Javid sunk back into his seat. "I'm sorry, Clive. You're right. I've broken my promise. I am so *terribly* sorry."

The ship jolted sharply. Lights flickered. Marie let out a scream and clung to both Javid and Clive.

"It won't matter much longer," Clive bellowed. "As soon as we're dead, that information capsule will open and the whole goddamned galaxy will know."

Another groan escaped Javid. "Oh, let us die, then. Quick, Great Creator. Quick!"

"Die?" Marie screeched through sudden darkness. "Don't you talk like that, Javid!"

The engines roared as the ship maneuvered to escape the enemy. Javid raised his voice above the noise. "There *is* no information capsule. I made that up. I am such a *wretched* soul!"

"*What?*" The lights flickered back on. Clive's eyes were full of surprise. "No information capsule?" He began to giggle and then burst into howling laughter until a tear squeezed from his eye. He ignored the sirens and red lights that began to flash from every bulkhead. Slapping a hand to his knee, he drew in a breath, and again burst into laughter. "Ah, you Rashmarians are really something," Clive gasped. "All right, we're square, old man." Clive jabbed a finger into his chest. "Anybody who can fool the great Whale Baker has got his respect."

Javid and Marie could only stare at him. Clive raised his voice over the blare of emergency sirens, "Don't worry my Princess. With that weasel around, we'll make it."

Seconds later they were thrown into complete darkness. The ship jolted. Marie screamed. She felt Clive grasp her hand. "Hang on sweetheart, because if we die, at least I'll be going to heaven with an angel."

"Are you calling me Angel?" she screeched. "That is a *direct* insult, Mr. Baker!"

*   *   *   *

Bill waited one interminable day for Raymond to return. He made a dozen trips from the spaceport to the hotel, each one more disquieting.

"You worry like a child," his cabby patronized.

Bill hoped the cabby was right. He hadn't told his cabby the real reasons behind his fear. After his relay, he'd lost complete contact with Fringe ground control. Bill thought he would be sick if he dwelt on the possibility of capture, or the total annihilation of the Fringe base.

Then there was the second concern. It was nothing tangible. It was *in*tangible and definite. Space & Aviation Control, without prior warning, announced that all traffic in and out of Dorian air space would be coming to a complete halt for a few hours in order to make emergency recalibrations of all the trajectories. The bizarre announcement didn't get past Bill. He knew that the maintenance would get delayed for hours, then days, then indefinitely. The Telexans were on their way!

First, he sent the FC freighter back to Enderal, then his resourceful Fringe crew managed to confirm a liftoff time just before the shut down. At all costs he had to find Raymond before the 1600 hour deadline.

Bill was checking for messages at the hotel desk when through the lobby doors, he saw Raymond stepping out of a cab. He didn't wait for his driver to open the door. He didn't use a cane. Raymond stood tall, looking around as if the place were some architectural wonder. He didn't favor a hip, and Bill Tripp's jaw dropped. Raymond strode, smooth-gaited, into the lobby toward the body-guard who stood looking as though was seeing ghost.

"He wasn't kidding!" Bill said in astonishment.

"About the Healer?" Raymond shook his head. "No, he wasn't. But, there will be time for stories later. First, I believe there are pressing matters at hand?"

"There are, indeed," Bill smiled, gripping his boss's hand in a hearty shake. "It's awfully good to have you back, Sir."

At the spaceport, both cabbies begged for a visit from them again soon. Raymond promised he'd bring his entire family. He truly wanted to thank the Healer in a more fitting manner than by running about the jungle howling and scream-ing like a wild man.

Bill's heart raced as he strapped himself into the pilot's seat. The control tower was already demanding a reconfirmation of his security clearance codes, license numbers, description of passengers, crew, and cargo. After an unnerving pause, he was given lift-off clearance. Bill glanced at Raymond in relief, and threw his weight against the levers.

*   *   *   *

Marie's scream continued beyond the sudden silencing of the sirens. The lighting suddenly was restored. Marie wrenched her hand from Clive's and gave him a gloating look.

"I'm still alive, Clive," Javid reminded. "So stay away from my boss."

"Yeah, yeah."

Richard strode back toward them, waving a hand through the acrid smoke escaping from a fizzling component. He stopped in front of Marie and asked, "Are you all right?"

"Yeah," Clive answered. "What happened out there?"

"The last ship in pursuit decided on a suicide run," Richard said. "We nailed him just before impact."

"Excellent work, Commander!" Clive said before leaning over Marie to grimace at Javid. "Nice girl, but she's really not my type."

"You're right about that!" Javid retorted.

"Stop it, you two!" Marie hissed.

"What's the problem?"

"Nothing." Marie glared at Clive.

"Well, the best thing for my willies is to do something." Clive growled while releasing his harness. "Can I help on the bridge, Commander?"

"Yes. We could use your help."

"I'd love a hot drink, sir." Javid pleaded.

Richard pointed Javid toward the galley, then released Marie's harness.

"Oh, Richard. I'm sorry," she croaked. "You almost didn't get away because of me."

"It wasn't your fault. I should never have let you go to the village at a time like this." He looked at her, hair wind-blown, cheeks and arms revealing signs of a rough trip back to base. He found himself smiling as he fingered the chimes of a wrist bracelet. "What are these?"

Marie gasped. "Oh! I completely forgot. I was given these for the dance."

He helped her from the jumpseat. "I can see that you had a wonderful time."

She turned her wrists over to set the armlets tinkling. "Maybe the timing was off, but you were right. It was something I could never have imagined." She looked at him with shimmering, enlightened eyes. "I saw my father's face, Richard. It was like he was right there in the dust. He warned me, told me to run, then a laser hit the ground right where I'd been dancing."

Richard looked at her, aghast. One of the lasers had hit the village? He supposed the TRA would have picked up heavy life-form readings there.

A tear rolled down Marie's cheek. "The little boy's mother was killed. She was so young. And now I'm not there to help. We just left them and ran off to save ourselves!"

"Ah, baby." He swallowed bitterly. He'd known the boy's mother. "You did the right thing. The boy will be fine. The village will take care of him, and Chief Ungu knows that I will help as soon as I get back."

"I'm glad to hear that," she wept.

He wrapped an arm around her shoulder and guided her towards his quarters. "You should know that Javid played a major role in the Rashmarian mission," he said. "Without his electronic recorder, the whole mission would have failed."

"What recorder? Are you saying that Boro didn't—didn't survive?"

"Oh, no! Boro's fine, but he damaged his microprocessor in a fall."

Once in the stateroom, Marie could do nothing but sit listlessly on the berth while he removed the chimes. He held her to his chest, soothing away her sobs. It felt strange not to be on the bridge, dashing around like a warlord in his glory. It felt even stranger to be captivated by a woman who'd soon be gone from his life forever. Oh, they may have reunions now and again, if peace could prevail, if he didn't end up in a Telexan prison for the rest of his life. He closed his eyes and pressed his cheek against the skein of her hair.

When she slept, Richard returned to the bridge. He checked on their status.

"We're clear, Commander," an officer reported, keeping his eyes on the multiple screens before him.

Richard nodded. "All right. We lay low until we're sure we're clear, then we head quietly towards the Saurian fleet."

He made his way over to Reese to get an update on the Telexan Armada's movements.

"We're in luck," Reese breathed. "The TRA haven't figured out why our boys were in their control center. They're following the exact flight plan in Javid's recorder."

Richard leaned closer to the screen. "Three hyperspace jumps and they emerge right at the Dorian corridor of the Sector 5 lanes. We weren't so far off in our calculations," Richard smirked, "but our best guess would have missed them by two parsecs."

"And look at the beauty of this," Reese tapped his commlink against the screen. "They're getting into position for their first jump."

"That gives the Saurian fleet plenty of time to move into position."

"And when that Armada comes out of hyperspace?…they'll see the whites of our eyes in their crosshairs!"

CHAPTER 52

Marie awoke in Richard's elegant stateroom after a lonely and restless sleep. Twisting with frustration, she opened her eyes only to see a plain beige ceiling a few feet above her head. There were no priests painted here, no subtle colors of the nebula, no humidity to bathe her lungs with her first waking breath.

She tried to sleep again but her mind was like a malfunctioning hologram. She could see the face of her father, full of warning. *Run…run.* From where had he appeared? Had he died? The mere thought of it terrified her. She blinked, then tore out of bed to run from the chilling visions.

She found a small lounge and was adding sweetener to her hot drink when someone called her name. She turned to see the hulk of Captain Boro's frame filling the doorway. His wounded leg was thickly bandaged and one arm rested in a sling. When he hobbled into the room, Marie cringed, still afraid of him despite a growing awe.

"Good day, ma'am," he said, fumbling at one of the dispensers. "I'm glad to see that you are well. I hear that Richard was afraid he'd lost you."

"Captain Boro," she blurted awkwardly. "Thank you for bringing Javid back to me." Unwillingly, she stared at the prosthesis. It looked better somehow. The natural side of his face had softened. "And, thank you for retrieving the information that the Fringe needed."

Boro shook his head. The tenderness in his voice seeped through the mechanical whine of the vocoder. "The credit is not mine. I would not have achieved success without Javid and his friend Clive Baker."

"Well, Javid is no ordinary beautician," she half joked. "By the way, how did Javid get an electronic recorder?"

"He said he picked it up on Iggid."

"He did?"

"Yes, along with a few other gadgets that became vital to our mission. We are all grateful. Good day, Miss Flechette."

Boro nodded and hobbled out of the lounge.

Marie sipped on her drink and smiled, amazed at Javid's ingenuity and fore-sight. As she contemplated the strange flow of events, she heard her name again. When she saw Igna, Marie's expression flattened. Igna made her way over to the dispenser, standing unnecessarily close. Marie moved away, taking a seat at one of the small tables. Without invitation, Igna sat herself across from her.

"So, what now, Princess?"

Marie glared at Igna. "I don't know. I'm not the politician here. Why don't you tell me?"

"What do you plan on doing with our Commander now that you're on your way home?"

"I don't plan on doing anything."

"Love him and leave him?"

Marie's nostrils flared. "What do you want, Igna?"

"I want to know what you're going to do about Commander Shaw."

"Why would you care?"

"He's smitten with you, that's why."

"My personal affairs are none of your business, Igna. And if he is smitten with me, that is his affair."

Igna's eyes narrowed. "So, the spoiled little princess uses her power to grab the outlander's heart."

Marie's hand dropped to the table. The scalding liquid splashed over the rim. "Oh, give it a rest, Igna. I realize that you're nursing a broken heart but things like this happen. We can't always foresee the outcome of events. I didn't plan this, you know." She flung an arm out. "None of it."

"All the more reason for you to stay out of our affairs."

Marie's furious gaze locked with Igna's.

Igna drew in an audible breath. "You haven't thought of the consequences, have you? You don't understand our life here in the Fringe. Do you think Rich-ard is just going to drop everything to go live with you in your castle? And, what about you? Are you going to leave that monstrous company of yours to live on a planet that cannot support the life you're accustomed to? Oh, sure, it's been fun for a while, but how long would you really last, Princess? Do you think that Rich-ard would actually move to Nix States? I don't think so. It would destroy him. It would take away who he is, his essence, his freedom, his success as a leader. We need him. And, much as I am not a fan of yours, your people need you. You're a leader in your own right. Good grief, you own a cosmetics company, and yet you've built, what, a dozen hospitals? There are thousands of planetary systems in Nixodonia, and you're friends with the *President*? You may not realize it, Marie, but you are one of the most powerful influences in Nix States. Face it, people do follow you. Why do you think the TRA chose *you* to sway the masses?"

Marie stared blankly at Igna.

"It wasn't an off-handed choice, Marie. Your empire is a key. Are you going to abandon all that for the sake of a life in a desolate part of the universe for a man you barely know?"

Marie didn't answer. In fact, her lips couldn't move. The words Igna said held water—water Marie wasn't sure she could swallow.

Igna rose. "This isn't a matter of infatuation that you can casually take or leave. People depend on you. People depend on Richard. Think about that."

Marie was left sitting with her spilled drink. The only part of her that moved was the blinking of her eyes.

Richard stood with Reese as they reviewed Bill Tripp's earlier message: the TRA ringleaders were to meet on Enderal in just a few standard days. The leaders nearly missed the excitement as the Saurian Fleet's admiral acknowledged that all twenty-five ships and their escorts were now on a new course to assume an ambush position. Presuming victory, the Fleet would then move toward Doria and attempt to destroy the base there.

Richard groaned. "You know, Reese, that leaves us stranded. There's no hope of catching up to them—or working our way back to the Blue Rift rendezvous point."

Reese frowned. "You're right, A jump back toward Vesperoiy would light us up like a supernova on TRA detectors." Reese clicked his commlink against a console. "Maybe we'll just have stay put until the Saurian fleet can immobilize the TRA Armada."

Richard thought for a moment. "We might have an option. Let's not forget that every TRA ringleader is going to be on Enderal in just a few days time."

Reese squinted. "We won't be less visible because we're moving toward Nix-odonia."

"No, but we can maybe get to Bill's relay ship. He's gone straight to Enderal, He told the relay ship's pilots to keep their position until they get word from us. Unlike this ship, it's small enough to avoid detection. We could rendezvous, switch ships, and keep the Telexans in hot pursuit of this flagship, maybe on some nonsensical sightseeing tour of the Nixodonian backwaters."

Reese's eyes lit with excitement, then his shoulders slumped. "But, we've made a mistake—the same one the TRA is about to make—having their entire governing body in one place! The evacuation managed to put all of our leaders on this ship. Boro, Igna, Hollis, you, me. If we don't make it to the relay ship, the Fringe will collapse."

"We can make it."

A new voice had the leaders twisting to look behind them. Clive Baker stood there, eyeing the two intently. "Look," Clive said. "The Lieutenant here has a point, but your plan, Commander, doesn't need to fail, either. The fact that both parties have their top dogs in easy target groups doesn't mean it can't be to your advantage. Sure, they could snuff the Fringe in one fell swoop, but really—you ought to do it to them first."

"Really." Reese sneered at the self-assured pilot.

"Really," Clive retorted, pointing to his chest. "I'm a trader with the Fringe, remember? I know every worm hole in and out of this slimy, back-assed piece of space and if anyone had paid any attention, you'd know that we're sitting right atop the Bakeet Clusters."

Reese glanced at the nearest star map. "So?"

Clive gave a twist of his lips. "So! There is an electromagnetic funnel through the Bakeet Clusters into which one can do an instant disappearing act—right through to Nix States."

The two leaders glanced at each other.

Clive pointed an imperative finger at the two. "But if anybody, and I mean *anybody*, tells the rest of my trading bloc that I blew the whistle on this back door, I myself will annihilate the Fringe in one fell swoop!"

CHAPTER 53

Bill Tripp's dilapidated freighter landed safely on Enderal. While en route, Raymond had made Bill tell and retell the story of their abduction, not missing the innuendo that Marie was smitten with the man responsible for her misadventure. Bill defended the Fringe leader's actions, ones that inadvertently saved Marie from the clutches of the TRA. It was hard to believe that what had started out as a messy engagement breakup had turned out to be just a piece of the puzzle in a brewing interstellar war.

Bill's shoulders slumped with relief as the helicopter landed behind the Flechette estate walls. At the house, the welcoming party included someone Bill thought he'd never see again. Spencer strode across the main foyer. Uncharacteristically, they grasped each other in a hug. Minutes later, Genevieve's helicopter arrived after another difficult day at FC. She entered the foyer and stopped, seized by the sight.

"Wait," Raymond said, putting a hand up to stop her advances.

She stood, dumfounded, while Raymond did a series of dance steps before scooping her into his arms. Bill and Spencer made themselves scarce as shrieks of triumph rose in crescendo.

Later that day, Bill reviewed his plans. He had two jobs: first, find the location of this meeting called by Angel Keem, and second, find someone in the police force whom he could trust.

His first assignment took him on a solitary trek into Enderal City. He was sure that Paul's villa would reveal at least some clues. It was late evening when he arrived at the back entrance of the villa. Taking a breath, he punched in the security code, praying it hadn't changed. To his relief, the huge door popped from its lock. Bill cautiously stepped into the courtyard. His mind flashed back to the party he and Marie had crashed. This time, the villa looked deserted.

His flashlight guided him through the litter-strewn kitchen. He hadn't taken a half dozen steps into the entertainment quarter when he heard a scraping sound. Several voices exploded in the kitchen behind him. Bill dove behind one of the beaten couches.

"...almost everybody has arrived. We're just waiting for General Keem"

"Sounds like Marchand cleaned up good at that hidden Fringe base."

"I heard Shaw's on the run." Laughter. "This coup will be just too easy!"

The group came into the living room and trotted up the stairs. Bill heard a thud. He waited until there was dead silence before rising from behind the couch. A *coup*? Preposterous. Especially without Marie to back their propaganda movement.

Bill moved stealthily to the kitchen. His trained eyes and fingers quickly discovered the edges of an access port. He couldn't find the gadget that might open the egress, but that wasn't important now. This was how they got in.

He took the stairs, stepping around litter and empty bottles obviously left as a distraction should the authorities get suspicious of Paul. He looked through every room but found nothing. They'd disappeared somewhere. He was rechecking the master suite when another group came up the stairs. Bill found cover behind the thick curtains. The conversation terrorized him.

"Sure, we'll succeed with the coup, but if Yousef Phoebe doesn't find Marie Flechette, we'll have to double our firepower."

Another voice. "Butchering a bunch of Nixodonians wouldn't pull at my heartstrings."

Laughter.

"Senator Black might like that idea. He'll be arriving planet-side shortly."

Bill's eyes widened. Senator Black? The man who controlled the manufacture of military spacecraft and their weaponry? But for whom, Bill wondered. Taking a risk, he peered around the curtain. Bill stopped breathing. Was every key person in this nation involved with Angel Keem? On the other side of the rumpled bed stood Ray Lapp, their National Security Advisor, and—no, not Joe Abby!

Bill wondered if Keeta Abby knew of the conspiracy. She was one of Marie's best friends! Or was she? Through his shock, Bill realized that this explained the ease with which arms flowed into Telexa. Joe was their Defense Secretary! Moving into his field of vision were three of Nix States' most influential lawyers, including Commissioner Rhodes!

Bill watched as the commissioner reached under a lighting sconce. The wall opened up. The group stepped into a lift while chatting casually about the take-over of Nixodonia. The panels snapped shut, their edges invisible in the splashy pattern of the bedroom's décor.

When Bill thought it was safe, he crept out of hiding, tiptoed around the bed and inspected the sconce. The twist of a refit nodule opened the wall. When he stepped inside the lift to inspect it, the panels closed behind him.

Bill experienced chilling panic as the lift plummeted downward at a gut wrenching speed. There was no selection box, no way to reverse his action. Before he had time to fear the consequences, the lift slowed to a halt, and the panels snapped open.

CHAPTER 54

Deep in the blackness of space, two ships rendezvoused and exchanged personnel. Eight of the flagship's complement transferred to the relay ship to join the two relay ship pilots. The tiny ship wasn't designed for ten crewmen, but everyone seemed adaptable. Marie felt that her contribution was to adapt as well. The passenger list included Richard and Reese, Captain Hollis, Igna, Boro and Javid. Clive Baker was also on the list, since his knowledge was now needed to guide them through the wormholes of Nixodonia.

Living arrangements were on a group basis and predominantly confined to the main hold as there was nowhere else to go except the cockpit. The back chambers were now filled with survival gear and weaponry. The main hold would take care of both the sleeping and eating arrangements—another unique experience for Marie.

Hours later, the group gathered for a meal. They formed a circle that centered around the food packets heaped in the middle of the floor. Marie munched on a hard piece of something that tasted like packed sawdust. Boro sat across from her, his bandaged leg sticking out, but his arm had practically healed. Igna leaned against the far bulkhead, creating a jag in the tight circle of friends. Marie put their recent conversation aside and decided to enjoy the atmosphere. "All we're missing is the campfire," she jested.

Clive grunted. "No thanks. I know what a campfire will do to a ship's floor, and it ain't a pretty sight."

Javid burst into laughter. "Oh yes, I'd almost forgotten. The TRA set up camp in the rear quarter of Clive's ship," he explained to the group, "waiting to ambush us. Their camp was an awful eyesore to poor Clive, even though the rest of the ship looked like a charred potato skin."

"I wonder what happened to *my* ship," Boro added. "Hopefully Dowlar was able to escape back to the caves with it."

"Dowlar," Javid murmured. "I'd know if he were dead. I don't feel that he is."

"That guy?" Clive bellowed. "Nothin'll ever kill him."

"I'm sure your brother has found a way to safety," Marie comforted.

Javid sighed, "You'll meet Dowlar some day. I know you will."

"Ah, that means she's coming back for a visit," Richard said, smiling at Marie. She leaned against him, wondering about the emptiness of her act, wondering if she ever would, or could, return to the Fringe.

"Well, I think everyone should be commended for a job well done," Reese said, entering the hold from the cockpit. "No detection, and we're on our way." He sat cross-legged and rummaged through the packets. "Aw, did you guys eat all the protein bars?"

The sharing of stories went late into the night. Javid talked of life on Rashmar before its invasion. He was about to divulge how Clive got to Rashmar the first time when Clive broke in and told the story himself, frustrating Javid's attempt to exaggerate the story. Clive went on to tell a shocked audience of his acquaintance with Lola Phoebe, and then to reduce the hysteria, tried to redeem himself by saying that she'd been a great lover, and worth the price. That remark brought a groan of disbelief from the group now sprawled out on the deck floor.

Richard, Reese, and Boro told hilarious tales of when they were young lads with visions of grandeur. It was plainly obvious that they had no regrets about leaving behind their youth to take on the realities of those childhood dreams.

Slowly the stories dwindled and yawns began to inundate the conversations. Systematically, they stretched out on their mats in the same places they'd just eaten.

Marie lay on her side with Richard's arm around her. Half asleep, he pulled her closer. She heard him take in a deep breath, then drop into a deep slumber. The smile on her face felt permanent as she lay, unable to release her mind to sleep. She glanced around at the mounds beneath sleeping rugs, and her mind slipped back. Too many countless nights had been spent alone with no sibling or friend to share stories like these into the wee hours. She suddenly realized that it was loneliness that had driven her to invest herself so heavily into FC, and then to acting. She needed to avoid the loneliness that crushed her soul, without ever knowing it plagued her in the first place. But here, on the hard floor, she found an answer. She'd never experienced friends who shared food and drink with their fingers, friends who'd been comrades for as long as she'd been alive. Even Igna couldn't help laughing at the stories by the end of the evening. She had inched closer to Boro, and he'd given her room to wiggle in.

Now, lying quietly in Richard's arms, Marie sensed an awakening. She knew she'd never been happier. She'd discovered the natural scent of her skin, what her stomach could tolerate, the shock of sharing a common lavatory. Mostly, she had discovered that she was a woman of worth. Exposed to those around her were her triumphs and defeats, her ecstasy and pain, and her humanity, stripped of the glamour that had fashioned the Princess of Nixodonia. Here she stood alone, a creature of her godhead, no better, no worse. And she loved deeply.

Finally, she closed her eyes. The smile on her lips tightened. A tear escaped. It trickled down the bridge of her nose and splashed onto Richard's arm.

CHAPTER 55

To Bill's utter relief, the elevator that had plummeted him to the core of Enderal opened onto a vacant anteroom that exited in two directions. One side was glassed off, the offices in behind darkened for the evening hours. He quickly moved down the other hallway but came to an abrupt halt. The hallway suddenly turned into a catwalk. Peering around the corner, Bill found himself looking into an immense, sophisticated control room. Judging by the rate of decent, they were at a serious depth, yet the place looked like central control on G2. The catwalk that stretched before him was one level above the main floor. The ceiling vaulted upward another level, accommodating the large star maps on the opposite wall. The floor crawled with at least two hundred people. He saw the group that had just been in Paul's bedroom milling about with an even greater collection of Nix States' elite. They meandered comfortably amongst the most sophisticated equipment imaginable.

Bill dug into his jacket and pulled out his miniature filming unit. He made smooth arcs around the room, up, then down. The catwalk wrapped itself around the room, leading to a third level in some areas. The magnification capabilities of his filming unit would reveal more detail than he could perceive with his eyes so he let the unit soak up what it could, and made himself scarce. On his way back, he was forced into the narrow corridor of the glass-partitioned offices as another group stepped out of the elevator. His hiding place gave him a clue as to how to open the lift doors. Peering through the warping effect of the glass walls, he saw someone leave. A woman. She opened the port with a handheld device. He'd find one of those later.

He easily jigged his way into one of the offices. There was nothing of interest save the blinking lights of a communication unit. That was it! He studied the communicator, obviously run by the same person on a regular basis. Little notes were posted everywhere, trinkets, the picture of a child—and a list of other secretaries and their extensions. He chose one. No answer. The second one did answer. Bill cleared his throat. "Ah, yeah! What was the time for the general meeting again?" A tired voice drawled, "I'm sorry, sir. Who's speaking?"

"This is Senator Yousef Phoebe." Bill grunted. "My wife and I are arguing about the time and date of the meeting."

"Yes sir!" she snapped. "It's the 25th, sir. Twenty-two hundred hours."

In exactly two days time, Bill thought anxiously. "I thought so," he grunted, and hung up. He glanced again at the elevator doors. The gods blessed him again. A small man dressed in a maintenance uniform stood alone, pointing his gadget toward the doors. When the worker stepped in, Bill pounded him to the inside wall of the lift silencing him before the panels slid shut. Back in Paul's bedroom, he dragged the maintenance man's limp body out of the elevator, thankful that no one waited to go below.

He had to dispose of the body. All he needed was two days. Unfortunately, the smell of his victim would attract attention before then. Throwing the thin frame over his shoulders, Bill made his way down the stairs and headed towards the back entrance. In the kitchen, an interesting solution caught his eye. Two large beverage refrigerators stood along one wall, blinking little red lights at their bases. Both were mostly empty, and cold! Grunting, Bill stuffed the body into the largest of the refrigerators. He wrenched at the handle until it snapped off and took the broken end with him.

CHAPTER 56

The next morning the relay ship landed on Enderal. Everyone stayed on board until Bill could make his way quietly to the ship stationed in the freighter section of the spaceport. Entering the main hold, Bill first greeted Marie, grasping her in a tight embrace. "Welcome home, Marie," he said.

"I'm so glad you're safe," she breathed. "And, my parents...?"

"Yes, they know you're all right. And, your father? He saw a healer on Doria and—"

"He's *healed*?" She gasped. "I knew it! I knew something had happened. I saw a vision of him when I was at the native village."

"The village?" Bill asked curiously.

Yes, I'll tell you later. Did this Healer find out what was the matter with Papa?"

Bill stiffened, then found no reason to keep the truth from her "Yes You're father had been poisoned, Marie—very slowly—by Paul."

"*Poisoned*?"

"To keep him from checking on the Dorian operations."

"Not to mention creating a little distraction while stealing my cosmetics codes!" Marie's limbs liquefied in anger. "And all that crap about how wonderful a movie career would be for me!" She covered her eyes. Richard stepped behind Marie to place a hand of comfort on her shoulder. Bill reached out to shake hands with the Commander. The two muttered to each other about jobs well done.

Bill took in a breath. "I may as well tell all of you the rest of it."

Marie looked apprehensive. "Tell us what?"

"Paul is Angel Keem's son."

"The General's son?" Javid blurted, pushing his way through the tall bodies in the hold.

"Javid? What the—it *was* you on Rashmar!" Bill blurted.

Javid grasped the bodyguard's hand for a vigorous shake. "Didn't I tell you that I'd be of more help if you left me on the *Starquest*."

Richard stepped in. "Come to the security terminal, Bill. We're all anxious to hear more about this underground headquarters you found last night."

Marie took a few moments to shed feelings of disgust. General Keem's son! Richard was right about having no chance against such manipulation, but the time of reckoning was at hand. Bracing herself, she joined the others in the cockpit for Bill's briefing.

Bill's unit was plugged into a monitor where the covert bowels of Enderal were revealed. After weighing the options, an unspoken feeling of helplessness pervaded the group. The TRA's general meeting was only ten hours away. What could they do?

Suddenly, Igna jumped up and walked to the front of the group. "I have a suggestion, Commander." He gave her the floor and she pointed at the screen displaying the underground control room.

"Mr. Tripp has shown us that we can easily access this area," she said. "I have the munitions on board, which, if effectively placed, could destroy the complex while still giving us time to escape. The explosions would surprise them enough to render them easy targets, especially when they try to escape." She pointed to what seemed to be a main exit. "We can place detonators here." Igna pointed to the catwalk. "And all along here. Their sequence could herd the escaping rebels into here." She pointed to the exit that showed a smaller room beyond the main floor. "If the rebels are intent enough on the meeting, taking out the catwalk guards should be relatively easy." She indicated on her fingers. "If we can capture the key TRA leaders, destroy their armada *and* contain the Dorian base, we might be able to put this affair to rest."

The group sat in stunned silence.

Richard stood, jaw clenched. "Unless anyone can think of another option, I support it."

In minutes, the decision was unanimous for Igna's plan.

Marie found herself sick with panic when Richard spoke again.

"Very good. I, Reese and you three will execute the plan." He nodded to Igna, Boro and Captain Hollis. "Tripp and Baker, we could use your help, but—"

The two joined in before Richard had finished his sentence.

Marie watched in horror as the people she loved finalized what was nothing less than a suicide plan. She clutched at her middle, wondering if they understood that their lives might end before the night was over. She listened to Richard coolly tell the fate of the rest of them. She and Javid would stay aboard the ship with the two pilots and await their return. Marie reached over and grasped Javid's hand.

"I have a friend who's willing to stand by," Bill informed. "He's chief of Enderal City's Secret Service, and he has no love for the Telexans, I can tell you of that." Bill gave a twisted smile. "On top of it, he owes me a couple."

All the plans were efficiently wrapped up. Igna disappeared to the back with Boro and Clive to prepare the weapons. The others reviewed Bill's tapes again and again. Marie felt light years from Richard. His responsibilities were enormous. All of their lives were in his hands. She wished she could hold him and tell him everything would be fine, but she didn't believe that for a minute.

There was still an hour to wait before the team could safely depart for the underground bunker. When Richard suggested that they go to the crew section of the terminal for some real food and a clean up, there was a small cheer. The two pilots offered to stay on board so Richard squeezed the rest of them into the ship's fortified ground shuttle. The vehicle was hydraulically lowered to the tarmac. It meandered, unnoticed, amongst the landing gear of hundreds of freighters strewn about the busy port. The lounge smelled of stale smoke and urine. The male-dominated, ill-kept locker rooms made Marie's skin crawl. Having known only the Super Elite lounge, she was shocked to know that such places existed at the Enderal Spaceport. She stiffened when Reese's commlink shrieked.

"Code Red." it crackled.

Marie glanced nervously at her companions. That was the danger signal! Were they in trouble already? Richard hustled them into an empty locker room and closed the door. Boro threw his large back against it.

"Damn," Reese swore. He flicked on the commlink. The pilot's voice came over the tiny rod. "They're coming to check our passenger list. Stay put! We're authorized for only four bodies. Not sure who suspects we have more."

The little stick went dead. They waited nearly fifteen minutes before the rod lit up again.

"Two can come back. They didn't search the ship, but they said they'd be back. Boro and Igna, come for the ammo." The rod went dead.

"Damn! I hope someone didn't get curious about where our ship originated," Hollis muttered. "Too close a look at those Nixodonian shipping licenses and we're finished."

"We're still okay," Richard affirmed. "They're probably just beginning to wonder about all those VIPs landing for no apparent reason. Boro, Igna, take the shuttle and go load up."

The process took over half an hour, during which time Marie escaped to a dirty cubicle and vomited. Wobbling, she returned to the group just as Boro and Igna returned. Richard gathered them together. "We're getting out of here. All of us. They're going to search the ship. We can't go back...so we have to stick together."

They escaped the spaceport by simply mixing with the myriad vehicles that crowded through the ransacked shipping gate. The shuttle cruised through Enderal city without incident, its shielded windows protecting them from view. Bill guided them to an industrial sector of the city where he found them shelter in an abandoned warehouse. Once inside, the group piled out of the vehicle and milled close to each other in one corner of the cavernous storage shed. Having become accustomed to the jungle heat, Marie felt Enderal's winter chill penetrate her bones. She could only hope that the chill would cool her frazzling nerves.

Suddenly, her fear was gone. An unfamiliar serenity began to flow over her, as if some natural defense system emerged of its own volition to help her face the situation at hand. The lines of strain on her face softened as she gazed quietly about the dimness of the shed.

Reese could feel the strain on their Commander in regards to Marie and Javid. Knowing Richard was too emotionally involved to see the situation clearly, Reese took the decision into his own hands. "You were right, earlier, Richard," he said. "We need to stick together. It will be too dangerous to leave Marie and Javid here alone."

Boro stepped in "Good. I wanted to ask if Javid would join my team, anyway. I'll need him to help me set these detonators. Clive and I are too tall for that cat-walk railing."

Reese suddenly pulled out a thin triangular device and tossed it to Marie. Instinctively, she clutched it out of the air.

"I can't manage that thing and do my job as well," he said to her. "Do you think you can you operate this controller?"

Marie nodded numbly before finding her tongue. "Yes. If you tell me what it's for."

He stepped toward her. "See that button? It's a callback button. We'll station you along the back catwalk where you will have the most optimal view of the whole room. Also, you'll be closest to the lift. If things turn sour, one of us will either tell you directly, or signal you like this," Reese made a negative signal with his hands. "At that point, you'll push this button, which will activate our vibrator badges. Javid, you won't have a receiver, so keep a close eye on Boro. If Marie sets this off, we will rendezvous at the lift."

Marie's heart pounded as she held the black wedge. The past weeks had hardened her a great deal, but this was by far the greatest test of her strength and courage. She nodded before they changed their minds, or she changed hers. A vote was cast and everyone agreed to the new plan. Except Richard.

"Are you sure you're capable of this?"

Marie found herself turning numbly toward his voice. She spoke clearly to him and to the others. "I have been implicated in this horror for a long time, years in fact. It's both my wish and my duty to fight back. If I am to die, I want to die fighting for our freedom."

CHAPTER 57

Richard parked the crowded ground shuttle a short distance from the villa's back gate. Everyone craned their necks to see through the one-way windshield. Igna sat back, muttering that a briefing would be smarter than smashing skulls.

Marie found a moment to lock eyes with Igna, and gambled. "I was impressed with your suggestion and planning this morning, Igna."

"It's my job."

"I know. But you're good at it. I earnestly pray that it works."

Igna stared blankly a moment, then showed a hint of a smile. "Take care of yourself down there," she said. "I won't have time to look out for civilians."

Marie returned the smile. "I will."

The moment was upon them. The meeting below was scheduled to start in thirty minutes. The detonators were to be set during the ten minutes prior to the meeting when all the rebels would hopefully be on the floor socializing before the call to order. Marie dared not dwell on the narrow margin of success.

Entering the litter-strewn kitchen assaulted Marie's senses. Entering the master bedroom made gall rise in her throat. The bed was a rumpled mess and she knew that Paul's night with Susie hadn't been his last tussle here. Richard caught her eye. She made a gesture toward the bed. He raised an eyebrow and visibly held back a laugh. Marie flushed and glared back.

They descended in two groups, the first led by Reese, the second by Richard. Quivering with adrenaline, Marie leaned her head against the lift wall and breathed deeply. She was surprised to suddenly find Richard's hand in hers. He squeezed it and bent down to whisper in her ear.

"I love you, Marie. Please stay alive for me."

She cast him a quick glance but said nothing. Would he stay alive for her? She couldn't think about the enormous odds against any of them surviving. The doors opened and they bolted to the right, finding the others hiding in the offices. Most of the plans were finalized with eye contact and nods. Marie couldn't keep up with the body language but nodded mechanically as the hasty session ended. She then watched Javid and Clive accept their share of explosives from Boro. A sickening panic rose in her chest. She clasped the black wedge that threatened to slip from her damp palm.

They crept out of the offices. The two groups split up as they reached the catwalk. Reese and Igna took cover to the left, Boro with Javid and Clive to the right. Marie moved along the back catwalk with Richard. Hollis went ahead to clear their path. Marie cringed as she stepped over the dead body of a watchman en route to her vantage point.

They joined Hollis before moving quietly to an area that expanded behind them. Richard told Marie to crouch behind the upper mechanisms of a hydraulic lift. From there she watched Richard himself down two more guards to secure the rear catwalk for them. Marie swallowed and said a silent prayer for the dead and those who would die yet tonight. She'd never witnessed violence, and wondered about the crazy nature of humans whose greatest task in life was to protect themselves from each other.

Her own murderous feelings arose when she glanced down to behold the control room floor. There was no time to marvel at its size and complexity. Her breath sucked in forcibly as she began to recognize those milling about on the crowded main floor.

There must be three hundred of them, she thought in astonishment. Yousef Phoebe, Senator Black; the blond hair of her *friends* Ray Lapp and Joe Abby! And—Paul. Closer to the front, Henrie Marchand, Lola Phoebe. All acquaintances of her family? A movie role dropped into her eager lap? A Benefit Gala with a guest list enviable of kings?

A movement caught her eye. She saw a flash of Igna's tall figure silently take out a guard and appear in his clothing a moment later. Marie continued to scan the catwalks that circled the control room, disappearing behind the large star maps and computer screens at the front of the room. She saw Boro slip behind the star maps and thought she recognized Javid reach above the protection of the railing to stick a detonator to the wall.

Hollis's fair cheeks were flushed when he crept back to her hiding spot. "I need time to cover two more exits we didn't know about, or this won't work."

Marie looked at Captain Hollis, horrified. "But, there are only a few minutes left." She looked down at the wedge in her hand.

"Don't push that button yet."

Richard crept back to join them, brow wet, long wisps of hair pasted to it. He took Marie's hand and checked the unit. He glanced at Hollis.

"There are two more exits we didn't know about," Hollis whispered hoarsely to Richard who absently fumbled for more charges and handed them to Hollis.

Their attention was diverted to the floor as the crowd was silenced and the meeting called to order. Marie recognized the pockmarked face of the man who took the podium. So this was the infamous Angel Keem.

Marie glanced at Richard whose face showed visible strain. She reached out and touched his hair, fearing it would be the last such caress. His dark eyes looked at her woefully for a time that seemed like both an eternity, and a nano-second. Then he looked back at Hollis.

"Are your other charges up?"

"Yes." He tilted his head. "But I can't get to those new exits until that guard turns."

Abruptly, the guard spun and continued his beat in the opposite direction, his attention focused on the activity below. Without another word, Hollis crept away. An indication by Igna from behind one of the star maps caught Richard's eye.

"Damn, she needs more time, too."

Marie's mind strained with a plan that had begun to formulate in her mind. Her body vibrated with the possibility of it.

"You need more time? Maybe I can provide it."

"What are you talking about?"

Marie's ashen face portrayed an outer calm she herself didn't understand. Inside her head, the plan that she was concocting spelled certain death for her, but a chance for the mission to succeed.

"You asked me once if I was an actress."

His eyes widened. "And?"

"I'll prove to you that I am."

"This is no time to prove anything, my love," he said hastily. She was in shock! She was too calm. He knew he shouldn't have allowed her to come.

"I'm going down there. I'll give you the time you need. Give me a signal to clear out if you get a chance. If not, know that I loved you with every fiber of my being, Richard."

He blinked, and glanced about the room anxiously. He was aware that those below had begun to clue in to the fact that something was amiss. Richard spoke incisively. "Push the button, Marie." To his utter shock, she yanked the wedge out of his reach.

"No! We can't stop now, Richard. There won't *be* another chance."

The sentry turned for his return beat and came face to face with a young, red-headed officer dressed in a uniform that didn't belong to the Telexan Revolutionary Army. The guard let out a short yelp before falling. A thud on the catwalk resounded throughout the control room.

Hollis dropped beside the body, hoping the height of the catwalk would hide his presence, but he'd definitely been heard. The floor came to a nervous hush. The bellowing of Angel Keem's voice echoed off the high ceiling.

"What's going on up there?"

"I'm going down, Richard."

"Don't be crazy!"

"Take the unit. Now! Or I'm going to drop it!"

"Guard?" the General called loudly. "Where's the guard who's supposed to be up there?"

Richard grabbed for the tumbling wedge as Marie wrenched from his grasp. She scrambled out of his reach and stood up. Tall and proud, she strode to the catwalk railing and leaned over it. She called aloud to those below.

Horrified, Richard could do nothing but watch.

"He's dead," Marie spat stridently. "I killed him, just like I'm going to kill Paul Lambert when I get my hands on him."

She walked with angry purpose to the companionway that led to the main floor. Stopping half-way, she shouted at a stunned audience. "So where is he, the little weasel. It's taken me forever to find this quaint hideout and it has *not* been an easy search. I want to see him, now!"

Madness brewed in her eyes. Her motions were erratic as she stomped down the rest of the stairs. Two guards were immediately upon her. She struck out at them.

"Let go of me, you mindless idiots. I want to talk to my fiancé. Now!" She lunged at the guards. They retreated, looking for orders but receiving none.

"Paul?" She called again, her eyes searching the crowd. "Come out here, you little bastard."

She approached the back row of the assembly. They parted in stunned amazement. Suddenly, from the thick of the crowd stepped one Paul Lambert, his look that of utter disbelief.

"There you are, you little slime. Think I wouldn't find you? Think you could just leave me to the fate of some sex-hungry pirate?" she screamed hysterically, not knowing that a few days on a tiny freighter rendered her look perfect for the part. "Where the hell have you been?"

"What are you doing here?" he asked, his unblinking stare revealing dilated pupils.

"What am I doing here?" she asked with disbelief. Her foot swung out and landed a deft blow on his shin.

He stumbled backward, howling.

She spoke between clenched teeth. "So smart you think you are, throwing me to some deranged pirate as what, punishment for leaving you? Well, it was a bad idea. I ended up on some filthy vessel, raped, tortured and starved! But see? I got away and found myself in Telexa, that pit hole you told me about. The pit hole you've been part of all along. Oh don't look so shocked, Paul Lambert Keem!"

Someone had to grasp the agent to prevent him from crumbling. A murmur rippled through the crowd. Marie rattled on, her gaze locked on Paul, yet unable to ignore those closing in on her. Yousef Phoebe to her left, Joe Abby creeping in on her right. Somehow she kept her focus despite the excess adrenaline pulsing through her overwrought body.

"I might have forgiven you for that ugly bitch you were with that night, but pirates?"

"How did you get in here?"

"The same way I got in the night you were supposed to be at our engagement party, you fool. You could have at least changed the sheets on the goddamned bed!" She lashed out, slapping him hard across the face. It was enough to grab the attention of the crowd a minute longer.

"I found out a lot of things on that little side trip. Things you should have told me a long time ago, Paul. But no! You were so bent on using me that you missed seeing that I was looking for a way out as well. Hell, I would have joined you!" She laughed weakly. "What do you think?" she added, her gaze raking the crowd. "Maybe we should have our engagement party right here. Most of you were there that night, weren't you? Playing your two-faced charades." She gave a pitiful laugh. "And now I know your secrets. You should have been more careful because now that I'm here, I'm going to stay. You people owe me more than you know."

She didn't miss their distrust as they shot nervous glances about the control room. She glanced up to see Clive and Igna pace the catwalk in TRA vests. "There's no one else, sir," Clive grunted to Angel Keem.

"Very true," she agreed. "Do you think I'd let someone follow me down here? That I would share such a secret? I cover my tracks better than this clown does." She tossed her head. "I saw my ticket to the throne while I was in Telexa. I saw that movie you went to so much trouble to make." She laughed. "Do you think I'm so patriotic? I hate Pao Knabon."

She stepped toward Paul. Her thoughts struggled to sort themselves and make plausible sense. "My darling, your cunning and my power could have given us everything. But we were too smart for each other. We managed to outwit each other. So what are we going to do now, huh?"

The crowd parted. In the periphery of her vision, someone stepped forward. She let her gaze linger on Paul's for a moment before slowly turning to face General Keem. He was a vile-looking man. "So," she drawled, "this is he. The infamous General Keem."

"And you my lovely, the famous Marie Flechette. What a pleasure to finally meet you."

"The pleasure is mine."

"I see you are not altogether pleased with my son."

"Not altogether," she conceded.

"Perhaps you would be happier at my side, then."

Marie saw the lust in his eyes and the lascivious curl of his lip.

"We could talk about that throne you saw in your pretty little mind."

Paul suddenly found his voice. "I didn't send those pirates after her. Everybody knows that."

Marie spun toward Paul. "Really? Then who did?"

"The Fringe."

It was a new voice, but Marie recognized it.

"The what?" She tried to propel disbelief into her voice as she turned slowly to see Henrie Marchand standing beside Angel Keem.

"Well, if it isn't the great director himself. "Follow me." You even had me fooled." *Hurry, Richard*, her mind screamed.

"She's lying," Henrie said bluntly.

General Keem defended her. "I think she's resourceful."

Marie gave a sensual smile intended for the General, but her eyes were locked on Marchand's.

"How could I be lying? I'm here, in the flesh." She spread her hands. "I'm not a hologram this time, Henrie."

"You went to the Fringe, and you're not working alone." Henrie said, his eyes glancing suspiciously at the catwalks.

She spat her defense. "I went to hell, Henrie. And now, I've come back to haunt you, my dearest director."

The General stepped forward and took Marie's hand, raising it in a gesture of honor. "You will come with me, and we will see what kind of reparation we can offer you for your troubles." He bent down and planted wet lips on the back of her hand. Marie's mind went wild with panic.

"She's lying, General." Henrie said flatly, catching Marie's eyes, throwing her off guard.

The General seemed to reconsider. Still holding her hand, he looked at the director. "Yousef Phoebe has trusted your intuition before. However, you'd best not be wrongfully accusing my new First Lady."

Marie's insides convulsed. Panic spread up her chest, cutting off her breath. She forced down her rising shoulders and continued her cool stare. But Henrie dealt her another blow. "I know acting when I see it. I taught her." He held her paralyzed gaze. "How did you know that Paul was Angel Keem's son?"

"I escaped to Telexa—I found connections." Her voice was losing its edge. "It seemed everyone knew over there."

"Oh, I don't think so. But I think the Fringe might be smarter than we think. Where did you get that jumpsuit, Marie? Telexa doesn't hand out clothing like that to civilians. And you made another serious mistake." There was a stir amongst the rebel group. "*Angel's Test* isn't due to be released in Telexa for another three days."

A massive explosion rocked the catwalk behind the star maps, sending one of the tall, thin structures on a deadly fall to the ground. Screams erupted. As Angel Keem spun, a thin orange bolt sliced cleanly through his shoulder, singeing a hole through the Reptilian emblem. The General let out a hideous scream. His hand slipped from Marie's as he slumped to the floor.

A split second later, Marie spun and took giant leaps toward the companionway. Hands were on her, tearing her grip off the handrail, taking her down hard against the stairs. Suddenly, her assailant's grip failed. The body slumped on top of her and she realized that he was dead. Marshaling strength, she heaved the body off her legs. Marie was deafened by a second explosion.

Mayhem erupted. Panicking rebels fired aimlessly at invisible targets. Others lost their minds, becoming claustrophobic in the underground bunker and trampling over top of her in their panic to escape up the stairs. She stumbled and staggered, climbing only one step. A pair of angry hands gripped her throat, squeezing. Again, someone looked out for her, and whoever killed that antagonist took out the one below him as well. Marie managed one more step up as the bodies went down. An ear-piercing voice made her blood curdle. In terror her legs weakened.

"Come back here, you bitch!" Paul screamed.

She glanced back to see him at the bottom of the stairs, tearing at his own people to get to her, now half-way up the stairs. He scrambled over the bodies, and lunged for one of her ankles. Marie couldn't advance for the dead and wounded piled on the narrow stairway. She shook her leg violently but she couldn't loosen his grip.

Another explosion along the far wall filled one of the exits with debris. Marie realized that charges at both the new exits had been laid, herding the rebels into Reese's trap at the main exit. Immediately following a series of other small blasts, parts of the ceiling collapsed, sending shards of roofing material down upon her. She fell on the legs of a dead rebel. Regardless, Marie grasped at the railing and pulled with all her might to haul herself higher.

Paul didn't react to the explosions. He remained focused on his hold of her ankle. A laser blast disintegrated part of the railing near Paul's head but he was left unharmed. Finding renewed passion, Paul used her leg to haul himself up. His familiar hands clung to her, then one arm wrapped itself around her middle in a vice grip. The cluttered stairs were of no concern to him. He hauled her over bleeding and broken bodies to the catwalk above. Terrorized, Marie fought wildly, her attempts too feeble against his inflexible grip. On the catwalk, he hauled her to her feet, and slammed a blaster to her head.

"Now we'll talk," he yelled in her ear over the uproar of the fighting. Marie was crushed to his chest as Paul slipped about on the blood-smeared catwalk as he pulled her backward. "Tell me the truth, Marie. Would you have joined me?"

Was it too late to keep up the charade? He was stoned silly—and this, she realized was to her advantage. "Yes, Paul, I would have."

"Say that again?"

Another explosion rocked the back wall of the control room sending vibrations through the catwalk.

She screamed.

He roared, "We're going to die, you and I."

"No," Marie shrieked. "We can still get away. Just you and me."

"We can?" He began to laugh hysterically. "No we can't. I hate you, Marie Flechette. I always have. You had your castle and your doting parents and all those stupid fans."

His grip tightened sickeningly across her abdomen.

"You had everything you wanted. Henrie is wrong. You didn't lie. I know you better than that. You came here for more, didn't you?" He gave her waist a vicious tug and shoved the blaster more painfully against her temple. "Didn't you?" The war continued around them, but he took no notice. He took no notice of the fire that had engulfed a fallen star map and inched up another. He didn't notice the bodies of his comrades strewn between work stations on the control room floor. He took no notice of a white-haired figure dashing toward them and taking cover at the far end of the catwalk.

Her lips formed a tight, hard line. *Hurry Richard!*

"All that time you were lying to me, Marie. You didn't love me."

She found her voice. "You didn't love me either but at least I didn't cheat on you!" She twisted her neck to catch his eyes but they were lost in the distance.

"Well that's nice, but I had fun, with darling little Susie and a hundred others." He laughed pitifully. "I had to have something! First I walked in my father's shadow, and then I was ordered to walk in yours! I couldn't do it, Marie. I couldn't pretend to love you when I hated you so much. You had choices. I didn't." He put his temple against hers on one side and aligned the barrel of the blaster on the other. The detonation would explode both their skulls.

"No, Paul. You're wrong," she cried desperately. "What choices? I can't do anything without guards everywhere. I can't say anything without it being twisted and bastardized."

She must buy time. Buy time.

"You've seen it happen, Paul. I tolerate lies, ridicule and glorification all at once. The galaxy dictates my integrity, and the government my morality. I didn't even go to a normal school, Paul. I didn't even get to do that!"

She wanted to choke. Unable to face the awful truths of her own life. The realizations unleashed in uncontrollable sobbing. The only choice she had ever really made for herself was Paul. And that had been nothing but a disaster fueled by her own denial.

Paul's heavy breathing matched hers. "I went to school," he said. "My father sent me to places where I learned to kill people, how to steal and cheat, and seduce powerful women. I scored pretty high, Marie. I did. But I guess, in the final analysis, I failed. Then again, maybe I haven't." It was as if he'd achieved enlightenment of his own, sick mind. "No. Ha, ha! No, my lovely, I'm not going to fail."

Richard didn't feel like he was getting any closer to Marie. The rebels fought hard. His blaster fired automatically toward the floor, felling one more man. He'd lost touch with his emotion in the horror of it. Blood was everywhere, the room was filling with smoke, and still the rebels fought on. He had no idea where the others were. He didn't know who was alive or dead. His muscles burned with the exertion of holding the smoldering blaster, vomiting death with every pull of his finger. His legs cramped with the endless creeping along the catwalks, the thin metal sheath being the only separation between life and death. Over its glinting silver edge, he continued to herd the remainder of those on the floor toward Reese's trap. Somewhere in his dazed mind he knew he was getting closer to Marie, but would he make it in time?

Igna completed her mission. She had cleared the rebels from her end of the control room. She could see Reese at the other end, successfully bringing some of them to surrender. She also saw a flash of Clive Baker helping Reese confine them. A glimmer of hope arose in her heart when she saw that Bill's extra troops had arrived and were helping Reese. She choked in the smoke that had begun to descend dangerously from the ceiling and knew she had little time to get back to safety.

Then she saw Richard. He looked as if he were in control of the situation, so why was he creeping back into the bowels of the control room? Was he hurt? Was he stumbling? Her eyes suddenly caught sight of Marie being held prisoner by Paul Lambert near her end of the control room. There was no way Richard could reach her in time! Lambert had a gun to Marie's head and looked mad enough to use it. Igna lunged on long legs down the catwalk, but took the metal stairs that would bring her both higher into the thickening smoke, but hidden from Paul.

A great creak, followed by a yawning screech marked the release of a beam from the ceiling. It remained attached at one end and swung down in a graceful, deadly ark, missing the catwalk railing by just inches. It swung silently and ominously past Marie and Paul. With the short distraction, Igna got herself into position. Hands shaking, she dug at the throat of her jumpsuit and yanked up the cotton chemise. She pulled it over her nose and raggedly sucked in big gasps of air.

"Listen to what you are saying. Listen to me," Marie cried. "We're the same Paul." She witnessed a ceiling support swing dangerously close. She somehow prevented her mind from tearing off into madness when she realized Paul was oblivious to the swooping beam. Another opportunity. "Pri...prisoners of our birth."

"Yah, well I found an escape. I found those lovely little pills, and no one can stop me from taking trips wherever I want to go." Paul staggered back, nearly throwing them both to the slimy catwalk. "Not my father, not Henrie, not even you."

"But we can escape, Paul. Right now. You and me. We can start again."

"Sure." He gave a sinister laugh. "But not in this universe. You're right, Marie Flechette, Queen of the Cosmos, Princess of the Galaxy. We can escape, and I know the way."

She heard the cock on the blaster click into firing position.

"No, not like that!" she screamed in desperation. Suddenly, Richard's form, shrouded in smoke, streaked towards them from the far end of the catwalk. Her voice exploded. "*Richard!*"

Paul stiffened. "Who's Richard? Who are you calling, my love?" He shoved the blaster hard into her temple but raised his head to look.

Marie was too overwhelmed to think up another diversion. She closed her eyes tightly, panting in small cries.

Paul cried out to no one. Perhaps he cried out to the ghosts he saw all around him. "Don't come any closer. We're escaping. It's too late to save us."

Richard burst from the smoke. Sliding to a stop, he raised his blaster. Marie felt herself pulled violently against Paul's chest, creating his shield. The blaster left her temple and swung out in front of them. He fired.

The catwalk gave way, sending Richard sprawling, his feet tangled in the catwalk railing. The bolt from Paul's blaster sizzled past his head. In a mad frenzy, Richard tried to recover control of his own blaster but before he could draw another bead, the barrel of Paul's weapon was trained on him again. Without success, Marie struggled to throw Paul off balance.

Then from above, Igna's deadly aim caught Paul in the shoulder. His arm jerked as if being pulled outward by an invisible rope. The weapon arced over the railing and disappeared into the control room below. Horror and disillusionment filled his cry as Paul crashed to his knees.

Marie tore from his grasp and hurled herself against the wall, hands slapped against it for support. Richard untangled himself from the railing and sprinted toward her.

Wide-eyed, Marie stared down at Paul, his body writhing, his wide eyes fixed on the ceiling. "Marie," he called out. Blood poured profusely from his chest. A gurgling noise developed in his throat. "You're cheating me! I *hate* you, you bitch. I hate...you."

Richard reached Marie and she fell against him, sobbing, her eyes still magnetized to Paul's flailing limbs. Igna made her way down the companionway and staggered over to them.

"I hate you all," the Telexan screamed at them from the floor.

"Come on," Richard wheezed. The smoke was nearly impenetrable now.

Marie called out to Paul as Richard pulled her from the scene. "I'm sorry, Paul. I'm sorry for you." But her empathy was lost in the ravages of war. Igna grasped one of Marie's arms. Richard took the other and they hurried down the catwalk.

The angled stretch of catwalk where Richard had eluded death only moments ago supported them as they crawled along its tilted railing. It scorched their hands as the flames licked up from below. Safely on the other side, the three ran in the direction of the lift.

Behind them, the control room roared out its voice of flame, crackling, thundering. It filled the floor with acrid, blackened smoke, spreading the smell of charred flesh in sickening billows toward them.

Escaping down the short hall brought them quickly to the anteroom of the lift. To their utter relief, there stood Reese, Clive and Javid. They looked distraught and haggard, but their eyes brightened at the sight of their comrades. There were no formalities except for Igna's collapsing against Boro's chest when he appeared in the anteroom immediately afterward.

"Where's Bill?" Richard asked.

"He's okay. He's gone to get a few more police troops. He should be back by—"

The lift doors snapped opened and Bill stepped out with a half dozen officers who immediately donned masks and spread out. Richard gave Bill a solid slap on the shoulder. "Good to see you, my friend."

Bill touched Marie's cheek. "Are you okay?"

She nodded.

"That was a brave thing you did," he said.

"That was a reckless thing she did," Richard cut in, shocking the already traumatized group.

"It worked," Reese retorted. "We lost one. We could all be dead by now."

"One?" Bill's face blanched beneath sooty smears.

"Hollis," Boro muttered, holding a shaken Igna to his chest. "He got caught in the fire."

Bill slumped. "Oh, no."

Marie whimpered as the news dropped like molten lead on her heart.

Igna burst into tears. "I didn't think those star maps would ignite like that!"

There was a tremulous hiatus before Bill reestablished the group's solidarity. "You'd better all get out of here, quickly," he warned. "We need to get the prisoners out and stop the fires before we lose too much evidence."

Richard's group silently crowded into the lift as Bill donned a mask and disappeared from sight. The only sound inside the lift was that of hard breathing and a litany of coughing. Igna coughed the hardest. She slid to a crouch, slumping against Boro's leg. Boro cupped her head in his blood-smeared palm and pressed it against his thigh comfortingly.

Javid's gaze moved from Clive to Reese. They seemed to share his sense of disbelief at having wasted so many lives in the name of vanquishing evil. Javid then looked at Marie who stood alone, the corner of the lift her sole support. The Commander stood nearby, but avoided contact with her. The Commander's gaze trained steadily on the floor, his arms crossed, his head bent in exhaustion. Javid's heart broke as he read the anguish of abandonment on Marie's face. When a tear escaped her eye, Javid had to look away.

CHAPTER 58

Outside the villa's gates Marie had to shield her eyes against the whirling lights of security vehicles crowding the narrow alley. She could see Richard a few paces away barking at an official. "I need medical help for my crew," he shouted. An oxygen mask was shoved over his face.

"Are you Commander Shaw?" Richard nodded a positive response.

"You have acted outside of your jurisdiction, Commander."

Marie was only vaguely curious about the statement. She was dazed by the killings, dazed by Richard's reaction to her plan, which in the end had worked. She sneered. She hadn't done it for him, or for her own glory. She had done it for the group. And now Hollis was dead. Paul was dead. All those people were dead!

An officer approached her and stopped, momentarily shocked. Screeching hideously, he reached and grabbed her forearm.

"This is Marie Flechette! What the—? Lieutenant! Lieutenant. We have Marie Flechette."

Bedlam erupted around her.

"Where did she come from?" It was a woman's voice. "Look, she's bruised, her clothes are full of—ahhh, blood! It's everywhere."

Another voice squealed. "Glory to the Creator, that's Marie Flechette." The litany went on.

Reese and Clive stepped forward to protect her but were stopped at gunpoint. Reese swung and smashed an officer in the jaw. He was immediately tackled to the ground.

"Stop it!" Marie yelled at the officers.

"Reese, Clive, stop. I'll take care of this."

Marie could hear Richard shouting as he was shackled, blasters shoved against his chest. Marie was taken by the elbow towards him.

"Are you a prisoner of this man?"

Stunned, she glared at Richard, momentarily speechless.

"Did he do this to you? Who exactly are these people?"

Then she realized what was happening. Richard—of the barbaric Fringe—had just killed a number of high-ranking Nixodonian officials, and furthermore, had in his possession the kidnapped dignitary. She was angry but with two blasters at his chest she put aside her animosities.

"No He didn't do this to me," she answered. "This is the Fringe Commander."

"Where is your bodyguard, Bill Tripp? Didn't he call us to the scene?" The blasters raised.

"He's…no, wait! Commander Shaw did not do anything wrong. These are my friends. Bill is with us."

"With Fringe troops?"

"That is the pirate!" someone shouted. "The one who attacked the *Starquest!*"

Boro was immediately put under arrest.

"Wait." Marie cried.

Suddenly, everyone but herself and Javid were in shackles. A crowd surrounded her and began moving her in a human wave toward a medic van. She argued hotly with the commanding officers before forcing them to a stop as they passed Richard who was trying in vain to explain his position.

"Let him go," she ordered. The officer looked at her blankly. "Ma'am, this man is a criminal. He is outside of his jurisdiction and—"

"You listen to me," she said firmly. Finally Marie understood the power bestowed on her by what she had believed to be nothing more than a title. "Do you know who I am?" She spoke in a tone that hushed the crowd. "I don't think you do. Any of you!"

She meant it. She didn't know who she was herself at the moment. Fighting to grasp the situation at hand, she looked at the crowd and firmly took control.

"I am a member of the Presidential High Court, and upon me is bequeathed the power to free this man. I hereby place Commander Shaw and his officers under my protection until this matter is cleared up." Trembling, she held her ground. "He and these others are solely responsible for crushing a military coup against the Knabon administration that would have happened right under your arrogant noses had we not been here in *your* jurisdiction, to save *your* asses!"

Silence drenched the scene.

"Now," she added with spurious calm, "I order the release of Commander Shaw and his complement to my custody."

Slowly, the surprised officers began releasing the group. Another official approached her, his lip twitching with derision. "If this is the case, Miss Flechette, I'll need to know what you want done with your charges. But I must inform you that the Vice President has been advised of this situation and has ordered your group to be detained here until further notice."

"Vice—where is President Knabon?"

"He's already in protective custody, ma'am."

The wimp, she huffed! "Fine, get the Vice President on-line for me. Then contact my parents. Inform them that I'll need transportation back to the Flechette estate for eight—I mean, seven persons. My party will remain at our estate until further arrangements can be made with Commissioner Rhodes' successor in regards to their release from Nixodonia."

"Successor, ma'am?"

Marie frowned. "Yes. I'm afraid you'll be pulling our illustrious Commissioner out of that death trap." She thumbed toward the villa gates where officers were overseeing the emergence of the rebels from the underground bunker.

As the officer dismissed himself to carry out her orders, Marie's attention was drawn to the villa gates where Ray Lapp, his eyes round with shock, was being escorted toward the prison van. Next came Senator Black, Henrie Marchand, and a shrieking Lola Phoebe. Clive had either missed his mark, or had chosen to spare her. Perhaps there'd simply been enough bloodshed.

Marie wrapped her arms around herself as Angel Keem was hoisted out on a stretcher. Behind him was a beak-nosed man, shackled and in shock. "My poor General," he kept repeating.

The General was surrounded by medics administering emergency care. He moaned and rolled about the narrow cot, face ashen, the wound critical. Even in his serious condition, they were taking no chances. Both ankles were shackled to the stretcher.

So many of the ringleaders had survived. Marie wondered how many of the shrouded bodies being carried through the gates had been shields for their leaders?

An officer approached.

"Someone insists on seeing you, ma'am. He claims to be a personal friend."

She looked over at the policemen who where holding back a gathering crowd. They let one man through. Immediately she recognized the shocking red hair of Ken Lass.

"Ken, what are you doing here? We are not *personal* friends!"

"Marie, my *ghaud*, we thought we'd never see you again! You look awful! Has someone taken a look at you? A doctor, I mean?"

"Officer, take—"

He grasped her arm, "Wait. Listen I'm really glad you're alive, but just one statement. Please? I've been hounded day and night. You owe me at least a— hello Ken, yes it was awful."

"I owe you nothing!"

His mouth dropped open. "Wow, what happened to you? Well, I mean, I know what happened down there," he pointed a finger at the ground, "that's if you'll confirm it for me, but, Marie, you've *changed*."

"You can tell your people that I was well taken care of and that the Fringe Federation is solely responsible for the freedom of Nix States."

"The Fringe Federation doesn't exist, Marie," he mocked.

"Write it, Ken. And then you can warn your people that I will not be giving a public statement any time soon."

"They are not my people, Marie. They're your people. And they want to know what happened to you. If you don't give me at least a hint, I'll have to—"

"Officer, take this man away." Her request was firm.

"I was right about Paul. Remember that!" he shouted as they dragged him away.

Marie cupped her hands over her ears and forced herself to stay calm. She jumped when someone grasped her in a rugged hug. To her relief, it was Bill. She clung to him desperately.

"It's all finished down there," he said, rocking her in his arms.

Her body trembled, the tears flowed. He guided her to the medic van where Boro was receiving treatment. Boro gave her a grim smile.

"You didn't do anything like that to me, Boro," Marie told him urgently. "I didn't—"

"Please. No need." He cocked his head. "Thank you for saving us from this mob."

Igna was lying on a stretcher only a few feet away. She reached over and clutched Marie's hand. "Thanks kid," she hissed between dried lips.

Marie stammered out her own words of gratitude. "You saved my life, Igna."

Igna's grip tightened. "You did a hell of a job for a civilian." Her lips curled into a feeble smile. "Don't ever let anybody tell you you're not an actress."

A call from the senior officer diverted Marie's attention. "It's the Vice President, Ma'am."

A few minutes later, Marie removed a headset. Good. It was settled. She turned and noticed a guard direct a vehicle into the alley. From it stepped Raymond and Genevieve. Marie took a few lunging strides in their direction, but the sight of her father's robust frame brought her to an abrupt halt. It was as if the past two years hadn't existed. The vision of his face in the dust returned to her again. It occurred to her only now that that face hadn't been twisted in pain, but had been the same healthy one she saw now.

"Oh, Great Creator," she whispered, and ran into her parent's arms.

CHAPTER 59

Richard assessed the scene without expression as the helicopter began its descent within the walls of an immense property. The estate was more like a small city. The main house was larger than his government building on Vesperoiy. A secondary collection of buildings and gardens sprawled out behind the house, connected by tree-lined roads. He remembered reading about the Presidential visit here just before she'd embarked on the *Starquest*. He'd had an eye on her for two months by that time. He certainly hadn't foreseen falling in love with the woman!

His attention was drawn to the front of the property where tens of thousands crowded the at front gates. This also looked like small city, with tents and semi-permanent shacks set up everywhere. Bonfires dotted the encampment, mingling with the more powerful beams of numerous security vehicles obviously called in to monitor the situation. Her public influence fully dawned on him at that moment. The public wouldn't yet know of her arrival on Enderal, so these fans must have been here for a while, probably since her kidnapping.

It now felt ridiculous. The Princess of the Galaxy had gone from being his prisoner, to his being hers! He let out a breath. Why the hell was he so mad about everything? Was it a reaction to the mass murder they'd just executed. It wasn't supposed to have happened that way.

Inside the mansion, Richard found himself gawking at the Grand Hall entrance. He could not imagine the Marie he'd come to know walking these halls. Yet, she walked about as if the place was an extension of herself, hugging the half dozen people who'd gathered for an impromptu welcoming party. The Fringe group looked uncomfortable, except Igna whose crooked smile revealed her delight. Marie breezed back to Richard, but her smile faltered when she saw his scowl.

"I'd like to show you your quarters, Commander," she said.

So formal. And no sharing of beds at the Flechette mansion? He nodded and followed her up the staircase. He took off his soiled jacket and flung it on a powder blue chair. Marie stood at the door.

"Sorry, no priests painted on the ceilings here."

"No, there certainly aren't," he agreed.

Marie stiffened. "I don't know what you're so angry about, Richard, but I wish you'd just come out and say it. Surely it isn't about what I did down there?"

"You put yourself in great danger."

"I was in danger already. You put yourself in danger coming after me. You didn't have to do that."

"Don't be ridiculous!"

"Don't be ridiculous? I did my part. That's all. So, what is it? You can't stand to see who I really am, what I am capable of, where I live?"

He gave her an icy stare.

"You are who you are, Marie, but you're right." He ran a hand through his hair. "You're home now. I need to accept that."

Was he telling her it was over, or was she telling him?

"Fine, I'm home. The least you can do is have the decency to accept my home, as I accepted yours."

He turned slowly to face her. The only semblance of the physical Marie he knew was in the crumpled jumpsuit she still wore. Otherwise her features had taken on a radiance that told the world of her joy of being home, of being free. Wasn't that to be expected? His shoulders dropped and he opened his arms to her.

"I'm so sorry," he whispered. "Please come to me, one last time?"

Marie stood a moment. One last time? Regardless, she couldn't resist and stepped into his embrace. He rocked her gently as she clung to him before the chasm between their ways of life began to crack them apart like a monstrous earthquake.

"I'm not that unfamiliar with the high life," Richard murmured in her ear, as if to lighten the burden. "In truth, I'm impressed with your home. And, we're not altogether hopeless in the Fringe, you know. Perhaps someday you can check out the charm of Vesperoiy."

The charm of Vesperoiy. The Fringe's governing planet. Marie looked at Richard and smiled. "Perhaps." She left the room before he could see her cry.

CHAPTER 60

The next morning, breakfast was served in the guest dining room. The room was bright and airy, the food delicious. Richard was too hungry to scoff at the exquisite presentation, the fine linens or the abundance of choice.

Marie wasn't with them and he missed her until it hurt. On the other hand, he wished he could just leave and never see her again. Instead, he had to suffer the torture of being in this mansion a few days longer. Everywhere he turned, he would see either Marie herself, or pictures of her, or hear the drone from the sea of fans outside the estate gates. Now he understood why the fans were here. They believed that she would lay down her life for them, and now she had!

Grabbing his coffee, he excused himself and went out onto the balcony. He meant to get some air, but rather, below him in the courtyard, he witnessed Marie and her parents welcoming the Central States Investigators. She approached them with the dignity of a queen. In return, they treated her like one. They bowed deeply and asked a dozen questions about her well being before turning to the resurrected patriarch and his wife. He'd had no idea! She wasn't the pop culture icon he'd thought he'd kidnapped. No, this woman garnered the respect of an entire nation. He'd shared a bed with her in a rocky hovel. The dream was over.

An hour later, Marie reentered the fireside chamber and looked somberly at the group. "Some decisions have been made," she told them. "Javid, Bill and me will give our statements here at the estate. Everyone else, including Clive and the two pilots, will be leaving in the morning for our governing planet, G2. You will all give your formal statements to the Central Investigation Bureau there. Richard, I have requested safe passage for you and your officers back to the Fringe on your Flagship once everything is settled. Clive, after your questioning, you'll be escorted back to Iggid. I have asked amnesty for the acts against the *Starquest*, and for my abduction. I have assurance that these requests will be honored."

"We save their goddamned asses and we need permission to go back to our own country?" Reese exploded.

Marie glared at him. "They have to save face somehow, Reese," she said flatly. "They did, however, give me some exciting news. The Saurian Fleet defeated the Telexan Armada while still in Fringe space. There were virtually no casualties to the Saurians."

Shocked silence ensued before rejoicing burst from the group. Even Richard was visibly pleased. His head dropped back with a hard pull of his fingers through his hair.

"Have they gone on to Doria?" Reese asked.

"Yes, although the new General of the Space Naval Force was a bit surprised at what was left of the Nixodonian arsenal, he is preparing a fleet to help contain the Dorian base. I think they are relying heavily on Saurian support. They're hoping you'll accede to that, Richard."

There was a tense silence before Richard burst out, "You tell them it's on condition that they stop treating us like criminals. And it will be just that—backup." He looked at her steadily. "I don't want one more life lost for the Nixodonian cause."

"When you get to G2, you can tell them yourself, Commander. But first, let me finish. The firefighting forces you brought down to the bunker with you, Bill, saved much of the equipment. The computers containing the list of the Nixodonian underground was salvaged."

"They found the entire list?" Richard asked, skeptically.

"I don't know that for certain, but a roundup is already in progress."

"Well goody for Nix States," Boro sneered. "They get to clean their underwear without even knowing it was soiled in the first place!"

"Sometimes gaining independence isn't all glory," Marie retorted to a group of sobering faces. "Yes, independence. A recognized nation is what you'll get from this."

Still, they scowled with contempt.

"Isn't that what you wanted?" She was taken aback by the group's brooding silence. "I haven't heard from President Knabon yet, but the Vice President has informed me that negotiations have started in regards to granting the Fringe its independence."

"Negotiations?" Richard asked. "With whom? We're all here. They don't need to grant us anything. They just have to accept the reality that the Fringe doesn't belong to them."

"Richard, even in its wretched state you can't fight the power of Nix States. It's in your interest to play their game. Accept graciously. That is solid advice, Commander."

Reese leaned toward Richard and muttered surreptitiously in Richard's ear. Richard seemed to lower his guard.

"We're all shaken by this," Marie ground out, "and I understand that your custody here isn't easy to swallow. However, it's the best I can do." Her mouth formed a stern line. "You'll be leaving for G2 tomorrow. In the meantime, the property is at your disposal. Please stay within its walls." She turned and left the room.

*   *   *   *

Marie regretted having offered to be last to give her statement to the investigators. Had she anticipated the intensity of their interrogation she may have exercised her option to bow out. All those questions drove her to tears and those tears pooled in her eyes as she made her way to her private wing.

She trudged down the hall, away from where Richard would be sleeping. She hadn't even had a chance to bid him good night. Maybe it didn't matter. He had probably adopted the right attitude—to lighten the final blow.

She declined the nightly offer from Reebe for a massage. All three of her girls had survived and were home. That's all that she cared about tonight. Alone, she entered her quarters and gazed at the familiar decor that Richard hadn't laid eyes on. Oh, how quick she was to vacillate. She closed her eyes, hoping to ease her turmoil. Instead, vivid memories began to dance behind her eyelids.

Instantly succumbing to the need to grieve, she walked over to a closet larger than her whole suite on the nebular planet, and found the worn leather boots and the freshly laundered jumpsuit that she'd refused to let Reebe throw away. These would be the only things to remind her that any of it had actually happened. She wished she had the tribal bracelets with her now but they were still aboard the impounded relay ship.

Daring to relish its significance, Marie pulled out the long gold chain from beneath the collar of her evening jacket. With a finger, she traced the words and whispered, "We glorify you, oh Resplendent, oh Loving, oh Bountiful Universe." Grasping the treasure tightly to her bosom, Marie lay fully clothed across the bed. With the jumpsuit tucked under her head as a pillow, she sobbed until sleep overtook her.

Richard hadn't even undressed. He sat on the edge of the bed, hands drooping between his knees. With his head slumped forward he found himself childishly muttering the conversation he would like to be having with the patriarch, Raymond Flechette.

"This may come as a surprise to you, but I'm in love with your daughter, and I want to take her back with me. No, no—I'd like to ask you for her hand in marriage. No, that's too blunt. Ah—I shouldn't hide it any longer. Marie means the universe to me. Do you mind if I stay in touch with her?"

Richard shot to his feet and cursed. "You fool, Shaw," he grunted "What are you going to say? Can you find it in yourself to forgive the way I sent out my payrolled pirate—under your roof this very night—to pillage the *Starquest* in the sole conquest of your daughter? Can you find it in yourself to forgive this certain Captain Boro, who happens to be one of my good friends, not to mention one of my best officers, for killing one of your bodyguards, then damned near killing your daughter before I got my hands on her?"

"Might you," he said aloud to the wall while giving a dramatic shake of a finger, "might you forgive the way I have totally ignored her since she so bravely laid her life on the line for us all?" He slapped a hand to his forehead. "For how I've ignored her since we arrived at this castle of yours because this is my way of making this easier on *her*? Ahhhh!" The Commander in Chief of the Fringe Federation felt like a total fool.

"But wait," He continued in monologue while pacing the plush carpet. "I provided her with decent accommodation." He groaned. "Yeah! A hole in a rock. But, I fed her well…okay, so some of it was aborigine food." He paused. "Very good mind you. And I didn't question her too harshly." Richard spun at the far end of the room. "Not only that, I taught her some self-esteem," His voice rose. "I let her go out into the jungle and gave her the courage to swim in a pool all by herself. I gave her the joy of playing with children, never mind that they were stark naked!"

Richard plunked down on the powder blue chair. "No, Shaw. No." He ran a hand through his white hair. His gaze shifted when a creamy strand fell across the corner of one eye. He wondered what the patriarch thought of that? "No. Just keep doing what you are doing, Shaw. Just let it go. You promised to give her life? Well, I suppose this is it."

CHAPTER 61

She's back, folks. Not with the fanfare she deserves, nor in anger toward those who assaulted her. No, she's come home with all of her desperadoes in tow, exalting the very people who injured her. She even befriended the infamous Captain Boro. Our loving heiress then hid the pirate and his pals behind the ominous iron curtain of the Flechette estate.

But, is this so bad? Is it bad that the Fringe, once considered a barren piece of space, will now become its own nation? Is it bad that, in the birth pains of that aspiration, one hundred and nine people lost their lives in the secret rebel bunker beneath our very own city? Perhaps it's a very good thing that in Marie's shrewd decision to dump her small-time boyfriend, she inadvertently exposed the massive treachery of Angel Keem and all of his very surprising followers. Is it so bad that our princess won't give a statement unless everyone with her on that doomed night, Nixodonian or not, is granted the same privilege? No. I think we owe Marie Flechette all the homage, love, and respect due her. It is said that she laid her life on the line for her friends and countrymen, giving time for those with her to carry out their self-appointed task. Yes, it was a horror, but as great a horror as losing our freedom to a ruthless dictator? We hardly think so. Crude as the execution of this monumental task turned out to be, we are ever grateful to Marie Flechette and the Fringe Federation for their acts of heroism.

But, beware! There is a message to be had, here. For all of you planning on marriage, perhaps it is wise to investigate carefully what treasures might lie beneath the surface of the one you think you love.

—Celebrity Quest

CHAPTER 62

"Everybody, into the van," Bill yelled. "Marie first."

Marie was quickly guided by Spencer into the security van, not into the luxury cruiser in which she'd arrived at Enderal Lake Park. Her attempt to meet her fans in order to promote the new FC Benefit Foundation hospitals went drastically wrong. She had been shaking hands, holding the babies, touching the elderly, when a small explosive hurled through the air. It erupted just a few yards away, right near Anne Amaaka who shrieked and cursed all at once. Angry men shouted at Marie, "Get out of here. You don't belong in Nixodonia!"

It was the third such incident. She'd been home only a month.

"It's all right," Bill consoled as the van arrived at the FC estate. He took off his headset. "No one is hurt. The head count was twenty-five thousand. Only three are under arrest."

She looked at him, eyes brimming. "Oh Bill. Will it ever end?"

A few days Later, Marie's thinning figure slumped in a large library chair. The firelight reflected off her pale skin. Her fingers clutched weakly to a heavy glass tumbler filled with a strong drink. She chided herself for her choice of glass, its circumference engraved with an intricate design similar to the priest's goblets. She should let it all go, but something in her couldn't. The weight of the pendant had become almost too much to bear, yet she couldn't set it aside either. Besides, the pendant had been a gift. That was all.

"Ah, here you are." Raymond strode into the library and sat opposite her. "How are you?"

"I'm fine. I still can't get used to how well you look!"

"We've been through a lot you and me," he concurred. "In fact, there's something I need to talk to you about." The sudden change in his voice frightened Marie. "I made a promise to your mother before I left for Doria. I promised her that I would sort out this mess we called Flechette Cosmetics if I came back alive."

Marie straightened. "What do you mean?"

"The Healer showed me that I've lost something very precious, something I believed I had in my early adult life. Something I taught you once. It was an unshakable trust that the universe itself supports us."

Marie couldn't breathe. Unwillingly her mind filled with Richard's voice. *You have beliefs in the universe as your source of truth as well.* Had these beliefs really been a part of her youth? Had they all forgotten them?

"When FC became so famous," Raymond continued, "I forgot those teachings and I put my trust in the company. That's when it all started to go wrong. When you were kidnapped, I realized my mistakes. Gen had always warned me about the dangers of fame, but I couldn't see any harm in it. I now feel responsible for your troubles. I molded your identity before you had a chance to know it for yourself. When I was lying on that jungle mat, I feared I'd never be able to ask your forgiveness. I didn't think I'd never see you again."

"Oh, Papa, please! Don't take responsibility for my decisions! If you need forgiveness you have it, but—" Desperately, Marie found herself hoping to redirect the path she knew her father was taking. She'd lost Richard. She could *not* lose FC. "Is it the TRA's influence that bothers you? Do you think FC would have failed without their meddling?"

Raymond shook his head. "The TRA did nothing but grab onto an opportunity. We had a winner. It was I who created the monster."

"*Monster?*" She stood. "Papa! There would have been no monster without their influence. There may not have even been a winner." She suddenly saw her father's weakness. Could even her hero delude himself into believing that he was solely responsible for the company's success? For her galactic success? Suddenly, she realized her own failure. Had she not succumbed to the same sins?

Raymond sighed. "Perhaps the word is a bit harsh, but not as harsh as the truth. Believe me, darling. My arrogance would have been as bold, whatever our level of success."

Marie sat down, sensing that he, too, had grappled with life itself, yet he spoke of the opposite.

"I walked with death a long time before I would acknowledge it. Finally, I was forced to look it in the face. But death is my companion now, someone to walk with, to keep me from getting consumed by my inner self and regress into a man with no will. Sure, I created power here." He opened his palms. "But what kind of power? It's only the skill of conviction, really. I see now that the only power I have is the power of my decisions, and with death as my companion, each one I make is final. I have no time to vacillate. My decision now is to reconnect with my spiritual world. This one," he glanced about, "I have surely exhausted."

Marie felt faint. "Are you telling me you want to dismantle FC?"

He smiled. "No, darling. Nothing that drastic."

Marie breathed. "You're scaring me, Papa? Surely you're not ready to quit."

"No, but we certainly won't be expanding! However, I think we should reduce the overall size of FC, before it consumes us again."

"Do I have a say in how this will be done?"

"Of course. In fact, I'm here to make you an offer."

Marie's fear twisted into anxious trepidation.

"You're already groomed for the presidency. You can accept it anytime you wish."

Marie blinked, then laughed aloud. "Oh please, not *that*. Look at you! We would have hardly talked of passing on the presidency had you not been sick." She reached over and grasped his hand. "Yes, I want the position some day, but *truly*, I'm not ready now."

Genevieve suddenly entered the library. "Am I missing a party?"

Marie was still laughing. "I've just told Papa that's he's going to be President for a very long time."

Genevieve poured them all a fresh drink. "I'm afraid my news isn't as joyful. It seems the TRA has retreated back to Telexa, but they still have firm control of the power there."

"Even without General Keem?"

"His second-in-command has taken over. It seems that they infiltrated the government there the same way they did here, except that the collaborators in Telexa are still alive and well."

"And untouched," Marie muttered.

"I'm sorry, darling, but the news gets worse. The TRA have released *Angel's Test* in Telexa. Bill just told me that the movie's theme has infiltrated Nixodonia and that's what caused the upset this afternoon at the Enderal Lake Park."

Marie rubbed vigorously at her temples. "It will take months, maybe years, to convince everyone that I would *never* betray Nix States."

"And you may never succeed," her father said, solemnly, "but we know the statistics. Eighty percent do believe you, and more will be convinced with time."

"It's so overwhelming," she whispered.

"Maybe you should just concentrate on getting some rest before the honor ceremonies at the Presidential House," Genevieve said, handing her a drink. "We leave in just three days, darling."

Marie agreed. The President had wanted to honor Javid, Clive, Bill and herself for their part in overthrowing the military coup. She would have declined had it not been for the boys. They really deserved the recognition. As for herself, she'd been headline news since her return and couldn't wait for the frenzy to die down.

"I still don't understand why the Fringe wasn't invited." Genevieve said.

Raymond frowned. "I'm told that the ceremony's intention is to boost national pride. Inviting the Fringe would apparently defeat the purpose."

Marie shook her head. "Only four more years of Pao reign. Do you think we'll survive?"

The Flechette delegation arrived on G2 in a fanfare that would have excited Marie in former times. Today she felt crushed by the millions who pressed on her entourage. Inside the Presidential House, the activity was scarcely more sane. One bright light was the reunion with Clive Baker. Javid nearly jumped into Clive's arms. Despite their somewhat rocky beginnings, Marie felt as though she was welcoming her brother.

Clive gave the back of her hand a gallant kiss. "It's very good to see you again, Lady Marie." He grinned. "I want to give you a hug and say you look ravishing, but the boss," he tossed his head toward Javid, "has told me to keep my hands off!"

Marie winked at Javid. "Don't mind him. He's only wants to protect my hair."

"Just a minute!" Javid cried.

"So," Marie said, laughing, "tell your *boss* that I insist on a dance later."

"Oh, goody. I've never danced with a Princess before."

"And you won't now, either."

"No, no!" He waggled a finger. "I have now witnessed this phenomena with my own eyes."

"Then you need re-education, dear Clive. This is a not a kingdom, it's a democracy."

He gave a crooked smile. "Yeah, right. Rumor has it that Johnas is on his father's heels to the presidency. Won't that make the fourth Knabon in a row? Sound's like we're being hoodwinked, but seeing as that's our lot, I vote that this here dynasty has itself a Princess."

Shaking her head, Marie accepted his guiding elbow as the procession moved on. Javid trotted beside Clive, whispering imperatively that he was to behave himself. This was *not* an Iggid brothel.

Marie's annoyance with the affair began with the speeches. She was shocked when most of the emphasis was placed on her. President Knabon told a crowd of gasping aristocrats about Marie's courage during the attack of the *Starquest* and her unselfish act in the rebel bunker. She forced a smile when asked to stand for the great applause. She annoyed the President in return by insisting that the boys stand with her. They well deserved the honor, along with the handsome monetary reward.

The gala that followed did little but wear her out. Members of the High Court pried endlessly for details about her kidnapping. On-going questions about the unusual Fringe Commander and her association with him threw her heart into turmoil. It became increasingly harder keep to it to herself.

"I don't want anybody to know about Richard and me," she confessed to Bill as they danced together for the third time. "It will be pure torture if that story gets out."

"Don't worry. If Javid or Clive slip up, I'll have their heads. But," he raised an eyebrow, "Richard is not your latest passion according to the fan magazines. Anne just told me that there are a lot of eyes on me these days. I don't mind being a diversion, but maybe you should dance with someone else."

"Ah—your wish is granted," she whispered as the President himself cut in. She gave a nod to dismiss Bill, and imparted a pleasant smile to Pao Knabon. He began a waltz with her.

"It is good to have you home again, Miss Flechette."

"It's very good to be home, Mr. President. My comrades and I are grateful for this celebration. I'm also glad to hear that Nix States has recognized the Fringe's independence."

"The Fringe certainly deserves it," the President acknowledged. "The Senate has also renounced occupation of the Sector 5 lanes and will officially give their control back to the Fringe Federation. It seemed that Yousef Phoebe was responsible for their takeover in the first place. The whole affair has been quite a shock, but thanks to you, Nix States will remain at peace."

"I hardly worked alone, Mr. President."

"True, but it was *your* courage that put this ordeal to rest."

"You *will* crush the TRA, won't you Mr. President?"

"When we are strong enough, yes. We will help the Fringe with that task."

"Help the Fringe? But—the TRA is too strong!"

"They won't be once the Fringe destroys their Rashmarian base. With their main base down, the TRA will struggle for a very long time."

Marie glanced at Javid who milled about the crowds, fully enjoying the attention lavished on him. Rashmar would soon suffer another blow and she prayed for the safety of his people. She glanced at the President. "If I understand correctly, such a mission will be very dangerous. Captain Boro told me that many stolen Nixodonian ships are guarding that planet."

"And so, if the Fringe Federation is everything it says it is, we'll have our ships back in no time."

Marie gasped. "You expect the Fringe Federation to return your ships?"

His laugh hinted of mockery. "Ah, my dear. That is simply the price of independence."

She barely heard his next words.

"You know, my lovely, Johnas has been amazed by your strength through this ordeal. He would love to get to know you better. He's right over there."

Pao nodded toward the edge of the dance floor where the tall and not so fair Johnas Knabon stood gawking stupidly while his father did his dirty work.

"Oh, I'm flattered, but I will need some time to recover—"

"Take all the time you need, my dear. But think about it seriously. Your marriage to my son would be a great asset to our nation."

How did he consider such a union an asset, Marie wondered. Would he use her influence the way the TRA had hoped, to sway the masses into one more Knabon administration? This man was so incredibly vain he deserved to lose his nation.

"I'll consider it," she said through a tight smile.

As the President stepped away, she nodded to Bill who returned before Johnas could step in. She placed her hand at his elbow and asked him to take her for some refreshment. As they stepped off the dance floor, Marie discreetly expelled a breath. "Thank you."

He smiled cheerfully. "I thought you were enjoying yourself."

"Immensely." She glowered at the President. "I don't trust that man. He's suggesting that I marry Johnas because it would be an asset to Nixodonia."

Bill guffawed. "Johnas? Now that would certainly quell rumors about me!"

"I'd rather they be rumors about you."

"Oh, I don't know." Bill suddenly sobered. "I've just received something that I hope will challenge you more than rumors about me." With a frown, Bill pulled an envelope from his pocket. "The man has integrity after all."

Oh, please, not Johnas, Marie thought, opening the envelope with trembling fingers.

Congratulations on the Presidential honor you are receiving this evening, Marie. Javid, Clive, Bill and you are well deserving of the acknowledgment. Thank you for your help in restoring peace to our galaxy. All of us here in the Fringe Federation are eternally grateful for everything that you did.

—*Sincerely, Richard Shaw*

Unable to breathe, she quickly tucked the envelope into her handbag. She grasped Bill's hand as the music struck up again. He looked deeply into her eyes.

"I'll always love you. You know that."

Marie nodded almost imperceptibly. "I know."

Bill touched the moisture at the corner of her eye. He glanced down at the envelope whose corner protruded from the beaded satchel before recapturing her gaze.

"I pray that you make choices that bring you happiness, my love."

*   *   *   *

Genevieve floated about the elegant stateroom of the FC shuttle on its way back to Enderal.

"That was wonderful, wasn't it? Bill and Javid looking like kings in those silk embroidered suits. And that Clive Baker. He's such a clown. And, ah! To see our Marie standing up there, stunning, as usual. I was so proud of her."

"Yes, and you, my lovely, were ravishing." Raymond kissed her lightly as he breezed by while removing his formal overcoat.

"Marie was disappointed that her begging failed to invite the Fringe officers."

"Knabon honors his own, I suppose. Granted, Shaw did save our nation, but there were ulterior motives, remember?…His own ass?"

"You're too hard on him, Raymond. I thought the Fringe Commander was very charming. Incredible hair. I'm surprised Marie didn't fall for him. Incredible eyes, too."

"What do you mean, surprised. She did fall for him. Then what? The minute he gets her home, he treats her like he doesn't know her."

Genevieve's mouth gaped open. "She did?"

"No, he did."

"She told you she fell for the man?"

"No, Bill did."

"Bill fell for the man?"

Raymond laughed. "No. Bill told me that Marie was smitten with the Incredible Commander in Chief of the Fringe Federation. Yes, those were his words."

"Bill Tripp told you that? What on earth happened out there? Now, this is incredible."

"Be prepared," he muttered. "We're going to have to get used to it."

"Used to what?"

Raymond huffed. "Don't you think that the Incredible Commander tried too hard to keep his eyes off our daughter? I tried that with you, remember? And Marie, Great *Creator*! She's been a bit too despondent, don't you think?" In one artful move, Raymond scooped up his wife. "Oooh, I haven't been able to do that in two years."

He tossed her on the bed.

"Too bad Paul is gone," she giggled. "I'd like to sneak you some of those pills—and slow you down again!"

CHAPTER 63

Only days after receiving her Presidential honor for bravery, Marie Flechette was seen in swimwear at the Enderal City Lake Park yesterday flanked by dozens of Secret Service men, Bill Tripp in charge. Her relationship with the bodyguard remains strong and there is speculation of intimacy between the two. FC headquarters denies any such allegations and Mr. Tripp will remain at his regular post despite his substantial monetary reward from the Presidential House.

No one is quite certain of Marie's reasons for being at the park. There were no official ceremonies scheduled and it would seem unlikely that Miss Flechette would want to use the lake for a public swim. To our amazement, that was exactly her intention. Attempts to interview the heiress were thwarted by her security staff, so we will have to wait longer to find out what really happened during her kidnapping that has caused such a drastic change in our princess. There have been no statements from the heiress and her squad of Fringe-Nixodonian warriors, as was hoped, and she has yet to follow through on a request for a private interview with us. Yes, she has done her best to reach out, but her silence on this matter is not what is known, loved, or remembered by her fans.

But come on folks, let's keep holding our breaths. If there's one thing we do know, we know that Marie Flechette will rise again.

—Celebrity Quest

Marie knew that Anne Amaaka had been waiting a long time. Finally she made it back to her office, letting Anne rush in right behind.

"Anne, you'll be so happy," Marie chirped. "I finally chose all the models for the new magazine spread."

"Yes that is wonderful," Anne said flatly, "but…"

Marie turned "But, what?"

Anne pressed fingers against her forehead. "It's Ken Lass. He's been on me day and night, begging me to give you one last try."

Marie slumped into her office chair. With less vehemence than Anne expected, Marie said simply, "I can't."

"What do you mean, you can't?"

"I'm telling you! I'm declining Ken's request for an interview."

Wearily, Anne leaned her hands on the edge of Marie's desk. "We were friends once, Marie. Now I feel like I barely know you. You've been back nearly three months and you've said nothing, not even to me. Good gracious, your fans have a right to know what happened to you."

"What more do they want to know? They know everything already."

"They want to know what it was like for you, how you felt, what you did all that time. Surely you didn't just sit in your cell once the Fringe Commander granted you freedom."

Marie pointed a finger. "It wasn't a cell! And truly, Anne, one thing I did learn is that I need to keep my personal life just that. Personal."

"Your kidnapping was hardly a personal affair, Marie! It affected us all. *Celebrity Quest* has followed you from birth. Great Creator, they deserve a little consideration."

"It was their choice to follow me from birth, Anne. And as for consideration, they certainly didn't consider my feelings when they published those articles about Paul."

"Those stories turned out to be true."

"And, so is this. I've changed my mind. No interview."

The argument died very suddenly. Marie took in great gasps as her composure crumbled. After that outlandish affair at the Presidential House she'd tried even harder to bury her memories. It hadn't worked and she wondered how long it would take to forget.

"Well fine," Anne huffed. "But, if you don't want public life, what *do* you want?"

"Oh, Great Creator," Marie cried quietly. Looking up at Anne, she burst into tears. "All I want is to be left alone, Anne. I'm not even sure I want this anymore." She let a palm whack against the pile of work on her desk. "All I want is to swim in the pool, and hold my little brown boy. I want to see the sky turn all colors after sundown and eat in the mess hall with the gang. I want to run in the jungle, and watch the sun dance on the water. I want to hear the mechanic play his Zeeta and see what the merry-making is like there now. I want to talk to Chief Ungu, and ask him to teach me to hear from the stars like he does, just with his soul. I did that once you know, with the help of the smoke. But mostly, mostly," she sniffed, "I need to talk to the gods in the eclipse and ask their forgiveness for renouncing them."

Anne gaped at Marie. "What on *earth* are you talking about?"

"See what I mean? You can't begin to understand. No one would, and that is why I can't talk to you, or to them, or to anybody."

"Anne, would you excuse us, please." Genevieve stood in the doorway, surprising both women. Anne glanced back at Marie with a wide-eyed look before leaving the room.

"Oh, dear, you weren't supposed to hear that." Marie let her head drop into her hand.

"Why not?" Genevieve asked, walking slowly toward her daughter.

Marie waved a hand weakly through the air. "Because, I have to forget about it."

"You can't forget about an experience like that! If you deny it, it will only come back to haunt you. It seems it already has." Genevieve sat down on one of the couches. "You know, I've been listening to you since you came home. Your decision to keep your feelings from the press is a fair and wise decision, but you're also refusing to honor and explore those changes for yourself. You want to be the same old Marie again, but you're not. Oh, my darling, I don't expect you to share everything with me, but please remember; I will always listen without judgment. I'm worried about you."

"Don't worry about me! I'm here now. Just a thing that eats and breathes this company." Marie's words shot out too hastily. "Wait. I didn't mean it that way. This is where I want to be. It's where I belong. I can't let a couple of weeks on some unscheduled *holiday* change my entire life!"

Genevieve leaned into the softness of the couch. "Tell me about the little brown boy."

"Who? Oh him. He was just one of the children who would come to the jungle pool with the other children. It was his mother who died the night that I saw Papa's face in the dust. It was awful, Maman."

"Go back, Marie."

Marie looked at her mother in surprise. "What?"

"Go back. There's something there you haven't finished with, and whatever it is, it's eating you up."

Marie laughed hollowly. "I can't go back."

"Why not? Because the company can't go on without you? It can, Marie. And you need to know that you're always free to go."

"You've never forced me to stay. I'm here of my own free will."

Genevieve shrugged. "I believe that. Where else would you go? Everything is here for you. You're the envy of the galaxy. You wouldn't go out and look for a life of your own, because—well, because what could be better than Flechette Cosmetics?"

"Nothing. And I don't need any more diversions."

"So the Great Creator sent you away. He made you look elsewhere, to places you'd have never gone of your own volition. Goodness, Marie, you've had thirty-three years of your life here. Surely it's time to do something different."

"I can't just leave! Look at all this." She spread her hands to the work on her desk. "Who would take care of this?"

"It's taken care of."

"Wha—"

"Your father and I. We worked out a little contingency plan—you know, in case you never returned. In case *he* didn't survive. It can still be implemented."

Marie blanched. "But, but, the Fringe is so far away."

Genevieve shrugged. "My home planet is farther than Kutar 2. It never stopped me from being with the man I loved."

Marie stared at her mother.

"I keep having this crazy notion that there's someone waiting for you out there."

"You do?"

"Yes. Oh, what's his name? You know, that white-haired fellow. Commander Boro, is it?"

"No. It's Richard Sh—"

Marie's eyes widened, realizing her mother's bluff. Genevieve began to giggle. Marie followed in a burst of hysterical laughter that took on the function of opening a release valve too long under pressure.

When the women finally composed themselves, Genevieve stood and removed an envelope from her briefcase. "And if that doesn't convince you, this might." She winked at her daughter. "I'll let you relish this one on your own."

Genevieve handed Marie the envelope and strode out of the room. Marie fingered the envelope. Richard? With trembling hands, she recklessly tore it open and quickly scanned the words, too anxious to read it from start to finish.

...Johnas Ismal, son of our most exalted President, Pao. F. Knabon requests your hand in marriage, for the glory of the people, and the love of our great nation, Nixodonian States...

The letter fell to the floor, accompanied by a loud shriek.

CHAPTER 64

Marie found Javid in the central courtyard of the main complex sitting pensively beside one of the fountains. She approached him slowly, afraid she might be disturbing a meditation. Without turning her way, he addressed her.

"Hello, Marie." His voice was laden with sadness, yet when he turned to look at her, she could see joy in his eyes.

"Javid," Marie said nervously. "Is something wrong?"

He blinked. "You haven't heard?"

"Heard what?"

"About Rashmar. The Fringe Forces destroyed the Reptilian base. Clive called just an hour ago to tell me about it."

"Oh...my," she breathed, fully shocked by the news.

"I'm sorry, I thought you knew, but I guess word won't be out yet."

Unsteadily, she sat down on the stone edge of the fountain, facing him.

"Oh, my beloved Javid." She stopped for fear that her composure would dissolve altogether. Anguish filled her heart for a loss she had hoped never to suffer. She swallowed hard. "There's no need to ask my permission to resign, Javid. You're free to go at any time. I'm so happy that you finally get to go home!"

"Ah, thank you, my lady. But please, don't send me away too quickly. It could be weeks before it's safe for me to return. Just the same, leaving here will be difficult. I've spent many wonderful years in your employ, and many hours sitting right on this bench, wondering if I would ever see Rashmar again. There were times when I thought it wouldn't matter, but deep inside, my need to go back has never ebbed."

He clasped his hands and smiled widely.

"And now, I am even more blessed because I know what to expect, who's there, what things are like now." He cocked his head. "Well, I did know until this final invasion. But it doesn't matter. Most of the damage was in the valley. We'll fix it up, and then Dowlar and I will begin anew. Clive said that Commander Shaw asked the Rashmarians to stay in the caves during the invasion. He wanted none of us harmed."

Marie's throat ached. "That's such good news."

Javid caught her eye. "And you?"

She glanced down. With the toe of her shoe she ground down a small shoot appearing between the cracks of the cobblestone. "Oh, I don't know. I'm back at the top of my game, yet it feels like I've taken a step backward, like I'm going nowhere."

Javid folded his arms. "Where would you like to go?"

"I don't know, but it seems that I have at least one option."

He raised an eyebrow. "An option?"

Marie smiled tightly. "Yes. Johnas Knabon just asked for my hand in marriage—by courier!"

Javid roared. "Ah, how I love the jesting gods of Rashmar."

"When you get back there, you can tell your gods that I'm not very taken by their pranks."

"I'll scold them as soon as I get home," Javid laughed, but his heart ached terribly. Oh, if she only knew how much he would miss her. "Clive said he'd take me back to Rashmar when the time came. And, oh yes! I must tell you! He's coming in just a few days! He wants to take us for a spin in one of his new ships."

"Is that safe?" she teased.

"The reward money allowed him to set up quite a trade business," Javid grinned, "under the name of *Whale Freighting*, if you can believe it."

Marie smiled. "Yes, I can believe it." Eyes cast downward, she regretted the smear she'd made of the innocent green shoot. "Oh Javid, after you're gone, who will guide me?"

He spread his palms and looked at them piteously. "These hands and this heart have forgotten their lessons. I, too, must seek my teacher, and therefore I can no longer teach you." He shook his head forlornly. "A man cannot teach what he does not know."

Marie wanted to disagree, but the words remained lodged in her throat.

"You have nothing to fear," he encouraged. "Just continue to follow your heart and you will walk your destined path. Believe in yourself. Trust in your dreams.

"However," he added swiftly, "if you truly wish for guidance in regards to this present dilemma, take my personal, and presently unenlightened advice. Say no to Johnas."

*   *   *   *

The jesting gods of Rashmar!

Just three days later, Marie found herself feverishly pacing the library floor while ruminating over Javid's words from their talk at the fountain. Follow her heart? Fine. But how?

She had just seen Javid and Clive off by helicopter to the Enderal spaceport. Javid had received word that he could safely return to Rashmar and Clive had offered to take him in his new freighter.

Marie would have to inspect Clive's new fleet later. She had pressing duties to attend to, yet all she could do was pace. How she needed Javid now, and he'd been gone for only an hour. He was so wrong about her ability to make intelligent decisions for herself. Already, she needed his help to calm the heart that vacillated so painfully in her chest. Spinning on her heel, she resumed her walk. Marie scowled and swore to herself again that she'd made her final decision: to reduce her public duties in order to head the new FC magazine that she herself was creating.

Her pacing stopped. Perhaps she vacillated because this wasn't her final choice, but another band-aid solution. Her soul would end up like an embalmed corpse if she continued to suppress her festering emotional wounds. She clutched at her hair and wailed in despair.

Follow your heart. Believe in your dreams. What dream could Marie Flechette possibly have? She had it all—didn't she?

In the solitude of the Flechette library, a voice echoed off the bookcase. The air stirred, the flames in the hearth rose and danced. Marie came to a trembling stillness. Her eyes darted about, searching for the author of the voice. But she found that the voice had come from within, deep from the cavern of her soul—a place that was as mysterious as it was frightening. Marie was enticed to listen. It was only a whisper, but she knew it was the voice of her deepest essence, reminding her of her own words.

I will come if I am called.

*   *   *   *

"Ha! Check her out," Clive cackled with delight as he showed Javid around the cockpit of his new freighter. "Brand spanking new. Ain't she a beauty? Wait till you fly her. Noiseless, smooth, just like an eagle soaring for the sheer joy of it."

Javid brought his nose closer to the glittering instrument panel. "All these strange knobs! I'll have to learn piloting all over again."

"Naw! They're just fancy versions of the old technology. Here, sit down. I'll show you."

Before Javid's bottom had quite settled into the impeccable leather seat he found his heart in his throat. An alarm began to shriek.

"What is *that*?" Javid cried out. Seeing the confusion on Clive's face terrorized Javid even more. Clive was already cranking and flipping at controls before his buttocks hit his own seat.

"An emergency? What the—"

Your departure has been temporarily denied. Please stand by.

The two looked at each other, wide-eyed.

"Shouldn't all those TRA fellows be in jail by now?" Javid whimpered.

"Strap in buddy. We're taking off, permission or not!"

With trembling fingers, Javid pressed on the button that would secure him to the copilot's seat. The two froze as the speakers boomed again. *Please stand by. Urgent message pending.*

"Message?" Clive stared, hypnotized to the small readout screen. He suddenly burst out laughing. Javid craned his neck to catch a glimpse of the screen meant only for the pilot.

"No silly. Your screen is over there."

In front of him, clear as day, a little message bleeped in a gentle, crimson hue. *Might you have room for a stowaway? Can you be hijacked to Vesperoiy?*

Clive looked at Javid. "Now, who might want passage to the Fringe's governing planet?"

Javid shrugged. "A woman looking to follow her heart, perhaps?"

Clive grinned widely. "That good-looking High Court member, ya think?"

"I would think so."

"Now *this* is what I call a diplomatic mission!"

CHAPTER 65

Vesperoiy was greener than Marie had expected. It seemed that Richard had a thing for tropical flair. The view from the transportation unit that whisked her to the government buildings invoked such vivid memories of the nebular planet that her stomach sucked back in nervous spasms. During the voyage across the stars, she'd twice tried to make contact with Richard. But with a complete deflation of her ego, she'd cut off both transmissions. She thought that just facing him would be easier.

On arrival at the parliament buildings, she was informed that Commander Shaw was not on the premises. Thinking quickly, she asked if she could see Lieutenant Reese Mondiran. Before the attendant could say no, she showed her Nixodonian High Court identification. Eyes widened, and the man quickly began to make calls. After what seemed like an interminable few seconds, the attendant said, "The Lieutenant will see you at once, ma'am."

Marie walked through the security gates and around a large fountain that graced the center of the front gardens. Two giant stone-carved serpents reached high into the air, spouting funnels of water that splashed over their eroded scales to a fish-laden pond below. Directly behind the fountain stood the main building where she was to find Reese. Constructed of huge stone blocks, the building exuded an essence of masculine solidity, made effeminate by hordes of flowering vines that crawled over a good portion of the building's facade. Marie mounted the long steps, noting the sign above the huge columns of the stone canopy. Its newness clashed with the weathered look of the building.

Fringe Federation House of Parliament.

She smiled, knowing the sense of accomplishment they must have felt on the day of its erection. Marie entered the building. She stood on a spacious mosaic floor that featured a wide central staircase boasting corpulent stone railings and stout spindles. The stairs led to a massive second floor balcony that curved along the back wall of the foyer. The wall was punctuated with a dozen office doors, addressing the true nature of this magnificent building. She continued to survey the domed ceiling with its full circle of prism glass windows. Shards of light exploded into giant rainbows, painting the walls and staircase like the runaway brush of an edified artist.

Richard hadn't lied. Marie instantly fell in love with the welcoming charm of the building, complete with the pervasive, musty smell of tropical air. Marie looked up when she heard her name. Reese came down from the balcony two steps at a time and strode toward her, hand extended in greeting. His handsome features brought on a wave of nostalgia, something intangible from a sea of infinity that evoked a timeless sense of belonging deep within her soul.

"Well, I'll be!" Reese breathed excitedly. "I can't believe my eyes. Richard didn't tell me you were coming, the selfish rat."

"He doesn't know, Reese."

His smile waned. "He doesn't...know?"

"I came with Javid and Clive."

"The boys are here with you? That's fantastic!" Reese glanced behind her. "Where are they?"

"They're still at the spaceport. We're just here for a visit, but first, congratulations on your victory at Rashmar. Javid was so excited by the news!"

Reese frowned. "It will be a week or two before he can go back."

"Yes, we know." Marie floundered. "We were all going to tour the Fringe for a while."

"I see," he said, although it was obvious that he didn't. "Come on up to my office and we'll talk."

He led her up the well-worn stairs to a room directly off the circular balcony. The office radiated its ancient charm with huge windows arching toward an engraved ceiling. One window was being tickled by the leaves of a massive tree swaying lightly in the breeze of a central courtyard.

"It is really good to see you, Marie." Reese said. "Richard will be shocked. Can I offer you something to drink?"

"How shocked?"

Reese straightened. The look of wonder turned to one of clarification. "Ah, I see."

"I was going to contact him...and I guess I should have tried harder, because I now understand that he's not here."

"I'm expecting him any minute, actually," Reese said buoyantly.

Marie should have foreseen her own reaction. Her heart made a nauseating leap into her throat. Not one of her plans seemed clear or intelligent now.

"He spent the morning on a military excursion just outside the city."

"Oh, Reese!" Marie wrung her hands. "I really shouldn't be bothering him like this. I know he must be very busy now, with the independence and all."

"Bothering him?"

"So, perhaps I can ask you. I just wanted permission to go to the nebula and rest for a while. Visit Chief Ungu and the village. Things have been awfully hectic on Enderal, and—"

"Go to the nebula? You mean, alone?"

"Well, not exactly. Javid and Clive would come with me, and we would need passage on one of your military ships, of course." Her face paled very suddenly. "Oh my! It didn't occur to me that the base might still be in a state of repair. Are...are you even using the base?"

A smile crept up one corner of Reese's lips. "Well, it is still a bit of a mess, but yes, it's operational."

Marie let out her breath. "Ah. That's wonderful. So, can I get permission from you, then?"

Reese leaned his hips against the desk and folded his arms. "No."

Marie flushed. "No?"

The following sequence of events happened with stupefying speed. First, the black-clad figure of Igna appeared in the office doorway. She looked out of place toting a bundle of documents instead of explosives. "Well," she said flatly. "It's about time you got here. His next threat was to cut off his hair."

Igna disappeared down the hallway.

Seconds later, the tall figure of Captain Boro stepped into the room. Marie held her breath as a flood of mixed emotions washed over her. And yet, the pirate looked wonderful! His polished prosthesis glinted colorfully off the lights; his natural skin glowed with health. The corner of his mouth wrinkled against the metal as he gave her a wide smile. "Ah, my Lady, what a wonderful surprise!" He'd no sooner said that before popping his head out the doorway. "Major Cello," he called out. "If you have a moment...?" And he was gone.

Reese shook his head. "We're going to have to separate those two."

Marie had only the time to look wide-eyed at him before a bellowing voice exploded in the foyer below. Even through the incensed overtones, Marie recognized Richard's voice.

"Don't worry," Reese assured her. "You won't make him more angry than he already is."

She missed his jesting tone and gaped at him in shock. The voice became clearer as Richard stormed up the stairs of his government building, followed by a sea of staff members trying to explain that his ship couldn't be ready in twenty hours. Marie heard him move down the hall and stop at the adjacent office.

"Has there been a response to my message?" his voice asked.

"No, Commander," a woman said.

"I sent it two days ago."

"I'm aware of that, Commander."

"Call a general meeting. I'll be gone for the next three weeks. Lieutenant Mondiran will be in charge."

In a louder voice, the Commander bellowed, "*Reese?*"

"In heeere," Reese called out, wearily.

Marie spun toward the door and clashed eyes with the stormy, deep blue gaze of Richard Shaw. He stopped so quickly that his white hair fell forward before his mouth dropped open. They stared at each other in cataleptic shock.

Reese cleared his throat. "Your message has just arrived, sir."

He sprang from the desk and strode toward the door, first stopping between the two paralyzed figures. "I'll dismiss myself."

There was no response so Reese strode out the door, closing it behind him.

Marie trembled. "I—I didn't get your message. I must have been on my way here."

"Oh, *glory* to the Great Creator," Richard breathed, taking one lunging stride before stopping abruptly. "Tell me that you came back to me—for me. Ah—to visit me. Anything!"

"Oh Richard. I did," she said, coming to the final realization herself. "I was going crazy."

"Oh, my love," Richard confessed, "you weren't the only one."

In one great leap he reached her open arms and clasped her to his chest. His lips crushed down on hers, devouring her in a kiss that would defy the power of outside forces to tear them apart again. They clutched and rocked, whispered and giggled.

Panting, Richard said, "You have no idea how good it is to have you here in my arms. I never should have let you go, especially the way I did."

"You did what you had to do, and you were right! I couldn't have abandoned my family, or FC, or the responsibilities to my country. I was forced to take the time I needed to sort it out."

"Interesting. I forced myself into the same dilemma," Richard admitted. "I was about to fly to Enderal to try to make impossible arrangements for us to see each other regularly."

She smiled. "My heart tells me that regular arrangements simply won't work."

His grip tightened. "Be careful. I'm still a barbarian, you know. And, barbarians have a reputation for imprisoning beautiful women. My record is now proven."

She laughed. "Ironically, it was that imprisonment that showed me freedom. And, Richard," she hesitated. "I just can't do it anymore."

He hesitated. "Do what?"

She thought it would be difficult to say, but the words spilled out. "Life at FC just isn't part of my flesh and blood anymore."

He couldn't hope to believe her. "What are you saying, Marie?"

"I'm not exactly sure myself, but Chief Ungu invited me to learn from him. I need to understand myself better, find out who I really am, where I belong. *Untangle the mystery, untie the knot,* like I used to sing. I think that Chief Ungu could help me achieve that."

"I can arrange it for you, if you like," he said carefully.

Her gaze had become elusive. "There's something else," she said. "There's a challenge to be met here."

Richard looked into her eyes. "A challenge?"

"I need to see if Igna is wrong, if you're wrong." She bit her lip. "I need to know if I'm just dreaming or if I can get *accustomed* to this kind of life, like they would say."

Richard straightened slowly. "Is there any room in that life for me?"

She spread her arms. "All the room you can possibly imagine."

They clasped and kissed again and again. Finally, Richard relaxed his hold.

"I have a suggestion," he ventured. "Let me help you with the first leg of your journey—and of course, being a High Court member from a visiting country, my personal escort to the nebula would not only be proper, but necessary."

She tossed back her head and laughed.

"And, if the good Chief Ungu could be patient for a just few days longer, perhaps I could entice you to join me for a swim—or two—in a certain jungle pool?"

She met his smiling eyes. "Well, all right. But, be gentle with me, you savage."

EPILOGUE

NEWS FLASH: An unexpected alliance has been made in regards to our princess, Marie Flechette.

First, we must acknowledge that Marie's refusal to accept a public offer of matrimony to our democratic leader's son, Johnas Knabon, was taken as a serious blow to the Presidential House, but the blow was not as great as the one that followed. The secrets of Marie's adventures during her kidnapping have finally come to light. We have just received an official announcement of her engagement to Richard Shaw, Commander in Chief of the Fringe Federation. This news is a surprise to all of us, not just to the Presidency. The patriarch, Raymond Flechette, has made it clear that his support of the Presidential House will continue, as will his daughter's duties as a High Court member. Mr. Flechette added that Nix States should consider the marriage of his daughter to the Fringe leader a show of strength toward a better alliance between the two nations. Nevertheless, there are tangible resentments from select government officials who still regard the Fringe Federation's independence as a bureaucratic blunder, not supported by the Nixodonian people. Cool it, guys. Much as we're all sad to see Marie Flechette leave us, we should be grateful that her ties with her homeland remain strong. Should not galactic peace be the ultimate goal? Will that not be augmented by her alliance to the Fringe? We all agree that Shaw is a step up from Lambert, and although we may expect to see Marie disembark from a Fringe freighter in a jungle suit the next time she sets foot on Enderal, we believe that she will be happy, and at peace.

Now that is truly what should be celebrated as a Solar Sensation

—Celebrity Quest

The End

978-0-595-36162-5
0-595-36162-5

Printed in the United States
41226LVS00004B/1-78